Demons FOREVER

PEACHVILLE HIGH DEMONS
BOOK 6

SARRA CANNON

Demons Forever
Copyright © 2012 by Sarra Cannon

Printed in the United States of America.

Cover Design by Robin Ludwig Design, Inc.
Editing Services by Janet Bessey at Dragonfly Editing
Formatting by Inkstain Interior Book Designing
www.InkstainFormatting.com

BOOKS BY SARRA CANNON:

YOUNG ADULT

PEACHVILLE HIGH DEMONS SERIES:

Beautiful Demons
Inner Demons
Bitter Demons
Shadow Demons
Rival Demons
Demons Forever

A Demon's Wrath: Part 1
A Demon's Wrath: Part 2

ETERNAL SORROWS SERIES:

Death's Awakening
Sorrow's Gift

NEW ADULT

FAIRHOPE SERIES:

The Trouble With Goodbye
The Moment We Began
A Season For Hope
The Fear Of Letting Go

Sacrifice Me

—For Andrew
I wanted you all my life,
Prayed for you with all my heart,
And will love you with all that I am.
Forever.

A CASTLE AND A CROWN

CHEERS ECHOED THROUGH the streets of the domed city. Breathless, I stared down at the crowd. Was this really all for me? My ears rang and time seemed to stand still. I blinked, unable to make sense of this scene.

My father, the King of the South, stood next to me, fist raised high in the air. A ghost. A vision.

A demon.

Never in a million years did I think this could be my truth. How many times had I wondered about him? How many times had I dreamed he would show up at the door of my latest foster home and claim me? Take me away to his big house in suburbia where we would have a dog and a pool and a real life together?

And I'd thought that was dreaming big.

I didn't even know how to wrap my mind around the thought of a castle and a crown. Much less the fact that I was not completely human.

Jackson's hand squeezed mine, and I was instantly grateful he was here with me. He was the anchor holding my feet to the ground.

I squeezed back.

"We love you, Princess," someone shouted from below.

Me? A princess? Disbelief shot through me, making me so dizzy I had to grip the railing to stay upright.

I breathed in, warmth snaking across my cheeks. I wanted to duck my head. To hide in embarrassment. But I also wanted to smile and wave and giggle like a child on Christmas morning. My father was alive!

I had a thousand questions to ask him, but for now, the roar of the crowd washed over me like a wave. Inside, I tumbled end over end, one moment feeling as if I might drown and the next thinking I might float away.

Somewhere in the distance, fireworks burst into the air. I followed it with my eyes, raising my chin toward the domed sky as it erupted in a flash of greens and blues.

When the sky cleared, a tiny speck of darkness descended toward us. At first, I thought it was part of the festivities. But as it drew closer, its inky blackness expanded and grew, blotting out the light of the distant suns. The crowd gasped as the sky grew dark, all eyes turned upward in fear and confusion.

The hand around my shoulder grew tense. I glanced at my father. His silver eyes darkened to a steel gray. He held his breath.

"What is it?" I asked in a whisper.

"I don't know," he said. "Get inside. Now."

He motioned to the guards at our back. They rushed forward and gripped my arms. I resisted, unable to turn my eyes away, but they pushed me back into the safety of the throne room. Jackson stayed on the balcony, his eyes lifted to a growing darkness.

I pulled away from the guards, my heart racing. What was going on? Why did everyone look so afraid? I thought they'd said the dome was safe?

Trembling, I hugged my arms close to my chest and stared out through the archway. I watched genuine fear flash in my father's eyes. Beneath his silver beard, his jaw tensed. He lifted his arm like a shield above his head as a massive explosion rocked the domed city.

The tile beneath my feet shook from the force of the blow and my ears rang. I stumbled backward and fell onto the steps leading up to the throne. Screams echoed against the high ceilings and my blood went cold. Outside, the sky turned black as night. An oily darkness slipped down across the smooth surface of the dome, blocking any view of the forest beyond.

Time moved in slow motion.

I stood, panic rising in my stomach as both Jackson and my father followed something with their eyes. Their heads moved in unison as the gasps and screams below grew louder.

I pushed forward, running past the stunned guards to see it for myself.

Before I could reach the balcony, I saw what it was they'd been watching. A single drop of black liquid splashed across the solid stone railing, inches from the king. With a hiss, it ate through the rock in seconds. Then, a cascade of drops fell around them and the balcony gave way.

I shouted and reached forward, Jackson's eyes searching for mine as he fell.

THERE WAS NO ANSWER

*T*HE DOMED CITY erupted into chaos.

Shouts sounded in the distance as hunters poured through the city's front gate, the dome's magical seal broken. Spells flashed as demons and humans banded together against them.

I lunged forward, hands outstretched toward the falling balcony. In the instant before they fell onto the stone steps below, Jackson and the king both shifted to smoke. One black as night. The other white as a cloud. They coiled and circled up toward me, rushing past. Hands gripped me tight and pulled me with them as part of the floor collapsed and crumbled to the ground.

Out of breath, we landed on the steps of the shining silver throne.

"What's happening?" I asked. "I thought the dome was safe from witch's magic."

My father shook his head. "Some kind of bomb. Or acid. They must have figured out a way to damage the outer shield," he said. "They've cracked a piece of the dome, disrupting the protection spell. Harper, we have to get you to a safe place."

He motioned to the guards who had dragged me inside moments earlier. They were at my side in the blink of an eye.

I stepped back. "No, I want to fight."

"I don't have time to argue with you about this," he said. "Jackson, help these men get her downstairs. The dungeons three levels down will be the safest place. They were built ages ago with very strong stone."

Jackson sucked in a tense breath. "Yes sir."

I opened my mouth to protest, but Jackson's hand gripped my forearm and squeezed. When our eyes met, he shook his head to silence me. I had no idea what he was thinking, but I had to trust him. We didn't have time to talk this out. The battle outside grew louder and closer.

My father's eyes darted toward the gaping hole in the castle wall.

"Go," I said. "We'll be fine."

He turned to me, his silver eyes clouded with worry. "Get to safety. I'll find you as soon as this is over."

My stomach flipped as he shifted to white smoke and disappeared through the missing wall. Would I ever see him again? I couldn't lose him now, minutes after I found out he even existed.

The guards turned, ready to usher me downstairs to the dungeons.

"I'll make sure she gets down there," Jackson said, pulling me close to him. "Your city needs you now."

One of the guards, a tall demon with dark brown hair and bulging muscles, threw a glance toward the battle. "We have our orders."

"Don't waste your time on us," I said. "Go. We'll find our way down."

The second guard drew his sword from his belt. "Take the stairway behind you all the way down to the dungeons on the lowest level. You'll be safe there," he said.

My heart thundered in my chest. A flash of green shot across the throne room, hitting the far wall. I covered my face as sparks erupted and fell to the floor.

Jackson pulled me toward the staircase, and I ran with him. Once we started our descent, the guards shifted and flew out to join the fight.

As soon as the guards disappeared from sight, I pulled my arm away from Jackson and turned back toward the battle. "What are you doing?" I shouted. "We have to help them."

"Harper, you have to listen to me." He placed a hand on my face. "I know you want to go out there, but you've barely had any time to recover from the last fight. We need to get you—"

Before he could finish, a fiery bomb exploded by our feet. The force of it destroyed the area around us and sent us flying in separate directions. I lifted my arms to shield my face from the heat as I fell hard onto the marble floor. Wincing, I pushed up, coughing and clawing my way through debris.

Something nearby caught fire, and I struggled to find Jackson through the flames.

I shouted his name, but there was no answer.

Which way to the stairs? Disoriented, I stumbled over the broken floor and fell to my knees. I cursed and tried to stand again. In front of me, a figure emerged from the blaze. I lifted my eyes, hoping to see Jackson's familiar face.

My breath caught in my throat and I scrambled backward. It wasn't Jackson who had found me.

It was a hunter.

SHE WANTS IT BACK

*T*HE HUNTER'S HOLLOW eyes bored into me, her face twisted up in a terrible grimace.

"Looks like I win the prize," she said, moving closer. "Won't my priestess be proud?"

Priestess Winter.

Bile rose in my throat. Of course she was behind this whole thing. But how had she found me so fast? How had she been able to get through the dome's protective shield? It was as if she'd been watching me this whole time. Waiting for the chance to make her move.

Part of me had been hoping this attack had nothing to do with me. That it was just bad timing. But I guess, deep down, I knew better. Priestess Winter was never going to let me go. She would keep coming after me no matter where I tried to hide. And she wouldn't stop until I was dead and the Peachville line ran through the blood of another family.

I glanced around for any sign of Jackson, but I didn't see him anywhere. Panic twisted my stomach. Was he hurt?

The hunter cackled and raised her hands to me, sending a spell rushing forward.

Distracted, I couldn't think fast enough to protect myself. The spell hit me head-on, the force of it sending me backward again. This time, the back of my skull slammed hard into the marble floor. I cried out and curled into a little ball.

Another whoosh of air pushed past, this time lifting debris all around me, forming four tight walls that locked me in place.

"I don't know why they say you're so hard to capture," the hunter said, hovering just beside the makeshift cage. Her face was grotesque. Covered in a slimy fluid that reeked of decay. "This was my easiest catch in decades."

I clutched my throbbing head and rocked back and forth. I needed to get out of this trap, but I couldn't think straight. Blackness flowed over me and threatened to pull me under. I wanted to close my eyes and give in to it. I wanted to forget the pain that coursed through me.

"Why?" I shouted in my delirium. "Why won't she just leave me alone?"

"You took something that belongs to her." The hunter crouched low, her rancid breath turning my stomach. "She wants it back."

I shook my head. No, she was wrong. I didn't have anything that belonged to Priestess Winter. Then, through the haze of pain, I remembered.

The ring.

The diary Andros gave us when we left the Underground had led us to the sapphire ring. A ring of great power that acted like an anchor here in the shadow world, connecting all of the blue demon gates to the original. Without that ring, the Order wouldn't be able to pull demons through the blue portals.

And without it, Jackson and I wouldn't be able to reverse the spell that kept Aerden and me bound to Peachville.

I couldn't let her take the ring.

With sheer force of will, I pushed the pain from my mind. Carefully, I stood, my legs trembling at first, then finding their strength.

The hunter laughed. "Where do you think you're going?" she asked. She moved closer to the cage of stone and debris. "You'll never escape, no matter how hard you try."

I concentrated on my power, remembering back to the moment in the field when I'd shifted into smoke. I'd taken the form of my demon half to save myself once before, so maybe I could do it again. I focused on the feeling I remembered. Weightlessness. A loss of body and self.

But nothing happened.

The hunter studied me with narrowed eyes. "What's wrong? Can't remember how to use your power?" she asked. "You're such a child."

Did she know what I was? Who I was?

I took a deep breath in and released it slowly, trying to ground myself. To connect to the core of my power. I could feel the human side of my power buzzing in my veins, but where was the demon half? If I could somehow find a way to shift and control that side of my powers, I would be free. I would have the advantage.

Only it wouldn't come.

Tears pushed through to the surface, stinging my eyes. I was so exhausted. We'd been traveling for days and it had taken everything I had just to fight the three hunters near the blue stones. I'd barely survived their attack. Jackson was right. I needed more time to recover. I should have gone downstairs to the dungeons with him. I should have rested and let my father deal with these witches.

Above me, the heavy rocks pressed down. I used what little power I still had running through my veins to lift up, hoping to break the hunter's cage and set myself free long enough to get away, but the rocks wouldn't budge an inch.

Had I really come all this way just to be captured here in my father's castle?

If they took me now, I would never have a chance to know him or ask him all the questions I longed to have answers to. I shook my head and tightened my fists. There was no way I was going to let that happen.

I am stronger than this.

The hunter circled me like a beast watching its prey. She laughed and celebrated her catch, but before she could get all the way back around to the front, I pulled into myself, accessing a well of power deep within, then pushed out with everything I had.

As I lifted upward, the debris and stone holding me captive broke into a thousand pieces and flew out in every direction. The hunter screamed and rushed toward me.

I glanced up, looking for anything I could use against her.

An iron chandelier with six burning torches hung from the high ceiling above. I reached up into the air and grabbed hold of it with my mind. With all the power I had left inside, I pulled downward. I tore the heavy chandelier from the ceiling and brought it down on the hunter's head, the force of it smashing her skull with a loud crack.

She fell to the ground like a broken doll. Thick black blood oozed from a hole in the side of her head. Her arms and legs twitched twice, then fell limp at her sides.

Exhausted, my power spent, I dropped to my knees.

I turned my eyes toward the blown-out castle wall. The battle continued outside. Shouts sounded. Several fires blazed across rooftops, their smoke mingling with the smoke of demons shifting and moving through the semi-darkness. Spells flashed and cracked.

I blinked, struggling to see as my vision faded to black and my body hit the floor.

YOU GET THAT FROM
YOUR MOTHER

$\mathscr{S}$OMEONE SHOOK ME **from my sleep.**

Startled, I jerked up. A man with worried eyes and a silver beard stared down at me. At first, I didn't recognize him. Fear pumped through my heart. Then, relief flooded my veins. My father. We were in his castle and we had been attacked. But he was alive.

I sucked in a nervous breath. "Is it over?" I asked, my head still throbbing. "Did we win?"

My father crouched next to me on the floor. "Yes" he said, his voice tired and strained. Soot covered his face and his eyes were ringed with fatigue. "There were a few casualties on both sides, but we finally drove the surviving hunters from the dome. Much of the city was destroyed, so there will be a lot of work ahead in the next few days. We need to fortify the city's entrance and find a way to patch the crack at the top of the barrier."

I looked around, wondering where I was and how I had gotten there.

I was in a cell, the iron gate wide open. Under me, stiff straw scratched at my clothes. Someone must have brought me down here to the dungeon after I passed out.

I swallowed, my heart thudding in my throat. "Where's Jackson?" I started to stand, but my legs wouldn't hold me. "Is he okay?"

My father put a hand on my shoulder. "He's fine," he said. "Don't push yourself. I sent him upstairs to help heal some of the wounded. He said a hunter trapped him upstairs in the throne room, then came after you. When you killed her, it set him free and he brought you down here until the battle ended."

I sighed in relief, then leaned back against the cold stone wall. "Thank god."

"I should have brought you down here myself." He ran a hand through his hair. "I never would have forgiven myself if something had happened to you. How are you feeling?"

I reached up to touch the sore spot on the back of my head and winced. "I hit my head pretty hard," I said. "Other than that, I think I'm just tired."

My father leaned forward and placed his hands on my head. I flinched as an electric wave washed over me, then relaxed as the pain disappeared in an instant. This felt different from when Jackson had healed me in the past. Infinitely more powerful and not at all cold like Jackson's power.

"Wow," I said, the pounding in my head completely gone. "How did you do that?"

He gave me a small smile, then sat down next to me, back against the wall and hands on his knees. "Healing is one of my strongest powers," he said. "You'll be glad to know I paid a brief visit to the little boy you brought with you."

I brightened. "How's he doing?"

"He was pretty badly hurt, but he's recovering nicely," he said. "He should be ready for visitors in a few days. To be honest, I was actually surprised to learn healing wasn't one of your powers, but you never know exactly which abilities will get passed from one generation to the next."

We sat in silence for a moment. I thought of the destroyed throne room and the damage that consumed a large portion of the city.

"Did you even know this was possible?" I asked. "The explosion? Has the Order attacked the city like this before?"

He ran his hand across his forehead. "Never to this extent," he said. "We had some warning that the Order had been working on a spell that would damage our barrier, but until today I had no idea how far they'd come."

The fear in his voice scared me. If the king was afraid, shouldn't we all be terrified of what might happen?

"This is my fault," I said.

My father sighed and drew his eyebrows close together in the middle. "You can't blame yourself for this," he said. "The Order has had its eye on this city since I created it."

I stared down at the blue stone glittering on my finger. "You don't understand. I took something very valuable to the Order," I said. "I had no idea they'd come after it this fast, though."

He looked down at the ring and gasped, his eyes wide. "The anchor," he said. "May I see it?"

I pulled the ring from my finger and placed it in his hand. He turned it over and around, studying each detail. Every mark and facet.

"Incredible," he said. "We've been looking for this for ages. Where did you find it?"

I explained to him about the diary we'd been given. "It belonged to one of the original members of the Order," I said. "The entries explained the importance of the ring and how it had been hidden here in the shadow world to act as an anchor that would allow additional gates to be opened. Jackson and I went looking for it, and along the way, we discovered that each ring was hidden in a place of power. A place where stones of the same kind were grouped together. A gem dealer near the borderlands told us we could find a blue stone quarry here in the Southern Kingdom."

"But we've searched that blue quarry a thousand times," he said. "We've never seen any sign of the anchor."

"I think the hiding place revealed itself to me because I'm the prima futura of a blue demon gate," I said. "Not even Jackson could see the special pedestal that held the ring, but for some reason, I was drawn to it. It appeared when I got close enough, only the ring wasn't there. I think the pedestal triggered some kind of attack from three hunters who were guarding the ring."

"Amazing," he said. "I have seen other documents that spoke of this ring, but never before have I seen one with my own eyes."

"I'm pretty sure that ring is the reason the Order attacked the city today. I can't imagine Priestess Winter sent those hunters here just for me."

Unless the Order already knew I was half demon. I had no idea what that might mean in terms of the demon gate's power, but I wondered if that was the reason Priestess Winter had gone through so much trouble to transfer Peachville's prima line to another family rather than kill me outright. As I saw in Aldeen, sometimes she'd rather kill an entire town than deal with a prima who didn't follow the rules.

I shivered at the memory.

"I'm going to put this ring in my vault and make sure there are extra guards stationed with both you and the ring at all times," my father said. "We can't take any chances."

A sick feeling rolled around in my stomach. I wanted to trust him, but that ring was too important to our cause to let it out of my sight. He moved to place it in his pocket, but I reached out and gently touched his arm.

Surprised, he paused and raised an eyebrow.

"I'm sorry," I said, pulling my hand away. He might have been my father, but he was also a king. There were probably rules about being too familiar. "It's just that we went through a lot to get that ring. We need it."

He closed his fist around it. "Harper, I understand you've been through some tough battles," he said. "But you need to understand how important this ring is to all demons. With it, the blue demon gates are useless to the Order of Shadows."

"I know," I said, biting my lip. "But holding onto the ring only prevents the Order from bringing more demons through to the other side."

"Do you understand how many lives we could save if we could do that? How many rituals we could prevent?" he asked. "What could be more important than that?"

My chest tightened.

"Freeing the demons who are already trapped in the human world," I said.

The king stood and cleared his throat. "We all know there's nothing we can do for those who have already been taken," he said, a hard edge to his tone. "We have to concentrate on saving the demons who are still here in the shadow world."

"That's not true," I said, pushing against the wall to stand. Was he really so quick to give up on those who'd already been enslaved? "According to the diary we read, if we perform the original gate opening ceremony in reverse, we can close a demon gate forever. If we do that, it will break the bonds created by that portal. That means every demon tied to a witch in that gate town would go free and no one would have to die."

"That's impossible," he said. "Where did you say you found this information?"

"A diary," I said, crossing to him. "One of the five original sisters who created the Order kept a journal. A detailed history that includes rituals and information about different spells that were used to create the Order's power."

"Demons have been looking for a way to free the enslaved demons for two centuries," he said, shaking his head. "If a diary like that existed, I would have already known about it."

Warmth crawled up my neck. Was he calling me a liar?

"I can show you the journal if you don't believe me," I said.

"How can you be sure it's real and not something created to lead you down the wrong path?" he asked.

"I can't prove it's real, but I can tell you that it led me to the ring in the first place. And if there's any chance the ritual reversal might work, I will do everything in my power to perform it. Even if I have to risk my life by going back to Peachville."

The king paced the length of the cell, rubbing his beard. "I understand why you want to free yourself and Jackson's brother from the Peachville gate, but this war goes much deeper than one demon or one gate. We can't risk letting that ring get back into the hands of the Order."

I clenched my jaw tight. This was my first real conversation with my father, a man I'd dreamed of meeting my entire life, and he was already pissing me off.

"Peachville's just the beginning. If the ritual works there, it will work everywhere. With this ring, we could close all of the blue gates forever and free thousands of demons who are in captivity," I said. "Isn't it worth the risk if we can free so many demons and humans from the Order's slavery?"

My father sighed. "We can talk about this later," he said, his voice tired. "For now, let's get you up to your room. You have to be exhausted."

I swallowed. "Can I have my ring back?"

He turned back to me, worry creasing his forehead. "I think I'll keep it for now," he said. "That way I can make sure it's safe."

I crossed my arms in front of my chest. "I know you're my father, but that doesn't automatically mean I can trust you," I said. "The ring is rightfully mine. I need you to promise me that if I ever ask for it again, you'll hand it over without question."

He seemed to consider it for a moment, then released some of the tension in his shoulders and nodded. "I guess I should have expected you to be independent and stubborn," he said with a sad smile. "You get that from your mother."

My breath caught in my throat. A heavy silence filled the space between us. It was the first time he'd mentioned my mother. I wanted to ask him about her, but I was too scared to open that door between us.

"Now, let me take you to your rooms," he said, holding his arm out to me. "Thankfully the back side of the castle was not damaged."

I hesitated. Was I was doing the right thing by letting him keep the blue ring? Could I really trust him to give it back?

After a moment, I finally placed my arm in his.

IT'S COMPLICATED

*J*FOLLOWED MY FATHER up the stairs, past the main floor where more than a dozen people worked on the repairs.

Through the broken wall, a sliver of sunlight shone through the oily remains of the Order's attack.

"Harper, your room is up on the top floor," my father said. "In fact, I've had this room ready for you for the past sixteen years, just in case."

His words blossomed in my heart. He'd had a room for me? All these years of moving from one foster home to another, sharing rooms with other kids and never knowing how long I'd even stay in one place and all this time, a room had been waiting for me. It didn't seem real.

I gasped as he stopped in front of a large golden door. Shimmering on its surface was a beautiful painting of a white rose.

The door opened on its own as I approached, as if to welcome me home.

My father stepped back to let me pass, a gentle smile on his face and the hint of a tear in his eyes.

I stepped inside and my hand went to my mouth. The entryway was gorgeous. Perfect white roses were arranged in a large pink vase that sat on top of an intricately carved table. The floor glittered with multicolored stones embedded beneath clear glass tile.

Above my head, crystal lamps hovered in the air, unattached to any wires or switches.

"Go on," he said. "You have three rooms all to yourself up here."

My eyes grew wide. Was he serious? That was practically like my own house.

Like a giddy child, I moved through the foyer into the living room area, anxious to explore my new space. A space that had waited here for me all my life.

A thick black rug lay across the glittering floor. It looked like some kind of fur, and I couldn't resist leaning down to run my hand over its soft surface.

"Magdonear fur," my father said, naming an animal I'd never heard of. "When I was younger, I used to hunt quite a bit in the mountain areas. I had this made just for you when I realized how much you liked black."

I stood, my hand going to my heart. He knew I liked black? How?

My lips fell open, the room forgotten for a moment. I couldn't even think straight enough to figure out how to put words to my questions. "When?" I asked. "How long have you been—"

"Watching you?" He completed my thought. "I've been searching for you from the moment I found out you existed, but your mother did a good job of hiding you. When you came to Peachville, it was both the happiest day and the saddest day of my life."

I tilted my head and looked at him, puzzled. "Why both?"

He moved into the room and put his hands on the back of a leather chair in the small seating area. "The happiest because I'd finally found you," he said. "And the saddest because that meant the Order had found you too."

I swallowed, my mouth dry. "Why didn't you come for me?"

"It's complicated," the king said. He pushed off from the chair and moved toward the next room, avoiding the question completely. "We'll have plenty of time for talking about these kinds of things. Why don't we get you settled so you can get some rest? I'm sure you're anxious to get cleaned up, too."

I took a deep breath and pushed my disappointment to the back of my mind. I followed my father into the bedroom.

One look and it took my breath away.

The walls from floor to ceiling were made of dark stones in various sizes. A square mahogany bed decorated with inlaid pearl panels and draped with sheer golden curtains took up the right half of the room. A fire roared in the large stone fireplace to my left.

Even the ceiling in here was a work of art. An abstract mosaic created with pieces of golden-colored gemstones sparkled in the light of three large floating chandeliers.

My favorite part, though, was that the entire far side of the room was open to the outside. The same golden curtains that hung over the bed also draped across four separate archways. The light fabric swayed in a gentle breeze, caressing the floor with a whisper-soft touch. I pushed through them and stepped onto a large stone balcony overlooking the castle's gardens.

A white marble fountain flowed in the square below. The garden burst to life with flowers of every color, including an entire section of my mother's favorite white roses. Their fragrant smell reached me all the way up here at the top of the castle, and I breathed in, wondering if my mother had ever visited here. Had she even known my father was a demon king?

I knew from reading her journal that he had once been a married man living in Peachville. He'd had a wife and daughter there when my mother fell in love with him and got pregnant. Why had a demon king been living in Peachville, pretending to be a normal man? And what about my half-sister? Was she still living there in Peachville? I wanted so badly to ask, but he'd avoided every single question I'd asked about my mother or his past. I didn't want to push him away.

"What do you think?" he asked, joining me on the balcony.

"I love it," I said. "This is such a gorgeous castle. Did you design all of this yourself?"

My father looked out across the gardens. "Yes. The original castle where I grew up was destroyed in an attack around the time you were born," he said. "The dungeons down below were the only rooms that survived. When I returned to the shadow world, I had to basically start from scratch. That's when I built the domed city and this castle. I invited everyone in my kingdom to live under the safety of our dome."

He leaned over, resting his arms against the thick stone railing. Worry flashed in his eyes.

"Only, it's not so safe anymore," he said. "I guess I knew eventually the Order would find a way inside, but I didn't think it would happen so soon."

"Do you think you'll be able to repair it?" I asked.

"Yes, but what then?" He lifted his eyes to the top of the dome. A thin layer of black residue still clung to it. A large crack ran through the center at the very top. "What's to stop them from attacking again? I have to figure out a way to make my people feel safe. They count on me."

He sounded tired. I wanted to comfort him, but I didn't know how. He was still a stranger to me.

"We'll help however we can," I said. I had no idea how long Jackson and I would stay here, but I knew we would both do everything in our power to make it safe. Especially since the attack might have never happened if it wasn't for me.

The king straightened. "Thank you," he said. "But for now I'll leave you to get settled in. I need to meet with my council and the head of the guards so we can discuss our plans to rebuild."

I followed him back into the bedroom.

"Oh, and I'll have your handmaiden join you shortly," he said. "She's currently helping to clean the throne room, but I know she's been anxious to meet you."

"Handmaiden?" I asked.

"A sweet demon girl named Tulianne," he said, crossing through to the living room. "Don't hesitate to let her know if you need anything at all. I'm afraid I might not be around a lot in the coming days. There will be a lot of work to do around the city."

Disappointment flooded through me. "I had hoped we'd have some time to talk," I said. "I have so many questions about my mother and how you came to know her. And I'd like to talk to you about our plan to get back to Peachville."

At the mention of Peachville, my father turned sharply back to me, his face serious and stern. "Going back to that town is not an option," he said. "Not for many years. We need to fortify the city first and make sure you're safe from any attack. Then, after a few years, when the Order has backed off a little, we can revisit the idea of you going back there."

I bristled at his harsh tone. Was I a prisoner here now? "That's not really a decision you can make for me," I said, lifting my chin. If he'd really been watching me all this time, hadn't he learned I wasn't really one to follow the rules?

I swallowed hard and waited for his reaction.

My father narrowed his eyes at me. "Of course not," he said. I saw his hand move to the pocket that held the Order's blue ring. "I only hope you'll see the importance of staying here inside the dome where you'll be safe."

Where he could keep a closer eye on me. Wasn't that what he'd really intended to say? I was glad he cared about my safety, but I wasn't used to having a parent. And I certainly didn't want to have to start following his orders just because he was my dad.

He opened his mouth as if to say something else, but quickly closed it again. Instead, he gave a short bow, then shifted to smoke and disappeared from the room in the blink of an eye.

ALL THESE QUESTIONS

ACKSON HUGGED ME tight as we stood on the balcony looking out over the gardens below. My father had prepared a room for him down in the guard's quarters, but he'd come looking for me as soon as he was done in the healing rooms.

The three suns had started to set, their light fading rapidly.

"How are you feeling?" he asked.

I leaned against him, burying my head in his chest. "It's been the single most insane day of my life."

I'd never experienced so many highs and lows in such a short period of time. I was happy to have found my father, but still in shock about the fact that he was a demon king. Then there was the attack and my father's determination to keep me here. It was all so much to take in.

"Maybe you should get some rest," he said. "It was hard to really sleep down there in the dungeons."

"I know," I said with a laugh. "The bed up here sure looks a lot more comfortable than a heap of straw. I'm just not sure I can sleep. My mind is spinning with all this. He wouldn't even answer a single personal question the whole time we were together."

Jackson kissed the top of my head. "Give him time," he said. "This can't be easy for him, either."

I hadn't thought of it from my father's perspective. Was it hard for him to have me show up here like this? I guess answering a lot of questions after such a long battle might not be easy, especially when I wanted to ask him about very personal things like how, exactly, he'd come to know my mother and why he'd abandoned her all those years ago. In her journal, she'd said he broke things off abruptly, just telling her one day he couldn't see her anymore. Of course, she hadn't told him she was pregnant, but why had he left her in the first place?

Did it have something to do with his wife? Or his other daughter?

He'd said he built this castle sometime close to when I was born. Was that the reason he left Peachville? I shook my head, unable to get a grip on all these questions.

"I just hope he doesn't avoid me forever," I said. "I've waited too long to have this chance. He owes me this much. Especially if he's been watching me since I first came to Peachville months ago."

Just knowing he'd been keeping an eye on me made my heart hurt. Why hadn't he come for me? Why did he let me get pulled into the Order's grasp? They'd tried to kill me! If Jackson and Mary Anne and Lea hadn't risked their lives to pull me through the portal, I would have died never even knowing who my father was. Why hadn't my father intervened and tried to save my life?

The question stung. Did he even care about me?

But when I thought about the rooms he'd had prepared for me and the look on his face when I'd first walked into his throne room, I knew the truth. He cared about me. I could see it in his eyes. Maybe he just didn't know how to express it. Or maybe he'd had his reasons for not coming to Peachville to save me.

I hoped he'd be ready to talk about it soon. If he avoided me for too long, I might completely lose my mind.

"It's going to be okay," Jackson said, pulling me closer. "Time is a different thing for demons. We're immortal. A day is nothing to someone like your father. Try to be patient. I'm sure he'll come around."

Would he?

I thought about the sapphire ring. Now that he had it, my father had more control over me than I wanted. He'd promised to give it back to me if I asked, but could I trust him to live up to his word? Or would he keep it from me so that I would be forced to stay here in his castle?

Only time would tell.

Still, as the suns set beyond the cracked dome, I couldn't help but wonder just how much time we had left before the Order attacked again.

SUCH A DIFFERENT LIFE

*T*HE FOLLOWING MORNING, I awoke as the door to my bedroom pushed open.

Panic rushed through me. I jumped up, ready to fight. A short, dark-skinned girl pushed through carrying a basket of food. I relaxed and laughed in relief.

"You scared me to death," I said, clutching my chest. My heart raced.

"I'm so sorry, Princess," she said. Worry crinkled her face. "I never meant to scare you. I knocked, but when I heard no answer, I thought you must still be sleeping. I wanted to leave this basket of breads and pastries for you."

"It's fine," I said. "I'm just glad you're you, and not a hunter."

"Goodness, no," she said. She crossed to the left side of the room and set the basket on a mahogany table surrounded by high-backed chairs covered in tan leather. "My name is Tulianne. The king told me you would be expecting me."

I smiled and held my hand out to her. "I'm Harper," I said.

She smiled shyly and ducked her head. "I know who you are," she said, tentatively taking my hand. Instead of shaking it, though, she curtsied and bowed her head. "The king brought me here many years ago and I have trained to serve you. I cannot tell you how joyful I am to have you here after all this time."

"Are you serious?" I asked. "You trained for me?" It completely blew my mind to think about someone training for years just to serve me. Could this be real?

"I have trained in how to braid hair and sew dresses," she said. "I helped to decorate your rooms, and I work every day to keep them clean. Also, at your father's direction, I have put fresh white roses in your room every single day for the past seventeen years."

My mouth fell open. I couldn't believe she'd been here for seventeen years. The king must have brought her here right after my mother died.

"I have also spent much of my time, lately, learning everything I could about you," she said. She moved to the bed and began to make up the sheets. Only instead of using her hands, she used magic. Within seconds, the bed looked exactly as it had when I'd arrived, each pillow perfectly placed.

"That's insane," I said, unable to hide my shock. "This is your only job?"

"Yes," she said in all seriousness.

"I appreciate all that you've done, but I really don't need a handmaiden," I said. Just the thought of having someone make my bed and bring me food was so strange. I was used to doing everything for myself. "I'm sure there's something more important you could do rather than waiting on me hand and foot."

Her face fell and she looked like she was about to cry. "Please do not send me away, Princess," she said. "Being chosen to serve you has been the great honor of my life. It would break my heart to be dismissed, but if that is what you wish..."

Her voice trailed off, and guilt shot through me. I hadn't meant to upset her. I stepped closer to her and put my hand on her arm.

"I'm sorry," I said. "I didn't mean it personally. I'm just not used to being treated like this. I grew up learning to fend for myself. I only meant that I don't want you to go to any trouble."

"Trust me," she said, her face lighting up again. "You are no trouble to me. Every princess must have a faithful handmaiden. I am your devoted servant for life, as long as you will accept me. I will happily do anything you need."

"Thank you," I said. I couldn't help but like her. I could tell from these brief moments together she was a genuinely kind person. "It will be nice to have a good friend here in the city."

She lowered her head again, as if wanting to hide her smile. "You are too kind, Princess Harper," she said softly. "I am here to serve you. You are not obligated to treat me as a friend."

"Other than Jackson and the little boy who came here with us, you're my only friend here in the city," I said. "I hope we'll get to know each other very well for as long as I'm here."

She lifted her eyes to mine. "You do not plan to stay here?"

I shrugged and walked over to investigate the goodies she'd brought for breakfast. I'd been so exhausted the night before; I completely forgot to eat before I passed out in my new bed. I didn't even remember Jackson leaving.

"I don't know yet," I said. "Life is a little bit confusing right now, to say the least."

I picked a sugary pastry filled with chocolate and cherries. The flavors filled my mouth with sweetness and I moaned.

"Is something wrong?" Tulianne asked.

"Are you kidding? This is seriously the most delicious thing I have ever tasted in my life." I took another bite, having to restrain myself from shoving the whole thing in my mouth at once.

"I am pleased," she said, beaming from ear to ear. "This is one of my special recipes."

"I love it," I said between bites. I was already looking through the basket to see what else was in there. "Did you make all this yourself?"

She nodded. "I love to bake," she said. "I knew you would be hungry after such a long journey and after yesterday's attack."

"Thank you," I said. "These are delicious."

"I will bring them for you each morning," she said.

I laughed and covered my mouth. "You'll make me fat if I eat this every day, but it's so good I almost don't care."

"If there is anything else you would prefer, simply let me know and I will bring it to you," she said. "The kitchens are always fully stocked with meats and fruits and all kinds of fresh foods."

"I'm sure anything you make will be fine," I said.

The idea of having a handmaiden was going to take some serious getting used to. I would feel weird asking her to fetch me some food or brush my hair or clean my room. Maybe that was normal for a princess, but I still hadn't even wrapped my head around that whole thing yet.

Still, it would be nice to have someone besides Jackson to talk to.

"Can I ask you a question?" I asked, picking another pastry from the basket.

"Anything."

I motioned to the leather chairs around the table. "Here, have a seat," I said.

I sat down, but Tulianne kept standing. She bit her lip, looking worried.

"What?" I asked.

"A girl in my position is not usually permitted to sit down in the presence of her mistress," she said.

"Why not?" I asked. "Is that some kind of rule you have to follow?"

"It is an unspoken rule," she said. "I do not want to intrude on your time or your space."

"You're not intruding," I said. "I'd much rather sit and talk to you than be alone up here in this big room."

She eyed the empty chair.

"I understand if you have something else you need to do," I said. "But I'd love to spend some time with you if you want to hang out for a bit."

She smiled. It was infectious. So sweet and pure. Her chocolate-colored skin seemed to glow from within when she smiled. "Thank you," she said. "I would love that."

She sat down, crossing her legs neatly under her chair and placing her hands in her lap.

"Feel free to eat any of this food too. I'll never able to eat all this," I said. I pushed the basket toward her.

She studied my face for a moment to make sure I was serious, then carefully put her hand in the basket. She removed a small loaf of white bread and set it on a napkin on the table.

"What would you like to talk about?" she asked. She folded her hands back in her lap, not even taking a bite of her bread.

I considered her question. I desperately wanted to ask her about my father, but I decided it was probably more polite to ask her something about herself.

"Do you have family here in the city?" I asked.

Her face darkened. "No," she said. "Many in my family chose to stay in our small village in the outerlands instead of coming here to the domed city."

"How come you came here, then?" I asked, hoping it wasn't too personal of a question.

"I came here for you," she said. "The king was visiting our village years ago when I was just a young girl of fifty. He stayed overnight at the inn my father and mother owned. I used to serve him the same soup and homemade bread every night. We would sometimes exchange pleasant words. When his visit was over, he told me he had a young daughter who may someday come to live in his castle. He said if I was willing, he would like for me to come to the castle to serve as your handmaiden. This is a great honor to my people, and I could not refuse."

I listened to her story in awe. She'd lived such a different life. I couldn't imagine growing up surrounded by a family I loved, then leaving them for a princess I'd never met.

"Do you go back to visit your family often?" I asked.

She shook her head. "My mother is no longer with us," she said, "and I have not been back to see my father and the rest of our people in many years. It is too dangerous to leave the city and travel such a long way."

The sadness in her voice nearly broke my heart.

"It must be very hard to be so far from the people you love," I said.

"Yes, but at the same time they are the ones who stubbornly refuse to come to the dome," she said. "I believe it is foolish to take such risks."

Her speech patterns reminded me of Essex, Mary Anne's boyfriend in the Underground. He came from a small village in the far north while Tulianne came from the south, yet they sounded so similar. The thought of Mary Anne in love brought a smile to my face.

"What makes you smile, Princess?"

"Your English reminds me of a friend," I said. Thinking of him made me realize I should contact Mary Anne now that we were settled somewhere. When we left the Underground, we'd exchanged communication stones that were supposed to work kind of like cell phones. They only had so many uses in them before they wouldn't work anymore, so I hadn't thought it was important enough to call her, yet. Now, though, I really wanted to fill her in on everything that had happened.

She'd probably never let me live this demon princess thing down. Maybe I would skip that part for now.

"A good friend, I hope," Tulianne said.

"Yes, a very dear friend," I said. I turned my attention back to this small demon girl who had left everything behind to come here for me. "Thank you for coming here."

"You do not need to thank me," she said. "It is truly my pleasure, and I am very happy that you have finally come home."

Home. The word seemed strange in association with this foreign place. Would this ever feel like home?

I didn't plan on staying here long enough to find out. All I really wanted to do was get back to Peachville. For the first time, there was a real chance of closing the gate and setting both me and Aerden free. We needed to get to work collecting the ritual items so we could perform the binding spell in reverse.

Maybe once we'd succeeded, Jackson and I both could come back here to spend more time with my father.

Of course, once Aerden was free, maybe Jackson would want to go back and live with his parents in the Northern Kingdom. Something told me his family wouldn't take too kindly to having me move in with them. The half-demon, half-human princess of their rival kingdom? Not exactly daughter-in-law of the year.

"I can see you have much on your mind," Tulianne said. "Let me leave you to your thoughts. I should get back to the kitchens and to my work in the gardens before the whole morning passes."

I walked with her through the living room and into the small foyer. "It was nice to talk to you, Tuli," I said. The nickname just popped out of my mouth, and I liked the sound of it. The shorter name seemed to fit her so well. "Do you mind if I call you Tuli?"

She smiled and looked down at her feet. "I love it," she said. "It is what my mother used to call me."

"Good," I said, wondering if something bad had happened to her mother. "It fits you."

She paused near the door. "Thank you, Princess."

"For what?" I asked.

She lifted her eyes to mine, and for the first time, I noticed how beautiful they were. A light, clear violet that contrasted well with her dark skin and deep brown hair.

"For treating me as you would a friend," she said. "It is the greatest joy of my life."

She bowed her head and curtsied. Then, with a shy smile, she turned and left me alone with my thoughts.

EXACTLY WHO YOU ARE

THE FOLLOWING AFTERNOON, my father sent word that he'd like to have a private dinner with me.

My stomach flip-flopped, making me jittery and slightly insane. I called Tuli up to my room to help me figure out what to wear. Jackson lay back on my bed while I paraded various outfits in front of him. Dresses. My torn jeans. One felt way too overdressed while the other felt ratty and awful.

"A princess is allowed to be a little overdressed for a dinner in the presence of the king," Tuli said. Then, her face brightened and she clapped her hands together. "I think I might have just the thing."

She disappeared into the huge walk-in closet, then emerged with a green silk gown draped over her arm.

I scrunched my nose up. "Don't you think that's going to be too much for a random dinner?" I asked. "Maybe I should just wear my jeans."

She clenched her jaw and pressed her lips together in a tight line. With a shake of her head, she lifted the dress and motioned for me to go into the bathroom.

Jackson laughed. "I agree with Tuli," he said. "If you've got all these gorgeous handmade dresses in your closet, why not make the most of it?"

"I'll be right back," I said, rolling my eyes at him. There was no way I was going to wear a fancy green silk dress to dinner tonight. I would feel ridiculous.

In the bathroom, I looked around for a screen or some other place to change.

Tuli laughed. "There is no reason to be modest around me," she said. "Part of my responsibility is to help you dress. I promise you can feel safe around me."

Embarrassed, I removed my clothes and stepped into the green dress as Tulianne used her magic to start six separate braids in my hair. I had no idea how she kept them all going at once.

"That's amazing," I said, watching her. "I can only ever lift four things at once. If I even try adding a fifth to the mix, everything falls apart."

She smiled and also used her magic to lift the dress up and fasten it around my neck. "It is merely a matter of practice," she said. "Besides, I am sure you are only being modest. Everyone here in the kingdom knows you have great power."

"You're wrong," I said. "I barely even know how to use my magic. I wish I could learn more about it. Especially the demon side of my powers. I don't even know the first thing about them."

"Perhaps you can ask the king about training while you are here, to master both sides of your power," she said. "He has many guards who work with your kind."

"My kind?"

"Half-demon, half-human," she said. "Many humans have left your homeland to come here over the years, so there are many children like you in the city. We call them hybrids.

Learning to use both sides of your power at once is quite a challenge from what I hear."

She finished the braids and coiled them up against my head in an intricate pattern. She fastened them with golden clips that glittered against my blonde hair.

"How can they practice both when the dome protective seal only allows pure demon magic?" I asked.

"There are training rooms below the throne room where both types of magic can be used," she said. She stepped back to survey my outfit. She reached out toward the scrap of white fabric tied around my wrist, but I pulled away.

"I never take that off," I said.

"I am sorry, Princess," she said. "I did not realize it was important to you."

I'm sure the ratty piece looked strange to her, and completely out of place with this gorgeous dress, but I had vowed to never take it off. It was my reminder of the evil the Order was truly capable of.

"I am thinking you need one final touch."

Tuli lifted a gold chain and long, dangling emerald earrings from a box across the room and floated them toward us with a simple wave. She handed the earrings to me and while I put them on, she fastened the golden chain in my hair in such a way that it almost looked like a crown with a single teardrop-shaped emerald hanging down across my forehead.

I gasped when I looked into the mirror. For the first time in my life, I actually looked like a princess. It was almost too much to take.

"This isn't me," I said in a whisper. "I'm not this girl."

Tulianne leaned close.

"Now, you are the one who is wrong," she said with a knowing smile. "This is exactly who you are."

THEY FOUND YOU FIRST

NERVES KNOTTED IN my stomach.

This would be my first dinner alone with my father. My first real chance to ask him questions about my mother and about his life in Peachville.

As I made my way to the dining hall, I had to wipe my hands on the skirt of my beautiful green dress at least four times. I tried to breathe deeply and calm my heart, but the air stuck in my throat. I took my steps slowly, the gravity of the moment weighing heavily on my mind.

I didn't want to mess this up.

Even in the short time I'd spent with him, I'd learned that my father, the king, could shut down fast if I pressed too hard. Jackson explained that it was part of the demon culture to be patient, while humans were always in a hurry. Demons had hundreds of years to say what they meant or to figure out the truth of their own feelings. Humans never knew if tomorrow would come. It was something I couldn't quite understand and move past.

I might be half-demon, but I had never had the luxury of time. Not the way my father had.

Besides, I felt like I'd waited long enough already.

Two women in plain black dresses stood at the entrance to the dining hall. They smiled as I approached. I blushed from nerves and embarrassment. I wasn't used to being treated like royalty, and I suddenly felt silly in this fancy dress and these green jewels.

"Princess Harper," the woman on the left said. She had short black hair and beautiful blue eyes that sparkled when she talked. "Let me show you to your seat."

I smiled and tugged at my dress.

She bowed and led me through the entrance into a gorgeous room with high ceilings and the most beautiful long wooden table I'd ever seen. The dark wood shone in the light of the orbs that danced near the ceiling. The floor in this room was a deep slate gray and my shoes clacked against it as I walked.

There were twenty chairs seated around the grand table, but only two places had been set for dinner. I walked to the head of the table where ivory place mats were covered with ornate silverware, fine china with a deep blue pattern etched across it, and crystal goblets filled with water.

"Thank you," I said.

A man in a black suit pulled my chair out for me. He made the motions with his hands, but he never actually touched the wood of the chair's frame. Instead, the chair moved by magic. He bowed as I thanked him and sat down, the chair sliding perfectly under me.

I cleared my throat, then took a sip of water. My hand trembled slightly, so I gripped the goblet tighter, hoping no one noticed.

I stared at the empty place next to me.

"The king is still in the throne room with the head of the council," the woman said.

"Oh," I said. "Do you think he's still planning to come?"

"I'm sure he will do his best to spend time with his lovely daughter," she said. She stepped back toward the wall, taking her place beside the other servants dressed in black.

I placed my hands in my lap and crossed my ankles under the table. It was so strange having all these people here to wait on me. I would much rather have been able to just wear my comfy jeans and meet my dad at some fast food place. We could talk over a milkshake and fries or something.

I took another sip of water.

The servants behind me straightened. I looked around, wondering what was going on, then swallowed hard as I saw the king walk through the door.

With a comfortable confidence, he made his way across the room, eyes trained on me.

"Harper," he said. He held his hand out to me and I moved to stand. "No, no need to stand, my dear."

He nodded and the same man who had helped me earlier pulled the chair out. My father sat down next to me, propping his elbows on the table and clasping his hands together.

"You look beautiful," he said. "How are you settling in?"

"Great," I said. My voice came out with a weird croak, and I cleared my throat. "Tulianne is very sweet."

"I'm glad you are getting along fine," he said. "If there's ever anything you need, you just let her know."

Around us, the servants moved with grace and precision, and in less than a minute our plates were full. I watched my father closely and did my best to copy his actions. When he picked up his fork and started to eat, I did the same. I speared a deep red strawberry. The tart flavor made the sides of my cheeks pucker, but I tried not to make a funny face.

I was completely out of my league here. I'd never even eaten at an expensive restaurant, much less at a king's table. I didn't want to make a mistake and look stupid in front of all these people.

I would have much rather spent time with my father somewhere we could both feel comfortable.

"Have you had a chance to explore much of the city?" he asked. "It's a shame so much of it was damaged in the attack, but everyone's been working nonstop to get things back in order."

I finished chewing, then brought my hand in front of my mouth, hoping I didn't have any strawberry seeds stuck in my teeth. "Not yet," I said. "I've mostly just been in my rooms."

A smiled tugged at one corner of his mouth. "I hope you're pleased with your accommodations."

"Are you kidding?" I asked. "They're amazing. The balcony is my favorite part. I love the view of the gardens. I can smell the flowers all the way up in my bedroom."

I wanted to mention the white roses. To ask him about my mother, but I remembered Jackson's advice and took it slow. Small talk might be driving me crazy, but at least we were talking.

"That's wonderful," my father said.

"There was a really nice breeze last night," I said. "But how exactly does that work? If the dome keeps everything out, how come I can feel the wind?"

"The weather here inside the dome is almost always perfect. When it storms outside, we can still hear the thunder and see the rain falling against the barrier, but nothing gets through," he said. "The wind and even the warmth of the sun are actually spells cast to make everyone feel at home here. Every once in a while, we will cast a rain spell that only rains in the gardens and grassy areas so they get properly watered."

Nothing gets through. I winced as I remembered those drops of black acid falling through the crack in the dome. Could I ask him about that? Or would that put too much tension in the whole conversation?

I decided to go for it and say what was on my mind, figuring it wasn't really a personal question.

"Do you know how the Order was able to crack the dome?" I asked. "Is it fixed yet?"

My father sighed and nodded to a servant who quickly brought a bottle of wine to the table. "The crack has been patched, but we're still working to recreate the protective spell that keeps witches from casting human magic within the dome," he said. "It should be finished by morning."

"That's great," I said, relieved.

"Sure, until the Order attacks again," he said. "As long as we keep you and the ring here, I'm sure they'll be watching and waiting for the next chance to attack."

I looked down at my plate, not sure I had the appetite for all this food. "I don't want to put your people in danger," I said.

The king set his fork down and stared at me. When I looked up, our eyes met. "Harper, these are your people too," he said. "They would all willingly lay down their lives for their princess. Don't you know that?"

I shook my head. "They barely even know me."

"They adore you." He took a long drink of red wine. "Please, promise me you won't leave the safety of the dome. You belong here. You're my daughter, and my armies are dedicated to keeping you safe."

The strength of his words hit me hard in the chest. A whole army to protect me? I would rather take them to Peachville with me instead of staying here doing nothing to fight. Was my father expecting me to stay here forever?

"Can I ask you something?" I said.

He drew in a tense breath. "Yes."

I paused, unsure how best to word this. "Did you know the Order tried to kill me?"

He cleared his throat and drank down the rest of his wine. The servant at his side refilled it instantly. "I knew they had you in captivity," he said. "But I only found out about their attempt to transfer your line after you had already been brought here to the shadow world."

"Is that why you didn't come for me?" My plan to make small talk and avoid the hard questions flew right out the window. I couldn't help myself.

"Harper..." His voice grew quiet. He looked around at all of the servants in the room, then leaned forward. "I'm not sure this is really the best time to talk about this. We'll have plenty of time later to talk about anything you want."

My hands went numb from clasping them together so hard under the table. "When? I know you don't really want to talk about all of this, but I have so many questions," I said. "I am trying to be patient and understand that demons aren't always in a rush because of the whole immortal thing. It's just that I've been in the dark pretty much my whole life and now I've finally found someone who knows the truth about me."

My father looked down at his hands, his shoulders tensing.

"I know this is hard," I said. I knew I was going too far, but once I'd started talking, it was impossible to stop. "It's hard for me too, but if we're ever going to have a real relationship, we're going to have to be able to talk to each other now instead of pushing the important conversations off until later." I took a deep breath, trying to still the wild beating of my heart. "Why can't we talk about this now?"

After several long breaths, he finally nodded his head. "I know it must have been difficult growing up without a mother and father," he said. He talked slower than normal, giving each word weight. "Events in my own life forced me back here to the shadow world much sooner than I'd planned, and I had to break things off with your mother. I had no idea she was pregnant at the time, but when she was killed..."

He didn't speak for a moment, and I didn't breathe. Time stood still between us as I waited for him to continue.

"I searched for you," he said, looking over at me. "I tried to find you before the Order could get their hands on you, but I failed. They found you first. By the time I realized it, you were already a part of their world, I couldn't just swoop in and take you away."

"Why not?" I asked, my voice uncertain and weak.

"I was afraid if the Order found out you were my daughter, it would put your life in greater danger," he said with a heavy sigh. "Of course, it turned out you were in danger anyway, long before they ever found out you were a hybrid. I should have just come for you, but I vowed a long time ago not to interfere in the human world."

"So they didn't know about my demon side this whole time?" I asked.

"No one knew," he said. "Until you shifted while fighting those hunters, the only people who knew your identity were a few of the guards on my council and my oldest daughter."

My eyes widened and my heart skipped a beat. It was the first time he'd mentioned my half-sister. All I knew about her from my mother's journal was that she was about six years older than me and had jet black hair.

"She's still in Peachville?" I asked.

"My daughter?" He raised his eyebrows. "Oh yes, in fact you've already met her."

I opened my mouth, nearly jumping out of my seat to find out who she was.

But before I could ask him another question, three guards burst through the door. I wanted to scream in frustration, but as I turned, I saw the fear in their eyes.

"I'm sorry for interrupting your dinner, sire," one guard said with a sideways glance at me.

The king pushed back his chair and stood. "Has there been another attack?"

"It's Gregory, Your Highness," the guard said.

I recognized the name instantly. He was the guard who had found me right after Jackson and I fought with the hunters a few days ago. He was the one who brought us here to my father's castle.

"What happened to him?" I asked.

The guard turned to me. His lower lip trembled slightly. "He's been taken."

THE ACTIONS OF
EVIL PEOPLE

"*I* NEED EVERYONE ELSE to leave the room," the king said. I had no idea if that applied to me or not, but I wanted to hear what these guards were going to say. I stayed.

The servants all rushed out, leaving me, my father and the three guards.

"Tell me what happened."

The king paced the room as the head guard filled him in.

"As you know, Gregory and his men went to the outerlands yesterday to answer to reports of more attacks," he said. "He took six men with him. A few minutes ago, one of these men, Xeran, showed up at the gates of the city, mutilated almost beyond recognition."

The guard glanced at me nervously, probably wondering if this was an appropriate discussion to have in front of a princess.

"I must go to him," the king said, moving toward the door. "Maybe I can help him heal."

The guard stepped in front of him and shook his head. "Xeran is dead, sire. He passed away within minutes of arriving," he said. "It must have taken every last ounce of his life to get back here to tell us what happened."

The king paused, his muscles grown rigid. "Tell me what he said."

"He said they never even made it to the outerlands. They were ambushed by a group of hunters along the way. They were grossly outnumbered and taken by surprise," the guard explained. "He said it was a massacre. They killed everyone else, but took Gregory for their prisoner. Unharmed. Xeran pretended to be dead until the hunters left, then he made his way here."

"Why would they want Gregory?" I asked, standing.

"That's the real question, isn't it?" my father asked, pacing again. "As a personal friend of mine and a member of my council, Gregory was privy to many of my secrets, including the fact that you're my daughter."

"But everyone in the city knows who I am now," I said. "Why take him specifically?"

"That's what I need to find out," he said. "Did Xeran say where the hunters were taking him? Did they give any clue or mention anything that might lead us to where they're keeping Gregory?"

The guard shook his head. "No, he didn't mention anything like that," he said. "Only that when they left, they went north toward the borderlands."

My father sighed. "I'm sorry, Harper, but I'm going to have to cut our dinner short," he said. "In fact, I might have to be gone for a while."

"Are you going after him?" I asked. I wanted to go. To be a part of the action and to find out the truth for myself, but I knew he would never agree to that.

"Yes. If there's any chance Gregory is still here in the shadow world, I have to try to find him," he said. He looked to the group of guards. "Gather a task force. No less than twenty men. Tell

47

them to pack light and meet me by the front entrance in an hour."

The three guards bowed, then left the room.

"Is there anything I can do to help?" I asked when we were alone again. "I feel responsible for all this."

My father took my hands in his.

"I've been fighting this war since long before you were born," he said. "None of this is your fault. How could you be responsible for the actions of evil people?"

I stared down at our hands. "Not fighting back makes me responsible, doesn't it?"

"You shouldn't be so hard on yourself all the time," he said. "A lot of girls would have been seduced by their glamorous lifestyle and their power, but you refused to give in to all of that. You're a fighter, Harper. Otherwise, you wouldn't even be here. You would be at cheerleading practice, happily following their plan for your future."

I looked up at him. "I want to bring them down," I said. "They deserve to pay for what they've done to this world."

"And they will," he said. "Finding the ring was a good start. Over time, we'll be able to do more, but first you need to grow and learn to use your powers more efficiently."

I nodded. I knew he was right.

"Promise me you'll stay," he said, squeezing my hands. "Train with my guards. Get to know the castle and the city around you. When I get back, we'll throw you a real welcome home party. Something fit for a princess."

As much as I wanted to get back to Peachville, I also wanted to stay here and have the chance to finish our conversation. There was still so much I didn't know.

Besides, maybe he was right. Maybe I needed time to train and learn to use my powers.

"Okay," I said. "I'll stay. For now."

He smiled, then kissed my forehead. The intimate gesture brought tears to my eyes.

"I need to get going." He released my hands and walked to the door of the dining room. Before he left, he turned, his silver eyes gleaming. "It's good to have you home."

I WASN'T SURPRISED TO HEAR HER NAME

*I*T WAS WEEKS before my father returned to the domed city.

While he was gone, Jackson and I spent our mornings in training and our afternoons exploring the city. We'd met nearly everyone by now and life inside the dome had settled into a schedule.

There had been no more attacks on the city, but reports of hunters in the outerlands had everyone on edge.

When the king finally returned, it was with a heavy heart.

Tuli was the one who told me he was back. I ran to the throne room, wanting to throw my arms around his neck and welcome him home, but the sadness in his eyes held me back.

"You didn't find Gregory?" I asked.

He sighed and sat down on the silver throne. "No," he said. "We tracked him all the way to the borderlands, but it seems the hunters passed him off to another witch. She took him into the human world."

I stepped closer. "Are you going to go after him?"

My father shook his head. "I told you. I vowed not to interfere in the human world ever again," he said. "Going over there only leads to more problems and more loss. Once someone's been taken by the Order, there's no getting them back."

I couldn't believe he would abandon his friend like that, but after all the time that had passed, what were the chances Gregory was even still alive? I felt sick just thinking about it.

"Did you find out what they wanted from him?"

"We were able to capture one of the hunters who abducted him," my father said. "We questioned her, but all we learned was that Priestess Winter wanted him delivered straight to her in the human world. The hunter didn't know why."

Priestess Winter. I wasn't surprised to hear her name.

"She had to have been after some piece of information she knew Gregory would have," he said. "He was a good man. He wouldn't have shared what he knew willingly, but there's no telling what kind of dark magic she might have used to torture him. I have to assume he told her everything."

I shivered. What had she done to him? And what exactly had she wanted from him?

"That means she knows now that I'm your daughter," I said. "Do you think that's what she was after?"

"There's no way to know for sure, but yes, I imagine she knows about our relationship now," he said. "That's only going to make her more determined to capture you. She'll stop at nothing to steal the essence of your power and transfer it to someone else."

"A new prima?"

"Maybe," he said.

"If she kills me during a ritual and transfers the prima line to another girl, would that give the new witch the demon half of my power too?" I asked. "In addition to making her Prima?"

"I don't think it would be that easy," he said. "The way I understand it, the ritual she tried to perform on you before only transfers the bloodline, not the true essence of the witch. She'd have to plan something more elaborate if she wanted to capture your demon spirit as well."

"Like what?" A cold fear slithered down my spine.

"She could be planning to use a soul stone to trap your essence first," he said.

I gasped. I hadn't thought about her using a soul stone on me. I'd seen what one of those stones had done to Caroline, the future from Cypress, when the crow witch had kidnapped her. It had almost killed her.

"This is why it's more important than ever that you don't go back to Peachville," he said. "Not under any circumstances."

After hearing all this, I was kind of inclined to agree with him. I didn't want to die. Still, I knew we couldn't leave Aerden there, trapped inside a statue for all eternity.

Members of the palace council entered the throne room, cutting off the rest of our conversation.

"If you'll excuse us, I need to fill the council in on what happened," he told me. "We'll talk later."

Later.

I was really starting to hate that word.

EVERYTHING YOU
THINK YOU ARE

OVER THE NEXT several weeks, I immersed myself in my training. If Priestess Winter was determined to come after me, she was going to be in for the fight of her life.

Or at least the fight of mine.

In the training room, Piotrek, one of the guards who'd been working with me, lunged forward. I shifted into my demon form and became weightless.

Airborne.

I was smoke and space. Nothingness. Not in my body, yet fully whole.

I whipped from one side of the room to the other, dodging in and out of the hands that reached for me. Fingertips grazed my arm, bringing my awareness back to my human body. I shifted before I was ready, falling from the air like a sack of rocks. I landed hard on the stone floor of the training room.

"Are you all right?" Jackson rushed to my side. "That looked like it hurt."

I winced and rubbed my hip. "I'm fine," I said. "Probably just another bruise to add to the collection."

Piotrek turned and smiled. "You're already so much better than when we started a few weeks ago," he said, offering me his hand. "Think about the first time you and I sparred. You were barely able to shift."

I took his hand and pulled myself up.

He was right, but that didn't make it any less frustrating. I'd had weeks of intense training. I thought I would be so much better at this by now.

Shifting into demon form was such a strange sensation. The first time it happened against the hunters, it was shift or die. Some kind of survival instinct that kicked in. But when someone asked me to shift on demand?

Impossible.

My first training session with Piotrek and Liroth, another of my father's palace guards, had been spent doing nothing more than learning how to shift and connect with the demon side of my power. Even now, nearly four weeks later, I still hadn't mastered it.

Hell, I still had a hard time believing it was possible. Most of the time, the idea of being part-demon felt more like a dream than a truth. Much less the idea of being a demon princess. Everyone here treated me like royalty, but I still felt like the same old Harper. I still felt vulnerable and weak.

"Let's go, again," Piotrek said. He moved into fighting stance, his feet planted firmly on the stone below and his hands up, almost like a boxer. "This time we'll practice how to transition quickly in order to avoid a spell."

Jackson and Liroth stood back, watching.

I closed my eyes and drew in a slow, deliberate breath. The room stopped spinning as I tried to find my core demon power. When I'd learned to connect to my human witch power, I'd had to become grounded. I needed to feel the humming of the earth beneath my body in order to use my magic.

The demon side of my ability was the opposite. Instead of feeling heavy and grounded, I needed to be light and weightless. I needed to connect to the invisible energy of the air around me. To become a part of it. To forget myself completely.

I breathed in and out, losing my sense of body. My sense of self. I became other. Something totally different from everything I thought I knew about myself before I came here.

Each time the transition began, a split second of panic seized me. A fear of the unknown, as if letting go in such an extreme way would mean the loss of who I was. Over the weeks of practice, I had struggled to not give in to the panic, to let the transition take me.

I opened my eyes just as my body transformed into white smoke and air. I flew up toward the ceiling, then spiraled down, transitioning back to my human form just before my feet hit the ground.

Piotrek threw a bolt of lightning at my newly reformed body and I shifted again, letting the heat of it pass through me as if I were nothing more than a ghost. I smiled. Finally we were getting somewhere.

"See? You're really becoming a pro at this," he said. "The more you practice, the faster you'll be able to switch forms. It will start to become second nature to you, I promise."

I leaned over, hands on my knees as I struggled to catch my breath. I hoped he was right. I knew deep in my heart that once it came down to a real fight, my ability to shift could very well mean the difference between life and death.

"Okay," I said. "One more time?"

I lifted my head to find the three guys had all grown tense, their faces turned toward the door.

I followed their stares, my heart leaping in my throat, nearly choking me. My father stepped into the room.

He wore all black, his silver eyes bright in contrast.

I'd never seen him down in this part of the castle before. To be honest, I'd barely seen him at all since that day in the throne room when he'd first come home from his search. He'd been gone a lot lately, and I'd started to think maybe he was avoiding me.

I wondered if he could hear my heart pounding in my chest.

"Sir," Piotrek said with a bow. "We weren't expecting you."

The king's boots echoed against the stone floor as he crossed to where we stood. "I got home earlier than expected," he said. "The skirmish in the outerlands is finally over. For now."

I swallowed hard as the king's eyes found my own. There was a hard edge to them that made my stomach twist. I looked away.

"Glad to hear it, sir," Liroth said, then nervously cleared his throat.

Jackson came up behind me and put his hand on my shoulder. Normally, the solid warmth of his touch would have eased my nerves, but today it didn't really help.

Why had my father sought me out like this? Was something wrong?

An awkward silence hung in the air, everyone waiting to hear the king's intentions. It was too much for me. If I didn't say something, I was seriously going to explode.

"Did you need something?" I asked, my voice coming out colder than I intended. "We were just in the middle of an exercise."

The king cleared his throat and looked at me. "Actually, I'd like to spar with you," he said, bowing slightly. "If that's okay?"

My head snapped up. He'd definitely caught me by surprise. I tried to act cool and collected, but inside, my heart raced wildly. This was definitely a first. "Sure," I said. "No problem."

Piotrek moved toward the center of the room and got in starting position. "What should we try?" he asked. "We could—"

"I'm sorry, I didn't make myself clear," the king said. His voice was loud and carried easily through the training room. "I'd like to spar with Harper, alone."

My breath caught in my chest. I wasn't ready for this. Was he trying to give me a heart attack?

He met my stare, and I looked away, biting my lower lip.

"I'm not sure I've had enough time to train for this." My throat had gone dry. "I'm not very good yet."

The king didn't respond. He simply raised an eyebrow and looked at the three other guys in the room, waiting for his order to be obeyed. Liroth bowed and walked toward the door. Piotrek threw me a sympathetic look, then followed.

Jackson didn't move. "I think I'll stay," he said.

If I hadn't been so nervous, I might have smiled. Jackson was always trying to protect me, even from my own father. As much as I wanted him to stay, I was also curious about why my father wanted to be alone with me. Was he finally ready to answer questions about my mother? About his life in Peachville? Or had he found out something about Gregory's disappearance? I needed to know.

"I'll be fine," I said, clearing my throat.

Jackson turned to me. "Are you sure?" he whispered. "Because, I'll stay if you need me."

I squeezed his hand. "I'm sure," I said. "I'll meet you upstairs later?"

He nodded, glanced at the king one last time, then reluctantly left the room.

I tugged at the hem of my shirt and tapped my foot inside my shoe. The air between us was electric, filled with the buzz of a thousand unspoken questions.

I waited for him to speak, silence stretching out between us.

"Choose a weapon," he said finally.

I jerked my head up to meet his gaze, surprised. "A weapon?"

"Yes," he said, motioning to the back wall.

Along a series of pegs and stands on the back wall was a collection of weapons ranging from spears to knives to shields. I'd noticed them before, but I'd never actually used any of them.

"What for?"

I knew it was a stupid question, but it just sort of popped out of my mouth before I had a chance to sensor myself.

"For fighting," he said, smiling as he stepped back toward the wall. He looked over the selection carefully, then picked up a long spear with a very pointed silver tip.

I swallowed. Was he serious?

With nervous steps, I walked to the wall. There were so many different kinds of weapons to choose from. It looked like the stuff from fantasy novels or movies about medieval times. Long swords. Scythes. Shields made of iron. I didn't know the first thing about weapons like this, much less which one would be best in a duel against a spear.

"Choose any of them," he said. "There is no right or wrong answer here. It's all a learning process."

He sounded amused.

Meanwhile, I felt like I was going to pass out. There might not have been a right or wrong answer, but for some reason, I wanted him to see how hard I'd been working. I wanted to impress him.

And I hated that I felt that way.

I reached out and took hold of a medium-sized sword with a series of beautiful stones encrusted in the hilt. Something about it caught my eye and drew me toward it. I thought I would be able to hold the sword in one hand since it was much smaller than some of the longer ones up there. The moment I pulled it from its spot on the wall, however, it nearly fell to the floor. I hadn't expected it to be so heavy and the weight of it pulled me forward.

"A powerful choice," he said, eyeing me strangely.

Embarrassed, I pulled the sword up, this time with both hands clasped firmly around the hilt.

The king moved to the center of the training circle and assumed a fighting stance.

I joined him, hands trembling. "What are the rules?" I asked.

"No rules," he said. "Just stay alive."

I stared, wide-eyed. Stay alive? What kind of a rule was that? Was he actually going to try to kill me?

I didn't have time to question him. He stepped forward, his spear slicing through the space between us.

On instinct, I threw my sword out to block him, then jumped to the side. It wasn't my most graceful moment, but at least I wasn't dead.

"Still thinking like a human, I see."

Warmth flared up through my chest. Was that supposed to be some kind of insult? What exactly did he expect? As far as I knew, I'd been purely human my whole life. This demon princess thing was still kind of freaking me out, even after a month and a half.

We circled around the area like boxers in a ring, our eyes locked. I kept my sword out in front of me as I waited for him to strike again.

In a flash, he disappeared from sight, and I spun around wildly. Fear gripped my heart.

Where did he go?

A whoosh of air behind me. I couldn't turn fast enough. The tip of the spear pressed against my side, piercing the skin ever so slightly. The pain caused me to jump, my hand going to the wound.

When I pulled my hand back, red blood coated my fingers.

"What the hell?" I shouted, not really thinking about who I was talking to.

My father withdrew his spear and slapped the wooden end against the stone floor. "Don't complain," he said, his face stern. "You wanted to learn? So learn. Adapt."

My face grew hot with embarrassment. I was relatively new at this and he'd been alive for how many hundreds of years? How was I supposed to fight against a king?

"Again." He lifted his spear toward me.

Part of me wanted to give up, but could I really give him the satisfaction? With renewed determination, I met his gaze, sword ready.

I decided to be the one to strike first this time. I circled for a moment, then twirled and shifted to white smoke. I was surprised when the sword went with me so easily. As long as I was holding it in my hand, it became a part of my disappearing act.

Struggling to hold on to my concentration, I flew high then descended as quickly as I could, my sword pointed directly at the top of his shoulder.

A rush of disbelief pushed through me as I grew closer to him. He didn't move. I was actually going to hit him. Then, at the last second, he shifted and was behind me, forcing me to the ground. He wedged his weapon behind my neck, trapping me at a strange and painful angle.

Tears of anger threatened to come to the surface. Why was he doing this?

"Get up," he said. He withdrew his spear and stepped back.

I didn't want to get up. I wanted to disappear forever.

I gritted my teeth and stood, searching for the strength of will to turn and face him. I would not let him see me cry.

A wisp of white smoke appeared in front of me and I turned before he shifted back. I wasn't ready. Not yet. I swiped at my eyes, then placed both hands back on the jeweled hilt of my sword. "Okay," I said, facing him.

With a roar, he pivoted, spear slicing through the air toward me. I shifted into my demon form as the tip of his weapon reached the spot where my arm had just been. I whooshed around toward his back and attempted to strike him, but he recovered too fast and blocked me. Our weapons clashed against each other and he pushed me backward. My back hit the stone wall, and I winced.

I glared at him, but he smirked as if this was all just a game.

"The problem is speed," he said. "You have to learn to let go of your human body and embrace the demon side. Shifting into a shadow is like forgetting yourself. Stop trying so hard. Just let go. The faster you learn to switch between them, the stronger you'll be."

Sweat gathered at the nape of my neck. The sword weighed heavy in my hands. My jaw tensed as he lifted his spear again and disappeared in a cloud of white.

I heard a rush of air behind me and let go of my body. I shifted into nothingness. I flew in a figure-eight, swirling around him just as he took solid form. I reformed beside him and swung the large sword toward his legs. He jumped, my weapon barely missing him. Before I could recover, his spear came down hard beside my foot.

"Better," he said.

Better, but not good enough. I knew that if he'd wanted to, he could have killed me half a dozen times already.

Frustrated, I stood up and stepped back. I suddenly wanted to beat him. I wanted him to know he couldn't avoid me for weeks on end and then waltz in here like nothing was wrong.

He moved to pick up his spear and I attacked. I surged forward, half-human, half-demon, sword raised. The tip of my weapon slid across the flesh of his arm as I flew past. Triumphant, I stopped and turned back to see his expression.

Only, he was gone.

I turned my head from side-to-side, searching for him. Energy hummed above my head and I looked up as he descended from above. From the tips of his fingers, coils of demon smoke extended, then wrapped around my body like ropes. I dropped my sword and struggled against the bindings.

Humiliation and fury ripped through me. I couldn't do this. "Fine, I'm not good enough," I said. "Are you happy now? Just let me go."

The king stepped in front of me, eyes meeting mine. "That's truly what you believe, isn't it?" he asked. "So, what? You're just going to give up?"

The fears and frustrations of the past couple months fell upon my shoulders like a shroud. When I'd first come here, he'd promised to answer all my questions.

Later.

But instead of opening up to me, he'd grown more and more distant. As time stretched on, he seemed to find new excuses for staying away. I knew his search for Gregory and for information about the Order's plans was important, but wasn't I important too? Couldn't he set aside even one or two hours of non-fighting time to hang out with me?

I had completely lost my patience.

I drew into myself, bending over and pulling my arms tight to my chest. With one swift and powerful movement, I raised up. The vaporous rope that held me broke apart, and I was free. Blue flames roared on the tips of my fingers. I pushed my palms out toward where my father stood and flames flashed across the floor, rising up to trap him inside a cage made of fire.

I staggered backward, gasping for air. I'd manipulated fire with my witch's magic before, but this was different. I had no idea I could do something like that with my demon magic. I dropped my hands and the fire dissipated. I stared down at them, trembling.

My father crossed the room and waited until I lifted my eyes to his.

"Everything you think you are. Everything you believe you're capable of," he said, his eyes dancing with life. "You've just barely scratched the surface."

WHERE WE'RE HEADED

COOL EVENING BREEZE blew my hair back off my shoulders.

I stood on my third floor balcony looking out over the garden behind the castle. My mother's beloved white roses swayed in the wind. I wished she was here now. Maybe she could explain to me why my father was the way he was. Why he closed up so fast and was so afraid of getting close to anyone.

Behind me, familiar footsteps brought a smile to my face. I didn't turn around. I just waited for his strong arms to circle my waist. When they finally did, I closed my eyes and leaned against him.

"How did it go?" Jackson asked. His warm breath caressed my neck.

I didn't even know how to answer. There was so much I still hadn't worked through. "We fought with weapons," I said.

Jackson pulled away and came up beside me, his eyes wide. "He really sparred with you?" he asked. "Didn't you guys talk at all?"

"Yes, and we sort of argued," I said, frowning. "I think. He's a difficult man to understand."

"Maybe that's because he's not a man," Jackson said. He raised an eyebrow. "Did you kick his ass?"

I rolled my eyes and playfully pushed his shoulder, not even sure how to answer that.

"Well, did you?" he insisted.

"It was weird," I said, searching for the words to explain what happened in the training room. "He pushed me to the limit, and I just got so angry. I wanted to give up. But then I started thinking about everything I'd been through just to get here, and I raged on him. I don't even know what happened."

Jackson pulled back, then his face wrinkled with concern. He stared down at a spot on my side. "What did happen? Did he hurt you?"

I looked down. Blood coated the side of my shirt. "Oh, I almost forgot about that," I said. "I've got so many scratches and bruises from the training lately, I barely even noticed."

"Did your father do that to you?"

He crouched down and lifted my shirt a little to get a better look at the wound.

"It's only a scratch," I said.

"Harper, your whole side is bruised and bloodied," he said, standing. "Why didn't you tell me how bad it had gotten?"

I lowered my shirt. "I didn't want you to worry about me," I said. "Or worse, tell me to stop training for a while. I need this."

"I know you do," he said. "But there's no reason for you to be in pain all the time."

He took my hand and pulled me through the archway, back into my bedroom.

"I want to get a better look," Jackson said. He motioned for me to lie back on the bed. "Take off your shirt."

A hot blush flared on my cheeks.

He laughed. "I just want to see where you're hurt."

Slowly, I pulled my shirt off and lay down on the bed. Jackson crawled on beside me. He ran a hand along my bare skin, so soft it made me shiver. I closed my eyes, my heart racing at his touch.

With gentle movements, his fingers traced the outline of every single bruise and scratch across my torso, my arms, and my shoulders. I shivered as his touch sent a shocking chill through each wound, one by one. When he reached the spot on my hip where I'd fallen earlier in training, he leaned over, his breath icy against my flesh. I sucked in a shaking breath as his lips brushed against my skin.

I felt an intense flash of cold, then relief as the throbbing pain melted away.

"Better?" He moved beside me on the bed.

"Much," I said. I glanced down at my body and gasped to find every mark had faded to almost nothing. The wound from my father's spear had stopped bleeding and was now only a tiny scratch. I pulled my shirt back on and sighed. "I wish healing was one of my gifts."

"You heal in other ways." Jackson took my hand in his and brought it to his heart. "Before I met you, I was completely broken."

I blushed again, hyper-aware of how close we were. I took his hand in mine, our fingers entwined.

"What's going to happen to us?" I asked.

He frowned. "What do you mean?"

I shrugged and studied our hands. "I mean despite what my father wants, we can't stay here forever," I said. "Haven't we stayed long enough? What about Aerden? If we don't do something, sooner or later the Order will come after me again and we might lose our chance at setting him free."

"They can't get to you in here," he said. "Your father's council put a new protection spell on the dome. Even if they could crack it again, we would still be able to fight back before they could get to you."

I raised my eyebrows and shook my head. "Don't underestimate the Order of Shadows," I said. "You know that better than anyone."

Jackson sighed. "You're right, but it's safer here than anywhere else right now," he said. "And Aerden's not going anywhere."

"I know, but aren't you anxious to find out if the reversal spell even works?"

"The only problem is that finding out whether it works or not means going back to Peachville," he said. "And we can't do that. It's too dangerous."

I sighed and flopped back on the bed. I stared up at the gemstones on the ceiling. I let them hypnotize me as I tried to think of a new approach to this subject.

Jackson and I had been having this same conversation for weeks. And it always came down to this. We had to go back if we wanted to reverse the ritual. But we couldn't go back because it was too dangerous.

"We just keep going in circles," Jackson said, echoing my thoughts. "I wish we could find a way to free Aerden without risking your life at the same time."

"The thing is," I said, turning again to face him, "this goes so much deeper than me or Aerden. It's about all the innocent demons enslaved by the Order of Shadows. All the humans who have had their choices taken from them. It's time for someone to stand against the Order. You and I both know that's where we're headed, regardless of danger. And the longer we stay here, the more we put everyone in this city in the Order's path."

His eyes searched mine. "What are you saying? That you want to leave now?"

I sighed and snuggled closer to him. "I don't know," I said. "I was willing to stay here this long because I thought I'd eventually have a chance to really talk to my father and ask him all these questions swimming around in my head. But it's been weeks and he keeps pushing me away. I don't know that he'll ever open to me. It feels like we're just wasting time."

"Let's give it another week, now that he's home," he said. "Your father's throwing you that welcoming dance in a week, right?"

I nodded. Despite my protests at having a party in my honor, my father had insisted on throwing a formal ball here at the castle to officially welcome me to the city.

"Let's at least wait until that's over," he said. "Give him a chance to turn things around. Then we can talk about what to do next, okay?"

"Okay." I ran my index finger along his jawline. "I love you," I whispered.

"I love you, too," he said. "You're my life now, Harper. We're in this together until the end, for better or for worse."

His words made my heart soar. Then he kissed me and the world around us slipped away like a forgotten dream.

BEYOND THE BARRIER

THE NEXT AFTERNOON, Jackson and I walked down to the edge of the domed city to visit the school. It was a mixed school where demons, humans, and hybrid children all played and learned together. I had been coming here to spend time with the kids every afternoon for weeks. It was one of my favorite parts of living under the dome.

As we approached the playground, a young boy ran up to me and threw his skinny arms around one of my legs. I laughed as Jackson scooped him up and twirled him around. It was so amazing to finally see the boy healed and healthy again.

When we'd first seen him in the deserted village in the Northern Kingdom, I had no idea how much I would come to care for the little guy. He'd been so strong and brave to stand up to the hunters for me, and I was terrified he would die from his injuries. Thankfully, my father's healing powers had saved him just in time.

A few weeks ago, he'd actually started talking and had told us that his name was Ryder. When I asked him what had happened to his parents and his village, he'd told me the hunters had taken them all away.

How many demons had been stolen from this world for the sake of the Order's power and greed? Now, watching Ryder with Jackson, my heart ached with regret. I wanted so badly to be able to help reunite him with his family, but I had no idea where to even start. There was no guarantee his parents were still alive or that I could free them even if they were.

"Harper, come push me," Ryder said when Jackson finally put him down. He smiled and took off running toward the row of swing sets near the dome's border.

I leaned over and planted a soft kiss on Jackson's cheek. "I'll be by the swings."

"Have fun," he said, then headed over to where a group of kids were playing magic games.

The border of the domed city was clear, as if the city lived inside a bubble. You could see and feel the edge of the barrier as if it was made of glass, but it was much stronger than glass could ever be.

I stepped close to the border and pushed Ryder in his swing. He giggled as I pushed him higher and higher.

That's when something out in the woods just beyond the barrier caught my eye. At first, I assumed it was some kind of animal. A deer, maybe. I hardly paid it any attention.

Then, the figure stumbled out from the protection of the trees and fell to the ground.

I sucked in a pained breath and brought my hand up to my mouth to stifle a scream.

It can't be.

I stopped pushing and walked as close to the dome's border as I could get. I squinted toward the bloodied figure and my hands went numb at the sight.

It was Mary Anne.

A HATRED SO DEEP

I TOOK OFF IN a frantic run. I had to get to her. To help her.

The guards at the dome's entrance crossed spears as I approached.

"I'm sorry, Harper, you know the rules," the first guard said. His name was Everett, I think. I'd seen him here before, and I knew he was one of the king's trusted guards. Strong and tall.

"You don't understand," I said, out of breath. "I have to get out there."

"The king said not to let you outside the dome," Everett said. He stepped in front of me. He was human with bulging muscles under his uniform. He clenched his jaw and didn't take his eyes off my face for one second.

I didn't care if I had to lift this guy with my own two hands to move him out of the way. There was no way I was going to let Mary Anne suffer out there in the woods.

What had she been thinking? Had she been attacked by hunters? Why didn't she contact me on the communication stones? I hadn't talked to her in a few weeks, but she definitely hadn't mentioned heading this way.

Was Essex with her? Surely she wouldn't have left without him? Panic seized my heart. What if he'd been hurt?

"I don't care what the king said," I argued, my pulse racing. "My friend is hurt out there, and I need to help her."

The two guards turned to see who I was talking about.

"I don't see anyone," the second guard said. I had no idea what his name was, but I recognized him as one of the hybrids on my father's guard. Half-demon, half-human. Just like me.

"Here, I'll show you," I said. I moved away from the entrance and pointed toward the edge of the woods. "Come here. See her there by the trees? She's injured and she needs help."

The two guards both lowered their spears and took a few steps toward me to get a better look.

I seized the opportunity and shifted, turning to smoke as I zipped past them and through the city's gate so fast they didn't have time to stop me or even realize what was happening.

I reached Mary Anne's side in a matter of seconds. I shifted back to human form and reached out to her, planning to pick her up and rush her back inside the safety of the dome.

"Mary Anne?" I reached for her, then quickly pulled my hand back as if it had been bitten by a snake.

Her face elongated, morphing into an entirely new face. It happened so fast. One second I was sick with worry. The next I was filled with fear.

I recognized this person. Her amber-colored pixie haircut. Her dark green eyes.

She snarled up at me, then shifted into an orange and black tiger, her fur matted and dirty, not at all like the sleek and beautiful animal I'd faced all those months ago when we'd first come to the shadow world. This tiger's eyes were filled with a hatred so deep and ugly it took my breath away.

I shifted and headed for the entrance to the city. This whole thing had been a setup. How could I have been so stupid? I needed to get back to the safety of the dome.

Before I could slip back through, a solid black barrier formed over the only entrance to the city like a door with no key. The king's guards ran up just as the wall formed, locking them in.

And locking me out.

LOST WITHOUT HER

I TURNED, PREPARED TO fight.

A trio of witches emerged from the trees to join the tiger. I didn't recognize them, but I had a good feeling I knew who had sent them.

The orange tiger shifted back to her human form and the four of them surrounded me. My back pressed hard against the solid black barrier. I swallowed and tried to remember to breathe.

"We have some unfinished business, you and I," the tiger witch said. Her amber hair stood straight up, wild as the look in her eyes.

"I'm not going back to Peachville with you," I said. I touched the blood-stained white scrap of fabric tied around my wrist. A piece of the dress the Order had forced me to wear when they tried to kill me. I would never be their prisoner again. I'd rather die fighting.

"Who said we were here to take you back?" she asked, circling me.

"I know Priestess Winter doesn't want you to kill me," I said. "We've been through this before, remember?"

Her eyes widened and filled with a level of anger and madness I'd never seen before. "How dare you bring that up to me now," she said through clenched teeth. "My sister died by your hand that day. Do you really think I care what Priestess Winter wants? I'll just tell her you died while we were trying to capture you. What can she do? Kill me?"

The tiger witch laughed, but there was no joy in the sound. Its emptiness chilled me to the bone.

In that instant, I knew she wouldn't stop until one of us was dead.

I quickly sized up my enemies. The three witches she'd brought with her looked ragged. They wore stained clothes with rips in the knees and cuffs, as if they hadn't changed their clothes in weeks. Their matted hair and dirtied faces betrayed their state of mind. These were not witches who cared about their lives. They looked as if they had nothing at all to lose.

I had no doubt they would kill me if they got the chance. I widened my stance and lifted my hands.

The witch moved closer. So close I could smell the rancid meat on her breath. "I've been watching you for days, trying to figure out a way to lure you out here." She threw a glance over toward where the children stood, their faces pressed against the dome, fear in their eyes. "Always the same routine with these little ones. You're so predictable with your affection."

She shifted into a tiger so fast I barely knew what was happening. She extended her razor-sharp claws and swiped at my leg. I attempted to change forms, but I wasn't fast enough. Her claws sliced through my skin like knives. Warm blood flowed from my calf down into the dirt.

Her mouth opened and she lunged toward me. Just before she reached me, I managed to shift into demon form, reappearing behind her. From my fingertips, I shot out ropes of white smoke that curled around her body and lifted her up from the ground. I struggled to hold on, but one of the three witches who had come with her lashed out with a fireball so hot it burned my arm as it flew past.

I lost my concentration and cried out, grabbing my arm. One of the other witches lifted a large rock from the ground nearby, hurling it at me with a flick of her wrist. Disoriented, I tried to shift and failed. I couldn't focus. The rock slammed into my shoulder, knocking me to the ground.

Panic filled my chest. I was outnumbered, and I was losing.

What had I been doing all these weeks? Training so I could lose to a group of completely insane witches?

I wasn't about to let that happen.

But in order to win, I had to let go. I had to forget the pain and distractions of my human body in order to shift faster.

I pulled in a steady breath, then became the air around me, weightless and quick. I flew high, surveying the area. The woods were my best chance for cover. I still wasn't great at holding on to my demon form for very long, but I held it just long enough to get to the edge of the forest before I became human again.

The witches couldn't react fast enough. By the time they realized where I'd gone, I'd already lifted a fallen branch and hurled it toward them, my magical aim right on target. The trio fell to the ground, but the tiger witch shifted back to her feral form and managed to dart under the large branch.

She pounced on me, knocking me to the ground. I didn't have the focus to change again. My back hit the forest floor at high speed. I lost my breath. My head smacked against a boulder, and I nearly lost consciousness.

My eyes closed, but I fought against the darkness. I pried them open and glanced toward the dome. In the distance, Jackson pounded against the invisible barrier. His face wore the worry of a thousand days. His eyes urged me to get up and fight, but I struggled just to stay alert.

The tiger's fangs pierced the skin on my neck, ripping a scream from my throat.

I wasn't going to die like this. Not because of some stupid glamour trick. I remembered my father's words. *Shifting into a shadow is like forgetting yourself. Stop trying so hard. Just let go.*

So I did.

My body disappeared. The tiger's jaw slammed into the ground where I had been, but I was now behind her. Dizziness threatened to wash over me, so this time instead of trying to fight it, I gave in. I let it take me under and twist my insides. I forgot my human body and embraced this other me that had been hiding inside all these years.

I flew to a branch midway up the nearest tree. Using the force of my demon strength, a strength I hadn't even realized I possessed, I ripped a dozen long branches from the tree and sent them down around the tiger, trapping her inside.

When I was sure the branches would hold her for a moment, I turned my attention to the three witches who rushed toward her. I fell from the tree and shifted effortlessly, flying through the air faster than the wind itself.

Before the witches knew I was even there, I became human again and reached deep within the earth, pulling a sheet of dirt and rock up in front of them like a wall. They slammed against it, pushing it in my direction. It fell toward me and I struggled to hold it.

My heart beat with wild panic, seeing a way to defeat them. I didn't want to be a killer, but what choice had they left me? When it was either me or them, I couldn't afford to hesitate or show mercy. I had to be strong. I had to live.

With one giant magical push, I toppled the earth wall over them, crushing them into the ground.

Behind me, the tiger's roar gave me enough warning to shift and move just as she pounced. A single claw cut through my leg as I disappeared. The pain broke my focus, my body plunging hard onto the ground.

I scrambled backward, her teeth barely missing me. Frantic, I ripped a cluster of rocks from the ground, holding them over her head.

The tiger shifted to her witch form, cowering under the stones.

Why didn't she run?

I expected her to leap at me or growl or at least try to move out of the way of the crushing debris. Instead, she looked up at the stones above her.

"Do it," she said, her voice high-pitched and trembling. "If I'm going to die, I want it to be just like her. I want to feel what my sister felt in her final moments."

Guilt surged through me. I hadn't meant to kill her sister when we'd come into the shadow world, but I thought she'd killed Mary Anne. All I could think about at the time was revenge.

"I'm sorry," I said. The rocks hovered over her, and I didn't know whether to drop them or push them to the side. Was this another one of her tricks? "I know you don't believe me, but I never meant to kill your sister."

She turned to me then, her face softening for a moment. Her green eyes clear. "I'm lost without her," she whispered.

Then, something inside her cracked. Her eyes opened so wide, I thought they were going to pop out of her skull. Her mouth twisted up in a grotesque smile and she began to laugh.

I didn't know what to make of it. I half expected her to shift again and try to rip my throat out.

Instead, her insane laughter turned to sobs that shook her entire body. She threw herself against the ground, raking her nails furiously on the hard surface of the rocks. Blood trickled from her fingertips and she barely seemed to notice. Then, suddenly, the witch stopped moving, her eyes staring dead ahead. The rapid rise and fall of her chest the only indication she was even still alive.

Behind her, the black barrier that locked me out of the domed city dissipated into thin air.

Several guards rushed out to us. They seized the witch under her arms and dragged her inside the dome where her magic would be useless. I let the stones fall to the ground with a thud.

Jackson ran to me, falling onto his knees in the dirt. "Harper, are you okay?" He pulled me close. "Oh, god, what were you thinking?"

I couldn't answer. All I could do was watch as the guards carried the broken witch through the streets of the domed city.

YOU CARE TOO MUCH

"*W*HERE IS SHE?"

I expected to see the tiger witch here in the throne room, presented for some kind of sentencing. Instead, the room was bare. No guards or attendants. Only the king sitting on his throne. Waiting.

"I sent her to the dungeons," he said, no trace of a smile on his face.

"I don't want anyone to hurt her," I said, lifting my chin. "She's my prisoner, and I want to make sure she's being taken care of."

"She's my prisoner," my father said, his voice so loud it scared me. "I told you never to leave the boundaries of the domed city. You have expressly disobeyed me. You do not dare come into my throne room now and tell me what to do with a prisoner who attacked my city."

I stepped closer to the throne, refusing to back down. "You can't tell me what to do."

Even as the words left my mouth, I knew it was a childish thing to say. A daughter telling her father he had no authority over her. But I was still new to this whole having-a-parent thing.

"When you're here in the Southern Kingdom, you will do as I say." He stood. From his perch several steps up, he towered over me. His eyes darkened to a deep gray

"Or what?" I asked, crossing my arms. "You'll kick me out? You'll send me back to Peachville? Maybe I should go back there anyway. There's still a war going on whether you choose to fight or not."

My threat to leave seemed to curb his anger. The wrinkles on his forehead softened slightly. "Harper, you know I don't want you to leave," he said. "I just want you to understand that you have to be more careful. Once you're outside the domed city, you're vulnerable to whatever and whoever they want to send your way. They won't stop until you're captured or killed."

"I know," I said, not even sure why I was arguing with him. I guess I knew he was going to yell at me and wanted to beat him to the punch. "I made a mistake. This witch, she used a glamour to make herself look like my best friend, and I fell for it. It was stupid, but I have to be free to make my own mistakes without you yelling at me like I'm some ignorant child. I may technically be your daughter, but you've never once been a real father to me, so don't think you can just waltz into my life and start telling me what to do."

My outburst was probably the most honest I'd been with him since I first arrived in the Southern Kingdom, but there was still a huge wall up between us that I had no idea how to pull down.

"You can't expect that I'm going to be able to sit back and watch you get hurt," he said. "Not when I could do something to prevent it." He walked over to me and placed his hand on the bloody teethmarks at my neck. In an instant, the wounds healed over, leaving only dried blood and dirt behind.

"Tell me why you care about this prisoner so much anyway."

"I have a history with this tiger," I said. "I just want to know what you're planning to do with her."

81

"Tiger?" He cocked his head to the side, then nodded. "That's her spirit animal? A tiger?"

"Yes," I said. "I feel like I kind of owe her something."

"How so?"

I bit my lip. "I killed her twin sister," I said. "When we first came to the shadow world, the Order sent them after me. I got angry and lost control. I didn't mean to kill her, but my power was stronger than I expected it to be."

"And you think you owe her something because of it?" he asked. "Wasn't she trying to kill you?"

"It's not that cut and dried. I took away the one thing that was more precious to her than anything else," I said. "I do owe her."

My father put his arm around me. I stiffened at this first sign of affection in weeks.

"You have such a kind heart," he said. "But you have to realize that she and her sister put themselves at the service of the Order of Shadows. They were well aware of the danger that presented."

"So you think they deserved what happened to them?"

"They made a conscious choice to serve evil," he said. "They put themselves in that position."

"Well, I put myself in a terrible position today," I said. "I killed three witches to save myself. I don't even know their names or where they came from, but at some point, they were all probably just girls like me or Lark or Brooke. Girls who joined the cheerleading squad at their school because they wanted to know more about how their powers worked. Girls who had no idea what they were getting themselves into, until it was too late."

"How can you have such sympathy for those who choose to fight against you?"

"I know what the Order does to the recruits. I watched them pull my friend Brooke into a ritual room kicking and screaming and begging them not to go through with it. She was forced there against her will, no different from the demons who are pulled from this world to be slaves."

"It's very different," the king said. He turned away from me and began to pace in front of the steps up to the throne. "Maybe she didn't have a choice when she was being brought to her initiation, but what about afterward? Why doesn't anyone stand up against what's happening to the recruits? Why didn't your friend Brooke come to all of the recruits after her ceremony and warn you against what happened to her?"

I stood there, staring dumbly forward. I had no answer for him. I didn't understand it myself. Something changed about Brooke the night she was initiated. I didn't know if it had more to do with her loyalty to her family or her actual initiation, but she was never the same.

"I'll tell you why," he continued. "Power. Once a human witch feels a demon's strength inside of her and realizes just how much more powerful she has become, she's completely unwilling to let go. It's an addiction. Maybe she knows it's wrong, but she just can't seem to do anything to stop it."

His reasoning made sense, but I believed there was more to it than that.

"It's not that simple," I said. "Brooke's family has been a part of the Order of Shadows for generations. Speaking out would be a complete betrayal of everyone she loves. If she had come to us and told us to leave the cheerleading team or had explained even a little bit of what happened to her in that ritual room, who knows what the Order would have done to punish her? They might have killed her or turned her into a hunter for all we know. And it all would have been for nothing because they have the power to erase our memories."

"Just because it's dangerous doesn't mean she shouldn't fight against something that's wrong," he said.

"I agree with you," I said. "But I don't see you going into the human world to fight the Order. You said you refused to go there, because it's too dangerous. What's the difference?"

The room grew quiet except for the sound of my father's boots on the marble floor.

I had no idea what was going through his mind, but I hoped he heard what I was saying. If we ever planned to defeat the Order, we were going to have to be able to talk through our beliefs about them.

In my heart, I knew Brooke wasn't evil. But I also knew she wasn't strong enough to fight against everything, and everyone, she's ever loved.

Who would be?

He turned back to me, a sad smile on his face. "You want to know what the funny thing is?"

I stared ahead. "There's a funny thing?"

"I used to have this same argument with my own father, except I was the one arguing for human rights back then."

This bit of personal information took me by surprise. I wanted to ask him more about his father. About what had changed his mind about fighting in the human world, but he changed the subject before I had the chance.

"What would you have me do with this prisoner?" he asked.

I straightened. "Let me question her," I said. "She might be able to give us important information about Priestess Winter."

"Absolutely not," he said, slicing his hand through the air as if that added some kind of finality to his words.

"Why even ask me what you should do with her if you aren't even going to listen to me?" I said.

"I thought you might suggest something reasonable."

"Wanting to question her is perfectly reasonable." I crossed my arms in front of my chest. "She was very close to Priestess Winter."

"Harper, you just told me you killed this girl's twin sister. Do you not understand that everything she does is to get revenge on you? Do you honestly think she would tell you the truth? That you could trust her?"

I clenched my jaw. "Her spirit is broken," I explained. "She's vulnerable right now in a way she may not be in a week or more. If I go down there and talk to her, she might tell me something important while she still can. We don't have much time before she completely loses her mind, if she hasn't already."

"Or she might pull you into another trap by telling you something scary about what's happening back home."

My blood chilled in my veins. "What do you know about what's going on back there? Have you heard something?"

"See? You care too much. The Order knows that about you, and they will do whatever it takes to use it against you."

I sighed. I knew he was right. I'd just left the safety of the dome to save someone I thought was Mary Anne. But what else could I do? "I spent my whole life with no one to love and no one who loved me back," I said. "Now what? You expect me to go back to keeping everyone at arm's length so the Order can't use love against me?"

"That isn't what I said."

"Yes, it is," I argued. "But I can't do that. I can't turn my back on my friends and the people I love."

The king stopped his pacing and turned to look straight into my eyes. Silence filled the space between us; as if he wanted to share something but couldn't quite find the words.

"Then you'd better learn to be smarter about where you go and what you choose to believe," he said, finally finding his voice again. "Or you'll get yourself killed."

I swallowed, but my mouth had gone completely dry.

He was right. I'd been stupid to believe that was Mary Anne out there in the woods. If she had decided to leave the

Underground, she would have contacted me through the stones.

But maybe some good would come of it. Downstairs we now held a witch who had once been very important to Priestess Winter. When I disappeared from the Halloween Ball with Jackson and the other shadow demons, it was the tigers she had sent after me. When I was a prisoner on the third floor of Shadowford, the priestess had trusted the two tigers to watch over me. And when I was pulled through the portal to the shadow world, she sent the tigers to bring me home.

She trusted them and she kept them close. If anyone knew Priestess Winter's secrets, it was the tiger witch.

Somehow, I was going to have to get down there and pull them out of her. With or without my father's permission.

THE PEOPLE WE
LEFT BEHIND

*J*ACKSON WAITED FOR me in the garden, a notebook and
pencil on his lap.

"How did it go?"

I shrugged and sat down on the edge of the marble
fountain. "He treats me like an ignorant child."

"Well, in his defense, he is about five hundred years older
than you," Jackson said. He flipped his notebook over, hiding
the page from me.

I didn't even have the energy to ask him what he'd been
drawing.

I dipped my hand into the cool blue water. "He locked the
witch in the dungeon," I said. "He told me I couldn't go down
there to question her or anything."

"Did he say why?"

"He thinks she would try to manipulate me into another
trap," I said.

Jackson put his hand on my leg. "Harper. He's probably
right," he said. "She would do anything to hurt you. She's

fiercely loyal to the Order of Shadows and Priestess Winter, specifically. I doubt there's anything you could say to her that would make her break that loyalty, you know?"

I shook my head. "I'm not so sure about that," I said. "What if Priestess Winter wasn't even behind that attack today? There was something about the wild look in her eyes and the way her fur was all matted up. I got the feeling she'd gone rogue."

"That could all be part of the trap," he said. "There's no way to know."

I sighed. "I hate being stuck here in the shadow world, moving from safe house to safe house, avoiding all the action. I want to be doing something productive."

"You are," he said. "You've been training nonstop for weeks here, and it obviously paid off, right? You took on four very powerful witches today. Most people would have fallen within seconds, but you didn't. You beat them."

I looked down into the water of the fountain and a stray piece of hair fell over my eyes. With a touch so gentle, Jackson tucked the strand of hair behind my ear and bent over to kiss my cheek. Warmth rushed through my body, and I closed my eyes, taking in the feel of his lips on my skin.

Just knowing he believed in me made everything seem more manageable.

Still, I felt restless. "What good is all this training if I spend the rest of my life here, under the safety of some magical dome?"

I stood and took a familiar path through the garden. There were lots of flowers and beautiful blooming trees here, but the white roses were my favorite. I walked toward them and Jackson followed.

"What is it that you want to do?" Jackson asked. "If you go back to Peachville, you'll have the entire Order coming after you."

"Not the entire Order," I said. "There are people who would stand with me. I know it."

"Like who?"

"Like Lark and her mom. Mrs. King. Caroline and her mom from Cypress. I know I'm not the only one who would stand up against the Order of Shadows," I said. "Plus, didn't your shadow demon friends know other witches who want out? Other demon gate towns who are tired of using demons as slaves and having to obey the High Council?"

"Yes, but getting everyone to stand up and fight against them isn't going to be easy," Jackson said, quickening his pace to keep up with me. "Those women are afraid. They've seen what the Order has done to other towns that stood up against them. Towns like Aldeen."

I shivered, remembering the horrible scene Lea had shown me. Priestess Winter had killed all the witches from the Aldeen demon gate in one shot by killing their prima and pouring her blood onto the portal stone. The image of her death was etched into my memory like a nightmare.

"Aldeen was caught by surprise," I said. "If we all banded together, maybe we could be the ones to surprise Priestess Winter for a change. If we could perform the reversal of the gate ritual and free Aerden, we could prove to others that there is still a choice. Still a chance for a life of their own."

"We don't even know for sure the ritual will work," he said. "What will happen to us if it doesn't? We have to think smart, Harper. Priestess Winter has eyes everywhere. Even people you think are your friends could be her closest allies."

I stopped at the fence around the white rose garden, out of breath from walking so fast. I knew he was right. There were no clear lines to show good and evil, and I had no idea who I could really trust, no matter how much I wanted to think I did.

"Look," Jackson said, putting his hands on my shoulders and turning me to face him. "I know you want to take action, but rushing in without a good plan and without the skills or knowledge to defeat the Order would be foolish. I know it feels like we've been here for a long time, but we only just came to the shadow world a few months ago. We need to be patient, get our plan together before we just go in, guns blazing, so to speak."

I shook my head. "I feel so cut off from Peachville. We have no news about what's really happening over there. I guess that's part of why I wanted to try to talk to the tiger witch. To see if she could give me some clue about the state of things back home."

"I bet things are mostly the same," he said. "Except that we're gone and the Order is looking for us. Other than that, it's probably the same old stuff. Who knows if the people of Peachville even remember us? What if the priestess somehow made them all forget we ever existed?"

A dark feeling washed over me. Priestess Winter and the higher-ups in the Order were capable of almost anything. I didn't put any dark magic beyond their reach. They were always toying with people's lives, their emotions, their memories. And after I left, they had to have been very angry. I shuddered.

"What is it?" Jackson asked, pulling me close. "What's bothering you so much about being gone?"

I leaned my head against the solidness of his chest. "When you pulled me through to this world and saved my life, you took away some of the Order's power," I said. "When we found the ring, we took even more. Don't get me wrong, I'm happy we did it. But at the same time, I'm terrified."

"Of what?"

I thought about my friends. Courtney. Lark. Mrs. King. People I truly cared about. People the Order knew I had become close to. People they could use against me in the most horrible ways. My father was right. I did care too much.

"I'm terrified of what they'll do to the people we left behind."

A HERO LOCKED INSIDE

THE FOLLOWING MORNING, I awoke to shouts outside the castle.

I threw the covers off my legs and stood, squinting at the bright sunlight that streamed through the gauzy curtains. What in the world was going on out there? Was it another attack?

I only had a chance to take a few steps toward the patio when Tuli came rushing in from the hallway. "Princess Harper, wait, wait! Please do not step outside," she said. "I do not think anyone could see you from here, but we want to make sure you look your best today."

I would have been alarmed by her just crashing in like that except the smile on her face was as wide as I'd ever seen it.

"What's going on? Has something happened?"

She giggled. "The people of the city have gathered in the streets to celebrate your victory over the Order yesterday."

She practically skipped into the closet and came out moments later with a purple dress.

"What do you mean, celebrating?" I asked.

She held the dress up to my skin as if checking the color. "I mean the people of the city are outside the castle's front steps calling for you, singing your praises, bringing you flowers and gifts. Celebrating your battle with the witches yesterday," she said. "And I cannot let you go out there in your pajamas, so here, you are wearing this today."

My stomach fluttered.

"What are they expecting me to do?" I asked as Tuli pushed me toward the giant floor-length mirror in my bathroom. "Do I have to make some kind of speech or something?"

I traded my nightgown for the pretty purple dress. Its asymmetrical design looked great on me. Not that I wanted to go around wearing dresses all the time, but Tuli knew what she was doing when it came to fashion.

"Just be yourself," she said. "The people of the city are here to see Harper. They aren't expecting anything or anyone else. They simply want to show their appreciation."

"But that's what I don't understand," I said, wincing as she brushed through my wavy hair. I hadn't used any glamours to straighten my hair in a long time, but now I kind of missed them. Glamours had been so much easier. And less painful. "Appreciation for what?"

"For standing up against the Order, of course," she said. "The people champion your father's kindness and they appreciate that he has given them a safe haven to live with their families, but most of all, they are grateful to have a king who is willing to fight for them. They are uplifted to see that, like your father, you are willing to stand up against the Order and fight for what is right."

I shook my head. It had been foolish for me to go outside the domed city unprotected. I hadn't done it to be some kind of hero.

"But I didn't even realize they were from the Order when I left the city," I said. "I thought I was going outside to help a friend."

"It doesn't matter the reason for the fight," she said. "Many people saw what you did. There are not many who could stand against four witches. You fought like a real warrior yesterday."

Nervousness trickled through my veins, leaving me slightly shaky and weak in the knees. "I thought they'd be angry with me for bringing the attention of the Order here to the city."

"We live in a domed city, Princess. Drawing the attention of the Order is nothing new to them."

When she was done fiddling with my hair, she walked with me to the throne room where my father was waiting.

"You look lovely," he said, holding his arm out to me.

I looped my arm in his, wanting to hold tight to him like a little girl. "Thanks," I said, my voice uncertain.

I had no idea what to expect from the crowd outside. Did they really think I was some kind of hero for fighting those witches? I had only been trying to stay alive.

I took a deep breath, my trembling hands betraying my nerves. "Does this bother you?" I asked. "Their praise for something you thought was foolish."

"This isn't about me," he said. "Are you ready?"

I nodded, not sure I'd ever be ready, then walked with him to the balcony. The damage from that first attack nearly two months ago was gone and everything looked brand new. The steps of the castle were filled with flowers and gifts. The moment we came into view, someone in the crowd shouted and pointed up toward us. The loud cheers of the people below brought tears to my eyes.

I took my arm from his and eased closer to the balcony's edge. I leaned against the railing and stood higher on my tip-toes so that I could see everyone more clearly. Another cheer broke out, and I couldn't help but smile. I waved to the crowd below, unable to believe this was really happening to me.

I looked down at the mixture of humans, demons, and hybrids, hope radiating in their eyes. They believed in me. They really thought I was capable of doing something extraordinary.

Was I?

Or had I gotten in way over my head? I'd somehow managed to survive this long, but was it luck? Or was there really a hero locked inside of me? A warrior?

I touched the scrap of white fabric tied around my wrist. It was frayed at the edges and stained, but it was my talisman. My reminder of what the Order was truly all about.

I stared out at the people of my father's city and swore to myself I wouldn't let them down. I wouldn't let myself down. Somehow, I would find my way back to Peachville. And even if it took my entire lifetime, I would see the end of the Order of Shadows.

INNER DEMON

*T*HE REST OF the week went by in a blur. I threw myself into my training, spending almost every spare moment of my time down in the dungeons.

I'd been able to beat the tiger witch and her friends outside the dome, but the fight was way too close for comfort. Would I be so lucky next time? I still hadn't learned how to control the demon side of my power enough to use it to any real advantage in a fight.

If I was truly going to be a warrior, I would need full access to both sides of my power.

Jackson and I had agreed to wait until after my father's welcome home dance to make a decision about whether to stay here or go back to Peachville to try the ritual. As the week wore on and the day of the party approached, I began to feel more and more restless.

I wanted to go back to Peachville. There was no secret about that. I had never really been great at being patient, and I was dying to get back there and see if this spell would work or not. I also wanted to make sure my friends were safe. On the other hand, I knew I was still weak. In a one-on-one fight with

Priestess Winter, would I even last five seconds? The thought made me shiver.

How could one witch be so powerful she would make even a demon king nervous?

If I didn't learn to make the most of my hybrid powers, I knew I wouldn't stand a chance against a truly powerful witch. And I had no doubt that once she found out I was back in the human world, Priestess Winter would come after me with everything she had.

Piotrek and Liroth worked with me in the mornings, but in the afternoons, Jackson and I were alone in the training room.

"What do you want to work on today?" he asked. "More shields?"

I sighed and shook my head. I was exhausted and frustrated. I'd been practically killing myself for a week and didn't feel like I'd really made any progress.

"What's wrong?" he walked over to me and put his arms around me.

I rested my head against his shoulder. "I suck at this," I said. "We run the same drills every day and I'm still struggling."

"You're getting better," he said. "These things take time, Harper. You can't expect to master an entirely new form of magic in a couple months. Think of it this way. It's like someone who is paralyzed for years suddenly regains use of their legs. It's not like they'd be able to just stand up and start running a marathon. It would take months of intense therapy for them to learn how to even walk again; much less run. You have to give yourself more time."

I pushed away. "We don't have time," I said. "Every day we spend here in the safety of this dome, the Order is plotting against us. They're pulling more demons through their portals and recruiting more young girls to their cheerleading teams. Every day they get farther and farther ahead."

"And what exactly do you think we should do about it?" he asked. His jaw tensed. "We've talked about this a hundred times already. If we rush into something because we're impatient, we're going to get ourselves killed. Then who will stand against the Order?"

I kicked at the stone floor. "I wish I was improving faster, that's all," I said. "I know I'm getting better at switching from human to demon form, but the actual magic itself still feels strange to me."

"How so?" he said. "Let's talk it out."

I shrugged. "It's hard to explain. I mean, I can use both sides of my magic to create the same fire, but I still don't really understand why I would use one over the other in a fight."

"Okay, then let's try them both," he said. "One at a time. See if you can put into words how they're different. Then we'll figure out why you might use one in certain situations instead of the other."

I stared down at the floor. I was so used to magic coming easily to me. Sure, I'd worked hard, but most things only took me a few days to really master. Using demon magic was different. It scared me. Every time I started to use it, something inside me panicked, and I backed off.

I wanted to understand it, but at the same time, part of me wanted to just settle for using my normal witch magic and stay far away from the demon side of myself.

"Come on," he said. "We'll start easy."

He moved a training dummy to the middle of the room then came to stand beside me.

"Try to set the dummy on fire using the human half of your power," he said. "Really concentrate on how it feels and where your power comes from."

I breathed deep, taking a moment to really connect to the earth beneath my feet. I raised my hands, spreading my fingers wide as the tips erupted in flames. I drew them back and pushed forward, sending flames dancing through the air toward the dummy.

"What did that feel like?" Jackson asked.

"Safe," I said. "Controlled."

"What else?"

I thought of how Zara had taught me to focus using the image of a blue butterfly in the darkness of my mind. To clear everything else from my thoughts. "It felt grounded. Focused and calm."

Jackson nodded and waved a hand toward the training dummy. The flames disappeared and the dummy looked brand new again. "Now try using the other half of your power," he said. "The demon side."

I swallowed and shook my hands out, trying to get rid of my nerves. Accessing the demon side of my power was a lot more difficult. Most of the time in training, I couldn't really do it whenever I wanted. Most of the time, I spent half an hour trying to make it happen before I finally gave up.

I took a deep breath in and my heartbeat slowed. I imagined the flames on my fingertips, but they wouldn't come. I shook my hands again, then lifted them in front of me.

How could I do this? What was really different about the demon side of my power?

I thought about the times when I'd shifted easily or used my demon power without having to really think about it. First, against the hunters near the blue stones. I'd shifted in order to save my own life. Then, I'd used it again to break free of the hunter's cage in the throne room that first day we were attacked.

The first time I'd created fire with my demon power, I'd been arguing with my father.

Each time the demon side came easily I'd either been completely terrified of death or extremely angry. Feelings that were opposite of controlled and focused. There was nothing that felt safe about using my demon power. Instead, every time

I shifted forms, panic seized my whole body. In fact, when I was in demon form, the second I started to really focus on my body or power in any way, I tended to lose my form and shift back to human.

Maybe the key to accessing that demon side of my power was to let the panic take over. Maybe instead of calm and focused, I needed to feel passionate and fractured.

I opened my eyes wide and stared at the dummy in front of me. I imagined Priestess Winter's evil smile and the way her eyes gleamed as she ran her ritual knife across the throat of Aldeen's prima. I let fury fill my heart. I let it send my mind in a million directions. I let it bring me to the ledge. Then I fell. Instead of controlling myself, I gave my inner demon free rein to feel.

Somewhere in the core of myself, I felt a strange power bloom. It started as a kernel of fire, then spread out in a wide circle, exploding until it consumed me from head to toe. Flames ran down my arms and covered my hands, much stronger and brighter than the human flames from a few minutes ago.

I pushed my hands forward, sending the flames across the room. The training dummy erupted, fire blazing high up toward the ceiling.

Power danced inside me. The loss of control scared the crap out of me, but it excited me at the same time.

Instead of draining me, this power fed me.

Jackson placed a warm hand on my shoulder and the flames died. I stumbled backward, shaking my head.

"Whoa," he said. "That was intense."

I laughed, almost drunk with it. "I've never been able to do that before," I said. "That was incredible."

"How was it different?" he asked.

I struggled for a way to explain it. It was more sensation than something I could put words to. Still, I wanted to try. "This was wild," I said. "Passionate and free. Instead of controlled and meticulous, this power was all about letting go. Instead of a single image in my mind, I felt this deeper. Almost as if it was primal. Does any of that make sense?"

Jackson's eyebrow rose slightly. "Yes, it does," he said.

"Is that the way it feels when you cast your magic?"

He seemed to think about that for a second. "I think it's different for me," he said. "Since it's the only kind of magic I have, I don't really know anything else. It's just natural for me. I'm not going to have the same kind of sensations you do, because I don't have anything to compare it to."

I nodded. "That makes sense," I said. "Does it feel different to use your demon magic here than when you use it in the human world?"

"Good question," he said. "When we go back, you'll need to be prepared for the difference. Here, demon power comes from within. As if the fuel for it lies in some well deep inside. When a demon casts in the human world, though, the power is drawn from outside. Everything around you that's alive can become a fuel source. Trees. Animals. People."

"Does that make it harder?"

"Sometimes," he said. "It can be both an advantage and a disadvantage."

"How so?"

"Well, an advantage because we can pull from the witches we're fighting," he said. "If you can find a witch's life source, you can use your magic to drain her and weaken her."

"And the disadvantage?"

"The more powerful spells take a lot of energy to cast," he said. "If you've already used up most of the life fuel in an area, it's a lot harder to use those bigger spells. Or if you're in an area where there's not a lot of life to pull from. Like a desert or something."

I nodded. In theory, I understood what he was saying, but I had a feeling it was the kind of thing I needed to experience for myself to truly understand.

"Do you want to keep going?" he asked. "Or should we call it a night? Tomorrow's going to be a big day."

I sighed. "Yeah, I guess you're right. I'm not looking forward to this party at all."

He grabbed his backpack, then put his arm around me and escorted me out of the room. "It's important to your father," he said. "All you have to do is smile and say hello to everyone and act like the beautiful princess that you are. Easy, right?"

I groaned. It sounded like torture. All those people staring at me and expecting me to look and act a certain way. Definitely not my thing.

"I don't know about easy, but I'm sure I'll survive it," I said, pausing on the step above him. "Then we'll talk about our plans, right? After the dance?"

He nodded. "Then we'll talk."

I kissed him on the nose and he laughed.

"I'll see you tomorrow then," I said with a curtsey.

He bowed to me. "See you tomorrow, my beautiful princess."

THEY NEVER RETURN

HE MORNING OF the dance arrived, and all I wanted to do was keep training. I'd made a real breakthrough the day before, and I was anxious to get back down there and practice. I'd planned on trying to get a few hours in before I had to start getting ready, but Tulianne woke me up bright and early with a full schedule of pampering that would have made the most experienced debutante wide-eyed.

Apparently getting ready for a ball was an all-day event for a princess.

"You really don't have to give me a massage," I told her when she brought out the tray of oils and aromatherapy herbs. "I can just take a shower and be done with it."

"Nonsense," she said. "A princess must show up at a ball in her honor looking relaxed and at her most beautiful."

"Can't we just perform some kind of glamour that would make me look relaxed and beautiful? You guys can do glamours with demon magic right?" All this attention was making me incredibly uncomfortable.

"Why would we perform a glamour on someone like you?" she said. "All that would do is hide your natural beauty."

I snorted. Natural beauty apparently took all day to create. Still, the massage felt pretty good and maybe Tuli was right. I needed to relax. I'd been putting a lot of pressure on myself lately.

After the massage, Tuli drew a steaming hot bath and filled the large tub to the top with bubbles. She brought me a glass of juice made from an exotic fruit that only existed here in this world. It tasted like a mix of strawberries and peaches. Only sweeter.

Once I was settled in, she turned to leave.

"Wait," I said. "Can you stay? Talk to me for a while?"

She smiled and I could see the hint of a blush on her dark cheeks. "You want to talk?"

"Yes," I said. I'd come to enjoy our talks. So much of my time in the shadow world had been spent in hiding. I liked talking to Tuli because she showed me a different perspective to what life was like here. "I mean, you don't have to or anything. If you've got something else you need to be doing, I totally understand."

She shook her head and came to sit on one of the marble steps leading up to the tub. "I have nothing else to do," she said. "I just thought you might prefer some privacy."

I laughed. "Believe me, all I would do is sit in here and stress out about what this party is going to be like."

"Why stress?" she asked. "You don't like parties?"

Wow. Where did I even begin? "Parties back in Peachville were always a disaster," I said. "Someone almost always died or got kidnapped or something awful. Trust me, if I could live the rest of my life without another party, I would be a happy girl."

Tuli frowned. "I am sorry to hear this," she said. "I am sure your father did not intend to upset you."

I shook my head. "It's really not that big of a deal," I said. "I'm sure everything will be fine as long as I don't trip and fall or say something stupid."

"You will be just fine," she said with a smile.

"I'm not a very good princess," I said. "I'm too clumsy and awkward."

"I think you are a perfect princess," she said. "And everyone in the kingdom agrees with me."

My stomach flipped over. "They expect me to be their warrior," I said, running my hand across the mountain of bubbles around me. "I'm not even sure what that means. Do they want me to be like my father and live to protect them? If it were up to me, I'd take an army to the human world and fight the Order head on. What do you think the people want?"

Tuli's eyes darted to the door. "I do not think I should speak against the king."

"Trust me, Tuli, no one is here but you and me, and I promise I can keep a secret," I said. "I'd really like to know what you think. What the people here really want instead of just what my father thinks they want."

She brought her hands into her lap and fidgeted a bit, then took a deep breath in and out. "I think you are right that most of those who live here in the Southern Kingdom wish the king would be more aggressive," she said. "The king's army only fights when a village is attacked or when a hunter gets close to one of our cities. They never initiate the fight or go directly after the Order."

"Are there still a lot of demons living outside the dome?" I asked.

"Not a lot, but there are still a handful of villages who do not want to become a part of the domed city. They understand the risks, but they are not willing to give up their independence. For many, their ancestors have lived in a certain place for centuries," she said. "To leave their homes would be like admitting defeat. The king respects this. He sends out patrols and often visits these villages to make sure they are safe."

I floated closer to her and rested my arms on the side of the tub. "And are they? Safe, I mean."

She made a pained sound and closed her eyes. "I do not want to say anything against my king," she said. "He is a wonderful leader and he has done a lot for us here in the Southern Kingdom."

"But?"

"But those who live outside the city are not safe," she said. When she looked back up at me, her eyes were moist with tears. "My family comes from one of these villages. One of the lake-land villages in the deeper south. They refuse to leave our homeland, but..."

Tension filled her voice and her hands trembled.

"Did something happen to them?" I asked.

She nodded and a sob shook her body. Her head fell into her hands.

I grabbed a robe she had set out for me and got out of the tub. I put my arms around her and let her cry it out. My heart ached for her. It was obvious that whoever she had lost was someone she cared about tremendously.

When she calmed down, she swiped at her tear-stained face and pulled away. "I am sorry," she said. "You are supposed to be relaxing and here I am crying and burdening you with my sorrows."

"You are not a burden," I said. "I want to hear about what happened. I want to help if I can."

"No one can help," she said. "My mother was taken. My brother too. By hunters of the Order. There is no one who can save them now. Everyone knows that once a demon has been taken to the human world, they never return."

The sadness in her eyes broke my heart. I wanted to be able to help her, but I knew the awful truth of the situation. Her family members had become slaves. Forced to live inside the body of a witch somewhere on earth. It would be nearly impossible to find them, and even if we could find them, I had no idea if we could free them.

"I'm sorry." I didn't know what else to say to her. I didn't want to give her false hope, but what if the reversal ritual actually worked? How many lives could we save? "I wish there was something I could do."

"I wish that as well," she said. "My family has mourned my mother and little brother as if they are dead. I know there is nothing you can do for them, but I still have my father and my older sister who live in that village. The king tries to protect them by going after the hunters, but for every hunter his guards destroy or scare away, the Order sends two more in its place. No one is safe."

The Order never gave an inch. In every situation, they pushed and pushed and fought as hard as they could. They had no sympathy or care for family or for life and love. All they cared about was power. Sometimes, it seemed like the high priestesses of the Order actually enjoyed hurting others.

"Someday they'll pay for all the hurt they've caused," I said. "I promise."

Tulianne sniffed and gave me a weak smile. "This is why the people honor you," she said. "They can see in you the true spirit of a warrior. You are strong like your father, but your spirit has not been broken."

"Broken?" I asked. "What do you mean?"

"Nothing," she said, standing. "You should really start getting dressed. You don't want to be late to your own party."

I wanted to press her about what she'd meant, but she'd already disappeared into the bedroom.

A PRINCESS

"CAN I LOOK yet?" I asked.

Tuli giggled. "In a minute," she said. "I need to add a few finishing touches."

She'd spent the last hour dressing me and fiddling with my hair, but she refused to let me look in the mirror. "You are missing something."

"There's no possible way you've missed anything," I said with a laugh. "You've been working on me all day. What else can there possibly be?"

"Wait here one moment," she said. Mischief sparkled in her amethyst eyes. She disappeared into the large closet and emerged a second later with a large silver box.

"What's that?" I asked, eyeing the box.

"A gift from your father," she said. "He sent it with very strict instructions for me not to show it to you until tonight."

Excitement danced under my skin. Other than my necklace, which was now lost to me, I'd never gotten a gift from one of my parents.

"Here," she said. "Close your eyes and I will lead you to the mirror. Do not open them until I tell you."

I let out a nervous laugh, but did as she said. She steered me toward the full-length mirror in the corner of my room, and I was careful not to trip in my high-heels.

She stepped away from me, and I heard her take the top from the box. Then, I felt her come close to me and place something solid and slightly heavy onto my head.

I gasped and brought my hand up to my mouth. I knew what it was even before I opened my eyes. A strange fear consumed my body, tensing every muscle and making me hyper-aware of the weight at the top of my head.

"Open your eyes," she said in an excited whisper.

I almost told her I didn't want to. I almost told her to take it off. But I knew I couldn't change the expectations placed on me. I had to face my own truth.

I opened my eyes.

The crown sparkled with gorgeous dark blue sapphires and the clearest white diamonds. I reached up to lightly run my finger across the intricate design etched into the silver. I had never seen something so beautifully made in my entire life.

The blue of the sapphires matched the blue of my dress perfectly. Tulianne had worked for weeks to make this dress special for the ball tonight. The bodice fit perfectly, hugging me in all the right places, the neckline dipping low, but not too low. Layers of silk cascaded to the floor. A beautiful dusting of silver glitter sparkled across the right side of the skirt. Back in the human world, a dress like this would have cost thousands.

"What do you think?" she asked.

My breath caught in my throat and my mouth dropped open slightly. What did I think?

"For the first time in my life, I think I actually feel like a princess," I said.

How had I gotten here? Less than a year ago I was just a girl who couldn't stay out of trouble. I had no real home. No real friends. There was no one in the world who looked up to me or ever expected me to make anything of myself.

Yet, here I was.

"I never expected this to be my life," I said.

"Life is rarely what we expect it to be."

She was right. Even though I was only seventeen years old, I learned a long time ago that you never really knew what tomorrow would bring. Every time I thought I had my life figured out, something happened that turned everything upside down again. One day I was a foster kid in Atlanta, and the next I was in the car on the way to Shadowford. I never suspected moving to Peachville would be the beginning of the craziest, most unexpected year of my life.

I stepped back and took in my reflection. This may not have been the person, or demon, I ever expected to be, but this was me.

I was a princess.

THEIR NEXT MOVE

THE THRONE ROOM had been transformed into a fairy wonderland.

A thousand tiny lights sparkled near the ceiling like fireflies. Dark green vines curled up the stone walls, their yellow flowers fragrant and bright. The white marble floor had been covered with a lush green carpet.

I slipped my heels off my aching feet and dug my toes into the cool fake grass. I'd spent hours talking to the people of the city, being passed from group to group, dancing with anyone who asked for a moment alone with the princess.

As the crowd around me finally began to thin, I felt a warm hand caress my back.

"May I have this dance?" a familiar voice whispered in my ear.

The warmth of his breath on my bare neck sent shivers of pleasure from my head to my toes. I turned and the sight of him took my breath away.

Jackson bowed, then offered his hand to me. I curtsied and slipped my hand into his.

"I have never in my life seen anything so beautiful," he said as the music began.

I reached up to touch the delicate crown. "Isn't it gorgeous?"

His lips curled into a sexy half-smile and he raised one eyebrow. "I wasn't talking about the crown."

My face and neck grew warm, and I ducked my head to hide my red cheeks.

"I've missed you," he said, pulling me closer. The orchestra played a waltz, and Jackson twirled me around the dimly lit dance floor. "Do you have any idea how hard it was for me to stay away from you this long? All I've wanted to do was get you in my arms."

I smiled and pressed my cheek against his shoulder. "This is the only place I've wanted to be."

"The people of this city adore you," he said. "They believe in you."

"I hope I can live up to what they want me to be," I said.

"You already are everything they want you to be, Harper. Don't you see that?"

I pulled away enough to be able to look into his eyes. "We have to get serious about a plan to get home to Peachville," I said. "As much as I love it here, I can't help but feel like we're running out of time. I keep waiting for the Order to make their next move."

His eyes grew serious. "I know what you mean," he said. "But tonight I just want to feel your body close to mine. Tomorrow we can worry about a plan."

I closed my eyes and lost myself in the music and the feel of his strong arms around me.

A commotion near the throne pulled me from my dream state, but we were lost in the crowd. I couldn't see what was going on. Jackson and I continued to dance for a moment, but when a scream echoed through the hall, a knowing chill ran across my back.

I clasped Jackson's hand and ran toward the throne. A large group had clustered together around the steps, and Jackson and I had to force our way through. The orchestra stopped mid-song and was replaced by a chorus of gasps and screams and excited chatter.

"Please," I said. "I need to get through."

Panic crawled through my veins. Something terrible had happened. I could feel it in the air of the room.

Finally, we pushed through to the front. A bloodied figure knelt at my father's feet. The king looked straight at me with terrible fear written across his features. My eyes darted from him to the injured man as I stumbled up the steps, nearly tripping over my dress.

"I'm so sorry," the man said. "I did everything I could. I don't know how they figured it out, but they know."

The bloodied man nearly collapsed and the king crouched down to help hold him up. I rushed forward and propped him up on the other side.

That's when I saw his face more clearly.

Coach King.

I gasped. What was he doing here in the shadow world? This didn't make any sense. My mind reeled from shock. How was this possible? What had happened to him?

Coach King doubled over, crying out as a wave of pain seized his body.

"Hold on," the king said. "You've got to be strong now. Tell me, Roan, where have they taken her?"

"I don't know," Coach King said through clenched teeth. "I'm so sorry, my king. I have failed you. I tried to fight, but Priestess Winter, she was too strong. I tried, but I couldn't save her. They've taken her, my king."

I shook my head and tried to make sense of the scene unraveling before me. "I don't understand. Who have they taken?"

"My wife," he said. The coach struggled with those final words, then his body went limp. He was still breathing, but blood flowed freely from a wound in his side.

"Mrs. King?" I asked, not wanting to believe it. Was she still alive? What was going on? I felt sick.

My father placed a hand on my arm. "Yes," he said. "My oldest daughter."

I clutched my chest, my breath coming in rapid gulps. "What? What are you saying?"

"Harper." He paused. The expression in his silver eyes chilled me to the bone. "The Order's taken your sister."

MY SISTER

HE TRUTH OF what he'd said took a moment to sink in. I stood, speechless, unable to put the pieces together. Shock consumed me, my body frozen.

"Angela King is my daughter," the king said. "I'll explain everything later, I promise. For now, we need to get this man to one of the healing rooms upstairs."

Several guards materialized and placed Coach King's limp body on a black board that floated in the air. They shifted into white smoke, floating him across the room with great speed.

I couldn't move. I couldn't breathe. Jackson took my hand as I lowered myself onto the steps, not caring that the hem of my irreplaceable dress was now soaked in blood.

"Harper, are you all right?" he asked. He placed a hand on my face and forced my eyes to his. "It's going to be okay, do you hear me? We're going to get her back."

A viscous fear snaked up my spine as the realization of what just happened finally cracked through my shell of shock.

Mrs. King was my half-sister. She was the black-haired little girl my mother talked about in her journal. The daughter of my father and his wife in the human world. She was only a little girl when my mother met the King of the South and fell in love.

She was my sister.

Somehow the Order must have figured out who she was, and now they'd taken her. But where? And what were they planning to do to her?

"We have to find her," I said, my tongue finally working again. "We have to get to her before they do something awful to her."

My father shook his head. "We have to take this one step at a time," he said. He motioned to a group of guards who had gathered to wait for his commands. "Clear the castle. Let the council know I'm calling a meeting for tomorrow morning. Hopefully Roan will be well enough by morning to tell us the details of what happened."

"Roan?" I asked, leaning against Jackson so that I could stand.

"You know him as Coach King in your world," my father said. "He is one of my most faithful guards. I sent him to the human world years ago to watch after your sister. It's a long story, but there will be time for explanations tomorrow. For now, I need to get up to the healing room and give him my full attention."

I nodded, letting what little explanation he'd given soak in. "Please come get me if he starts talking," I said. "I want to know the details too."

"Harper—"

"Don't shut me out," I said, my tone harsh. "She's my sister, and I deserve to be a part of this."

"If there's time, I'll send for you," he said.

My father disappeared, his trail of white smoke following the same path as the guards who had taken Roan up to the healing rooms.

Jackson held me tight. "I should go too," he said. "His injuries were really bad. Maybe I can help in some way. Will you be all right? Or do you want me to stay?"

I pulled away, still numb. "Promise me you'll come find me when you're done," I said. "I want to know everything."

He kissed my cheek, then followed the others up the staircase.

I sat down on the cold stone steps and pulled my knees toward my chest. The Order had taken my sister. All this time, she'd been right there in front of me, and we'd never even realized we were related.

Or had she known all along?

I thought back over the time I'd spent in Peachville. The way her eyes widened when she saw the necklace I wore that first day at Peachville High. Her warnings about the demon tattoo and how the Order might be watching me. The way she fainted at the ceremony when Priestess Winter tried to take my life.

She must have known who I was this whole time. But why wouldn't she have told me?

I laid my head in my hands as tears began to fall. My worst fears had been realized. Now that I finally knew who my sister was, she might be lost to me forever.

EVERY SECOND
YOU WASTE

I SAT ALONE IN the empty throne room, the festive party atmosphere replaced with worry and fear and heartbreak. Why hadn't anyone come to tell me what was going on? Why weren't we already on our way to rescue her?

The longer I sat there, the angrier I became.

I paced back and forth in front of the throne, my ball gown swishing at my feet. Had Coach King survived? Had he been able to tell them anything?

Questions swirled around in my head.

Why had the Order taken her anyway? What was it Coach King had said when I first walked up?

I don't know how they figured it out, but they know.

The Order knew Mrs. King was my sister. They'd taken her because of me.

Hadn't my father told me this would happen? He'd said I cared too much and the Order would eventually use that against me. But I never imagined it would happen like this.

I pressed my palms to the side of my head and closed my eyes tight.

I had to save her.

This was all my fault. I was the one who had taken the sapphire ring. I was the one who had caused the blue demon gates to become inactive. Even if Priestess Winter had been willing to walk away from Peachville and leave things as they were for a while, there was no way she was going to overlook the fact that her blue portals were out of business.

Especially since her home gate was the first sapphire demon gate ever opened. According to the diary, it was the first of any stone to be opened, more than two hundred years ago.

I knew she'd stop at nothing to try to get the ring back from me.

But how had she found out about my sister? Had Gregory told her? My father had said Gregory knew a lot of his secrets. Maybe this was one of them. But if that was true, why didn't my father get her and bring her here where she would be safe?

My breaths grew thin and shallow.

I couldn't just stand here waiting for answers. Coach King might not be ready to talk, but I knew there was someone else here in the castle who had answers.

Priestess Winter's faithful servant.

The tiger witch. She was bound to know something. It couldn't be coincidence that she had come here to attack me only a week ago and now, after her failed attempt, my sister had been kidnapped. The two events had to be connected. And I was going to find out how.

My mind made up, I shifted into white smoke and flew down the staircase. I raced past the guard's quarters on the first sub-level and the training rooms on the second. Finally, three floors below the main level of the castle, I arrived at the dungeons.

Two guards stood watch just beyond the stairway. They straightened at my approach.

"Princess, is everything all right?" The guard on the right stepped forward. His eyes darted nervously to my bloodied skirt. "Do you need help?"

I lifted my chin. "I'm fine. I've come down to speak with the prisoner."

His eyebrows drew together. "Which prisoner?"

I paused. I hadn't thought about the fact that there might be other prisoners down here. When I'd been here before, during the attack on the dome, the cells had been empty.

"The witch who attacked me outside of the city the other day," I said. "The one with the short red hair. I have to talk to her. It's urgent."

He looked to the second guard, then back at me. "I'm sorry, Princess." He cleared his throat and shuffled his feet nervously. "The king has told us not to let anyone in to see her. Not even you."

I bit the inside of my lip, holding back a curse. "I don't care what my father told you," I said. "It's extremely important that I talk to her. It's a matter of life and death."

The second guard stepped forward. "Princess, my name is Arian," he said. He spoke deliberately, holding one hand toward me as if I were a wild dog he was trying to calm. "I can tell you're very upset. You aren't thinking clearly. Why don't you go upstairs? I can send for your handmaiden and have her make you some tea. You can speak with the king in the morning about the prisoner."

I wanted to scream. "I don't want any stupid tea," I said, louder than I intended. "What I want is to talk to the witch."

"I'm afraid that's not possible," the first guard said. "The king—"

"The king is my father. That makes me a princess," I said, stepping closer to him. "I am your superior, and I demand entrance to these cells."

Arian put his arm in front of his friend, pushing him back a few steps. "We cannot let you through."

I clenched my hands tight. Anger raced through my veins and before I even knew what I was doing, my fists were on fire. "Every second you waste could mean my sister's life," I said, my voice a low growl. "Let me through."

The first guard's forehead broke out in a sweat as he stared at my fiery hands. He nodded and stepped aside. "You'll find the witch in the last cell on the right," he said.

I raced past the two guards, turning right as I ran through the dungeon. I passed at least a dozen occupied cells before reaching the last. I slowed, gasping for air. My heart raced as I approached.

There, on a pallet of straw and dirty rags at the far side of her cell lay the tiger witch.

A COLD STONE WHERE HER HEART SHOULD BE

*T*HE WITCH'S EYES were open, but her stare was blank and lifeless. My hand trembled as I reached out to touch the iron bars that held her captive.

I swallowed, my mouth suddenly dry.

A deep growl rumbled from her like thunder on a stormy day.

"What do you want?" she asked. Her body was curled into a ball, her arms wrapped around her knees. Her face had become a tense snarl.

"I want answers," I said.

She laughed and sat up, pressing her back hard against the moist stone wall behind her. "Answers only lead to questions," she said. She rocked her head back and forth, thumping it against the stones. "Or haven't you learned that yet?"

"I want you to tell me how much Priestess Winter knows about me and my family," I said. "I want to know how she found out about my sister. Was it Gregory who told her?"

The tiger stopped banging her head and paused, her eyes growing wide and wild. "Gregory?" Then she smiled, her lips curling up so high I could see the pink of her gums. "You mean the handsome guard? Poor Gregory."

I gripped the bars tighter.

"Was it you who took him from the hunters?" I asked, my stomach sick. "Is he dead?"

She left her spot on the straw and got up on her hands and knees. Her head dipped low, but her eyes were still glued to my face. She crawled toward me very slowly, as if she had transformed to her tiger form. Only she hadn't. She couldn't.

Her magic was of no use here inside the dome.

"Poor Gregory, the guard," she said, her eyes gleaming with mischief. "So loyal and sweet. He screamed and cried and swore he'd never tell. Of course, that's what they all say. At first."

I closed my eyes. My chest grew tight, my breath ragged.

I didn't want to imagine the horrible things they must have done to him. "Why?" I asked.

The witch lifted her imagined paw and licked it. She ran her wrist across her auburn hair, then licked it again. "I'd been tracking you for days when Gregory found you," she said. "After that little stunt you pulled with the hunters, I finally understood how such a young girl like you could have such power."

"Wait. You were tracking me?" I asked. "How?"

She laughed. "Did you forget you had one of the Order's tattoos on your back?"

I shook my head. "It doesn't work here," I said, reaching back to touch the spot on my lower back where Brooke had put the tattoo. "I would have felt it."

The witch clucked her tongue. "People are always underestimating the Order," she said. "Priestess Winter is very resourceful. She found a way to track the tattoo. It wasn't that hard, really."

I closed my eyes. It was me who had brought them here. No wonder the hunters had always found me so easily. I would have to find a way to deal with the tattoo, but for now I wanted answers about Gregory.

"You were there when I fought the hunters and Gregory came for me?"

"I saw you take the ring, but before I could even try to get it back, Gregory and his men appeared to bring you here. I wanted to know why he trusted you so quickly. A prima futura in the domed city? Unheard of. Priestess Winter was pleased with my catch. A dear friend of the king. A wealth of knowledge waiting to be unlocked."

"So she knows about me?" I asked. "About my father?"

She sat back against her legs. Her eyes traveled up and down my body. "A demon girl who wears a silver crown," she said. "She knew you were special, but she always thought it was the twins who made you strong."

Her eyes went glassy and she stared straight ahead, not seeing.

"Twins?" At first, I was confused. I thought she was talking about her own sister, but then I realized what she meant. Jackson and Aerden. Their presence in Peachville made the entire coven stronger. Maybe it even made all the blue demon gates stronger. That was why Priestess Winter didn't want to kill the town. She didn't care about me. She wanted the twins' power.

The tiger witch shut her eyes tight. A teardrop rolled down her cheek. "Twins have a rare bond," she said. "So much more powerful when they are together."

She was talking about herself now, but I felt none of the guilt that had plagued me before. She and her sister were evil. My father was right. They alone chose their fate.

"Imagine how angry she would have been if you had died," she said, her tears turning to hysterical laughter. "If she had lost a precious rarity like you. Half prima, half demon princess. She'll never stop until she rules you. Even if she has to force her way into your mind or rip your very soul from your body."

I shuddered.

"That's what she did to Gregory, in the end," the witch said, crawling closer to where I stood. "He loved his king so much, he refused to give up what he knew. Priestess Winter has magic at her disposal that would turn your insides. By the time she was done with him, his mind was jelly and his secrets were hers."

She cocked her head to the side and narrowed her eyes at me.

"What's happened, Princess?" she asked. "You wouldn't be down here wearing that crown and that blood if something terrible hadn't happened."

My hands began to tremble. I took a step back and clutched my skirt in my fists. "Don't you already know? My sister has been kidnapped," I said. "Where did she take her? Do you know what she plans to do with her?"

The witch moved with cat-like grace as she approached the limits of her cell. "I never knew you had a sister," she said. "This was not one of dear Gregory's precious secrets, but I'm glad to hear my priestess has discovered it. Maybe now you will understand some of what I felt when you took my sister from me."

"Tell me where Priestess Winter would have taken her," I demanded.

"She plans to make her a bird, perhaps? Trapped in a cage with no song to sing."

She laughed at her own humor, but I didn't understand. A bird? What was she talking about?

"Give me a real answer," I said. I tried to sound confident, but fear caused my voice to falter. "Where is she?"

The witch made a popping sound with her tongue. "Maybe she's with my sister," she said. "In heaven."

"No." I shook my head, refusing to believe it. "If she wanted her dead, she would have just killed her. Why take her prisoner unless she has some other use for her?"

"Bait, perhaps?" She scratched behind her ear. "Fishing for a demon princess. When I didn't come home and lay you on her doorstep, she must have moved on to plan B."

I placed a hand on my stomach, ill at the thought. "She sent you to capture me," I said, sorting through my thoughts. "And when you didn't come back, she knew you'd either been killed or taken captive. So she took my sister, knowing I'd come after her."

The witch raised an eyebrow at me. "It isn't that hard to figure out, is it?"

"If I give myself up, would she release my sister? Would she let her live?" I asked, stepping forward again, hands on the bars.

She laughed, low and deep. "You act as if Priestess Winter has a beating heart," she said. Her emerald eyes met mine. "You took something precious to her, so she repaid the favor. What else did you expect? Trust me; Priestess Winter has a cold stone where her heart should be. Or didn't you know? She didn't even allow me a day to mourn my sister's death before she sent me back after you."

I looked away. Those eyes sent chills through me.

Priestess Winter was never going to let my sister go. Just like she was never going to let me go.

"I'm going after her," I said, my mind made up. "You might as well tell me where she is. If it's really a trap, you won't mind sending me in the right direction."

The witch growled and slinked back toward her straw mat. She curled up the way I'd found her. "She's at Winterhaven," she said. "I'm sure they'll be expecting you."

I released the cold bars and stepped away.

Winterhaven. The Winter's home in Washington D.C. In order to save my sister, I would have to go right to the source. I would have to face an impossible enemy.

I walked away from the tiger witch's cell with a heavy heart.

Jackson and I had planned to make our choice after the dance, but now the choice had been made for us. It was time to go home.

SHE'LL NEVER STOP

*J*ACKSON TURNED AS I entered my chambers.

"Where have you been?" he asked. "I've been looking everywhere for you."

Early morning light streamed in through the golden curtains. Jackson stood near the archway. He still wore his tuxedo from the night before. His bow-tie lay undone across his neck and the first several buttons of his shirt were loose. His hair was messed up, as if he had run his hand through it a thousand times.

"I went to see the witch in the dungeons," I said. "How is Coach King? Is he going to survive?"

Jackson rubbed the back of his neck. "It doesn't look good," he said. "He's been asking to see you."

My lips parted. "He has?" I asked. I looked down at my dress. Blood and dirt caked the bottom of the skirt. "Should I go now? Is he awake?"

"He was asleep when I left," Jackson said. "But you don't want to wait too long. I don't think he'll survive for more than a day or two. Priestess Winter's daughter really did a number on him."

My heart skipped a beat. "Zara?"

Jackson's eyes met mine and he shook his head. "No," he said. "Of course not Zara. He said she was there but that it was her oldest sister, Selene, who stabbed him with one of their ritual knives."

I sat down on the edge of the bed, my legs wobbly. "I can't believe this is happening."

Jackson sat next to me and put his hand gently on my leg. "Did you find out anything from the witch?"

I reached up and unfastened the crown from my head. It had grown heavy over the past twelve hours. I took it off and held it in my lap, the gemstones glittering in the dim light. "Priestess Winter knows about me being half-demon. She knows I'm the king's daughter. She knows everything," I said. "She sent the tiger witch here to try to capture me, but when she never showed up back in the human world, Priestess Winter moved on to my sister. She knows I'll try to save her."

Jackson ran his hand through his hair. "So, it's a trap."

"It seems that way," I said. "And a good one too."

"What do you want to do?" His gorgeous green eyes searched mine. "I'm with you no matter what you decide."

I placed my hand on top of his. The warmth of his skin felt so good after being in the cold dungeon air. "How could I possibly turn my back on my sister?" I asked.

Without warning, the wave of emotions I'd been holding back overflowed and gushed forth from me. Hot tears spilled down my cheeks. I set the crown on the bed and stood just as Jackson threw his arms around me. He hugged me tight to his body as sobs stole my breath.

"I'm so sorry," he said. "We'll go after her. We'll get her back."

I nodded, my tears soaking into his collar. "We'll save my sister and then we'll save Aerden," I said. "The Order has to be stopped, Jackson. Priestess Winter has to be stopped. Now that she knows about me, she'll never stop until she has control of my power."

"We'll stop her together," he said. He held my shoulders and pulled back so that we could see each other's eyes. "We need a good plan. Your father's right about this being an impossible enemy. We won't win with force alone. We have to be smart."

The door to my room burst open and Tuli rushed in. She glanced at Jackson and ducked her head. "I am so sorry to interrupt, but you need to come soon, Princess," she said. She lifted her eyes and they were filled with sorrow and fear. "Roan, your sister's guardian, has taken a turn for the worst. He is in a great deal of pain, Princess, and he is asking to speak to you alone. I believe he is holding on until he sees you."

I wiped the tears from my face and nodded, a twinge of pain and sorrow tightening my chest. "Show me the way," I said.

With a heavy heart, I followed her toward the healing rooms, knowing these would be the last moments of Coach King's life.

ZARA'S GIFT

HE SMELL OF death hung in the air.

Coach King lay on a bed in the center of the room. He was covered with a blanket all the way up to his chin. His body shivered beneath it. I pulled another blanket from a stack near the door and laid it carefully over his body.

The coach opened his eyes to a slit. When he saw my face, his lower lip trembled and a tear fell across his temple and disappeared into the pillow beneath his head.

"She loved you so much." His voice was made of gravel and sand. "From the minute you first arrived in Peachville and she realized who you were, she never stopped talking about you."

He spoke of her as if she were already lost to us, forever.

"I'm going to get her back." I sat down on a small wooden chair beside the bed. "They won't kill her as long as they think they can use her to get to me."

He cleared his throat, then winced. His knees and shoulders lifted slightly as he scrunched his injured middle together. Finally, he relaxed again. "She wouldn't want you to come after her," he said. "She'd never forgive herself if anything happened to you."

"Don't worry about that now," I said. "You need to rest."

He turned his head to me and pulled one arm from under the blanket. He clasped my hand tight. "I have to tell you something before it's too late," he said. His eyes darted toward the cabinet in the far corner. "My jacket. The one I was wearing when I got here. I think it's in the cabinet. Can you get it for me?"

I stood and walked over to the cabinet. Inside, his blood-stained letterman jacket hung on a metal peg. I lifted it out and brought it over to him, confused as to why this jacket could be so important to him now.

"In the pocket," he said.

I dug into each pocket until finally, in one of the inside pockets, I found a folded piece of paper.

I held it out to him. "Is this what you want?"

He nodded. "Open it."

He pressed his head back against his pillow, his body going stick straight as a wave of pain washed over him. He reached out for my hand and gripped it hard.

When it had passed, I carefully unfolded the paper, breathless to see what was so important. Drawn with perfect precision was a picture of a crystal butterfly made of diamonds and blue stones. It looked so familiar, but I couldn't remember where I'd seen it.

"Where did you get this?" I asked.

"When the Winters came to my home, they were all there. The priestess and her three daughters," he said. "The youngest one, Zara, came up to me just as the others were pulling my wife from the house. She stuffed this into my pocket and told me I had to hold on until I could bring this to you. That you would remember her gift. She said it was the key to saving your sister."

A slow breath filled my lungs as I drew a hand to my lips. Zara's gift. I could see it now as clear as day. A small white box given to me after the Heritage ritual in the basement of

Winterhaven. The butterfly had a bobby pin attached so I could wear it in my hair, but I'd never actually had a chance to.

She never even hinted that the butterfly had any kind of special power.

"Did she say anything else?" I asked. "Did she tell you how it would help me?"

He swallowed hard and shook his head. "She only had the briefest moment to talk to me," he said. "Her sister told her to finish me off, but she let me live so I could give you this message. That's all I know."

His face contorted and he cried out.

I cringed and wished I could do something to help him. I had completely misunderstood him all this time. After everything that had happened with Tori and some of the other cheerleaders, I'd thought he was one of the bad guys. How could I have known he was a demon charged with guarding my sister?

I looked at him with fresh eyes. It had all been an act this whole time. A distraction to hide his true identity, perhaps. He had sacrificed his own life to protect my sister.

A debt I knew I would never be able to repay.

A bright red stain bloomed in the middle of the blanket that covered him. He clenched his teeth tight and shut his eyes. I stood and ran into the hallway to find a healer, but it was no use.

By the time I turned around, Coach King was gone.

THE FIRST BREATH

I RETURNED TO MY room, exhausted and heartbroken. I ran a bath, getting the water as hot as it would go. I stepped out of my ruined ball gown and took all the pins from my hair, letting the waves fall across my shoulders and down my back.

The image of Coach King's dead body lingered in my memory. I had never seen a demon die. In a way, it had been beautiful. When his body had gone still, a white mist lifted from it and a white light formed. It wasn't a blaring kind of light that would make your eyes burn, but it wasn't exactly dim either. I'd never seen anything like it.

His spirit hovered there for a moment, then shimmered and filled with color. A soul passing into what the demons called the Afterworld. Here in the shadow world, a demon's passing was usually of their own choosing. A way to move on and make room for the next generation. Roan, my father's friend and my sister's guardian, had not had a chance to choose his passing.

After a moment, only his body remained, his spirit gone from this place.

What would happen when I died? Would my spirit be lifted from me as a shimmering light?

I descended into the bath, letting it burn my skin.

I needed to wash away the stench of the dungeons and the memory of dried blood.

I closed my eyes and sank beneath the water. I let it surround me, welcoming the pain. I wanted to feel something. To ache on the outside as much as I did on the inside.

I was done with feeling numb. I was finished with patience and waiting. Now was the time for action.

I shed my fears and my doubts there in the water. I stripped away thoughts of impossible enemies and let the potential for defeat dissolve into nothingness.

When my lungs screamed for air, I finally rose and gulped it in. The first breath of a new life. A renewed purpose.

The Order had my sister. My flesh and blood.

And I was going to get her back.

WORTH DYING FOR

*M*Y FATHER SAT on the throne, his head resting in his hands.

I took a deep breath and walked over to him. He was obviously grieving, but I had no idea how to comfort him. "I'm sorry about your friend," I said, not sure what else I could say.

"I couldn't save him," he said. "All this power to heal and it still wasn't enough against those witches. In the human world, the metal from the ritual daggers becomes like a fast-working poison. By the time he got here, it was already too late. I couldn't save him without sacrificing myself."

I wanted to give him time to mourn, but we didn't have that luxury. "What do we do now?"

He looked up and searched my face. His shoulders slumped. "You want to go after her." He said it as a fact and not a question.

"Don't you?" I asked. "She's your daughter."

"It's not that simple," he said.

"Why not?" I took another step forward. "Why can't it be that simple?"

He sighed and gripped the throne. "I thought I made it clear to you what kind of enemy we're facing here," he said. "Once someone has been taken by the Order, they're as good as dead, Harper. There's nothing we can do for her now."

Heat flared in my chest. "So we leave her there to be tortured and killed while we sit here in our safe little cocoon waiting for the Order to find another way inside?" I shook my head. "I can't do that."

The king stood. "You have to let her go," he said, his voice booming. "I command it."

I raised my eyebrows. "I am not under your command," I said. "I've been on my own my entire life, making my own decisions. I may not have always made the best choices, but I'm still alive so I can't be doing too bad."

My father clenched his jaw and turned away.

"The Order almost killed me," I said. The truth hit me, nearly taking my breath away. "You may not have known their exact plans, but you knew they had captured me. You made the same choice then that you're making now, didn't you? You could have come for me."

"I wanted to," he said.

"Then why didn't you?" My lower lip trembled, and I pressed it tight to make it stop.

He turned back to me. "I've known many demons who tried to save their loved ones from the Order," he said. "Every single one of them is dead now."

"That's not a good enough reason to stop trying," I said. "Look at Jackson. He went after his brother and is still alive."

"And where *is* his brother?" The king formed a tight fist. "Is he free? No, he's still held captive by the same town that took him a hundred years ago."

"Yes, but as long as he's alive, there's hope," I said. "And what about me? I would have died that day if Jackson and Mary Anne and Lea hadn't come for me. They took a chance against the Order and they saved my life."

His shoulders tensed. "They got lucky," he said. "Besides, they only had to hold off the Order for a few seconds while they pulled you through the portal. They didn't have to fight an entire coven."

"The point is they risked everything and we all lived," I said. "They had a plan and they were smart. They didn't underestimate the Order. They went in with their eyes wide open, knowing they didn't have the power to stand and fight. If we go in with a solid plan, we could save her. I know we could."

"Don't be foolish," he said. He stepped toward me and grabbed my shoulders. "If you go there, you'll die and I'll have lost both my daughters. Priestess Winter, she's different. She's powerful beyond reason. All of the priestesses of the High Council are like this. They shouldn't be capable of such enormous power, but somehow they are stronger than an entire army of demons."

"Come with me," I said. "Together, we can beat Priestess Winter. Everyone has a weakness. She has to have something we can use against her. Once she's out of the way, we can reverse the portal binding spell and free the demons who are still alive. And if we can free Peachville, we can free everyone. We could change everything."

Tears formed in my father's silver eyes. He shook his head and pushed me away. "Going after the Order is a death wish," he said. "The best we can do is try to defend our homeland. I have a duty here to my people."

"You have a duty to your family," I said, my voice cracking slightly.

"If you go, I won't come after you." His jaw formed a hard line. "If you leave the safety of this dome, you're on your own."

I shook my head. "No. You're wrong. I'll have Jackson and my friends."

"Harper, you're going to get them all killed. Can't you see that?" he shouted.

"What I see is a king who has lived so long he's forgotten that some things are worth dying for."

I turned on my heel and walked out, refusing to allow a single tear to touch my cheek.

THE PATH CHOSEN

*A*NGER FUELED MY footsteps. I didn't even know where I was headed until I found myself standing in front of the door leading to the soldiers' quarters. My heart pounded. I knew women weren't typically allowed down here, but what good was being a princess if I couldn't break a few rules?

I threw the door open and stepped across the threshold.

A few guards stopped in their tracks. A short guy tugged nervously on his t-shirt, then ran his hands over his jeans as if to smooth them out.

"Can I help you, Princess?" His voice cracked a bit.

I lifted my chin. "I need to talk to Jackson," I said. "Can you show me to his room?"

The guy tossed a glance toward the back hallway, then bit his lower lip. "If you'd like, I can ask him to join you in your quarters when he's available?"

"I'd like to see him now," I said, my jaw tight.

The guard winced and lowered his head. Guilt slipped through a crack in my resolve. It wasn't this poor guy's fault I was angry. He hadn't done anything wrong, but I'd practically yelled at him for no reason.

I took a deep breath and relaxed my shoulders. I'd make a terrible ruler. I wasn't cut out for this shit. "I'm sorry," I said, doing my best to soften my expression. "I just really need to talk to him. I know I'm not really supposed to be down here, but it's important. Would you mind showing me where his room is?"

The short guy swallowed and nodded. "Sure," he said. He jerked his head toward the back hall. "I'll show you."

I forced a smile. "Thank you." My voice hitched on a tear. I held it back and walked slowly through the hallway.

Many of the doors down here stood wide open. Men of all ages sat together playing cards or listening to music. I felt like I'd invaded a college dorm.

They straightened as I walked past.

"He's here," the guard said. He motioned to a closed door near the end of the long hall.

"Thanks again," I said.

The guard turned to leave, then flipped back around to me. "Princess?"

"Yes?" I asked.

He stared down at the floor, shuffling his feet. "I'm sorry you lost your sister," he said.

I swallowed. "I didn't lose her," I said. "I'm going to get her back."

He looked up, eyes wide. "Oh," he said. He cleared his throat and stuffed his hands in his pockets. "I just meant that I lost two brothers to the Order, so I know how you're feeling."

I stared into his eyes, so full of sadness and compassion. "I'm sorry," I said, my earlier anger fading. Everywhere I turned there was someone else who had endured great loss. The Order had taken so much from so many, it broke my heart.

"Thank you," he said. His eyes filled with tears and he shifted and flew back down the hall.

I straightened my shoulders and turned back to the closed door. I lifted my hand and knocked, some of my confidence shaken.

"Not today, guys, I have some work to do," Jackson's voice called from behind the door.

"It's me," I said, leaning in to make sure he could hear me.

The door jerked open and Jackson pulled me into his arms. "Harper, are you okay?"

"My sister's been kidnapped," I said. "What do you think?"

He stepped out into the hallway and looked back toward the entrance. A large group of guys had come out into the hall to watch me, probably wondering what in the world had brought me into their space.

"Come in," he said. He pulled me into the room and shut the door. "You aren't supposed to be down here."

The room was small. Just big enough for a twin bed and a tiny desk that was built into the wall. There wasn't even a closet or a bathroom or anything in here. The bed was unmade, but Jackson quickly threw the comforter over the sheets and smoothed out a place for us to sit.

"I know," I said. "I didn't even really mean to come down here, but I didn't know where else to go."

"What's going on?" he asked.

"My father," I said. "He's so impossible."

"What happened?"

Jackson sat down on the bed, but I paced the small space in front of him.

"He won't even consider going after her," I said. "He said I needed to let her go. What the hell? He's this almighty king, but he's too afraid to fight for his own daughter's life? I don't understand it."

Jackson leaned forward, resting his elbows against his legs. "I can't say I'm surprised," he said.

I clenched my hands into fists. "Why is everyone so quick to give up around here? I thought shadow demons were supposed to be powerful and strong?" I said. "What happened to being brave? Or is everyone in this world completely chicken-shit?"

Jackson stood and ran a nervous hand through his hair. "You might not want to say that so loud," he pointed toward the door. "Remember where you are and who you're talking about."

"Let them hear me," I said, reaching for the door handle. "I want to know the truth. Why does everyone here refuse to fight?"

Jackson shifted and reappeared between me and the door. He took my hands and walked me back toward the bed. "That's not entirely fair," he said. "Everyone out there has lost someone important."

"I know. That's exactly what I'm talking about." I shrugged out of his embrace. "I don't understand why they don't all band together and go rescue the ones who have been taken. Everyone in this city has a terrible story about someone they love being taken. Why don't they fight back like you did? Why don't they force their way through and take them back?"

"I wasn't so successful, if you remember," Jackson said. "Before you came along, I'd been powerless for nearly fifty years. The Order is too strong, Harper. You know that. A lot of shadow demons have gone after their loved ones. They never come home. If it wasn't for the fact that my presence made Aerden stronger, I wouldn't have survived either."

I clenched my teeth and made a choked sound. "I'm not going to just let them take her," I said. "I can't do that."

"I know," he said.

I looked up at him. I hadn't expected him to agree with me. "So you'll come with me when I go?"

He took my hands again and this time I didn't pull away. "It's you and me, Harper." He leaned down and kissed my forehead, his lips warm and soft against my skin. "Until the day I die."

I put my arms around his waist and pressed my body against his, finding strength in his words.

"My father said I'll just get myself killed," I said. "Do you think he's right?"

Jackson hugged me tighter. "I've seen you fight your way through the most impossible situations," he said. "I think if anyone can save her, it's you."

I smiled and buried my face in his shirt. "Thank you," I whispered.

We stood together in silence, our hearts beating in unison. Our future uncertain, but the path chosen.

After a while, I pulled away and sat down on his bed. "Coach King died." I stared down at my hands.

Jackson's shoulders slumped and he leaned back against the stone wall. "I heard."

"I was there when he passed away," I said. "I've never seen anything like that before. It was beautiful in a way."

"You saw the lights?" he asked.

I nodded.

"When a demon passes into the Afterworld, you see their true soul's colors," he said. "The more beautiful the spirit, the more beautiful the lights."

"I always thought he was a jerk," I said. I slipped my shoes off and brought my feet up on to the bed and hugged my knees close to my chest. "I completely misjudged him. All he was ever doing was trying to protect my sister and keep tabs on the Order."

"What was it he wanted to talk to you about?" Jackson asked.

I reached into my pocket and pulled out the small square of paper Coach King had given me. I handed it to Jackson.

His mouth dropped open. "I've seen this hair pin," he said. "Where did he get this?"

"Zara gave it to him. She was supposed to finish him off and he thought she was coming over to strike the final blow. Instead, she handed him this drawing and told him to get it to me as soon as possible. She said it was the key to saving my sister," I said. "Where have you seen it?"

"I'll show you," Jackson said, standing. He crossed to his desk, opened the top drawer and pulled out his drawing pad. He flipped through a few pages, then handed it to me.

My eyes widened. "When did you draw this?"

"Two days ago," he said.

The drawing was a close-up of me in profile. The main detail of the picture was a beautifully ornate butterfly pin in my hair.

"I thought it was just another vision of you," he said. His lips turned up slightly in one corner. "I get them a lot. Visions of your face or your eyes. Nothing too specific as far as what's happening or what you're doing. Just pictures of you. I saw this butterfly so clearly, but wasn't sure how it was important."

I started to flip to the next page, but Jackson pulled the pad away from me.

"Don't," he said. "There are things in here I don't want you to see until you're really ready to see them."

I crossed my arms in front of my chest. I hated when he kept his drawings a secret from me, but I had too much on my mind to sit there and argue with him about it.

"The butterfly pin was a gift from Zara," I said. "After my Heritage ceremony at Winterhaven."

"Did she tell you anything about it? Does it have some kind of special magic attached to it?"

I shook my head and leaned back against the wall. "I have no idea," I said. "She never said a word about it except that it was a gift."

"Where is it now?" Jackson leaned against the edge of his desk.

"I put it in the drawer of that mirrored dressing table in my room at Shadowford," I said. "I never even wore it or anything, but who knows if my stuff is still there, or not? For all we know, the Order cleared everything out."

He brought a finger to his mouth, thinking. "I wish we had some clue as to why she wanted you to have it," he said. "Do you think we can really trust her?"

I thought about Zara's bruised face the last time I saw her. The day Priestess Winter almost killed me in the ritual room. I nodded. "Yes, I think we can."

Jackson stared down at the drawing. "Then we have to find that butterfly."

THE BEGINNING
OF THE END

"WHAT WE NEED is a plan," I said, nerves knotting in my stomach. If we were really going to do this, I knew it would be the most difficult thing I'd ever faced in my life. Hunters were nothing compared to Priestess Winter herself.

"And reinforcements," Jackson said.

I turned to him. "It's too dangerous. No one thinks we even have a chance," I said. "Who would possibly come?"

"Mary Anne for one," he said. "If we're going back to Peachville, she's going to want to come with us."

I rubbed my forehead. I hadn't even thought about Mary Anne coming along. We could certainly use her help, but was it fair to ask her to risk her life again? It wasn't like she was best friends with Mrs. King or anything.

Angela.

I was going to have to get used to thinking of her by her first name now. Angela King. I wasn't even sure I'd ever heard her first name before last night. But now she was more than just a teacher or a cheerleading instructor. She was my sister. I figured that put us on an automatic first-name basis.

"If Mary Anne comes, Essex will probably want to come too," he said. Then he cleared his throat. "Maybe Lea will come."

The mention of his ex-fiancee made heat flare across my cheeks. She was a princess like me. Well, not exactly like me because she was fully demon, but we had a lot more in common than I'd ever dreamed. She loved Jackson, I was sure of it. I wasn't so sure she'd want to help us. Or ever see me again, for that matter.

All three of them had stayed behind in the Underground. Would they really come with us back to Peachville to fight? "There's only one way to find out," I said. "The communication stones are up in my room. I'll have to go up and call."

"Tell Mary Anne they'll need to leave right away," Jackson said. "We don't know what the Order's plans are for your sister. We don't know how much time we have."

I shuddered at the thought of her trapped in some torture room at Winterhaven. I had no doubt the Order had taken her to get to me, but what were they planning to do with her?

Jackson was right. We had to hurry.

"If they hurt her..." Tears welled up in my eyes and I pressed my lips tight. They'd taken her because of me. I'd never forgive myself if she died.

"We'll get her back," Jackson said, taking my hand in his.

I looked into his green eyes and saw faith there. The fact that he believed in me made me love him even more.

"We'll save my sister," I said, squeezing his hand. "And then we'll save your brother."

The gravity of the statement nearly took my breath away. We'd spent months here in the shadow world avoiding the Order. Doing everything we could to stay hidden and stay alive. Still, through it all, I knew they would eventually catch up with us. I knew eventually we would have to fight.

It suddenly hit me that this was the moment. This was the beginning of the end for us. One way or another, we were about to start the journey that would lead us to freedom or to death.

THE WORLD TO ME

"*H*ARPER?"

The red stones glowed bright in my palm.

I smiled and pressed my free hand to my chest. It was so good to hear Mary Anne's voice.

"Hey," I said. "Can you talk? Something's happened."

"Of course," Mary Anne said. "Are you and Jackson all right?"

"We're fine," I said. I paused. Where did I even start? "Do you remember that I told you about my mother's journal and how she said my father was married to a woman in Peachville?"

"Yes."

"And they had a daughter?"

Mary Anne gasped. "Harper, are you saying you found your sister?"

I took a deep breath. Every time I thought about her, hot tears threatened to spill from my eyes. I needed to pull myself together and be strong for all our sakes.

"It's Mrs. King," I said. "The Order's kidnapped her."

"Oh, my god, are you serious?" she said. "I'm so sorry, Harper. We've got to go after her."

The anger and determination in her tone brought the tears even closer.

"I know it's not totally fair to ask you to come with us, but—"

"Bullshit," Mary Anne said. "I'm coming. Just tell me what to do."

I stared down at the small red stones that allowed me to talk to Mary Anne. Even though she was hundreds of miles away, I felt so close to her and so incredibly grateful to have a friend like her.

"You'll need to leave as soon as possible," I said. "Do you think Essex will come with you? I don't want you traveling alone."

"I will not leave her side," Essex said.

I hadn't realize he was there with her, but I was so relieved to hear him say he'd come with her. "Thank you. We can use all the help we can get." I swallowed my pride. "Will you ask Lea if she will come too?"

Mary Anne paused. "We can ask," she said. "I have to be honest with you, though. Lea's been kind of distant lately. She barely even talks to us anymore. I don't know if she'll even listen."

Mixed emotions rushed through me. Lea wasn't my favorite person in the world. Still, I knew she was important to Jackson. And she was powerful. We needed her help, especially if we survived long enough to attempt the ritual to free Aerden.

"At least try," I said. "Tell her we're going to try to free Jackson's brother. Maybe that will convince her to come."

I'd already explained the ritual reversal to Mary Anne last time we'd talked. We hadn't had a lot of time, but I'd managed to tell her we'd settled here in the Southern Kingdom and I'd found my father. What she didn't know was that he was a demon. Or that he was the king.

"How long do you think it will take us to get to you?"

"Essex, can you shift into demon form and carry Mary Anne with you?" I asked. "If you can travel that way, you could be here in a day. Maybe two at most."

"Yes. This is something I can do," he said. "We will move as fast as we can."

"Do we need to bring anything with us?" Mary Anne asked.

"Bags," I said, thinking of Essex's trade as a tailor. "We'll need to be able to move easily and travel light. Besides that, just bring anything you think you might need in the human world."

"We can do that," Mary Anne said. "We'll leave first thing in the morning."

"Thank you. This means the world to me," I said. "I'll have two guards waiting for you at the border. They'll escort you to the city. Please be careful. There are hunters everywhere these days. Keep your eyes open."

"Guards?" she asked. "How did you manage to get their help?"

I cleared my throat. "Piotrek and Liroth are their names and they'll show you where to go once you get into the city. There are a few things I haven't had a chance to explain just yet, but you'll see when you get here."

"We'll be there as soon as we can," Mary Anne said.

The light inside the stones faded as she disconnected, and I said a silent prayer that fate would make their journey swift and safe.

ON OUR SIDE

*J*ACKSON AND I sat alone at the dinner table.

My father hadn't joined us once since our argument in the throne room. In fact, he seemed to be avoiding me altogether. We hadn't spoken at all in two days.

I understood why he didn't want me to go after her alone. What I didn't understand was why he wasn't coming with me. The idea of a father who wouldn't risk everything for the life of his own daughters was beyond me. What was he so afraid of?

I knew I needed to let go of my anger and focus on the plan to save Angela. Still, I couldn't help but be disappointed in my father. Did he even care about me at all?

"You need to eat," Jackson said. "You're going to need your strength."

I realized I'd been pushing my food around instead of actually putting any of it in my mouth. I stabbed a piece of broccoli and forced it into my mouth. I didn't have much of an appetite these days, but I knew he was right. I couldn't live on fury alone.

"Let's go over the plan one more time," he said.

I started to list the things we'd talked about so far when a familiar voice in the hall caught my attention.

"I'm sure she won't mind if we interrupt her dinner. Trust me, she'd be more upset if you didn't tell her we were here."

Excitement flooded through me.

They're here!

I stood and ran toward the door, shoving it open and throwing my arms around my dear friend. "Oh, my god, I've missed you so much," I said, holding Mary Anne tight.

She tensed at my embrace for just a moment, then relaxed and hugged back. I knew she wasn't always the most affectionate person in the world, but I couldn't help it. I'd missed her with all my heart, and after that scare with the fake Mary Anne in the woods, I was so happy to see her here safe and sound.

Essex stood to the side and as soon as I let go of Mary Anne, I pulled him into a hug. He stiffened, then blushed. I laughed, thinking how perfect they were for each other.

"Come on," I said, laughing and taking Mary Anne's hand. I nodded to the guards who'd been stationed at the door. My father had them watching me like a hawk the past few days.

The guards bowed in recognition and turned back to their posts as I led Mary Anne and Essex into the dining room.

"So what's up with the castle and the guards and everything?" Mary Anne asked. "Is this where you're living?"

I scrunched my nose. She was going to be pissed that I hadn't told her yet. "Yes," I said, not sure how to explain this. "I told you I'd found my father?"

"Yeah, so what is he? Some kind of advisor or guard or something?"

"Not exactly," I said, biting my lip.

"He's the king," Jackson said. "He's a demon and he's the king. Harper wasn't sure how to tell you, but there it is. No big deal."

Mary Anne's eyes grew wide, her mouth dropped open. "You can't be serious."

I nodded and walked over to my place at the head of the table. "I know it's hard to believe," I said. "I still hardly believe it, myself."

"Wait a minute," Mary Anne said. "That makes you a demon?"

"Half demon," I said.

"A half demon daughter of a king," she said, shaking her head and falling into a chair one of the servants pulled out for her. "Holy crap, you're a princess."

She giggled, then covered her mouth, as if the sound had surprised her.

"I'm sorry, this is just a lot to take in," she said.

"Trust me, I completely understand," I said.

"Why didn't you tell me earlier?"

I shrugged. "I wasn't really sure it was something that should be public knowledge just yet," I said. "Plus, I figured it was the kind of thing you had to see to believe."

Mary Anne looked at me in astonishment, then smiled. "I always knew there was something special about you," she said. "I guess I'm not surprised."

I smiled back, relieved the truth was out there.

I sat back down at the table, but pushed my plate away. I was too excited to eat. "Can I get you guys anything for dinner? You have to be hungry."

"Sure," Mary Anne said. "I'm starving. We didn't bring much with us on the road. We wanted to pack as light as possible so nothing could hold us back."

I motioned to a servant waiting nearby and they disappeared into the kitchen to get more food.

"How was your trip?" Jackson asked.

"It was quite easy," Essex said. "We did not see a single hunter the entire way here. To be honest, it was strange to see the roads so clear."

I frowned. "Maybe the Order is concentrating all their efforts on attacking the villages here. We've had some trouble with hunters nearby."

"I'm glad you guys made it here safely," Jackson said.

"Did you make those?" I asked Essex, pointing to the two large backpacks they carried with them.

He beamed with pride, setting his down on the floor beside Mary Anne's. "Yes, I made them special for the trip," he said. "They have some secret compartments inside, and I imbued them with a type of magic that makes them feel much lighter than they actually are."

Mary Anne touched his leg. "It made the journey a lot easier."

I raised my eyebrow at her and she moved her hand, rolling her eyes. Still, I noticed a hint of a smile tugging at the corners of her lips.

"I'm so glad you're here safely," I said. "Did Piotrek and Liroth meet you at the border?"

"Yes," Mary Anne said. A servant placed a full plate in front of both her and Essex. "They were great. They brought us here to the castle, but said they had some others duties they had to attend to."

I made a mental note to find the two guards later and thank them.

Jackson cleared his throat. "Lea wouldn't come with you?"

Mary Anne and Essex exchanged a look so brief, I almost missed it.

"She's really busy with the Underground," Mary Anne said. She took a large bite of rice and took her time chewing it up. "She said she wants to help with Aerden, but she's not sure when she'll be able to get away."

There was more to it than that. I could feel it. "What's going on?" I asked.

"What do you mean?" Mary Anne scooped another bite of rice into her mouth.

"I mean, you're hiding something," I said. "I'm sure you're just trying to spare my feelings or whatever, but we don't have time for secrets or sympathy. What's the real reason she isn't coming? She hates me, doesn't she?"

Mary Anne and Essex looked at each other again and this time Essex bowed his head and stared down at his lap. Wow, was it really so bad?

"I honestly don't know what's going on with her lately," Mary Anne said. "After the two of you left, she became more and more distant. She spends all of her time with the Underground's leaders and she never makes time to see us anymore. I practically had to beg to get even five minutes alone with her to tell her we were leaving."

"They must be planning something big," Jackson said, shifting in his seat. "Any idea what it might be?"

Essex shook his head. "No, we have talked many hours about this, but we cannot figure out what must be going on inside the leadership," he said. "It seems the Resistance army has been training more than usual, though. Something is being planned, but the leaders have not shared their plan with the general population of the Underground."

"I can guess," Mary Anne said. "Personally, my suspicion is that they're planning some kind of massive attack in the human world."

"So why would they be keeping that such a secret?" I asked. "That's exactly what we're planning to do. We could work together. I don't see why they'd keep that from us."

Mary Anne shrugged.

Jackson shut his eyes. "Because it's possible their plan involves destroying all the demon gates." He slammed his hand against the table. The silverware jumped up and clanged back down with the force of the blow. "I thought I'd convinced them to move past that," he said.

I pressed my hands to my forehead and drew a deep breath in through my nose. As if we weren't already on a race against the clock. Now we might also have to deal with the Resistance? I thought they were on our side.

"Back when I was sitting in on the meetings, there were some demons on the committee who believed that if we could destroy all of the demon gates, we'd eventually also destroy the Order itself."

"But that would mean killing thousands of demons," I said. "Even if they didn't care about the humans who would die, why would they want to kill the demons too?"

"Collateral damage," he said. "Everyone agrees it's horrible, but some think it's the only way."

"And Lea?" I asked. "What does she think?

He frowned. "She was on the fence about it a lot of the time," he said. "She didn't necessarily agree with the tactics, but she said she couldn't really see a better plan of attack. The Order is just too strong. She thought the best way to weaken them would be to close the gates and diminish their numbers."

A frustrated sound escaped from my throat. "If we go around killing demons and witches without even trying to free them, how does that make us any better than the Order?"

"Hey, you're preaching to the choir here," Mary Anne said.

"I did not realize that was the plan," Essex said with a frown. "However, I can see why many of my kind might see an advantage to this line of reasoning. Over the past two hundred years, we have come to consider those who have been taken as already lost to us forever. We have never heard of any demon who escaped from the human world once they were imprisoned inside a human witch. To us, those demons are already dead."

"They aren't dead," I said, standing up and kicking my chair. "I've seen Aerden manifest to save my life more than once. He's the same, only trapped. That's the way it is for all the demons who have been taken. If their human host is still alive, so are they. And as long as they're alive, there's hope."

I felt bad about raising my voice. I knew Essex wasn't to blame here. Still, it made me so angry that they were just so willing to write their loved ones off without a fight.

"Many would see it as a mercy killing," he said. "You have to understand. We are accustomed to living for hundreds of years. When we pass away, usually it is by choice so that another generation may rise up and so that our power may be used for other purposes. When a demon is taken from this world into the human world, their life is shortened to maybe fifty or sixty years if they are lucky. Not a single day of this time is spent in freedom. It is torture for my kind."

I gripped the back of the chair and leaned forward. I'd never really considered what life must be like for the majority of the demons taken to live in the human world. Demons like Aerden who were tied to a prima's bloodline lived for possibly hundreds of years. Of course, he was forced to live as a slave, but at least he was alive. For the others, though, they only lived as long as their humans lived.

"How long do you think we have?" Mary Anne asked, looking to Jackson. "How long to free your brother before the Resistance begins attacking gates?"

Jackson ran a hand through his hair. "I'm not sure," he said. "That might not even be what they're planning. Maybe they've worked out a new plan."

"We can't risk waiting to find out. There's too much at stake and we're running out of time. We can't worry about the Resistance right now. It sucks that Lea wouldn't come, but we can do this without her. We have to." I looked each of them in the eyes, my heart racing in my chest. "Tomorrow, we go back to Peachville."

THE BEST CHANCE

*L*ATER THAT EVENING, the four of us sat in my living room, a map of Peachville drawn out on a large piece of paper in the middle of the floor. Jackson had spent part of the day drawing in the basic roadways and landmarks.

"My family's village is approximately here," Mary Anne said. She placed a red gemstone over the forest on the edge of town. "We can use that as our base camp. All I need to do is set up the protection spell again."

"You can do that?" I asked. "How will we all get in, though? Will we have to swear a blood oath?"

"Essex and I talked about this some before we left the Underground," Mary Anne said. "There might not be time to perform a blood oath ceremony every time we want to invite someone into our camp. Especially if we end up with a lot of people who want to help."

"What else can we do?" I asked. Using the crow village was a genius idea. I'd been scared we would end up running from the Order the whole time, always in danger. If there was a way Mary Anne could secure the crow village, we might be able to hide there undetected for a while.

"I will cast the spell that my family originally used as a barrier, only I'm going to alter it a tiny bit," she explained. "Instead of a blood oath to me or my family, a person wanting to get in will have to actually be carrying a drop of my blood."

I swallowed. "How are we going to get that to work?"

"Before we left, Essex made a set of blue wristbands that will work like keys to the village. He put a drop of my blood into each of the bands, so essentially anyone wearing one will be able to get in."

"What if someone steals some of the bands?" Jackson asked.

"We can't let that happen," Mary Anne said. "We'll have to guard them with our lives and only give them to people we completely trust."

I considered her plan. It was risky, but it was a really great idea. "Do you think the blood spell is strong enough to keep the Order out?"

"It's practically impenetrable," Mary Anne said. "A blood oath is one of the strongest types of magic. As long as we are careful with the bands, we'll be safe."

"Let's do it," I said. "As soon as we pass through to the human world, you two need to go straight to the village to set up the blood spell."

"What about you guys?" Mary Anne asked. "Where will you go?"

I looked to Jackson. "We're going straight to Shadowford."

He met my eyes and nodded. We'd already talked about this part of the plan. Jackson and I would go to Winterhaven alone.

"Wait a second," Mary Anne said. She sat up straighter. "You mean we came all this way and you don't want us to go with you to rescue Mrs. King?"

"Angela," I said.

Mary Anne reached out to touch my hand. "Angela."

"The less people we take to Winterhaven, the better," Jackson said. "If we go alone, maybe we can stay under the radar and rescue her before anyone knows we're there."

"They took her so you'd come after her," Mary Anne said. "They aren't going to let you just walk in and take her. They'll have traps set up everywhere."

"Maybe," I said. "But it won't do any good to have us all trapped there. If we don't show up at the crow village within a day or two, you can come back through to the shadow world and try to get more help. Besides, if we don't come back, we'll need you to try to perform the ritual reversal to free Aerden. If that works, it will change everything."

"So why don't we do the ritual first, then?"

"Because if it works, Priestess Winter is going to completely lose her shit," I said. "She'll be so angry, there's no telling what she might do. She might kill Angela just to get even."

Mary Anne bit her lip. "True," she said. "We have to get her out of there first, if we can."

"Exactly," I said. "And if we can't, then at least someone else will still be alive to try the ritual."

Jackson handed her the witch's journal Andros had given us. "The details of the ritual are in this book," he said. "I've marked the page."

"Do you think it will work?" Essex asked. "If demons can be freed from their prisons on earth, this will change everything about the way our people think. If we could see our families again..."

His voice drifted off and he stared down at his hands.

"It's the best chance we've ever had of defeating the Order and freeing our kind from slavery," Jackson said.

Mary Anne took the journal and tucked it away inside her backpack. "I'll hold onto it, but I expect you to come back and get it from me in the village," she said.

Silence filled the room. No one said it, but I knew we were all thinking the same thing. What if Jackson and I never came back from Winterhaven?

Jackson finally broke the tension. "Remember, once we get across the border to the human world, we have to be very careful not to cast any demon magic," he said. "Essex, Harper already knows this, but demon magic works differently in the human world. There, our magic is fueled by the living things around us. Trees, grass, even human life if that's the only source available. A simple spell will leave a noticeable mark in the grass that can be tracked. No shifting or casting of any kind once we go through. Not until it's absolutely necessary."

"I understand," Essex said.

"Aren't we forgetting something important?" Mary Anne asked.

"What?"

"How exactly are we planning to get back to Peachville?" she asked. "If the ring you took made the portals inactive, how will we get through?"

It was a good question. One Jackson and I had given a lot of thought to over the past few days. "There has to be another way through," I said. "Coach King managed to come through the night he was attacked. He wouldn't have been able to travel far with his injuries as bad as they were. There has to be another portal between Peachville and this domed city. A portal the Order doesn't know about."

"But where is it?"

"I don't know," I said.

I rubbed at the muscles in my neck. "Let's call it a night for now," I said. "We've been talking through this for hours. We all need to get some rest. We're going to need our energy tomorrow night."

"You're right," Mary Anne said. "I'm exhausted."

"We'll all stay here in Harper's room tonight," Jackson said. He stood and walked toward the bedroom door. "We'll come back to this with fresh eyes in the morning."

The three of them disappeared into my bedroom, but I sat there alone for a long time staring at the map, wondering how in the world we were going to find that portal.

TO FEEL CLOSER

I SAT ON THE couch staring at the map of Peachville.

It was late, and I knew I needed to get some sleep, but my mind wouldn't stop churning. We had to figure out how to get back to the human world. I could go to my father and ask him for the location of the portal, but I didn't think he would tell me. He didn't want me to go back, so he wasn't going to make it that easy.

The gate had to be somewhere here inside the domed city, and the other side must come out somewhere in Peachville. Coach King had been injured so badly, he wouldn't have been able to travel too far. If he'd come through somewhere far away from the domed city, he might have passed out or been intercepted by hunters before he got to the throne room.

My guess was that the portal was actually somewhere near the castle itself. But where?

I ran a hand through my hair and sighed.

We didn't have time to waste like this. Every second we stayed here in the shadow world was another second the Order had to torture my sister.

The outer door to my chambers opened, and I sat up, on full alert.

"It is just me, Princess." Tuli entered, carrying a stack of blankets and a single white rose. "I thought you might need these since you have so many people staying with you in your quarters this evening."

"Thank you," I said, taking the blankets from her. "What's the rose for?"

She raised an eyebrow and walked toward the middle of the room. "These were your mother's favorite flowers," she said. "I am told she loved them so much, she even had them planted at the lake near her home in the human world."

"Yes," I said, wondering why she had really come to my room this late at night.

Tuli came to stand in front of the large map of Peachville. "Your father loves them too," she said. "He takes very special care of his white rose garden."

I sat up.

"I think he spends so much of his time in the garden because it makes him feel closer to your mother." She paused. "If, for some reason, you wanted to feel closer to your mother," she said, "you might also take a stroll through the roses sometime. There is a particular spot near the back corner that is especially beautiful."

With that, she laid the white rose near the edge of the map.

I gasped, my eyes wide as I stared at the rose. Of course. It made perfect sense. The white roses at Brighton Lake bloomed all year long, despite the weather. They were magical roses, brought there from the shadow world. That had to be the secret to the portal.

Why didn't I see this sooner? The black roses also held special powers related to portals. When Jackson had pulled me through to the shadow world from the Peachville portal, there had been a ring of black roses around it. In order to close the portal temporarily, we'd had to cut down the roses.

The entrance to the Underground had also used black roses. It made sense the white roses held a similar power. Somehow, the white rose garden here connected to the roses near Shadowford.

"Why are you telling me this?" I asked in a hushed voice. I knew it must have taken great courage for her to go against the king's wishes.

Tuli looked at me, her violet eyes gleaming with tears. "Ever since my family disappeared, I have mourned them as if they were gone forever," she said. "You give me hope that someday I may see them again."

My heart overflowed with appreciation. "Thank you," I said. "I promise I will do everything I can to bring them back to you."

I pulled her into a hug. She squeezed me hard, then wiped away her tears. With a sad smile, she bowed and walked quickly from the room.

I got down on my knees in front of the map and picked up the white rose. I breathed in its sweet scent, then placed it down over the spot marked Brighton Lake.

A LIFE OF OUR OWN CHOOSING

I CRAWLED INTO BED next to Jackson. He opened his eyes and yawned.

"What time is it?" he asked, pulling me into his strong arms.

I pressed against him. He wasn't wearing a shirt and the feeling of his bare skin against mine sent warm tingles through my body.

"About three in the morning," I said. "This time tomorrow, we should be on our way to Winterhaven."

He sighed. "If we can figure out where the portal is in time," he said.

"It's in the white rose garden," I said.

Jackson sat up slightly. "Seriously? How do you know for sure?"

I smiled and placed a finger over my lips. "Shhh," I said. "Mary Anne and Essex are sleeping near the fireplace."

"How did you find the portal?" he asked, his voice low now.

"Tuli," I said. "Well, she didn't come right out and say it, but I know. Besides, it fits doesn't it? It comes out at Brighton Lake."

"The white roses at the lake," he said, laying back down and holding me tighter. "I don't know why I didn't think of that sooner. It seems obvious."

We snuggled closer and I breathed in the scent of him. I felt so safe here in his arms.

Part of me never wanted tomorrow to come.

"Is this how it felt the first time you went through the portal?" I asked him. "When you went after Aerden?"

"Not really," he said. "I was so angry back then. I wasn't thinking clearly or going in with any kind of plan. I was stupid back then."

"I'm angry," I said, "but it's more than that. What I feel isn't that kind of raw passion. It's more like focus. Like, I know what I need to do, and I'm resigned to it."

"I know what you mean," he said. "When I went after Aerden the first time, I just wanted to kill everyone in sight. I went in there thinking I would have to fight one battle and then it would all be over. This time, it's so much bigger than that. We're truly going to war this time. A war that could last for years."

I sighed. "Do you think we'll ever come back here?"

Jackson kissed the top of my head and ran his fingers through my hair slowly. "Someday, when the war is over. We'll be free of the Order of Shadows," he said. "Maybe we'll decide to rule the Southern Kingdom or maybe we'll live in the human world for a while, but someday, we'll have a life of our own choosing."

I pressed my body closer to his. "It sounds like a fairy tale," I said. "Tell me what else we'll do someday."

Jackson put his mouth close to my ear. "Someday, far in the future, after your father has passed on to the Afterworld, we'll have a child of our own. A son."

I sat up and peered through the darkness at his face. "Now I know it's a fairytale," I said. "You know as well as I do that women in the prima line can only have daughters."

Jackson smiled his half-smile and raised an eyebrow. "In the future, anything is possible," he said.

And I spent the rest of the evening dreaming he was right.

ONE WAY OR ANOTHER

I WOKE BEFORE THE others and left them sleeping while I walked out onto the balcony to watch the suns rise. I leaned over the cool stone banister and placed my chin in my hands.

Was I crazy for going back?

I was doing exactly what Priestess Winter wanted me to do. Expected me to do. I knew I was playing right into her hands, but what choice did I have?

What kind of traps would she have set up around my sister?

Would she block my magic so I would be defenseless? Was I really strong enough to survive? I shivered, thinking of all the possible dangers. Hopefully Zara's crystal butterfly would prove useful in rescuing my sister, but how? I prayed I could trust her and that Zara's note wasn't just another part of Priestess Winter's trap.

My head swam with information, worries, questions. My toe tapped against the stone floor. In less than twenty-four hours, it would be done.

One way or another.

Below me, footsteps sounded on the tiles of the garden path. I straightened and looked down to see who was taking a stroll in the garden at this early hour.

Silver hair caught the light and my stomach twisted with nerves. My father. He was headed for the white rose garden, a place I'd seen him go to think many times in the past weeks. I glanced back toward the bedroom, then decided they were fine in there without me for a few minutes.

I wanted to be snuggled in the crook of Jackson's arm, not arguing with my father. But I knew I had to talk to him. I had to ask him to give me the ring back. If Jackson and I survived, we'd need it to perform the ritual reversal and try to free Aerden. He'd taken it to put it somewhere safe, but he'd promised to give it back when I asked. It was time to find out if he could be trusted.

I took a deep breath. Then, as I released the air, I shifted into my demon form and flew toward the garden below. My feet landed beside the fountain where I'd spent so much of my time here at the castle. I reached into my pocket and withdrew a small red gemstone. It wasn't a coin, but it was the closest thing I had to one here in the shadow world.

I brought it to my lips and made a wish, then with trembling hands, I tossed it into the water.

YOU MIGHT NOT GET
ANOTHER CHANCE

M Y FATHER STOOD just outside the garden gate, his hands wrapped around the silver railing as he stared into a sea of white blossoms.

He didn't turn as I approached, even though I was sure he must have heard my footsteps.

I moved closer, placing my hands near his on the railing. It took me a moment to work up the courage to speak. "I wish you would come with me."

My father didn't answer or acknowledge me in any way, and for a moment, I was sure he was determined to ignore me. Then, as I turned to go, he finally spoke.

"I still remember the day I met your mother," he said.

I turned back, my heart racing.

"She was the most beautiful human I'd ever seen in my life," he said, a faint smile on his weathered face. "She was so young and full of life, but in her eyes, I saw an old soul. Wise beyond her years. Like you. She saw things the way they really were, and she was so determined to change things. She really wanted to make a difference."

I swallowed a lump in my throat.

"I tried to stay away from her," he said. "I already had a human family there in Peachville. A wife. A daughter. I didn't want to destroy all that I had built in the human world, but your mother, she was... irresistible. So beautiful."

I couldn't speak for fear he would stop. I could barely breathe. I'd been waiting for him to open up to me since the first day I'd come to the domed city.

"Claire." Her name was a whisper on his lips. A prayer. He closed his eyes. "I never should have left her there."

"You couldn't have known what would happen," I said.

"I know, but if I had stayed," he said, "or if I hadn't broken things off, at least she would have died knowing how much I loved her."

I drew in a nervous breath. "Why did you break things off with her?"

He sighed. "She was a prima futura," he said. "With her mother dead, she was going to be initiated as soon as she turned eighteen, and I didn't have any way to free her from that bond. There was no possible future for us and knowing that was torture."

"Is that why you left Peachville?"

"That was part of it," he said. He cleared his throat. "I already had plans to leave once I told her we were through, but I couldn't bring myself to walk away. Then, my father died and everything changed. It was my duty to come back here and take over as King of the South. If I had known about you or about the danger she was in, I never would have left you both there."

"What about Angela?" I asked. "You left her."

He nodded and pulled a hand through his hair. "She was safer there with her mother, a reputable member of the Order," he said. "No one there knew who I was or even that I was a demon. Claire was the only one who knew the truth."

My lips parted. My mother had known he was a demon. "Did she know you were a prince?"

"She knew everything," he said. "I even brought her here once to meet my father before he passed."

"What happened to him?" I asked.

He shook his head, his jaw tight. "He chose to cross into the human world to try to save someone he loved," he said. He gripped the railing so tight his knuckles turned white. "He thought he was strong enough to fight Priestess Winter. To force her to release someone he cared for very deeply. After he died, and then your mother, I knew it was useless to try to save anyone once the Order had them. I vowed that I would never be foolish like my father. He had a responsibility to his people. To me. And he threw it all away to save someone who simply couldn't be saved."

"That's why you won't go after Angela? Your own daughter?"

He looked toward the front of the castle. Toward the city beyond. "Everyone in this city has lost someone they love to the Order. A daughter. A father. A husband." He lowered his head. "They are powerless to go after them or to save them. If I abandon this city to go after my own daughter, what am I saying? That my family is more important than theirs? That I care more for this one girl than I do for any of them or their loved ones?"

I placed my hand over his and he turned to meet my eyes. "Then let's save them all," I said.

He looked away, pulling his hand from mine. "You're so much like your mother," he said. "Like I used to be when I was younger. Thinking you can change the way things are. Well, you can't. No one can. The Order is so much more powerful than you know. We've sent armies to fight them. Armies that have been slaughtered in a single afternoon. The best we can do is protect those who have not yet been taken. It's the only way."

"You're wrong," I said. "Things are different now."

"How?"

"We have the journal," I said. "A true account of the Order's beginnings, written by one of the five original sisters. A true path to freeing the demons who have been slaves for so long. If we can break the bond between the humans and demons, we can destroy the Order and save all of those who are still alive."

He closed his eyes and drew in a long breath. "I wish I could believe that."

Frustration became a raging river inside me. "I'll prove it to you," I said. "I'm going to save my sister, and then together, my friends and I are going to perform that ritual and you'll see. I only hope that once you see the truth, you'll find the courage to join me in freeing all the demon gates."

My father turned and started to say something, but then shook his head and looked away.

"If there's something you want to say to me, you better just say it." I looked out over the white roses. "You might not get another chance."

My words carried a weight that hung in the air between us. The future was so uncertain. I thought of my mother and how she never really knew that he had loved her. She died with a broken heart, not understanding the true reasons behind his actions.

Now, here he was years later, still regretting everything he kept from her. But would it make any difference in our relationship? Or was his heart so damaged he would never really let me in?

His silence said it all. I waited longer than I should have, wishing he would tell me he loved me. Wishing he would push past his fear of loss and find the courage to follow me to the human world. But he didn't say a word.

Instead, he reached into his pocket and pulled out the blue ring. He stared down at its glittering stone, turning it back and forth between his fingers.

Then, in one swift motion, he placed it on top of the silver railing and disappeared into the morning breeze.

I'LL SEE YOU SOON

ARY ANNE AND Essex sat on the floor of the bedroom, supplies and clothing spread out in front of them. They looked up as I entered.

"Hey, where have you been?" Mary Anne asked.

"Talking to my father," I said. I clutched the blue ring tight in my fist. His silence still stung. It felt like a betrayal. An abandonment.

My frown must have kept them from asking me a bunch of questions. Instead, they both turned back to their work, packing the four brown bags Essex had made for our journey.

"Where's Jackson?" I asked. The bed had been made and there was no sign of him.

"I think he went back down to his room to get a few things."

I walked over to where they sat and joined them. "Is there anything I can do to help?"

"I think we're just about done gathering all our supplies, but you can help us pack them all up," Mary Anne said. She handed me one of the backpacks. "Everything's arranged in piles. Just take one of each and put it in the bag."

SARRA CANNON

We worked the rest of the morning to get ready, taking a short break when Tuli brought in some muffins. In the afternoon, after all our work was done, Jackson and I took them on a tour of the domed city, introducing them to some of the friends I'd made over the past few months.

I didn't tell anyone we were leaving, but I think many of the people knew. I could see it in their eyes and the way they held on to my hand just a moment too long.

We made a special trip to the city's school to see Ryder. He was such a different child from that silent boy we'd found in the abandoned northern village. He laughed and played with the other kids and watching him, you'd never have guessed he'd suffered such great loss.

I was going to miss him with all my heart.

When we said goodbye, I pulled him close and hugged him tight. "You be a good boy, okay?"

"I promise," he said. He placed his small mouth near my ear and whispered, "I'll see you soon."

I stood and swiped at a tear as it rolled down my cheek. I smiled, hoping he hadn't seen. "See you soon," I repeated. I brought my fingers to my lips and kissed, then placed them against his cheek. "I love you."

"Love you, too," he said with a toothy smile. He gave Jackson a hug, too, then ran off to play with his friends.

"He seems sweet," Mary Anne said. "That's the little boy you found all alone on your way here?"

I nodded, sniffing as I held back my tears. "Come on," I said. "It's getting late. We should head back to the castle and get something to eat."

As we left the school, I glanced back and saw Ryder watching us from across the room. He placed his tiny fingers to his lips, then held them out toward me. Something he had seen Jackson and I do a hundred times.

I touched my cheek as if to accept his kiss, then followed the others through the door.

THE TATTOO

*T*HERE WAS ONE last order of business before we could make our way through the portal.

I had to get rid of my demon tattoo.

"I'm not looking forward to this," I said, pulling up the back of my shirt and laying down on the floor in my bathroom.

Jackson held a mortar and pestle in his hand and was using it to crush up black rose petals. "We don't have a choice," he said. "If you step through that portal to the human world, Priestess Winter will know you're back."

"Worse," I said. "She'll know where the portal is. That would put this whole town in danger."

I knew there was no choice, but the idea of having the magical ink sucked from my skin made me feel sick.

"How do you even know how to do this?" I asked.

"In the beginning of my time as a human, the Order tried to brand me with one of these marks," he said. "They wanted to keep track of me and make sure they knew where I was and what I was doing at all times."

He poured a little bit of water into the mortar and continued to mix up the paste.

"They did?" I asked. "I've never seen a tattoo on you before."

He raised an eyebrow. "Exactly."

I laughed. "You figured out a way to get rid of it?"

"I found the room on the third floor with all those spell books," he said. "I used to go up there in the middle of the night and memorize the ingredients to different potions. The Order had stolen my magic, but that didn't mean I couldn't create a little bit of magic for myself here and there."

I remembered the small closet in his room, filled with different exotic ingredients. I'd gone there to make a potion of my own, once upon a time.

"The tattoo is made from a special kind of ink," he said. "A sort of magical tracking device. The power inside the black roses will suck the ink from your skin. I'm not going to lie. This is going to hurt."

"Great," I mumbled, laying my head down against my forearms. "Let's just get it over with."

"When I rub the paste over the ink, you'll feel it move around and squirm," he said. "You'll want to touch it, but you have to be careful not to itch or scratch or touch it at all or the ink will soak into the skin on your hands."

I nodded, getting nervous.

"As soon as the ink is completely gone, let me know," he said. "I need to scrape the paste off with this stone and put it inside a living thing. That way, to the Order, it will seem like you're still here in the dome."

"How will I know when the ink is gone?"

"You'll know," he said with a laugh. "Ready?"

I took two deep breaths in and out. "Go," I said.

I heard stone scraping against stone, then jumped as the cold paste hit my skin. He slathered it across the length of my lower back. Immediately, the ink began to wiggle and writhe, swirling around like a cat chasing its tail.

Then it started to burn. I tensed and bit down hard.

The heat seared my skin, and I felt the overpowering urge to move. To reach back and scrape the paste from my skin. But I knew I had to stay still. I had to wait.

Just when I didn't think I could take it another second, the burning stopped.

I sighed in relief and gave Jackson a thumb's up. Quickly, he used the stone to scrape the rose paste from my back and transfer it to the soil of a potted plant next to him. I sat up, grabbing a cold cloth from the floor beside me and placing it on the burned spot on my back.

The plant trembled and shook, its leaves falling to the ground in a heap. Blue ink traveled up the length of its stalk. It swirled around, then finally settled, still and calm.

I shuddered, thinking how that stuff had been inside me for months.

"Thanks," I said. I looked in the mirror and saw a large red burn across my skin.

"Don't worry," he said, placing his hand on the spot. "That'll probably go away in a few days."

Icy power ran from his hand to my skin, relieving the burn.

I took a deep breath in, praying I'd still be alive to find out.

BACK TO PEACHVILLE

*H*OURS LATER, AFTER the suns had gone down, the four of us gathered in my chambers. Essex handed each of us a backpack full of supplies. He reached into his own and pulled out a handful of blue wristbands. He placed one on his own wrist, then passed them around.

"These will be your keys to Mary Anne's village in the trees," he said. Then, he handed me an extra one. "For your sister. I am very much looking forward to meeting her."

I smiled, grateful for his confidence and faith. I secured both bands around my wrist, right next to the white scrap of fabric that I'd worn for months, then took a final glance around the bedroom.

Truly a room fit for a princess. I hoped Jackson was right and that someday we would come back to the shadow world. Back to this castle.

"Ready?" I asked, energy buzzing through my veins.

Together, we stepped out onto the balcony.

"Thank you for coming with me," I said to them. "I have no idea what we're going to face, but I am so grateful to have you by my side."

"Don't sound so nervous," Mary Anne said. "We totally got this."

I laughed and she grabbed tight to Essex's hand. We stepped off the edge of the balcony and flew down to the garden below. We made our way through the gate and waded through the roses, careful not to crush them. As we walked, I felt a strange pull. Almost magnetic. I followed the feeling until we came upon a small circle of roses tucked away in the farthest corner.

It looked exactly like the entrance to the Underground, except these roses were white. This had to be it. Was I really ready for what awaited me on the other side?

I took a deep breath and tried to steady the galloping beat of my heart.

Then, I stepped into the circle and was sucked through the portal back to Peachville.

THE WOMAN IN THE WHEELCHAIR

*I*N A BREATH, we stood at the edge of Brighton Lake.

Toads and crickets and other tiny little beings went about their evening as if nothing had changed. Nearby, something jumped from the water, then disappeared again beneath the surface.

None of us said a word or dared to move.

It felt strange to be back in the human world after all these months. I felt like a memory of myself. My hand drifted to my throat, where my mother's necklace should have been. Without it, there would be no Aerden to protect me.

For the first time, maybe I was strong enough to protect myself.

I hugged Mary Anne and stared into her bright blue eyes, silently letting her know that this was where we parted ways. She nodded, then shifted into a black crow. She flew away and Essex took off at a run, following her deep into the woods.

Jackson grabbed my hand and squeezed.

We walked along the worn path toward Shadowford. We passed the area above the ritual room and I paused. I kind of wanted to go down the steps to look at the portal stone and see what it looked like now that the gate was inactive, but Jackson pulled me onward.

The smaller house where Ella Mae lived was dark and quiet. It was the middle of the night here, so our hope in coming at this time was that everyone would be asleep and wouldn't notice our presence.

So far, so good.

Getting into Shadowford itself wouldn't be a problem. Manipulating locks was so easy at this point, it was second nature. We avoided the automatic light attached to the shed and came around the back of the large white house. I quickly turned the lock with a flick of my hand and we walked into the kitchen of Shadowford Home.

Only the sound of the air conditioner disrupted the silence. Jackson's eyes met mine. We'd made it safely into the house without a single issue. When we'd talked about this day, we'd considered every possibility from an army waiting for us as we passed through the portal to a set of traps placed on the entryway to the house. The fact that it had been so easy to get this far made me uncomfortable.

Where was the Order? It had only been a few days since they'd taken my sister, but that was plenty of time to create a plan and to set up traps for me.

My nerves hung on edge.

Danger lay in front of us. I just didn't know when or where. It was the not knowing that made me queasy.

Jackson and I tiptoed through the kitchen, down the hall past Mrs. Shadowford's room, and finally up the large wooden staircase to the second floor. About halfway up, one of the stairs creaked and I winced, frozen in place as I waited. Nothing in the house moved. After a moment, I kept going, keeping my steps as light as possible.

Once upstairs, I headed straight to my old room. I stared openly, surprised to find it looked exactly the same. I don't know why I'd expected it to look any different. Maybe because I had changed so much since I'd last been here.

Jackson kept an eye on the hallway as I went to the dressing table and reached for the drawer where I kept the butterfly pin. For a split second, panic filled my heart. What if it wasn't here? What if someone had taken it?

But when I opened the drawer, there it was. The white box.

My hand trembled as I reached for it, knowing there was a possibility this was the trap we'd been waiting for. Could Zara be trusted?

Just in case, I closed my eyes and created a connection to the human side of my power, feeling the hum of the earth beneath me. To make sure I had control of my magic, I opened my eyes and held out my palm. A perfect orb of dim light formed instantly, illuminating the area in a circle around me.

I carefully picked up the box, not willing to believe Zara could be evil like her mother. I set it on the mirrored dressing table and pulled the top off. Nestled in a bed of white fluff, the blue butterfly sparkled. No monsters came out of the woodwork and no witches came flying through the doorway. I let out a sigh of relief.

I picked up the pin and moved it from side to side, watching as the blue crystals glittered in the dim light of my orb.

What was so important about this piece of jewelry? Why did Zara want me to wear it now? I had no idea what kind of power or magic these stones held, but she'd taken an awful risk to remind me of it. If her mother or her sisters had seen her give the secret note to Coach King, she would have been in serious trouble.

This butterfly had to be something special.

I gathered a small section of hair near my temple and slid the butterfly pendant over it. In the mirror, I recognized the image from Jackson's drawing. Proof that one way or another, I was exactly where I was meant to be.

"Let's get out of here," Jackson whispered. "Anything else you needed to grab while we're here? If so let's get it and go."

I glanced around. There was nothing here I felt all that connected to. Hand-me-down clothes. Scraps of ribbon. My cheerleading uniform. It was all a part of my old life. As if it was a different girl who lived here, once upon a time.

"No," I said, shaking my head. "I don't need any of this stuff."

"We should try to get upstairs then before it gets too late and everyone starts waking up," he said.

With quiet steps, we walked into the dark hallway.

Immediately, something felt off. As soon as I stepped out of the room, an ice-cold chill ran down my spine. Jackson must have felt it too, because his eyes grew wide as saucers and his lips parted.

I spun and looked down the length of the stairs at the woman in the wheelchair. Her eyes glowed a deep blue, dark as midnight on the ocean.

"Welcome home, Harper," Mrs. Shadowford said.

Very slowly, with deliberate movement, she placed both hands on the armrests of her chair.

Then, she stood up.

YOU LEFT ME HERE
TO ROT

I TOOK A STEP BACK.

Jackson gripped my arm. "Did you know she could walk?"

I shook my head. "I had no idea," I said. "But I don't like this one bit."

Without taking her eyes from my face, she began to make her way up the stairs. Her steps were slow, but focused.

"I don't either," Jackson said. "I think we should go."

"Where?" I asked. "I'm not leaving this house until I've gone through the Hall of Doorways. If we go up there, she'll just follow us." I planted my feet firmly on the floor, steadying my nerves and readying for battle. "If she's coming after us, we'll just have to stand and fight. I mean, she's a witch, but she's also an old lady. There're two of us. We'll just stun her or lock her in somewhere and head upstairs. It'll be fine."

I was impressed with how confident I managed to sound, despite the fact that my knees were jelly. The old lady had creeped me out from the moment I first saw her. I definitely did not want to stand here and wait for her to attack me, but if I was going to do this thing, I was going to do it one hundred percent. No backing down, no matter how scared I got.

Mrs. Shadowford placed her foot on the top step, then lifted herself level with the two of us. "I've been waiting for you," she said. "To be honest, I'm surprised to see you here, so eager to fight. So naïve and completely out of your league. I thought you would be too scared to come back, but it looks like Priestess Winter was right about you."

"I'm not afraid of you," I said. Not exactly a true statement, but I desperately wanted it to be true.

She laughed at me then. A full-toothed belly laugh that echoed through the hallway. Inside her mouth, her teeth were black and filled with a stench that hovered in the air like sewage. It was almost as if something inside her had begun to decay.

My stomach turned, and I had to struggle to keep from retching.

"You stupid girl," she said, licking her lips with her black tongue. "You should be very afraid of me. I may have been created to be a servant to your kind, but I can kill you just as easily as I could have protected you."

"Protected me?" I asked, narrowing my eyes at her. "When did you ever protect me?"

Mrs. Shadowford gripped the top of the banister with one hand as if to steady herself. "I never got a chance to protect you." A greenish liquid dribbled from the side of her wrinkled mouth as she spoke. "Your mother took you from me before I even knew you existed. She made me what I am, this old bag of bones. Then you. You left me here to rot."

She leaned over and spit, the dark green fluid dropping to the ground with a slick wet sound that brought the bitter taste of bile to the back of my throat. What the hell had happened to her?

"I don't know what you're talking about," I said. "My leaving didn't have anything to do with you."

"You stupid girl." She snarled at me, her teeth covered in grime. "You defy the Order when you don't even know the first thing about how the Order works."

"I know enough," I said.

She laughed then. A grotesque growl of a laugh that made the floorboards shake beneath my feet. "Trust me." She ran the back of her hand across her lips, smearing green ick across her cheek. "You've barely scratched the surface. There are secrets and truths that go deeper than you could ever imagine."

Something in the craziness of her eyes sent fear racing through my body. I'd always assumed Mrs. Shadowford was just a cranky old lady who'd inherited this house because she married my mother's uncle. I thought her only authority came from the fact that she ran this home for troubled girls. Now, I was beginning to question if I'd completely underestimated her this whole time.

"I would have been faithful to you," she said, hunching over slightly. "A faithful servant. I would have given you everything you ever wanted, if only you had been a good girl and done what you were told. Instead, you left me with nothing but this body, falling apart like a rotting corpse."

She laughed again, bending so far over that her body contorted into a strange crouch. She'd gone completely mad, her eyes focused on me with wild clarity. She didn't even blink or look away for one second.

My instinct was to step away from her. To run. But I couldn't leave. There was no way I was leaving here tonight until I'd found my sister.

She opened her mouth in a silent scream. Her head rolled back as her jaw opened wider and wider, coming unhinged as her wrinkled face split in two. She shed her skin like a snake, letting it fall to the ground in a withered heap.

I stepped back until my back hit the wall with a thud. Jackson gripped my hand and our eyes met in terror.

I had no words for the monster that stood before me. Its skin was scaly and green, glistening with wet goo. At first, it appeared as a pillar, stick straight. Then, where Mrs. Shadowford's legs used to be, eight clawed legs skittered across the floor, hinged like a spider. Its head held glossy blue eyes, and from her back, a long tail with a sharp stinger curled up toward the ceiling.

Beneath the monster, the pile of skin melted away into the floorboards, the stench of decay overwhelming as Mrs. Shadowford's body dissolved.

This new thing that had taken her place was like something out of a horror movie. Definitely not human. Definitely not demon. I'd never imagined anything like it, not even in my worst nightmares. It seemed like a cross between a scorpion and a spider. Only huge.

Jackson stepped in front, putting himself between me and the monster. "If you want to get to Harper, you'll have to go through me," he said. He lifted his left hand and it began to glow a bright, icy blue. Frost formed on his fingertips.

The monster opened its mouth and hissed. Its teeth were jagged points that looked like they could tear through the toughest metal without a second thought. It reared its head back, then thrust forward, heading straight for Jackson's chest.

Jackson pushed his energy toward the monster's head, encasing it in ice. She staggered backward.

"We have to get out of here," Jackson said, gripping my arm.

I stared at the grotesque monster as it flung its head from side to side. The ice around it had already begun to melt and drip onto the floor.

"We can't go anywhere," I said. I placed my hand over his for a second. "We have to get upstairs tonight or she'll tell them we were here and it will spoil everything. We have to fight this thing."

I had only looked away for a second, but that was long enough for her to regroup and lash out at me. One sharp claw embedded into my right thigh. Pain ripped through me and I fell to my knees. I pressed my hand against the wound. Blood oozed through my fingers.

The monster retracted her claw, then struck again.

My brain was seconds behind the action. I couldn't react fast enough. Jackson lunged toward me, shifting just as his hand touched my skin, bringing me with him as he flew down the stairs and into the foyer. He slammed the door behind us and quickly pushed the couch against it.

"That should give us a few seconds," he said. "Let me see that wound."

I lifted my fingers and winced as he ripped a wider hole in my jeans. He pressed firmly against the gaping hole the monster had left in my thigh, then closed his eyes.

"I couldn't shift fast enough," I said. "Dammit, why didn't I fight back?"

"Shhh." Jackson's face was tight.

I opened and closed my hands. He needed to hurry. A couch wasn't going to hold that thing for long.

Bitter cold flared up in my thigh and the pain slowed. When Jackson took his hand away, the bleeding had stopped, but the skin was still raw.

"Better?"

"Yes," I said. "But now what?"

"This thing is bad, Harper." He threw a nervous glance at the barricaded door. "I've never faced one myself, but I know Lea and the other shadow demons have fought something like her before. They called it a green scorpion, and now I understand why."

Thick claws clacked against the stairs.

My chest tightened. "What did they say about it?"

"It has venom in its tail, just like a real scorpion," he said. "If it gets in your system, it paralyzes you."

I scooted back. The scorpion had reached the bottom of the stairs and was now clawing at the wooden door.

"Did they mention how to kill it?"

"That's why I told you we should run," Jackson said. "They said they couldn't kill it. Its body is covered with a thick outer shell that acts like armor."

The pincer on the end of one of her front legs crashed through the door, splintering it into tiny pieces.

"Then we have to destroy the shell," I said.

The thing that used to be Mrs. Shadowford destroyed the rest of the barrier and crawled into the room, climbing onto the couch, stinger raised. Her glassy blue eyes moved from me to Jackson and back again.

I filled my lungs slowly, hearing my father's voice in my head. The only way to get ahead of the moment was to let go of my fear. Anticipate. Act instead of react.

I pushed fear-thoughts into a box in my mind and closed it. I didn't have time for worry. I didn't have time to wait for her to attack. Instead, I shifted, white smoke filling the air where my body used to be.

The transition took my breath away. I'd used my demon power in the shadow world, but it felt completely different here. Instead of charging my power from the ground and deep roots beneath the surface, I pulled from more immediate things. I felt energy soar at me from every living thing nearby, including the scorpion itself. I sucked it in and became full with it, flying faster than I ever had before. I hurled myself toward the scorpion, sending a rope of smoke around her neck and squeezing.

The monster bucked and pulled. I stumbled and almost lost my hold, but a second smokey rope joined mine, coiling around her neck. Jackson's black smoke.

I glanced at him and he was human, then demon, then human again. Charcoal-colored smoke hung like a haze around him. I gasped as his demon form came into view. In the shadow world, I'd taken a potion to make all demons appear as humans, but the potion didn't work here. I wasn't prepared for what I saw.

I lost my concentration. I stared at the mix between a winged gargoyle and a horned beast.

"Harper!" he shouted. Jackson took human form again and pointed to the sharp stinger coming straight for my head.

I let go of my hold on the scorpion and shifted just before she sank her stinger into my skin. I reappeared behind her, then created fire in my palms. Red-orange flames burned around my hands. I reached out and grabbed the scorpion's tail. She screeched as it burned through her outer shell. The stink of barbecued flesh filled the air.

Hope rushed through me. If I could destroy the shell, maybe I could kill the monster.

With a strong whip of her tail, she lifted me from the ground and sent me flying across the room. I shifted just before my head hit the wall, flew down the length of the wallpaper, and landed safely on the floor. Dizziness overcame me for a moment, but I knew I had to recover fast. Before she got a chance to strike me again.

I cartwheeled across the room, thankful, for the first time in my life, for my cheer training as the scorpion's claws sank into the floor where I had stood only moments before.

"Freeze her," I shouted.

Jackson lifted his hands and threw a blue light at the scorpion. Popping sounds filled the room as ice crept across the scorpion's body, starting at its tail and ending with its upraised head.

I had seen him fight this way before, and I knew someone encased in ice could be shattered and killed. I looked around for a weapon to use to shatter her before she thawed. I reached for a piece of the splintered door, ripping it from the rest of the wood.

I aimed for the beast's neck, then threw the makeshift stake as hard as I could. The sound of breaking glass filled the room as my weapon hit just below my mark. One of the scorpion monster's legs shattered and broke away from its body.

She thawed quickly and skittered toward me despite her missing leg, mouth open in an angry scream.

I jumped up, shifting just enough to hang in the air above her like a fog, my human form still visible. I sent a stream of hot flame down on her back, feeding it with more and more power.

The scorpion's protective shell began to disintegrate in the extreme heat. Underneath, her skin glistened and bubbled. She jerked her flaming head violently. I struggled to keep the flame going, but my power was drained.

Just when I thought I couldn't keep going, a girl appeared in the broken doorway. Her long blonde hair covered part of her face, but I recognized her instantly.

Courtney!

Her hands glowed red and she motioned for me to come to her. I flew across the room, reforming beside her. She placed both of her hands on my arm and energy poured into me like a waterfall. With renewed power, I strengthened the flames that surrounded the monster.

Jackson lifted dead flowers from a pink vase near the window, then tossed the moldy water onto the floor. He pulled his fingers together and lifted the water from the ground as if it were a string he could lift up in a straight line. He formed a long spear with the water, then blew his icy breath against it, freezing it in an instant.

He lifted the ice-spear and thrust it forward. Without its shell, the monster was vulnerable. The spear sank deep into the its flesh, right where its heart should be. The fire melted the weapon on contact, but it had done its job. The scorpion lifted her body into the air like a bucking horse, then fell flat against the pine floors, acid bubbling from its neck as dark green blood gushed onto the floor.

The monster's limbs seized, shaking violently before finally going still and cold.

Mrs. Shadowford was dead.

BRIGHTON MANOR

I BACKED AWAY AS a river of green blood spread across the wooden floor.

The three of us backed into the hallway. The stench of rot and decay was overwhelming and I had to cover my mouth. Jackson opened the front door and we stepped out onto the porch.

I hugged Courtney tight. "Thank you," I said. "You really saved us back there."

She smiled, then lowered her head to hide her face. "I'm glad you're home," she said. "I missed you."

"I missed you too. Thank god you showed up when you did. Thank you," I said. I was so happy to see her, but she couldn't stay here. If anyone found out she'd helped us, she would be in danger. "I need you to do something else for me."

"What?" She lifted her eyes to mine.

"Take the van and go straight to Lark's," I said. "Tell her what happened and that I'll be in touch soon. Her mom will be able to keep you safe. They'll figure out a story to tell the Order so no one will know you're on our side, okay?"

Her face tensed and she shook her head. "Where are you going?" she asked. "Can't I just go with you?"

Jackson coughed and leaned over, resting his hands against his knees. "It isn't safe," he said. "We don't want to drag you into this."

"But we'll need you soon," I said. "Mary Anne's back too, and she's setting up a special place for us to hide. I promise we'll come for you as soon as we can."

Courtney pushed her hair from her face and nodded. She disappeared into the house, then came back a few moments later with the keys to the van. She gave me a brief hug, then drove away.

"Holy shit, that was intense." I leaned against one of the white pillars. "I always thought Mrs. Shadowford was a monster, but I never knew it was literally true."

"I knew we might face some pretty scary stuff tonight, but that was disgusting."

I forced myself to swallow, even though the lingering smell of yuck made me want to puke. "So I get that she was a scorpion of some sort, but what exactly was she? I mean, was that just her spirit animal? Like the tiger witch?"

Jackson shook his head and straightened. "No, this was something different," he said. "Like I said, Lea's talked about them before. They aren't human. Lea didn't share all the details, but she said something about them being created by the Order to act as guardians or protectors of some sort."

"Well, whatever it was, I'm glad it's dead," I said. I walked over to the front steps and sat down, extending my legs so that I could get a better look at the gash in my thigh.

"How does it look?" Jackson asked, coming to sit beside me.

It was hard to tell with so much dried blood everywhere, but as long as it wasn't still bleeding, I was happy. "I'm fine. I just need a minute." I looked up at the big white house with its southern architecture and its never-ending secrets. "I guess we can stop calling this place Shadowford Plantation now, huh?"

Jackson twisted to follow my gaze. "It was never really hers anyway," he said. "This house has always rightfully belonged to you and your family."

It was such a strange thought. Yes, this house belonged to my family, but at what cost? The only reason it had ever been given to my family was because it was built for them by the Order when the gate here was created.

"It used to be called Brighton Manor," I said, thinking of all the women who had lived here before me. Besides my mother, had any of them been like me? Or had they all obeyed the Order like good primas should? I fiddled with the white fabric tied around my wrist and thought of the woman in white from my dreams. I wanted to think she was like me. That all my ancestors had been unwilling victims in the Order's games. "We should get upstairs. The sun should be coming up soon. I don't want to miss our chance to rescue my sister tonight."

"Are you sure you're up to it?" Jackson asked.

I narrowed my eyes at him. "Don't start with me."

He rolled his eyes and stood up. "I'm not trying to talk you out of anything. If you still want to go, I'll go," he said. "I just know that a wound like that can slow us down. We want to go in there with the best chance of getting back out."

I sighed and reached up for a helping hand. "I know. I'm sorry," I said. "But we talked about this. Tonight is our best chance. Especially now that Mrs. Shadowford is dead. I'm pretty sure the Order's going to notice something like that. They'll know we're here. Plus, we used enough demon magic to alert anyone within a hundred miles to our presence."

I looked around and noticed the ivy growing up the walls was curled and dead. Proof of our presence.

"Then let's go rescue your sister," he said.

I nodded and started up the stairs, but he pulled me back into his arms. His lips came down on mine in a sweet kiss.

"You did great in there, by the way."

I studied his supple lips, then lifted my eyes to his. "My reaction time was too slow."

"Only in the beginning," he said. He lifted one hand to my cheek and caressed my skin with the back of his knuckles. "No matter what happens from here on, I want to make sure you know how much I love you."

The warmth of a blush flourished under my skin, and I leaned into his hand. "I love you, too."

We stood there, staring into each other's eyes. My heart filled with his love and confidence. We both knew we were heading toward a war that could take decades to fight. We also knew we might not survive the night. No future was certain. The only thing we could count on was this. Us.

I pulled away and stepped inside the house.

"Let's go start a war."

SHE'S ALIVE

THE HALLWAY WAS eerily quiet.

The noise of Mrs. Shadowford's screeches still echoed in my ears. We stepped over a river of green as we made our way to the stairs. I refused to look at it. I could smell it; that was enough.

I took the stairs two at a time, Jackson on my heels.

Together, we walked to the end of the hall where the secret entrance to the third floor waited. Nerves gathered in the pit of my stomach. What would be waiting for us on the other side? Another scorpion monster? Priestess Winter herself?

My throat went dry. I coughed and straightened my shoulders. This was the point of no return.

I was ready.

I stepped into the secret passage and walked up the narrow staircase to the room with five doors. A single candle shone its light in the room, casting shadows against the walls. I turned to the door with a demon carved on its surface. The entrance to the Hall of Doorways.

"This way," I said.

The hall stretched out farther than I could see in the near darkness. My heart raced, but I moved forward with my chin high.

My hand raised to the butterfly pin in my hair. Zara had brought me down this hallway for my Heritage ceremony. That felt like a lifetime ago.

I kept walking, looking side to side at each doorway. Some had emblems or animals, while others were blank. I knew I was looking for a door with a butterfly, but I had no idea if there would be more than one. All of the women in the Winter family could shift into butterflies, but it was a common symbol. Even Lark had one form on her back when she'd gotten her tattoo.

There were probably thousands of families in the Order who could shift into butterflies.

I had to hope there was only one with a door.

After passing at least a hundred doors, I finally saw it. A blue butterfly engraved in the wood of a thick black door. Adrenaline rushed through my veins. This was it, I could feel it. I could feel her. A connection just as strong as the one I'd been able to create with Jackson in the Underground.

"She's here," I said. "I honestly don't know how I missed this before."

"Missed what?"

I turned to Jackson and smiled. "Missed my connection to her," I said, an excited fluttering in my chest. "I was so worried I wouldn't feel anything."

"What does it feel like?" he asked.

"It's amazing," I said. "I never knew what to look for before, but the second we walked up on this door, my blood began to hum. An energy that's, I don't know, somehow familiar. As if there's a piece of me that's separate and searching for a way back. She's alive, and she's somewhere behind this door."

Jackson stared at me with a glow in his eyes. "Do you think it's strong enough to find where they're keeping her?"

I closed my eyes and pictured Angela King. I could see her so clearly in my mind. Every detail of her face. Her jet black hair. I could hear her voice as if I had a recording of her in my memory. She was a part of me and now that I knew how to connect with that side of myself, I knew I would be able to find her.

"Yes," I said, hope rising up in my chest. "I can find her."

A HUNDRED HEARTBEATS

I CRINGED AT THE creaking sound that echoed through the hall as I opened the door to Winterhaven. If anyone was up at this hour, they would have heard that. We needed to act fast.

Moving to the center of the room, I sat down as Jackson paced between the five doors, ready in case anyone came through. I closed my eyes and concentrated on my sister. Our blood bond. Our demon bond.

At first, I could only feel that she was here in this house. Alive. I could tell she wasn't up here on the third floor with us, but nothing more specific was coming to me. I settled deeper into my meditation, letting the room itself fall away. I blocked the sound of Jackson's boots against the floor as he walked back and forth. I stilled my fears and my worries and all that was within my soul until it was just me and her.

Sisters.

It took me a moment to remember how to do this. I'd been able to follow Jackson through the Underground with this power, a sort of mental projection that allowed me to extend my consciousness beyond my body.

I sent my power out to search for her, my body firmly here in this room but my mind exploring the house below. I tried to remember the layout of the house from the time I was here before. I imagined walking down the large staircase and onto the second floor. I mentally searched the hallways, but I knew my sister wasn't being kept there. My connection to her urged me down, farther into Winterhaven.

The grand staircase led down to an opulent first floor. Everything was so clear in my mind, as if I had sent a ghost of myself down throughout the house. So far, I hadn't run into any other energy. If anyone was home, they had to have been asleep or in another part of the house.

I searched the main floor and my instinct brought me to another staircase off the kitchen. It led down to the basement. I remembered this path because it was the same one we had taken down to the room where my Heritage ritual took place all those months ago. Was my sister being kept somewhere in the basement?

I took a slow breath in, centering my mind so that I could push my vision farther into the bowels of the Winter's home. My magic extended, snaking down this third staircase like a long tentacle.

My arm erupted in goose bumps and a tingle went through my core. I was close to her. She was definitely somewhere on this basement level. My mental image of her strengthened and I chased the feeling of her down the hallway, past the ritual room and finally to a narrow wooden door. For some reason, I couldn't push my vision through that door, but I knew she was there. I knew I had found my sister.

The more I focused on her energy, the closer I felt to her. Even though I couldn't see through the final door, I could feel her fear. Terror gripped her spirit and I winced, almost losing our connection. I struggled to hang on as her fear intensified. Something was definitely wrong. I needed to get down to her fast.

Quickly, I pulled myself back through the space, retracing my steps and mapping out the path I had to take.

"I know where to find her," I said, standing. "She's all the way down in the basement, but I'm pretty sure I can get down there."

"Is she okay?"

I frowned. "I couldn't see her," I said. "There was a doorway I couldn't push through, but I need to hurry. Jackson, something down there had her completely terrified."

"Maybe we should shift and just get down there as fast as we can," Jackson said. "As long as we can get close enough to her for one of us to make contact with her skin, we can shift and bring her with us."

"I've thought of that," I said. "But if we go down there and it's a trap, then the Order has us both."

Jackson ran a hand through his hair. "So what are you suggesting we do?"

I knew he wasn't going to like this next part of my plan, but for me, it was the only thing that made any sense. It was the safest way.

I moved my weight from one foot to the other. "I need to go down there alone."

Jackson stepped toward me, eyes narrow. "Absolutely not. We're doing this together," he said. "I'm not going to let you go down there by yourself. We don't have any idea what kind of traps they might have set up."

"Listen, I know this isn't what you want, and I know we were planning to go together," I said. I placed my hands on his biceps. "But I didn't expect her to be all the way in the basement. It's too far. There's no way we're going to just walk through the house with no one noticing us, and it's too dangerous to shift into demon form and fly down there. It would pull too much energy from the life in this house. Someone would feel our presence too quickly and we'd be caught for sure. Besides, if it's a trap, then at least they'll only have one of us. If I don't come back, you can go for help."

"You can't do this on your own," he said. "If we can't both go, then let me go by myself."

"How is that better? You only have access to demon magic," I said. "Any magic you cast is going to be detectable. I can use the human side of my power to go invisible. It's our best chance. Besides, you don't even know how to get down there."

"I don't want you to go alone," he said. "How will I know if something's gone wrong?"

I walked over to him and placed my hand over his heart. His heartbeat was strong against my palm. "You'll feel it," I whispered.

The room around us was silent except for the pounding of my heart in my ears. I waited, watching the confusion and struggle in his eyes as he tried to decide what to do next. I knew he didn't want to let me go alone, but he had to also see the logic in my plan. If we both went down there, we'd be putting everything at risk. But did he believe in my strength enough to let me go?

He lifted his hand up to cover my heart and we stood there for more than a hundred heartbeats, our eyes locked.

"If I feel even for a second that you're in trouble, I'm coming down there," he said. He leaned toward me and pressed his forehead against mine. "Please be careful."

I threw my arms around him. "I will."

I kissed him, then turned to the door that led downstairs and into the main part of Winterhaven. I closed my eyes and took a deep breath, feeling my shoulders rise and fall as I relaxed and drew my witch's power into my body.

Blue energy poured into me and it felt so familiar as the glamour took hold. So much like home. I opened my eyes and lifted my hand in front of my eyes, watching it disappear.

WHERE GUESTS WERE NOT ALLOWED

I DIDN'T SEE A soul on the second floor.

I walked with the lightest of steps, careful to keep far away from anything I might bump or knock over. The last thing I needed right now was for my clumsiness to get me into trouble. I kept my magic on full alert like my demon training had taught me. Ready to act and embrace both sides of my magic if I had to.

At each turn, I paused to make sure my connection with my sister was still strong. I had a map in my head, but I also knew I couldn't afford to make any mistakes.

I made it down the grand staircase and headed toward the kitchen. As I looked around, I noticed that everything in this house was white with pops of blue. The floors were normal wooden floors for the most part, but all of the walls and ceilings were painted a pristine white. Almost every piece of furniture was white, and despite the number of children who must have grown up here, there wasn't a single marred edge or flaw to be seen.

A blue glass chandelier hung from the ceiling above the staircase. A blue and white vase held a bouquet of blue hydrangeas. A rug thrown across the floor downstairs was mostly white with a blue floral design.

How could someone so dark stand to be surrounded by so much light?

Priestess Winter was all about appearances, even down to the last detail here in her home. Everything about this place felt fake and manufactured. Created to give the impression of purity. Holiness. To me, it just felt cold and sterile.

She has a cold stone where her heart should be.

The tiger witch's words popped into my mind as I studied the house. Yes, Priestess Winter was cold. And calculating. I don't know why I hadn't noticed the chill in this place the first time I was here. I guess time and distance gave me some perspective on the kind of person she really was.

I felt my sister's energy below me, pulling me down to her. Could she feel that I was here? What was it she was so afraid of? I shuddered to think what Priestess Winter might have done to her.

Following her energy, I made my way through the living room toward the back of the house. I passed through the pristine kitchen and opened the door to the basement.

A dark staircase led downward. It was too dark at the bottom to really make anything out, but I knew I was close now. I hurried down the stairs, relying on memory to make my way in the darkness. I knew this part of the basement was beautifully finished. An extension of the house above, and not like a basement really at all. But when I finally reached the narrow wooden door where my vision had stopped, a feeling of darkness overcame me.

I had the distinct impression I was about to enter a part of Winterhaven where guests were not allowed.

Was this where I would find the priestess waiting for me? I had come too far too fast. Too easy. But I couldn't stop now.

My hand trembled as I reached for the doorknob. I turned it slowly, my heart racing in my chest. What horrors would I face behind this door?

The darkness beyond was suffocating. A black abyss.

Somewhere in the distance, water dripped. The air smelled mildewed down here, like a wet towel left in a dark place for far too long. Something skittered along the wall beside my head. I covered my mouth, stifling a scream.

I needed light.

I searched along the wall for a switch, but couldn't find one. My breath became rapid and my chest tightened. I knew I couldn't go any farther without my sight. I let my invisibility glamour fall away and conjured a dim white orb.

Dark gray cement walls rose up on either side of a slender hallway, closing me in tight. I gulped for air, desperate not to lose my connection with my sister's energy.

I walked as fast as my feet would carry me, but when I almost stumbled, I had to force myself to slow down.

So far, all I could see down here was this long, claustrophobic hallway. No doors or rooms. Just an endless path forward.

Finally, the hall opened up into a large square room with three new possible paths. A crossroads. I stood in the middle and had to choose. But which way?

I thought my connection to my sister was drawing me to the right, but when I took a few steps down that path, I felt her presence pull away. Confused, I stepped back into the middle. I took several deep breaths and concentrated again, releasing all of the tension from my body and letting my inner instincts take over.

Left. She had to be down the left hallway. But when I turned and started down the left hallway, I felt her pull away again.

Damn. What was I doing wrong?

Out of frustration, I picked the only other option and nearly took off at a run, but something stopped me. This wasn't right.

My sister wasn't down any of these hallways.

I clenched my jaw tight and wanted to slam my boot against a wall. Had I lost her somehow? What had I done wrong? Standing here in the center of this crossroads, I could clearly feel that Angela King was near, but the second I committed to any path, she grew distant.

So, where the hell was she? I'd gone every possible direction.

My skin began to tingle and my breath stopped in my chest.

Wait.

Not every direction.

Slowly, I lifted my eyes toward the ceiling. I hadn't gone up.

NO SONG TO SING

*A*BOVE ME, IRON cages hung from the tall ceiling. My hand flew to my mouth and my eyes widened. There had to be at least twenty cages up there, and from the looks of it, there was a body in every one of them.

It was too dark and too far up for me to tell exactly where my sister was, but I knew instantly she was in one of those cages.

She plans to make her a bird. Trapped in a cage with no song to sing.

Again, the voice of the tiger witch echoed in my memory. I shivered.

The bodies above me twitched. Jesus. What were they doing to these people? No one deserved this.

A drop fell from one of the cages and landed near my boot. This was the source of the drips I'd been hearing, but it wasn't water like I'd originally thought. It was blood. In horror, I yanked my foot out of a pool of sticky red. I looked up and saw that whoever was just above my head was bleeding rather badly.

Please don't be my sister.

But I already knew it was her. I could feel it deep in my bones and in my racing heart. She was hurt and losing blood. I counted back. She'd been here three full days already. Had she been bleeding this whole time? It was a miracle she was even still alive.

I had to get her down from there.

I looked to the edges of the room, searching the walls for some kind of lever system that would bring the cages down, but there was nothing. Whoever put her there must have flown her up there. I'd taught myself to levitate once upon a time, thankfully, and would have to use that magic again, here. I couldn't risk using my demon magic just yet. Not when I'd come so far without being detected.

I stilled the panic in my core and concentrated instead on lifting my body from the ground and up to the cage. It took a few tries. My hands trembled out of control and my knees had gone weak. These poor people. I knew my sister had only been here a couple of days, but what about everyone else? Some of these people could have been here for years.

I had to steady myself. If they caught me down here, they might decide to put me in one of the cages, too. I couldn't live a life like that. Besides, if Jackson felt that I was panicking or in trouble, he would risk everything to find me.

I breathed in and out. In and out. I let the horror of the situation fall to the back of my mind and focused only on my sister. She was the only one I had come here for. I would worry about the rest of these people later. For now, it was all about my sister.

My feet left the ground and I rose slowly toward the cage, levitating. I kept my eyes on the person above me, not daring to look at anyone else captive here. There was no telling what state I would find them in, and losing my concentration now would mean falling to the very hard cement floor. As I rose, matted black hair came into view. A single pale hand lay near the edge of the cage bars, streaked with dried blood.

Tears sprang up and my concentration faltered for a moment, but I forced myself to be strong.

I had to get her out of this place.

Once I was level with the hanging cages, I could see them in more detail. A small ledge jutted out beside the door to the cage. I lifted myself up to this ledge and grabbed onto the side of the cell.

The cage swung slightly as I placed my weight on it and I held on tight, my breath coming in ragged gasps.

My sister stirred. Her lips parted and she groaned, her forehead wrinkling in pain. Or fear. I tried the door, but it was locked tight. I crouched down close to her face.

"Mrs. King?" I cleared my throat. "Angela? Can you hear me? It's Harper."

I touched her hand. Her feverish skin beaded with sweat. Her hair was caked with blood and dirt. My chest ached. She was here because of me. How could someone put her in a place like this?

I reached my hand through the cage a little farther and shook her shoulder. "Angela, wake up. Come on, we've got to get out of here."

She groaned again. Her leg kicked out and she jerked her head violently to one side, smacking it against the bars. Every piece of me tensed. What had they done to her? She seemed to be locked in some kind of nightmare. Her eyes were still closed, but I could see them moving rapidly behind her closed lids.

What if I couldn't wake her up? Maybe leaving Jackson upstairs wasn't the best idea after all. There was no way I would be able to carry her. I don't know why this hadn't occurred to me earlier. I would have no choice but to shift with her and fly her up to the third floor. I would have to move incredibly fast if we were going to have any chance of escaping this place.

I stood and studied the door again. About halfway up on the right side, there was a keyhole. I tried to use my magic to flip the lock mechanism inside the iron enclosure, but it wouldn't budge. I looked around for something I could use to try to pick the lock manually, but what? Inside the cage, they had all but stripped my sister down to nothing. She was wearing a torn t-shirt and workout pants that were ripped and bloodied. She didn't have any jewelry on or anything in her hair.

Wait. I reached up to the butterfly bobby pin in my hair. Zara's gift. She'd said it was the key to getting my sister out of here. I had a feeling she hadn't meant it so literally, but I wasn't sure what else to do.

I pulled the jewel from my hair with shaking fingers, nearly dropping it down into the muck and blood below. I inserted it through the rusty keyhole and searched inside until the end of the bobby pin locked into the right place. I smiled through my tears. Thank goodness for my years as a delinquent.

Carefully, I turned the butterfly pin in the lock and held my breath as it clicked and the door to the cage fell open. I stuffed the pin back into my hair.

I crawled in and sat down beside Angela, leaving one leg outside to hold the door open.

"Angela," I said, I shook her harder this time. Still no response.

I looked around, not even knowing what I was looking for. I just wanted something, anything, that could help me wake her up. I desperately needed her to be conscious. I wasn't even sure I could carry her if I shifted and tried to take her with me that way. The only object I'd ever really shifted with before was the sword when I'd sparred with my father. I had to hope this would be as easy.

I thought of splashing water on her face, but there wasn't even any water here in the cage with her. I had no idea if she'd eaten or had anything to drink in days. How long could a person live without water?

Panic surged inside of me. I should have planned better. There had to be some way out of this.

Think.

There had to be some kind of clue I was overlooking. Steeling my nerves and stomach, I looked around at the faces in the other hanging cells. Almost all were women. And everyone was passed out just like my sister. I couldn't really see anyone else clearly, but I could tell there were two men among the crowd. Seventeen people in total. Three empty cages.

What were the odds everyone here would be asleep or passed out? Even though I had made some noise, no one had so much as stirred. And they all seemed to be dreaming just like Angela.

They were in some kind of trance or forced sleep. Probably to prevent them from using their magic to escape or fight back.

If it wasn't for the obvious nightmares, I would have said it was a blessing to be asleep. I knew from my time in the torture room at Shadowford that being awake in a prison like this would be horrifying.

I gripped my sister's hand and leaned my weary back against the iron bars. How could I break this magical spell that was keeping her asleep?

I wasn't a healer or someone who was naturally gifted at this sort of thing. I wasn't even sure it was possible for me to break the spell.

I placed my hands against her skin and visualized her waking up. I could feel some of my power flowing into her, but this only seemed to intensify whatever dream she'd been locked into.

The tears I'd been holding back began to flow down my cheeks. My only choice was to shift into my demon form and carry her with me. Since I'd never tried it with a person before, I wasn't exactly sure how it worked. The only thing I was sure of was that my demon power was bound to pull enough energy from my surroundings to let Priestess Winter know I was here. It would put both me and my sister in extreme danger. Jackson too.

This completely sucked.

But what else could I do? I was out of options and running out of time until dawn.

I wiped away my tears and gripped Angela's hand tight. I took a long, steady breath in, prepared to shift.

Just as I began to exhale and disappear into white smoke, a voice stopped me cold.

"I knew you would come for her," the woman said with a raspy laugh. "Harper the hero, risking everything for the people she loves. What noble bullshit."

I gasped, cold tingles crawling across my skin like spiders made of ice.

I recognized that voice. I turned in the direction of the sound, realizing with surprise it was coming from one of the nearby cages. I stared at the bloodied woman sitting up three cages over.

She wasn't wearing her pearls or makeup and her hair was shaved close to her head, but her eyes were the same cold blue I'd stared into many times with fear or disgust. I could tell from the contempt in her voice and her fevered stare that she blamed me for being held captive here.

And it was my fault. In a way.

She'd betrayed my mother and had her killed in an attempt to steal the power of the prima line. All I'd done was tell the priestess about her betrayal. Was it bad that I almost took joy in seeing her here like this?

I'd thought no one deserved this fate, but maybe I was wrong. If anyone deserved to be here, it was Lydia Ashworth.

ALL MAGIC HAS A COST

"*Y*OU PROBABLY THOUGHT I'd be dead by now," Lydia Ashworth said.

"Your own actions got you here," I said, leaning back against the bars. "Am I supposed to feel guilty about that?"

She laughed, then leaned forward as wet coughs wracked her body. I grimaced. That didn't sound good. Had she been here since the day the Order tried to kill me? That was months ago.

"I know this might come as a surprise to you, but I don't blame you for what you did," she said once her coughing had stopped. "I was headed to this place from the time I was fifteen years old. I tried to play their game, but I guess I always knew this is where it would all end."

I bit my bottom lip. Was she trying to gain my sympathy? She was the one who had made a pact with the crow witches. She was the one who had betrayed my mother and had her killed. She'd been playing with fire since before she was my age.

I was glad she'd finally gotten burned.

An awkward silence filled the room. The only sound was my heart beating wildly in my ears and the drip, drip, drip of blood on the floor below.

"I knew you'd come for her," Lydia said again. She adjusted her position and leaned back against the far side of her jail. She lifted one knee and rested her elbow against it. She gave me a sad smile and shook her head. "I was the one who picked Angela to be the cheer team trainer, if you can believe that. How stupid, right? I trusted her. She was such a rising star in the Order. Turns out she was a traitor this whole time. I had no idea she was a half-demon. Much less that she was our Prima Futura's sister."

My eyes widened and I leaned forward. "You knew? About our father? About me?"

"Yes," she said. "Well, not until recently. I could tell there was something special about you. You caught on to the magic so fast. Still, that could have just been talent or dumb luck. But after you escaped to the shadow world and had been gone a while, I knew there had to be something more to it. I've seen what Priestess Winter does to gates who defy her. I expected her to kill us all and move on. When she didn't, I figured it had to do with you somehow. You were still valuable to her in some way."

I shook my head. "That still doesn't tell me how you knew about my father."

"One of the Winter sisters told me," she said. "Honora, I think. She comes in here sometimes to bring a new prisoner or take someone away for questioning. I asked her why her mother hadn't destroyed the Peachville gate, and she told me you were a demon princess. I honestly thought she was kidding."

I looked around. "Why are you the only one awake in here?"

"I'm not a threat to them," she said, hanging her head. "They've already stripped my magic away. I'm a hollow shell at this point until they decide to make it official."

"Make what official?" I asked.

She lifted her head and stared straight into my eyes. "You don't know?" she asked. "They're going to turn me into a hunter."

A cold shiver ran up my arms and I pulled them closer to my chest.

"You probably think I deserve all this, and maybe I do," she said. "But if I do, so does Priestess Winter herself."

"What do you mean?"

"Don't you understand? The ceremony to transfer the prima line is dark magic," she said. "It's everything the Order says they stand against, yet it's exactly what they tried to do to you. Priestess Winter acts like she's such a saint. She pretends to follow the law of the Order, but she openly defied her own rules just to transfer the line to a new family. I mean, think about it Harper. She arrested me and threw me in this place for basically trying to perform the same dark magic she was casting. For me, it's illegal and blasphemous, but for her, it's fine."

I sat back. I hadn't considered that before now.

"You were worth the blasphemy for her, though," Lydia said. "Of course, after you were gone, she probably would have just altered everyone's memory to forget you ever existed. Then she could have gone back to her fake perfect life without a mark on her pristine record. People are much more likely to join an organization that seems pure and good than one that openly practices evil and kills its own members on a whim."

"You said you know what she does to a town that defies her," I said. "That's dark magic too."

Lydia sighed. "I know what she does to those towns. That doesn't mean the rest of the Order's witches know that. They see Priestess Winter as this blameless example of perfection. They practically worship her, never realizing she would kill them in an instant if it served her purpose."

Bitterness dripped from her words.

"Are you really so different?" I asked, my heart aching for my mother.

Lydia Ashworth laughed and raised her eyebrows. "No, I guess not," she said. "I've lived my life stepping over people to get what I want. Killing them if I had to. Hell, even being in this cage didn't stop me. Why do you think your sister's here in the first place?"

I looked down at my sister. She was still dreaming, her expression locked in fear.

I swallowed. "What are you talking about?"

"The Halloween Ball," she said. "When you accidentally unlocked my memories of your mother, I remembered who she'd been having an affair with. We were, after all, best friends. She'd told me everything. And since I knew who her lover was, or at least who he was pretending to be, I knew he had another daughter with his human wife. That made you sisters and it made Angela King a half-demon."

"And you thought knowing that could somehow save you?"

"When they took me away that day," she said. "They brought me here to rot. Of course, I had no idea the ceremony had failed. Shocking really, when you think about it. A young girl like you surviving despite all odds? Then apparently you kept surviving, even against the hunters. Priestess Winter came tearing in here about a week ago, so angry that she couldn't find a way to capture you. Yelling something about you killing her favorite cat. That's when I realized she had no idea about the valuable bait she had right there in Peachville."

My heart stopped. "You told her about my sister to try to save yourself."

"Yes. I told her," she said. She gestured at her cell. "She promised she'd let me go. I shouldn't have been surprised she was lying."

Rage boiled up inside of me. "First, you kill my mother," I said through clenched teeth. "And then you have my sister imprisoned?"

"Don't take it personally," she said. "I've been in too deep since I was a young girl. It's been nothing but bargaining and struggling to stay alive and to stay on top ever since. All I ever wanted was to be Prima. Is that really so much to ask?"

"It was your choice to get mixed up with the crows," I said. My fists were clenched so tight I'd lost all feeling in them. "Whatever fate they've got in store for you, I'm sure you deserve much worse."

"Is there a fate worse than becoming a hunter?" She looked at me, the fear in her eyes raw and real.

If I didn't hate her so much, I might have pitied her.

"Do you expect me to feel sorry for you?" My fingernails dug into my palms. "You deserve everything that's coming to you. It's really Drake and Lori I feel bad for. You might not have been the best mother in the world, but at least they had a mother."

A hysterical laugh escaped from her then. She banged the back of her head against the iron bars. "You're just too sweet for your own good, my dear," she said. "Always thinking of other people even when you're in danger. Well, I have news for you. Drake lost his real mother a long time ago."

My blood ran cold. "What do you mean his real mother?"

"Use your head, Harper. Do the math. Your mom and I were in the same class in school, right? So how did I have two children who are both older than you? I would have to have had them when I was what? Thirteen or younger?"

I lifted my hand to my forehead. She was right. How did I not realize this earlier? How come no one had ever mentioned that she wasn't Drake's real mom? "I had no idea," I said.

"No one does," she said. "That's the kicker. Not even Drake realizes it. He and Lori are my sister's kids, but now no one remembers I ever even had a sister. Memory altering spells can be very powerful, especially when they're mixed with the darker magics."

"Darker magic?" I asked the question, but was I really prepared for the answer? She'd already told me so much, I wasn't sure how much more I could handle. I wrapped my arms around my sister's trembling body.

"Priestess Winter may have acted like she was surprised by your announcement that I was working hand-in-hand with the crows, but that was all an act," she said. "She's known about that since the day your mother died. When it didn't work, I was terrified someone would come after me, but no one came. I actually thought I got away with it for a while. I was terrified when Priestess Winter came to me a few years later, well after my initiation ceremony, and told me she knew what I had done. Only she hadn't come to hurt me. She'd come to ask me for a favor."

"What kind of favor?"

"She wanted the crow's spell book," she said. "She wanted access to its dark magic. It was magic that had been lost to the Order for some time. Priestess Winter was eager to get it back."

A shiver ran down my spine. "So you stole the book from the crows?"

"Priestess Winter made a copy and I returned it before anyone had even noticed it was gone."

I knew the question I had to ask now, but the answer scared me. "What did you get in exchange?"

She smiled and ran a hand over her shaved head. "Two things. I wanted to be acting Prima in your absence," she said. "And second, I wanted my sister's life."

I shivered, a cold chill deep in my bones.

"Mariah. She was everything I wasn't. Beautiful, smart. Everyone loved her." Lydia beat her palm against her head with force. "She was nearly ten years older than I; and I was so incredibly jealous of her. Our parents were always asking me why I couldn't be more like Mariah. So, when I got the chance to have anything I wanted, I chose to have her life. I just didn't realize Priestess Winter would take it so literally."

I swallowed thick disgust. "What did she do?"

She cradled an imaginary child in her arms and a river of tears flowed down her cheeks. "I remember when Drake was just a tiny newborn. I was still in high school back then, and my sister lived in this beautiful house with her perfect husband and her perfect kids. I remember visiting them when Mariah brought Drake back from the hospital. He was so little and so fragile. I loved him instantly, but Mariah, she took it all for granted. She complained that he cried too much and that she wasn't getting enough sleep. She adored Lori, but she said she never wanted a boy. What good was a boy to the Order? She didn't understand what a gift she'd been given. She didn't understand how beautiful her life really was. I never would have taken it for granted the way she did."

"You stole her life," I said, my voice shaky.

Lydia sniffed and ran her hand under her nose. "I didn't mean to. I know you won't believe me, but it's true," she said. "I just meant that I wanted a life like hers, but Priestess Winter told me that the only way to cast such a powerful and permanent spell was to sacrifice something valuable. I didn't realize she meant my sister until it was too late."

Horror filled my veins and I looked away from her. Oh god, she had killed her own sister. The room began to spin. I wanted to throw up.

"The funny thing is that after everything I did for the Order, and for the Winter family, this is still where I ended up," she said. "I guess in the end, she realized I knew too much. At least she didn't put me into a nightmare sleep like the others. The only way to break it is to drink a potion. One no one knows the recipe for except the Winters."

I swallowed and looked down at my sister. "Do you know where they keep it?"

"It's no use," she said. "You'll never win against them, Harper. You know why? Because you aren't willing to use dark magic against them. Dark magic is the most powerful thing on earth. Priestess Winter will win every time."

The spells. Dark magic. "You said these spells are permanent?" I asked. "That you took over your sister's life forever, and no one even remembers her? I didn't know that was possible. I thought all magic lost power over time."

"There is so much you still have to learn about the Order and about the way magic works." She crawled to the front of her cage and leaned her head against the bars. "All magic has a cost, Harper. The greater the magic, the greater the cost. And dark magic? It costs the most of all. Don't let Priestess Winter fool you. She pretends to be a champion of rules and honor, but she's the most evil of us all."

She looked me straight in the eye and the sadness and despair I saw reflected there rocked me to the core. If there had ever been good in her, it was gone now.

"You were right about one thing, though."

"What's that?" I asked.

"I do deserve this," she said. "And Harper?"

"Yes?"

Her face softened and tears filled her eyes. "If you see my sweet Drake, will you tell him I love him?"

With that, Lydia Ashworth turned away, hiding her human face from me forever.

ANYONE COULD BE ANYONE

I BROUGHT A SHAKY hand to my forehead.

The Order had ruined so many lives. I knew Priestess Winter was evil, but the true extent of her power and influence hadn't really hit me until now. If she was capable of wiping out the memory of a person's entire existence, what else was she capable of?

People who had grown up with Lydia Ashworth had completely missed the fact that she was too young to have ever given birth to Lori and Drake. Her own husband didn't even remember that he had once loved another woman.

Who else in Peachville had made a similar sacrifice? How could I be sure anyone was really who they said they were?

Anyone could be anyone.

My chest tightened and my breath hitched. The room spun around me, and I leaned back against the cold iron bars, desperate to get my bearings. Was she right? Had I gotten too deep into something I didn't even know the first thing about? Every time I pulled a thread in the tapestry that was the truth about the Order, it led to something completely unexpected. Just when I thought I had a hold on the truth, another thread came loose and everything changed again.

How do you fight an enemy you don't even understand?

I sat there, paralyzed, staring at the shivering body of my sister. Panic seeped into my bones. Jackson and I had just declared war against something much more dangerous than I realized. This went so much further than just the slavery of demons. The deceit and lies involved went deeper than I could have ever imagined.

I rubbed my face and forced myself back into the moment. I had to get control of myself. This was just another example of the great evil Priestess Winter was capable of. I'd already seen the horror of her actions that day Lea showed me what happened in Aldeen. Was this really so much worse?

I had to get it together and get the hell out of here.

Still, my hands shook and my breath caught in my throat. How was I going to find the potion we needed to wake her up? I prayed Jackson would be able to find a recipe in the library upstairs.

I grasped her hand tight and took a deep breath.

Here goes nothing.

I connected to my demon power, my heart racing. I visualized the path I'd taken to get here. I would have to retrace my steps with lightning speed in order to get back to the Hall of Doorways before anyone could stop us.

I closed my eyes and let the fiery essence of my demon half burn within my soul. I shifted, taking Angela with me as I flew away from the cage and back through the hallway.

Adrenaline shot through me. For a few brief moments, I believed I could really do it. I could get her out of there without anyone seeing us. But before I reached the end of the long basement hallway, I smacked against an invisible barrier. The blow forced me back into my human form as I fell to the ground.

I heard a crack as Angela's head hit the cement beside me. I rushed over to her, my entire body aching and sore. Warm blood gushed from my nose.

Angela groaned and rolled to her side, still dreaming despite the pain.

I was only footsteps away from the stairs that led back up to the main house, but some kind of barrier had come up since I'd first come through here. This was the trap I'd been waiting for. When I lifted my eyes to the top of the stairs, my heart stopped cold.

Blue silk slippers descended the stairway, followed by a beautiful girl in jeans and a white ruffled shirt. American as apple pie with her pale skin, white-blonde hair and rosy cheeks. She smiled at me with her lips, but her eyes were cold and filled with contempt.

Honora.

I'd only met her briefly a couple of times, but I recognized her immediately. She was Zara's middle sister. A second.

Had she been watching me this whole time? Fear twisted in my gut, and I knew.

She'd been waiting for me.

THE BUTTERFLY

"*I* SUPPOSE IT'S POINTLESS to ask you to let me go," I said. Honora cocked her head to the side, her blue eyes wide. "This can't be much of a surprise to a smart young woman like you," she said, her voice sugary as cotton candy. "You had every chance to be a good prima, but it's your own choices that have brought you here. This isn't what anyone wanted for you."

"Of course not," I said. I searched my sister's head for the source of a new bleed, finally feeling a gash just behind her left ear from where she hit the floor. I needed to stall Honora. Distract her so I could stop the bleeding. "You all wanted me to bow down and be the Order's puppet. If you knew me at all, you would have known I could never be that person."

She lifted an eyebrow. "I don't know. You seemed to really enjoy compromising yourself in order to make the cheerleading team," she said. "After all, you knew Agnes wanted it more than anything. You didn't even hesitate, though. You squashed her dreams without a second thought."

My mouth fell open. "You do realize Agnes was a murderer, right?" I said. "That spot on the cheer team would have never been open if she hadn't killed Tori and tried to frame me for the murder. Am I really supposed to feel guilty about foiling her evil plan?"

Honora's smile lost some of its glow. "You didn't know that at the time. As far as you knew, she was one of your only friends. An innocent orphan girl who just wanted to be a cheerleader."

I applied pressure to Angela's wound, doing my best to stay focused on what was really important here. I wasn't about to apologize for betraying Agnes. What she did to me was way worse. Besides, we all knew the Order wasn't ever going to let Agnes onto the team anyway. Even if I hadn't decided to try out.

Honora straightened her pearl bracelet and tugged at her sweater. "We all thought you had potential. You could have been such a great prima. A real leader in Peachville. Imagine the power that could have been yours at such a young age.," she said. Her eyes glittered at the mention of power. It turned my stomach. "It's not too late, you know. It can still be yours if you want it."

I made a choking sound. "At what cost? My soul? My friends? My memories?" Bitterness swelled within me. "Do you really think power is worth all that to me?"

Honora's mouth fell open. "Yes," she said. "Everyone wants to be powerful."

"I just wanted to feel like I belonged to something," I said. I looked down at my sister. Her face twisted in some secret horror that made my heart ache. "I just wanted to have a family. Not that someone like you could ever understand that. You have to actually have a heart to care about other people."

I swallowed back tears. I knew this conversation had gone on long enough. Honora hadn't come here to talk. She'd come to destroy me. And I intended to be ready for her.

I took a deep breath, centering myself. I knew this battle would be my first true test. I connected first to the earth beneath my feet. Beneath the floor. Deep within the ground, a powerful energy flowed. I sucked it into myself, fueling my body for the fight to come.

"You shouldn't be so quick to throw it all away for people like her." She looked down at my sister, disgust written across her face. "Trust me, having sisters isn't all it's cracked up to be."

I studied her and wondered what she must have meant by that. Did she know Zara had betrayed them? I thought of the butterfly in my hair, but didn't dare bring attention to it.

"I'd like to judge that for myself," I said, praying Angela and I would make it out of here safely.

Honora shook her head. "She's never going to wake up," she said. "I've made sure of that."

Anger ran through me. I gripped Angela's hand. I wouldn't let her stay like this forever. Whatever they'd done to her, it was torture. I could see it in every grimace. Hear it in every moan. I had to save her.

"You'll need a potion to wake her up," she said. She placed her index finger on her chin and paced in front of me. "Of course, I'm sure mother would be happy to give your sister one. That is, if you were willing to make a trade."

I clenched my jaw tight. "What kind of a trade?"

"An even trade. You for her. If you agree to become Prima, all these nightmares go away," she said. She waved her hand and the air shimmered as the barrier between us disintegrated. She stepped closer and crouched down beside me. "We could even take away your memories and replace them with happier ones. We could make you forget about Jackson. You wouldn't even miss him. Besides, Zara's upstairs right now with Selene, making sure he can't come down here to save you."

My head snapped up. "What?"

Zara had betrayed us after all? This couldn't be happening.

"Think about it, Harper. You could still have your sister and your friends in the Order. You'd be rich, beautiful. You'd have so

much power and influence. It would be a dream life. I promise
you. You wouldn't remember any of this."

Was she serious about this? Did she really think I'd give up
so easily? Even after all that I'd been through?

"The only alternative is death," she whispered. She placed a
hand on my sister's arm and Angela's body convulsed in pain.
"For everyone you've ever loved."

Rage fueled my inner demon. I came alive with it, my hands
tingling. Every inch of my skin buzzed with it. "Becoming a
prima would be worse than death," I said.

Honora stood, a heavy sigh breaking from her lips. "Don't
be foolish, Harper," she said. "This won't end well for you."

I let go of Angela's hand and stood, my eyes locked on
Honora's face. She had become my first target. And once I'd
finished her, I would move on to anyone else who dared to
stand in my way. Even if I had to find Priestess Winter herself
and force the potion recipe from her mind.

I breathed in, feeding my power with two kinds of energy. I
was both witch and demon. The earth hummed beneath my
feet. Life-force pulsed in the air around me, animating my
demon side. I gathered it all in, ready to fight.

My hands burst into flame, and I sent a wave of red fire
toward Honora.

She lifted a single finger and my fire stopped, frozen in time
as if she'd merely pressed pause. The flames hovered in the air
between us for a brief moment. Then, she put her lips together
and blew, extinguishing the fire with a single breath.

My heart stopped. Shock weakened my knees and I
struggled to breathe.

She raised an eyebrow and waved her finger from side to
side, clucking her tongue. "You shouldn't have done that," she
said.

Before I had a chance to recover, she reared back, then pressed
her flat palm toward me. A great invisible force pushed through

the hallway. It hit me like a bulldozer. My legs came out from under me and I flew several feet backward, landing on my ass.

The impact jarred me. I shook my head, trying to get my bearings.

Down the hallway, Honora cursed. She had a strange expression on her face, as if she were confused. She tugged on her hair and frowned.

I scrambled to my feet as Honora reared back and threw a ball of light toward me like a baseball.

I lifted my forearm in front of me, forming a shield at the last possible second.

Honora's spell slammed into me. Her energy turned to black oil against my shield and a foul taste coated my tongue. Her darkness seeped into the shield and into me. Coughs shook my body, forcing me to bend over.

I clutched my chest and gasped for air, panic consuming me. I'd completely underestimated her. Was I strong enough to defeat her?

I had to try. For both mine and Jackson's sake.

From the corner of my eye, I saw a darkness swoop down on me from above like a bird. I screamed and crouched low to the ground as something brushed against my shoulder. A crow? I forced my eyes open, searching for familiar red eyes and knife-like talons. Instead, there was only shadow.

My shirt ripped at my shoulder, but whatever she'd sent after me hadn't been able to touch my skin.

Honora stomped her foot, an angry sound rumbling deep in her throat.

I straightened and gathered a new spell between my fingertips. I threw a bolt of white-hot lightning toward Honora. She caught it as if it were a baseball, then threw it right back at me. I exhaled, letting go of my human form. My body transformed to smoke as the lightning flew through me. I somersaulted through the air, then reformed closer to where she stood.

Surprise flashed in her eyes, but she recovered quickly. With a flick of her wrist, she sent a flock of shadowbirds toward me, their pointed claws outstretched.

I formed a circle of flames at my feet, then crouched and drew them up around me like a dome. The birds screeched as they burned. When the last shadow had died against my fire, I pulled the energy together into a single fireball, then hurled it toward Honora.

She moved to dodge it, but the fire grazed her skin. She cried out, clutching her arm. When she pulled her hand away, her skin was blackened. She spun toward me, fury in her eyes.

I took advantage of the moment and reached out to the earth deep beneath her feet. I planned to rip through the cement, pulling whatever vines and rocks and soil I could from under the house, but before I could do it, she spun her body around like a tornado, a large gust of air nearly knocked me down and broke my concentration.

Jesus. I didn't know she could do that.

I struggled against the wind, but managed to stay on my feet. She stopped spinning and stared at me, mouth open.

Rage reddened her face. Her entire body shook with tension. She pulled both hands up and away from her, forming tight fists that began to glow with a bright blue light.

Fear raced through me, and I tried to shift, but something about that light put me in a daze. I worked to close my eyes or look away, but I was helpless against it. Like a deer in headlights, I stared forward, unable to move.

She lifted her hands and shot the light toward me. Terror ripped through me as the light approached. I could feel the heat of it on my skin, but I could do nothing to protect myself or turn away. I screamed, bracing myself for the pain, knowing from the fury in her eyes that this was it for me. The end of it all.

The light made a direct hit, and although I felt the extreme power behind it, I felt no pain.

Honora stumbled backward, eyes bulging. Her shoulders slumped and she gasped for air. "What have you done?" she asked. "How did you resist that? I... I put everything into that spell."

She stuttered in fear and confusion. She leaned against the wall, her chest rising with each pained breath.

Confused, I studied my skin, patted my body to make sure I wasn't missing something. I hadn't done anything. I had no idea why I wasn't dead or in excruciating pain.

Then, something began to burn the skin near my temple. I reached up, confused. My hand touched the bobby pin in my hair.

Zara's gift. The crystal butterfly. Somehow, it had protected me from Honora's magic. It had been protecting me all along. That must have been why she seemed so angry and confused every time she tried to cast a spell at me.

The force of her light spell must have been too much for it. The butterfly burned so hot against my skin, I had to rip it from my hair and throw it to the ground. The blue stone in its center flashed bright, then faded and cracked.

Honora stumbled forward, eyes narrowed. She fell to her knees near the broken pin. "Where did you get that?"

I stared down at the butterfly in awe. I was wrong. Zara hadn't betrayed us. She must have put some kind of protection spell into the stone. How had she known back then that I would someday need it?

Tears of gratitude stung my eyes.

She had saved my life.

YOU WON'T REMEMBER
A THING

*S*HE GOT IT from me," Zara said.

She stood with Jackson at the bottom of the steps. The sight of the two of them together and safe made my heart soar. Hope filled me from head to toe. Were we actually going to make it out here alive?

Honora stood up, then stumbled against the wall, her power drained from the intensity of the fight. "You'll pay for this," she said, daggers in her eyes as she stared at Zara.

"Maybe," Zara said with a shrug. "Then again, maybe not. Jackson, can you hold her for a second please?"

Jackson sent coils of smoke at Honora, wrapping them around her. She struggled, but her strength was gone.

Zara stepped closer to her sister, then pulled a tiny vial from the small white purse she carried. Honora's eyes grew wide.

"What's that?"

"This?" Zara stared at the potion, then cut her eyes back toward her sister. "This is my insurance you won't tell mother about my trick with the butterfly pin. You won't remember a thing."

She lifted one hand toward her sister's throat in a claw like motion. Honora's head snapped backward, her mouth pulled open. Zara uncorked the small vial and poured it down her sister's throat, then forced her mouth shut until she swallowed it down.

"Good girl," she said. "Now, why don't you lie down and get some rest. You look tired, sister."

Honora went limp in Jackson's coils. He set her down gently, her eyes closing the moment she hit the ground.

I ran up and threw my arms around Zara. "Thank you," I said. "I would be dead if it wasn't for you."

Zara hugged me back. "I'm so glad it worked," she said. "I'll explain everything to you later, but we really need to get out of here as soon as possible. Selene is locked in a similar sleep upstairs, but I don't have a potion strong enough to hold my mother."

She turned to head back up the stairs.

"Wait," I said, crouching down to where Angela lay on the floor. "What about my sister?"

"I almost forgot," she said. She looked inside her little purse again, then pulled out a larger vial that glowed with an orange liquid. "Here. This potion should pull her from her sleep."

I took the vial and gently opened Angela's mouth. I poured the liquid down her throat and waited.

"How long will this take?" I asked. I felt the ticking of the clock.

"It should only take a moment," she said, glancing back up the stairs. "We need to hurry."

"I can carry her," Jackson said.

"What if the potion doesn't work?" I asked, tapping my foot.

Beside me, Angela stirred and my heart leapt. Her eyes fluttered open and she stared into my eyes. I nearly cried with joy.

She smiled and started to lift her hand toward my face, then her body went completely limp.

"What happened?" I asked. I shook her gently. "Angela, wake up."

Jackson turned to Zara. "The potion isn't working."

Zara shook her head. "It worked," she said. "She wouldn't have opened her eyes if it didn't. She's just too weak. I think she passed out."

"You'll have to carry her," I said. "We need to hurry."

Jackson nodded and picked Angela up into his arms. He shifted, flying up the stairs and around the corner out of sight. Zara nodded to me, then morphed into a small butterfly. With a silent prayer of thanks and disbelief, I looked down at Honora's still form, then shifted to smoke and followed them up toward the Hall of Doorways.

SHE COULDN'T HAVE TAKEN THAT NEWS WELL

THE FOUR OF us flew high above the tree-tops toward the crow village.

Zara flew as a butterfly and Jackson and I were in our demon form. Angela was still too weak to shift or fly, so Jackson carried her. We flew as fast as we could, careful to stay high enough up that we could pull energy from the growing leaves rather than something on the ground that would be much easier to track.

When we reached the crow village, Mary Anne paced, waiting at the entrance.

My body tingled as I passed through the barrier into the protected zone. I couldn't believe the difference in the village from the last time I'd been here. While some of the houses were still burned and in ruins, four of the houses on the far side of the circle had been completely fixed up. Mary Anne and Essex had been busy.

Jackson entered behind me, and Essex rushed over to help him carry my sister.

"Is she okay?" Mary Anne asked. She threw her arms around me. "You have no idea how happy I am to see you. I was so worried."

Essex nodded toward a small blue house up ahead. "We have set up a special room for your sister," he said. "It will be very comfortable for her while she is recovering."

"Thank you," I said. I started to follow them, then remembered Zara was still outside, unable to enter without one of the blue wristbands.

"What's she doing here?" Mary Anne asked, scowling.

"She's going to be living here," I said. "Do you have one of those blue bands I can give to her?"

"I'm not letting her in here." She crossed her arms in front of her chest. "She's one of them."

"You don't know what she did for us tonight. We can't leave her out there," I said.

"You're right. Now that she's seen this place, she'll probably go tell her mother where to find us," Mary Anne said. She looked around, a finger pressed to her lips. "We could set up a temporary jail down in the library."

I let my head fall back. "She's not going to tell her family," I said, anxious to get to my sister's bedside. "She saved our lives and helped us get out of there. Why would she have done that if she planned on turning us over to her family now?"

Mary Anne shrugged. "I don't pretend to understand everything the Order does," she said. "Maybe Priestess Winter wanted to know where your friends were hiding and sent her here as a spy. All I know for sure is the Winter family is our enemy, and I don't think we should let her in."

Outside the barrier, Zara conjured a small pink blanket out of thin air. She laid it on the ground and sat down, legs crossed.

She fluffed her skirt around her and smoothed her hair, not looking worried or concerned at all. In fact, she looked happy.

I held back a smile, then turned to Mary Anne. "Do you really want to go there?" I asked. "If we were judging everyone here by the actions of their family members, would you even allow yourself in here?"

Mary Anne frowned. "Point taken."

She pulled a blue wristband from her pocket and held it out to me.

"Can you give it to her?" I asked, already walking toward the house where they'd taken Angela. "I want to be there when my sister wakes up."

Mary Anne rolled her eyes, then nodded and stepped through the barrier toward Zara.

I took off in a jog, anxious to see how my sister was doing. The potion Zara gave her had pulled her from the nightmare sleep, but she'd been unconscious the whole way home. I knew she'd lost a lot of blood and we didn't exactly have the means to give her a transfusion up here. We couldn't take her to a hospital either. Not without risking everyone's lives.

I prayed Jackson's limited healing powers would be enough.

I climbed the steps up to the blue house and walked through the open door. "Hello?" I called.

"We're in here," Jackson said, poking his head from a door at the back of the house.

My heart pounded as I stepped into the room. Angela King lay on a queen-size bed in the middle of the room, her eyes closed, but her breath steady and strong. Someone had placed a tray of basic medical supplies on the bedside table. Bandages. Alcohol. A bottle of painkillers. There was even a small vase of purple flowers on the table.

I was touched by their thoughtfulness, but held back my tears.

I sat down on the edge of the bed and took her hand in mine. "She's burning up," I said. I placed my hand on her forehead and was alarmed by the heat. "Did you find a thermometer?"

Essex reached into a small black bag and pulled out a digital thermometer. I took it and placed it under my sister's tongue, already knowing she had a high fever.

When it beeped, I pulled the thermometer from her mouth and cringed. 102.2. Not life-threatening, but high. Too high.

"Is there running water?" I asked Essex. "Ice? Anything we can use to try to bring her fever down?"

Jackson moved to the other side of the bed and pulled up a chair. He sat down and placed a hand on the wound on her head. He closed his eyes.

Essex came back carrying a wet wash cloth and a bucket of ice. "Will these help?"

"Yes, thank you," I said, taking the washcloth from him. I placed the cloth over Angela's forehead and motioned for him to set the ice down on the table.

I waited in silence as Jackson went over Angela's wounds one-by-one. He wasn't a powerful enough healer to get rid of them completely, but he was able to stop most of the bleeding and hopefully take away some of her pain.

I bit my lip, clutching her hand in mine. "Should we take her back through the portal?" I asked. "Our father could heal her in an instant."

Jackson shook his head. "It's too risky," he said. "Every available witch is going to be searching for us. If anyone saw us pass through that portal, it would put the entire city in danger."

I lowered my head to her hand. He was right. I hadn't thought about what might happen if the Order found my father's secret portal. We couldn't risk it. Especially not so soon after we'd rescued her. Still, I knew I would have to at least try to get word to him that we'd gotten her out safely.

Maybe it would change his mind about what was possible in the fight against the Order.

I sighed. "I just want her to be okay."

"Thanks to you, she's going to live," he said.

"Thanks to Zara," I said. "I never would have survived down there if it hadn't been for her. Honora's power was so much stronger than I imagined."

"When I first saw her walk through the door at Winterhaven, I didn't know what to think," he said. "I had no idea if she was on our side or theirs, but she just walked right up to me and put her hand in mine. She told me exactly what we needed to do to make the memory potions and the one that would wake Angela up from that nightmare. I don't know how she found out I had experience with potion-making, but she knew."

"The Winters know everything," I said. "I think they must have spies everywhere."

"Maybe," he said. "When her sister Selene finally came to find us, we had the potion and everything ready for her. I think she was so surprised by Zara, she forgot to put up a fight. You were right about trusting Zara."

"For a minute there, I thought it was the other way around. It's so hard to know who to trust," I said. I thought about Lydia Ashworth's story. How she'd stolen her sister's life and how no one even knew or remembered. Who else was not as they seemed in Peachville?

I stared down at my sister. Even she had turned out to be someone completely different than I expected. I knew she was a good person, but she'd been one of the Order's trusted leaders for years. I smiled as I thought of how shocked Priestess Winter must have been when she found out the person training future initiates was a half-demon.

Probably not as shocked as she was when she found out we'd gotten away. She couldn't have taken that news well. So far, she'd avoided getting directly involved in my capture. She'd sent everyone from the tiger witch to hunters to her own daughters after me, but she'd never actually come after me herself. I had a feeling next time I wouldn't be so lucky.

Jackson stood and turned off the light in the room. He stood behind me and rubbed my shoulders. "Let me know if she wakes up," he said.

"Where are you going?"

"I'm going to help the others get the rest of the village set up," he said. "There's still a lot that needs to be done."

I knew I should offer to help, but I didn't want to leave Angela's side. I wanted to be here when she opened her eyes.

"I'll bring you some food in a little while," Jackson said. He kissed the top of my head. "Get some rest if you can."

I nodded and gave him a weak smile. "I'll try," I said, knowing it would be a very long time before I would allow myself the luxury of sleep.

I DON'T THINK
SHE'S ACTING

OVER THE NEXT few days, we each took turns sitting with Angela. I spent the most time there by far, but I took breaks to eat and stretch my legs every once in a while.

Essex came in late one afternoon and offered to take over while I got some dinner. "Mary Anne insists you need food to keep your energy strong," he said. "I will let you know if there is a change."

Reluctantly, I stood and stretched. I hated to leave her side, but we'd been here three full days and there'd been almost no change. I had already decided if she didn't wake up within a week, we were taking her through the portal to our father. Risk or no risk. We'd have to find a way.

"I'll be back in a few minutes," I said.

"Take your time," Essex said. He settled down in the chair next to the bed and opened a book he'd been reading. "Enjoy some food and you will be feeling better."

I smiled. He was really such a sweet guy. He was definitely a welcome addition to our group of friends.

I yawned and made my way outside.

I gasped. This entire side of the village had been transformed into a garden of pink and white blossoms. Zara walked among the flowers and as she placed her index finger on the petals, they lit up from within. Mary Anne stood off to the side with her arms crossed in front of her chest.

"You realize this is basically blasphemy, right?" Mary Anne said. "If my family was here, they would absolutely die to see it turned into a pink flower shop."

"Well, your family isn't here, are they?" Zara said, not pausing in her work to light up the village. "Besides, this place is depressing. We need to stay positive if we're going to have the energy to fight."

"And you think flowers will make us feel positive?"

"Of course," Zara said. "You'll see."

I had to smile as I watched them argue. They were such opposites, but at the same time, they had so much in common. They had both grown up around horrible, evil women, yet they had both somehow found the courage to stand up against them. They'd also both sacrificed everything in their lives to save me, and I had no idea how I would ever repay them.

"If you're going to light them up like that, can we at least make them a darker color?" Mary Anne asked, wrinkling her nose.

Zara brought a finger to her mouth, studying her flowers. "What about dark pink?"

With one wave of her hand, the flowers deepened in color.

Mary Anne threw her hands up in disgust. "How is that better? Pink is not a dark color," she said. "I meant something like deep red or blue or something."

"I think it's pretty," I said, stepping onto the black pathway that connected the houses.

"Whatever," Mary Anne said, glaring at Zara before she turned her attention to me. "How is she?"

I glanced back at the blue house. "She's still unconscious."

Mary Anne walked over and placed a sympathetic hand on my arm. "I'm sure she just needs some extra rest while her body heals," she said. "She's going to be fine."

"I hope so," I said. I turned to Zara. "Have you ever seen someone recover after taking the potion?"

She pressed her lips in a tight line, her shoulders slumped. "No, but that doesn't mean it isn't possible," she said. "I know they've woken people up before, but they usually only do it to torture them for more information."

I swallowed back my disgust. "How could you live there knowing your mother kept so many prisoners in the basement?"

I crossed over to a dining table that had been brought out from one of the larger houses and sat down. I propped my elbows on the table and cradled my head in my hands.

Zara and Mary Anne sat down across from me.

"My mother does many things I don't approve of," Zara said. Her clear blue eyes darkened. "That's why I had to find a way out."

"I don't understand how you put up with it for as long as you did," I said, wrinkling my forehead. "I would have gone insane if I had to see her every day, knowing what she was capable of."

Zara placed her hands in her lap and dipped her head. "Believe me, I have struggled with this for a very long time," she said. "Family is complicated."

"Tell me about it," I said. I'd only had a father for a couple of months and it had been amazing and awful at the same time.

She took a slow breath in, then looked around as if afraid someone else might be listening. "To be honest, I don't even know if Priestess Winter is really my mother."

I wondered if I'd heard her right. "What do you mean?" I asked. "Who else would she be?"

She folded her hands together and pressed them so tight they turned pink. "I'm not sure," she said. "She looks exactly like my mother, so at first I thought I was just crazy. But deep down, I know something is wrong about her. See, when I was really little, I had a great relationship with my mother. I think she kind of favored me over my older sisters."

There was a sadness to her smile. She sniffed and when she looked up, her blue eyes were full of big tears.

"I was afraid of the dark when I was little," she said, a quiver in her voice. "My grandmother said it was a terrible weakness. She told my mother not to spoil me by coming into my room to comfort me when I would cry. My mom would sneak into my room most nights anyway. It was our secret thing, and it always made me feel better."

Mary Anne and I listened, leaning forward against the table.

"Well, on my fifth birthday, my grandmother died," she said. She looked around again, reaching up to play with a loose strand of hair. "I knew I was supposed to mourn with everyone else, but to tell you the truth, I was kind of glad she was gone. She was mean to me, always saying that if I ever wanted to be a warrior like the other thirds in my family, I had to toughen up."

"So your mother took over as Prima?" Mary Anne asked.

Zara curled the hair around her finger, then uncurled it. With wide eyes, she nodded, one of the tears finally escaping down her cheek. She wiped it away with the back of her free hand. "She went through her final joining ceremony that same night," she said. "Of course, I was too young to attend. Back then, I didn't even understand what was going on. I knew the women in my family had magical abilities, but I had no idea about the demons. After my grandmother died, though, everyone started calling my mother Priestess Winter. She had all these new responsibilities and she hardly had any time for me. When she did see me, she was different."

"Different how?" I asked.

"Cold," she said. "And she stopped coming into my room at night. Even if I would cry. I used to wait for her after the lights went out, but she never came to comfort me again."

Mary Anne leaned back and shrugged, unimpressed. "That doesn't prove anything," she said. "She took on a new role that took up a lot of her time. She stopped babying you. What's the big deal?"

Zara dropped her hands into her lap. "She didn't just stop coming into my room at night. There was more to it than that. When I got home from school one day about a week later, I found her in my bedroom. She had completely changed it. She'd taken all the nightlights out and turned everything from a beautiful light pink to this dark jet black," she said.

"What's so wrong about that?" Mary Anne asked.

"I was horrified," Zara said. "It was like a cave in there, and at night it got very dark. My mother never would have done something like that. When I asked her why, she'd looked at me with such cold eyes. She told me I needed to toughen up."

Zara swallowed hard. When she spoke again, her hands had begun to tremble. "Her voice sounded exactly like my grand-mother's. It scared me."

"But don't you think that could just be due to the fact that she'd taken the prima demon into her body?" I asked. "I mean, maybe the demon changed her somehow?"

Zara shook her head. "I don't think so," she said. "When I was little, I didn't understand what was happening, but even when I learned more about the process of a witch's initiation into the Order, I knew there was more to it when it came to my mother. She was never herself again."

I thought of Brooke and how much she'd changed after her initiation too. "I've seen it happen before," I said. "People change after they take the demons inside them. I don't think it's so unusual."

Zara's shoulders stiffened. "You don't understand." Her voice cracked. "I may be young, but in my short lifetime, I've seen more than a hundred possessions. I've seen the way people change. Sure, the Order gives them a mission that might change their ambitions and dreams, but deep down, they're still the same person. I'm telling you my mother was gone after that day. I could feel it. She even started doing things only my grandmother used to do. Like the way she would scratch her nails against her skirt. Or how she always put exactly two teaspoons of sugar in her tea. My real mother never used to do those things. It was eerie."

"Wait a second," I said, trying to figure out just what she was suggesting here. "Are you saying the demon caused her to act like your grandmother?"

"Not exactly"

"So what are you saying, then? Exactly?" Mary Anne asked.

Zara pressed a hand to her chest. "I don't think she's acting," she said. She shook her head and twirled her hair around her finger nervously. "I don't know. This is the first time I've talked about it since I was a little girl. I tried to talk to my sisters about it back then, but they said I was being ridiculous. I know it sounds insane, but I can't help how I feel."

I tried to make sense of what she was telling us. "Zara, are you saying your mother somehow became possessed by your grandmother's spirit?"

She lifted her chin, but her lip trembled and for a second, I thought she might cry. "I don't know," she whispered. "I only know that after that day, my mother might as well have been the one who died."

Her words hung around us all like a cloud of sadness. Still, something about her story chilled me to the bone. What had really happened to Zara's mother? Was it the demon who had changed her? Or some other dark magic?

"I have wanted to get out of there for so long," Zara said. She sniffed, her nose running from crying. "I was so happy when they told me I was going to be guarding you and training you. The day I met you was one of the happiest days of my life."

I reached across the table and took her hand.

"Then, everything fell apart," she said. "I never expected my own mother to try to kill you."

"Can I ask you a question?"

She nodded. "Sure."

"How did you know to give me the crystal butterfly pin?" I asked. "If you didn't expect her to try to hurt me, how did you know I would need it?"

Zara smiled through her tears. "I created that butterfly for our training," she said. "You were learning so fast and we were so close to moving on to more dangerous spells, I thought it would be neat for you to have a sort of talisman. A shield against my magic. That way I could really test you by using real magic against you. If you messed up and any magic got through, the shield in the pin would protect you from getting hurt. It was never meant to be used in a real battle."

"How did you learn to do that?" Mary Anne asked. "Imbue stones with magic shields, I mean."

"I mostly taught myself," she said. "My sisters and I got the spell from my aunt's spell book when we were little. We used to take the stones from a box in the ritual room at Winterhaven. There are tons of them down there, just like the one I used. We would perform the spell to imbue the stones with a protection spell and then we could practice throwing fireballs and other magic at each other without worrying about getting hurt."

"Which is why Honora's spells couldn't hurt me." I shuddered to think of what would have happened if her spell had hit me. I might have been hanging in an iron cell in the basement of Winterhaven instead of sitting here talking about it.

"Yes," Zara said. "We never got to use it in training, and when I found out my mother's plan to lure you to Winterhaven, I prayed you still had it and that it would at least buy you some time if it came down to it."

I removed the butterfly pin from my pocket. The blue stone in the center was cracked in several places, but it still glimmered in the light from Zara's garden.

"Thank you," I said, meaning it in the deepest part of my heart. "I know you took a huge risk giving Coach King that note."

Zara squeezed my hand. "You took a risk coming back to save your sister," she said. "You had to have known it was a trap."

"It was foolish, I know, but I wouldn't have been able to live with myself if I hadn't at least tried to save her."

"Not foolish," Zara said, her eyes gleaming with tears. "Brave."

THE TYPICAL HUMAN LIFETIME

*S*OMETIME THAT NIGHT, I finally gave in to exhaustion and collapsed in a bedroom Jackson had set up for me. He'd picked out a gray house for the two of us to share and spent a lot of time making it livable. I hated being away from my sister's bedside, but I couldn't keep my eyes open another second.

Hours later, Jackson burst into my room, out of breath.

"What is it?" I asked, terror gripping my heart. Were we being attacked?

"She's awake," he said, a smile dancing in his green eyes. "Your sister's awake, and she's asking for you."

My heart skipped.

I jumped from the bed, ran down the stairs and out into the street. Zara's flowers were still bright, lighting up the entire village. Essex and Mary Anne sat in two chairs they had dragged from one of the houses nearby. I didn't even care about my tangled mess of hair or the fact that my clothes were probably crazy wrinkled. I just wanted to see my sister.

I wanted so badly to shift and travel to her faster than my legs could carry me, but we'd agreed not to use demon powers if we could help it. It was too easy to track. I ran instead, barreling up the steps to the small blue house. I tore down the hallway and pushed into the bedroom.

Zara sat by the bed, but stood when she saw me. She smiled and stepped quietly out of the room.

Angela King's eyes met mine and my heart overflowed. I sat down on the bed and took her hand. We couldn't stop staring at each other.

"Oh, Harper, I don't even know what to say." Tears filled her eyes as she gripped my hand tighter. "I want to yell at you for risking so much to come get me, but I also know I can never thank you enough for what you did."

"I couldn't just leave you there," I said. I wanted to throw my arms around her, but was scared I'd hurt her. "And after seeing what they were doing to you, I'm so glad we got you out of there. How are you feeling?"

She shuddered. "It was horrifying," she said. "I kept having the same nightmare over and over. Everyone and everything I've ever loved kept being ripped from me. It felt so real and so painful. I feel much better now. Just a few sore spots here and there."

"It's all my fault," I said, lowering my head. "If it wasn't for me, they never would have taken you."

Angela sat up straighter, and I helped her readjust the pillow behind her back. "You can't blame yourself for the actions of evil people," she said. "You aren't responsible for their choices."

Her words touched a place deep in my heart. They were an echo of something our father had told me. It was so easy to blame myself for all that had happened, but she was right. I couldn't control what others decided to do with their lives.

Our eyes met again and my heart fluttered.

"It's so strange to be sitting here with you like this and to know you're really my sister," I said. "I mean, I always dreamed of something like this, but I never thought it was really possible. And now to have finally met both my father and my sister? It's a dream come true."

"I wanted to tell you so badly," she said.

I swallowed. "How long have you known?"

She raised an eyebrow and smiled. "Since the first moment I saw you," she said. "Do you remember that day? You had just gotten to Peachville High and you passed out in front of the demon statue. I rushed over to help you up. When our hands touched and then I saw that necklace, I knew it was you. You have no idea how hard it was to keep it a secret."

"Why did you?" I asked, trying not to sound hurt.

"I couldn't tell anyone," she said. "The Order has ways to extract memories and secrets. Telling you would have put us both in danger. It was too risky. I couldn't draw any unnecessary attention to myself."

"I have so many questions," I said, not even knowing where to start.

"We have time," she said with a smile. "I'm sure you've figured out by now that our lives are going to be much longer than the typical human lifetime."

My eyes widened. I honestly hadn't even thought about that. "How much longer?"

"It depends on whether you spend more time here or in the shadow world," she said. "The more time we spend over there, the stronger our demon half becomes and the longer our life becomes."

I still had so much to learn. So many decisions to make.

"Why did you stay here?" I asked. "If you've known who you were all this time, why wouldn't you leave the Order behind and live with our father where he could keep you safe?"

Angela's eyes searched my face, a sad smile pulling at the corners of her mouth. "Because I knew eventually they would find you," she said. "If I was living in a castle in the shadow world, I wouldn't have any way to really help you or keep an eye on you. I stayed because I knew if I played their game and pretended to be a good member of the Order, training the initiates, I could be there for you whenever you came home. I could get close to you without looking suspicious."

"You did that for me?" I asked, my face warm.

"Our father wasn't happy about it," she said. "He wanted me to live in the shadow world where he could keep me from going through the initiation, but I couldn't abandon you like that."

"You'd never even met me."

"That didn't matter," she said. "You were my sister and I knew you'd come home someday. I wanted to be there when you did."

I didn't know what to say. I couldn't believe she'd gone through so much for all these years, waiting for me to return to Peachville.

"I always used to wonder if you'd look like me, "she said. "But you don't look like me at all. You definitely take after your mother. I was just a little girl when she used to babysit for me, but I thought she was the coolest. She was so beautiful and such a rebel. I was incredibly sad when she died. It was a really tough time for me. My father had just up and left our family out of the blue and we didn't know where he was, and then Claire died. I felt abandoned."

"I've been wondering about that," I said. "I tried talking to him about Mom and about you when I was living in his castle, but he's a hard man to get to know."

She laughed. "To say the least."

"He mentioned something about leaving Peachville just before Mom died," I said. "I didn't realize he didn't tell you where he was going."

"One day everything seemed fine, and the next, he was gone without a trace," she said. "At the time, my mother and I had no idea why."

"How did you find out who he was?" I asked. "Did he come back for you?"

"He showed up at my house just before I turned eighteen," she said. "My mom had a meeting with the Order, so I was home alone. There was a knock on the door and when I opened it, there he was. Like he'd never even left. His hair was lighter and his eyes had changed a little, but I knew it was my father."

My mouth fell open. "What did you say to him?" I asked. "I probably would have slammed the door in his face after what he'd done."

"I almost did," she said. "Something in his eyes stopped me, though. He looked so serious. He said he was there to tell me something very important, but that he couldn't stay long and I needed to listen very carefully."

"He told you about the Order?"

"Yes," she said. She smoothed the blanket over her legs and stared down at her hands. "It was a lot for me to take in at the time. I'd grown up thinking the Order was great, full of powerful, beautiful women. But as he talked, I realized everything he said made sense. The way the Order controlled everyone in town. The way my mother acted sometimes, keeping secrets from me about the initiation ritual. He told me everything that night. He told me about the demons, about who he was and why he'd had to go so suddenly."

I swallowed. "Something about his father dying?"

"His father died fighting the Order," Angela said. "He's never told me all of the details, but I know it happened here in the human world, in a town called Clement in Tennessee. After that happened, it was Father's duty to take over as ruler of the Southern Kingdom. He didn't have a choice but to leave us."

I took in a deep breath and let it out slowly. I tried to imagine what that must have been like for her, growing up without a father and then having him suddenly show up and tell her he was a demon king.

"He also told me about you," she said. "Of course, all of us girls on the cheerleading squad knew our town's prima was missing. We knew the story and that someday she would come back to us, but it wasn't until that night that I knew the prima was my own half-sister."

I sat back. "So all in that one night, you found out how evil the Order really is. How they enslaved demons and that you, in fact, were half demon. And at the same time, you had to find out that your half-sister was the future prima?"

"Yes," she said, nodding. "It was a lot to take in, but I had an important decision to make. I was only a few weeks away from my initiation. I had to decide whether to go back with my father to the shadow world or whether to go through with it and become a member of the Order of Shadows."

"I don't understand why he waited so long to tell you the truth," I said. "He should have given you more time to make up your mind."

"He felt the information put me in danger," she said. "He wanted to keep me safe and innocent as long as possible. Besides, it worked out in my favor."

I narrowed my eyes at her. "How?"

"If I had known when I was little what the Order was really all about, I never would have joined the cheerleading team in the first place. Instead, I gladly became one of them," she explained. "They trusted me, which allowed me to eventually become a leader within the Peachville Order. It put me in the perfect position so that when you finally did come home, I could be there waiting for you."

I still couldn't believe she'd chosen to stay in the Order and put her life at risk just to help me. No one had ever done something so selfless for me. "If it hadn't been for you, I would have felt so lost. And if you hadn't been there to warn me about how the demon tattoo allowed them to keep an eye on me, I probably wouldn't have ever been able to get my memory back. Everything would have turned out completely different."

I thought of the night I'd gone to the third floor to retrieve the recipe for the Elixir of Kendria. If I hadn't known to hide myself from the Order's watching eyes, they would have stopped me for sure.

"There were so many times I thought I was going to lose you," she said. "The Halloween Ball was the worst. I went looking for you, but I knew you could be anywhere. I hoped Jackson would be able to keep you safe, but as soon as I heard the Order had taken you prisoner, I thought I had lost you forever."

"The important thing is that we're together now," I said. "We have so much lost time to make up for."

"I have no idea how you survived against the hunters and everything Priestess Winter has thrown your way, but the fact that you actually broke into her house to save my life is honestly a little unbelievable," she said.

"I wouldn't have made it without Zara's help." I looked away. "And Coach King's."

She paused. "Roan?" she said. "I thought they killed him."

"Zara was supposed to finish him, but she didn't," I explained. "She gave him a note for me and let him go. He barely made it to the castle in time to tell us everything that happened."

She cleared her throat and swiped at her eyes. "Father couldn't save him?"

I shook my head. "I'm sorry."

"Roan and I have been together since I was eighteen. Father sent him to watch after me." She laughed through her tears. "It was his idea to use the last name King. Kind of a joke right under the nose of the Order."

"Did you love him?" I asked.

She sniffed. "In a way," she said. "We weren't in love with each other, if that's what you mean. But he was always looking out for me. Always paying attention to what was going on in the Order, trying to guess their next move or make sure no one was in a position to hurt me. I can't believe he's gone."

"They'll pay for what they've done. I'll make sure of that. I know Priestess Winter is going to send everything she has at me now," I said. "We need to be ready. Find a way to trick her or weaken her in some way."

"What are you thinking?" Angela said. "I assumed we were heading back to the Southern Kingdom for a while."

I shook my head. "We're not going to run," I said. "We're going to end this, one way or another. If you need to go there to rest and get better, I completely understand and we'll help you get there safely, but I'm in this now for real. I won't stop until I've destroyed the Order of Shadows."

My sister stared at me for a long moment, then nodded her head. "I'm not going anywhere," she said.

We clasped hands again, and I realized Honora had been wrong.

Having a sister was more than I ever dreamed it could be.

FAMILY TREE

*O*UR SMALL GROUP gathered in the middle of the village the next morning to share breakfast.

Angela was feeling much better already, her body healing rapidly now that she was awake.

"It's part of my power," she explained. "I can heal others, but I have also always been a very fast healer if I focus my energy inward."

Mary Anne and Essex had brought out more chairs and had even managed to scrounge a mismatched set of plates and glasses. There were six of us all together and we sat down to enjoy pancakes, eggs, bacon and orange juice.

"Where did we get all this food?" I asked. We certainly hadn't carried it here in our backpacks. "I thought we agreed no one should risk going into town unless it was an emergency."

Mary Anne laughed. "This is one of the perks of hiding out here in the village," she said. "My family members hated leaving the nest, so they always stockpiled food in this big freezer in the basement of the Crow Mother's house. I didn't mention it before because I wasn't sure any of the food would still be good. Turns out the freezer was still working this whole time."

"Wow," Jackson said. "This is incredible. How much is left in there?"

"Enough that we could feed at least fifty people for a month or longer," Mary Anne said.

My eyes grew wide. This was definitely good news. If we needed to, we could stay here indefinitely. Well, as long as no one discovered we were here.

I poured a tall cup of coffee and loaded it with cream and sugar. Then, I stood and clanged my spoon on the side of the mug to get everyone's attention. "I wanted to take a second to say thank you," I said. "You've all taken a huge risk by being here with me, and I want you to know how much I appreciate it."

Jackson placed his hand on mine and Zara smiled up at me.

"We want to be a part of this just as much as you do," Mary Anne said. "I want a front row seat to the destruction of the all-powerful Order of Shadows."

"We need a plan first," Angela said before taking a huge bite of her eggs.

"It all starts with Aerden," I said, looking to Jackson. I sat back down and loaded my plate with food. Now that my sister was feeling better, my appetite had returned in full force.

"In the shadow world, Harper and I came across a book," he explained. "A diary of one of the original creators of the Order."

Zara gasped, her fork clanging to her plate.

"What is it?" I asked.

"The diary. Did it have a butterfly engraved on the front?"

I swallowed, my mouth growing dry in an instant. "Yes," I said. "Do you know something about it?"

"I've heard my mother mention it specifically," she said. "You're right about it belonging to an original member of the Order. Alexandra, I think. The youngest."

Excitement shot through me. This was proof the book was real. And if the book was real, that meant the spell was real too.

Beneath the table, Jackson gripped my leg. "What else do you know about it?"

"In order to understand the origins of the book, you need to understand my family's history," she said. "There were five sisters who started the Order of Shadows. Young witches in a coven near D.C. where my family lives now. Eloisa was the oldest. The first Priestess Winter. I am her direct descendant. She's my great-great-great-grandmother or something like that."

Zara leaned over and reached under her chair into the small white bag she'd brought with her when she came. She pulled out a piece of white paper and a set of sparkly gel pens in various colors. "Here, I'll draw it out so it's easy to understand," she said. "Over a thousand years ago, a demon named Mythic came to our world and fell in love with a human woman named Aeliana."

She wrote their names at the top of the page. I remembered them from my first lessons about the Order's history.

"They had a daughter named Kallista. She was the first witch ever to exist, a half-demon, half-human hybrid. I'm going to skip all the stuff in between, but one of Kallista's direct descendants was a woman named Haven," she said. She wrote the name at the top of a family tree, then drew five lines out from that in different colors. "She was born just over two hundred years ago. Haven had five daughters, power-hungry sisters who created the Order of Shadows. Eloisa was the oldest. Then Hazel, Magda, Gladys, and finally Alexandra. Eloisa created the first demon gate, which is my home gate at Winterhaven."

"And the diary we found belonged to Alexandra?" I asked.

Zara circled her name on the page. "Yes. Her descendant is Priestess Love. She lives in Frankfurt, Germany where the fifth original gate was opened, and is the head priestess over all of the European demon gates."

My eyes widened and my hand went to my throat. "I didn't know there were gates in Europe," I said.

Zara's light blue eyes met mine. "Oh yes," she said. "The Order has gates all over the world."

I gasped. All over the world? I never realized how far the Order's power had spread. No wonder demons were so afraid of fighting back. The Order's influence stretched all across the human world and even into the shadow world. Who knew where else they might have already invaded? What if there were other dimensions with gates and portals here in this world?

Thinking of it took my breath away. Destroying the Order would take decades, if it was even possible at all.

I grabbed my drink from the table and placed the cool glass against my flushed skin. Every time I felt like I was getting a handle on things, I realized the Order was much bigger than I'd imagined.

"Can you explain to me about the gates?" I asked. I needed to understand the structure of the Order so I could bring them down, one by one if I had to. "How many are there? And how do you know which Priestess is in charge of which gate?"

"There are five priestesses who make up the High Council. Each one of the priestesses is a direct descendant of one of the five sisters," Zara said. "To begin with, each sister opened one gate of her own. These were the original gates which used five separate colored stones. Like I mentioned, Eloisa's gate was the first, a blue portal in D.C. at Winterhaven."

I listened carefully.

"These five original gates are by far the most powerful," she said. "Once the sisters learned to open additional portals of each color, they began opening gates all over the world."

"Using their rings as anchors," I said, putting it all together in my head.

"Yes. At first, they were each in charge of a color of gate. For example, the Winters were in charge of all the blue gates around the world," she explained. "However, that became difficult since they are spread out. In order to make it easier on themselves, they eventually decided to assign themselves regions instead. Since Priestess Winter's home is in the eastern part of the United States, she's in charge of all portals in the East. Since Priestess Love's home is in Europe, she's in charge of the European gates, and so on."

I nodded, feeling overwhelmed. My head was spinning with information.

"The five priestesses meet at least once a year to discuss policies and the state of their regions," Zara said. "Then, there's the High Priestess."

"Who is she? Another descendant of the sisters?" Mary Anne asked.

Zara shook her head. "To be honest, I'm not sure. There's a lot of mystery surrounding the High Priestess. My mother doesn't like to talk about her."

"Let's get back to the diary," Jackson said. "That's what is really important right now. You said it was Alexandra's diary?"

"Yes. Apparently Alexandra's descendant, Priestess Love, kept the journal a secret until a few years ago when it went missing. I know this because my mother was extremely angry about it when she found out," she said. "I've never seen her so mad."

The news brought a smile to Jackson's face. He looked up, our eyes meeting. "The diary is real," he said. "It's really going to work."

"What is?" Angela asked.

Jackson stood, his eyes gleaming with hope. "The spell that will free my brother."

A MAGICAL BATTERY

"THE DIARY SAYS that in order to reverse the magic that binds a prima to her demon, you must perform the original initiation spell backwards, using all of the original ritual items," I explained. I listed them using my fingers. "The cup. The ring. The necklace. The ritual dagger. And the master stone. If this works and we really are able to free Aerden, then Peachville is only the beginning."

"The first step will be finding the original items from the rituals," Jackson said. "Since these items are still used in the initiation ceremonies, I imagine they're guarded by the primas in each demon gate town."

Angela nodded. "Peachville's ritual items were always kept with Lydia Ashworth," she said. "When she was taken prisoner, the Order transferred them all to the Harris family."

Brooke. If Priestess Winter had succeeded in killing me several months ago, Brooke would be the prima futura right now.

"What about my necklace?" I asked, reaching to my throat. I'd had that necklace since I was a little girl, and I wanted it back. "They took it from me in that last ceremony."

Angela pressed her lips together and grimaced. "The Harris family got that too," she said. "I've seen Brooke wear it to school a couple times."

Anger rolled through me like a wave. The image of her prancing around wearing my necklace as if she was already Prima, made me sick to my stomach.

"What does the ritual involve?" Zara asked. "I've never seen a demon gate being opened for the first time. It's rarely done anymore."

"Why not?" I asked.

"I'm not certain," she said. "I think it might have something to do with the way the gates work. They have to be placed in areas where the magical barrier between the shadow world and the human world is weak. The two worlds must be close enough for the barrier to be brought down and the demons to pass through. I would guess the rituals have slowed because all the magical locations have already been used."

I nodded, bringing a hand to my mouth in thought. It made sense. "The ritual itself is pretty simple," I said. "Once we have the items we need, it's mostly just a matter of reciting the right words in the right order. We'll need five women from the town to stand on the five points of the star. We'll also need someone to act as priestess."

I looked at Zara and she brought her hands to her lap.

"I can do it," she said. "Who are the five women, though? Mary Anne, Angela and you. That's only three."

"I was thinking Lark and Courtney," I said. "We'll have to bring them up here and explain the ritual first, but I'm sure they'll help us. We might even be able to get a few others like Lark's mom to help just in case."

"What else do we need?" Mary Anne asked.

"We'll need people to stand guard in case Priestess Winter or other members of the Order show up to try and stop us," Jackson said. "I'll be in charge of leading that group."

Essex stood. "I will join you in this fight."

Jackson nodded. "Thank you. I'm hoping I can find my other shadow demon friends who are still here in the human world. Joost, Mordecai and the others," he said. "If anyone else has some ideas of who else we can ask for help, we'll need all the bodies we can get."

"What about the ritual items?" Angela asked. "The cup, the necklace and the dagger are with the Harris family, but what about the ring and the master stone?"

I patted my pocket. "I have the ring."

Angela gasped. "You do? I've never even seen a ring used in the rituals here. Where did you get it?"

"It was in the shadow world," I said. "The ring is part of the magic that allowed the Order to open multiple gates of the same color gemstone. The ring was placed in a special area of great power for the corresponding colored stone. They call it an anchor. When I found the blue ring and took it out of that area, all the blue gates became inactive."

"All except one," Zara said, her eyebrow raised. "The original blue gate at Winterhaven is still active."

"Yes," I said. "I thought that might be how it worked. The ring kept the additional gates open, but the original gate would be unaffected."

"What is the master stone?" Angela asked.

"We wondered that too," I said, looking at Jackson. "We decided it has to be the portal stone, right? It's the largest stone and all of the other ritual items have a chip of the portal stone inside them."

"Yes, it makes sense," Zara said.

It was reassuring to hear her agree with us on that. I had never specifically seen or heard the portal stone referred to as a master stone, so it made me nervous. I didn't like making assumptions about something like this since we'd likely only have one good shot at the ritual reversal. After that, the ritual room would be guarded and closed off at all times.

"I'd like to see if we can find more information on the master stone, just to be sure," I said. "Zara, maybe you could help with that?"

"Of course," she said.

"The first step is to get the three ritual items from the Harris house," I said. "Any ideas?"

"Why don't we just break in and take them?" Mary Anne asked. "There are six of us and we're pretty powerful. Brooke's older sisters have already graduated and left home, haven't they? So it would probably just be her and her mom there."

"The problem is we don't want anyone to suspect what we're planning," I said. "Right now, our main advantage is that Priestess Winter has no idea we have the diary or that we're planning to try to free Aerden. If she finds out we are gathering the ritual items, she'll guard the portal stone with an army. We'll have to wait until no one is home to take the items."

"That might be a problem," Angela said, cringing. "I know from our weekly meetings that after the items were moved to the Harris house, they had a security system installed in the house. Video surveillance cameras on the main doors. If you go inside, they'll see you. They'll know you were there and when they see the items are gone, they'll be able to guess what you're up to."

"So we have two problems," Mary Anne said. "We have to find a way to trick the video cameras, and we need to get the items in such a way no one knows they're gone until it's too late." Mary Anne asked.

"Exactly," I said.

Essex had been silent throughout most of the discussion, but he sat up now and cleared his throat. "I would like to make a suggestion, if I may," he said. "What if we were to make copies of the ritual items? Something that looks identical to the ones you will steal? Then we could switch them out and no one would know they were gone."

Jackson straightened. "That's a great idea," he said. "How do we do that, though? They'd have to be perfect copies for it to work."

"We can use glamours," I said, my heart racing. It felt good to be coming up with a real plan. The idea of finally being free of the Order's power was exhilarating. It was all beginning to feel so real.

"We can't glamour them indefinitely," Jackson said. "They'll lose the illusion the minute someone stops concentrating on them. I don't think we can afford to have someone hanging out there at Brooke's house all the time to keep up that one spell."

"I can create a glamour that will last many days even without concentration," Essex said.

Jackson furrowed his brow and stood up to pace the length of the table. "How?"

"By using the stones," he said. "Like the elders."

"You mean like a magical battery?" Jackson asked.

"Yes, this is what I mean." Essex looked around the table.

"Wait, I'm lost. Can you explain it?" I asked. "What kind of battery?"

Jackson came to stand behind his chair and placed his hands on the back of the seat. "You remember the soul stone Mary Anne's ancestor used to stay alive?"

How could I forget? I nodded, thinking of the crow witch and how she had been alive almost a hundred and twenty years through the use of a soul stone.

"The soul stone would draw a witch's essence and power from her body," he explained. "Then the crow witch used the stolen power as a type of battery to keep herself alive. Well, that was just a perverted version of the elder's magic Essex is talking about. In our culture, our elders choose when it's their time to move on to the Afterworld. Usually this happens when their child is ready to have a child of their own. During their passing, the elder pours a portion of their power and essence willingly into a stone similar to a soul stone. It's a type of voluntary sacrifice, representing love and a promise to future generations."

"And the stone?" Zara asked. "What happens to it?"

"It can be used for anything that takes power," Jackson said. "It's the elder's way of giving back to our world. Sometimes a stone can be used to power a certain spell for decades. The lights in a city, for example, or a protection spell around a home. Usually it's up to the family how to use the stone's power."

I listened carefully, trying to wrap my head around it. I turned to Essex. "So you're saying you can make a glamour last longer by using one of these stones to power it?"

"Yes," he said. "Except no one will have to pass away in order to make this magic work. If we all allow the stones to absorb even a very tiny portion of our power, it should be enough to run a simple glamour spell for at least a week."

Excitement rushed through me. "Where would we get the stones we need?"

Essex reached into his backpack. He pulled out a handful of different colored stones from the shadow world. I wanted to kiss him, I was so happy.

"This is awesome," I said.

"That solves the issue of the Order knowing we took the items," Jackson said. "We still have to figure out how we're going to get in there to switch them for the real items without being noticed by the cameras."

I had an idea, but I knew Jackson wasn't going to like it.

"I'm going to just walk in and get them," I said, my heart pounding.

Jackson groaned. "Of course you are."

"How do you plan on pulling that off?" Mary Anne asked.

I smiled. "I'm going to become Brooke Harris."

NO ONE WILL EVEN KNOW IT'S ME

"*I*T'S TOO RISKY," Jackson said. "You don't need to leave the crow village until it's time to perform the ritual."

I shook my head. "No one will even know it's me," I said. "Glamours are practically second nature to me now. All I have to do is copy Brooke's look."

Jackson stood and pushed his chair in toward the table. "I don't like it, Harper. I thought we decided you would stay here no matter what," he said. "If anything goes wrong and they find out it's you—"

"They won't," I said.

"What if Brooke comes home while you're there?" he said. "I think they'll notice if there are two Brookes walking around."

"I can help," Mary Anne said. "I'll use my crow form and watch out for Brooke. If I see her car drive up, I can warn Harper."

"And I can disappear if that happens," I said. "As long as I have an exit strategy, it shouldn't be too hard. We just need to spend some time watching her routine and make sure we know when she'll be gone."

"She's at school every morning by seven forty-five," Angela said. "Before I was taken, Brooke would always come to my office and say hello in the mornings."

"Great. What about the rest of her family? What are their routines?"

"Her older sisters have already moved out, so you won't have to worry about them," she said. "Her dad works at the bank, and they open at eight. He probably leaves earlier than Brooke in the mornings. It's her mom you might have to worry about."

I cringed. If my glamour was off even the tiniest bit, her mother would spot it in a heartbeat if she got a clear look at me.

"She's a stay-at-home mom?" Mary Anne asked.

Angela nodded. "I don't know if she has any set schedule, really."

"That could be a problem," Jackson said. "You can't go in there if her mom is home. If she sees you taking the ritual items, it's all over."

"Wait," Angela said, raising her eyebrows. "Laura goes running every morning. She's mentioned it several times. It used to annoy me, because she was always bragging about running no matter what the weather was like outside."

"Any idea what time in the morning?" I asked.

"I'm not sure," she said. "I just know she usually doesn't come in to the school on Fridays until about nine because she runs and then showers."

"Since the Harris' house is out in the country, we can go tomorrow morning and hide in the field across from her house. We'll keep a close eye on the three of them and wait until they've all left the house."

"Then what?" Jackson asked.

I shrugged. "Then I walk back into the house and switch out the ritual items."

"And what if Brooke's mom comes home while you're still there?"

"I'll just say I forgot something I needed for school. A book or something. Brooke carries a backpack to school right?"

Angela thought for a second, then nodded. "Yes, she has a blue messenger bag she carries."

"Perfect," I said. "Do you think you can describe it to Essex? If he could make a similar bag tonight, I can take that and glamour it to look like Brooke's tomorrow when she walks out to her car. I should be able to get a good enough look at her to copy her. I can hide the ritual items inside."

"I still don't like this," Jackson said. He gripped the back of his chair. "It's too quick. I think we should take a few days to scope it out and make sure of their routines and maybe find out where they're keeping the items in the house. What if you go in there and you can't find them? If her mom sees you, she's going to wonder what you're looking for."

"I can say I lost my shoe or something," I said. "If I can't find them within fifteen minutes or if she comes home, I can just leave. I don't want to put this off any longer. Every day we hide out here in the crow village is another day Priestess Winter is out looking for us. We have to move as fast as we can if we're going to have any chance of saving Aerden."

Jackson drew his hand through his hair and sighed. "Okay, but I'm coming with you."

I shook my head. "No, you have to stay here," I said. "If something does go wrong, I'll need you to come save me."

He tensed his jaw and took several deep breaths in and out. "If there's even the slightest hint that something is off. I mean, even just a feeling in your gut or Brooke's mom comes in and looks at you funny. Anything. You promise me you'll get the hell out of there, okay?"

I nodded and saluted. "Promise."

He smiled and rolled his eyes. "You're lucky you're so cute."

I stood and hugged him tight, grateful for every moment we had together. "I'm lucky for a lot of reasons."

LEAP OF FAITH

*A*FTER BREAKFAST, EVERYONE separated to work on various jobs. Essex and Mary Anne began on the ritual item replicas and the messenger bag. Zara sat alone at the big table writing out as much information as she could remember about her family tree. Jackson, Angela and I gathered in the living room of the large gray house where Jackson and I were staying.

"What can I do?" Angela asked. "Is there anything else we can do now to prepare for the ritual? Besides the items from Brooke's house, what else do we need?"

I went through a mental checklist of what we might need. I could only think of one other thing we'd need besides the ritual items, and I knew it wouldn't be an easy task. "People," I said.

"People?" Angela asked, sitting down on the leather couch at the center of the room.

"We need an army," I said. "The day we go to perform the ritual, I want to have as many people there protecting us as possible. That way if Priestess Winter shows up, she'll have to get through an army before she can stop us."

"The problem is how do we know who we can trust?" Jackson asked. He sat down in a recliner near the fireplace.

I grabbed a notebook and pencil and chose a spot on the floor, using the coffee table as a desk. "Yeah, that's the hard part. After what Lydia Ashworth told me, I'm scared there's really no way to know what's real and what isn't." I tapped the pencil on the surface of the wood table. "It's already hard enough to tell who is good and who is evil in this town. Now that we know people have been trading favors in exchange for permanent spells and glamours, it's just going to be harder to know who's even really who they say they are."

Angela sighed and rubbed her forehead. "I still can't believe she did that to her own sister," she said. "She betrayed everyone when you think about it."

My heart ached. My mother was dead because of Lydia Ashworth. Someone she trusted and loved as a friend. I shuddered. Trust was a tricky thing. You never really knew if someone could be trusted until you found out they'd already betrayed you.

"The best we can do is go with our gut," I said. "We need to make a list of everyone we think will truly stand by our side when it comes to fighting against Priestess Winter. Some names will be easy to add."

"You can put Joost, Mordecai, Erick, and Cristo on the list," Jackson said. "I know we can trust them and they'll stand by us through the fight."

"Do you know how to get in touch with them?" I asked. "They could be anywhere in the world right now."

"They used to leave me messages in the barn at Shadowford," he said. "I can leave something there just in case they are checking it from time to time. There are no guarantees, but it's worth a shot."

I wrote the names at the top of the list. "Courtney, Lark and her mom are on our side too," I said. "Who else?"

Angela named six women in the Peachville Order she said would stand against Priestess Winter.

"What about the Sullivans?" I asked.

"Who?" Jackson asked.

"The prima family from Cypress?" I asked. "After the ordeal with Caroline, Eloise said she thought of me as one of her own daughters. There's also a piece of their demon inside me. I want to trust them, but to ask them to join us puts them in a tough position."

"And if they die in an attack, the entire town of Cypress would die too," Angela said. "It's risky."

"Still, we need all the help we can get," I said. "I'm going to write them on the list and if they want to join us, maybe they can leave Meredith at home so the whole town isn't in danger. I don't think it will hurt to let them know our plans and let them make the decision on their own."

Jackson and Angela nodded. We continued to list anyone and everyone we could think of, and when we were finished, we had about fifteen names.

"I wish Lea had come," Jackson said.

Hearing her name made my stomach tighten. It was probably my fault she wasn't here.

"She made her choice," I said. "There's nothing we can do about that now."

Jackson looked toward the fireplace, a tight expression on his face. "No, there isn't."

I swallowed, pushing back a rush of jealousy. He had chosen me, so I knew he wasn't upset because he wanted to be with her. Still, it was obvious he cared for her and she had let him down.

"How are we going to let everyone know what we're planning?" Angela asked. "We can't possibly risk going around talking to all these people individually."

I bit my lip. She had a point. We needed to get everyone to one central location and explain our plan to everyone at once.

We could do the meeting here in the safety of the crow village. But how to get everyone here without going to talk to them?

Then, it hit me. I sat up on my knees, excitement dancing through my veins. "The shoes," I said.

Angela scrunched her eyebrows together. "What in the world are you talking about?"

"The cheerleading shoes," I said. "You used to put a memory spell inside them so that when we put them on, we'd automatically know the steps of a cheer or a dance, right?"

She nodded, but still looked confused.

"Could you put a similar spell on the wristbands Essex made?" I asked. "Something that would give people a memory of how to get here to the crow village?"

Her eyes grew wide and her lips parted. Then, she smiled, finally understanding what I meant. "Yes! I could put a movement spell on the wristbands so that when anyone put it on, they would know the steps to take to get here. They wouldn't necessarily understand where they were headed, or why, but the bands could bring them here or to any location we wanted."

"We could mail them out to the people we want to invite," I said. "Maybe we could include some kind of message to let them know it was a secret meeting with me. The wristband would allow them to get into the village. All they would have to do is put it on and follow the steps."

"Very smart," Jackson said. "Of course, once they get here, our secret hiding place won't be a secret anymore."

"It's a risk we're going to have to take," I said. "If we go anywhere else, we'll risk being discovered."

"At the meeting, we can ask everyone to make a decision about whether to help or not," Angela said. "If they decide they don't want to risk their lives for this, we can ask them to take a potion that will make them forget. That way Priestess Winter can't hold them responsible for keeping secrets, but we also won't have to worry about them telling anyone where we are or what we've got planned."

"Good idea," I said.

"I'll go talk to Essex and see if I can get started on the memory spells," Angela said, standing. "I'll have to imbue each one with specific directions from their house to the village. This could take some time."

I looked back over the small list of names. My stomach knotted. We were taking a huge risk trusting these people, but we needed the help. It was truly a leap of faith.

I carefully tore the list from the notebook and passed it to my sister, my hand trembling slightly as I let go.

THERE WASN'T A MINUTE TO WASTE

MARY ANNE AND I woke up super early to prepare for our trip to Brooke's.

I practiced my glamours, making myself look like Mary Anne, Angela and Zara until I felt confident I could replicate Brooke's body and clothes with nothing more than a brief glance as she walked to her car. The glamour had to be convincing enough to fool her mom if necessary.

My skin tingled. Getting the ritual items was vital to our entire plan. Without them, there was no hope of even attempting to free Aerden. Today had to be a success.

I glanced at the clock. Six-thirty. "You ready?" I asked Mary Anne. "We need to get over there early enough to make sure we don't miss anyone leaving the house."

Mary Anne pushed her hair behind her ear. "I'm ready," she said. "I'll shift to crow form and stay there until we get back unless you need me. Once you're inside, listen closely for my call. I'll fly onto the roof and make as much noise as possible if someone is coming back into the house."

I nodded and wiped my sweaty hands on my jeans. "Let's do this," I said.

Jackson stood in the doorway of our gray house, his arms crossed at his chest, worry in his eyes. I brought a hand to my lips and blew him a kiss from the bottom of the steps.

A weak smile tugged at one corner of his mouth. "Be careful," he said. "If you're not back here in two hours, I'm coming after you."

"We'll be back," I said.

I picked up my bag full of fake ritual items. They weren't exact copies yet. Essex had done most of the work and last night, the six of us had gathered around the stones and poured a small part of our energy inside. According to Essex, our gifted power would allow the items to hold their glamours for at least a week. As soon as I found the three ritual items in the Harris house, I would simply have to use my glamour magic to make our fakes look exactly the same before I put them in place.

By the time the stones lost their charge and the glamours faded, Aerden would already be free. Or not. Either way, the ritual would be over and we'd know.

All we had to do was get these items.

Mary Anne shifted into a small black crow, her blue eyes still large and bright. I had already created a strong connection to the core of my power, so becoming invisible only took a moment. Together, we stepped outside the barrier and flew toward the Harris house. I used levitation instead of my demon form so that it wouldn't leave a trail.

It only took us ten minutes to get there. We settled into the field across the street from the house and waited. We didn't dare talk or change from our current forms. There was zero room for error this morning.

Nothing happened for a long time, but finally around seven fifteen, the front door opened and Brooke's mom stepped onto the porch wearing black leggings and an oversized t-shirt. She stood on the porch for a few minutes stretching, then stuck her ear-buds in her ears and took off down the dirt road.

One down, two to go.

Angela had said Mrs. Harris ran five miles in the morning. At a decent pace, that meant we had about forty-five minutes before she'd be home. The clock was ticking. My toes danced inside my shoe.

When the door to the garage opened fifteen minutes later, I bit my lip to hold back my excitement. Mr. Harris' car backed out and as he drove away, I could see he was alone in the car.

Now there's just Brooke.

I had snagged a watch from one of the houses in the crow village and found myself constantly checking it. When Brooke finally emerged from the house, it was right at seven forty. That gave me less than twenty minutes to get in the house, find the three items, and get out.

I studied Brooke carefully. Every detail of her outfit was important. Dark skinny jeans. Leopard print ballet flats. Red button-up shirt with a leopard print scarf tied around her neck. Her dark brown hair hung loose down her back.

There was no sign of my mother's necklace and relief filled my heart. I didn't have a plan for what to do if she'd been wearing it today.

Seeing her again made a large lump form in my throat. There was a time when I thought she was a good friend. Someone I could trust and share my secrets with. I thought she cared about me back then.

But she'd just stood there while Priestess Winter tried to take my life.

She got into her car and drove away. I waited a full minute just to make sure she wasn't coming back for anything, then hurried across the road toward her house, still invisible.

I stepped around the side of the house, out of view of any cameras. I sat down on the pavement and concentrated on every detail of Brooke's outfit. Slowly, my body transformed. My hair became dark and straight. My clothing changed to match Brooke's exactly. I pulled a small mirror out of my messenger bag and smiled.

Perfect.

To the cameras, it would just look like Brooke had come home for a few minutes. It wouldn't send off any warning signals and hopefully no one would pay it any attention.

I stood and rubbed my sweaty palms against my jeans. I had about fifteen minutes left before Mrs. Harris should be home. There wasn't a minute to waste.

I strolled around the front of the house and turned the doorknob. The door was unlocked and I walked right in.

The entryway opened up into Brooke's large living room. It brought back strong memories of my first sleepover here. The night we'd all stayed up practicing cheers for my audition. Back then, I thought I'd just been incredibly lucky to have made some real friends here in Peachville. I'd believed this town was really my chance at starting over and having a better life.

I swallowed my regrets and started my search for the ritual items. I was sure they wouldn't be out in the open anywhere. When I'd seen the dagger at the Ashworth's house the night of the Homecoming dance, it had been locked in a black case in Lydia's office.

With a quick look around the single-story house, I found the office and looked for the case. After a couple of minutes, I couldn't find it anywhere. I needed to move on. I checked the master bedroom, thinking maybe Mrs. Harris had tucked it into her closet or under the bed. I looked everywhere, but there was no sign of the cup or the dagger in the bedroom.

Where else could they be? I tapped my toes nervously. Ten minutes left.

A growing panic welled up inside. Mrs. Harris could be back any minute now. What if she decided to take a shortcut or if she was an exceptionally fast runner? I had to hurry.

I decided to start in the living room and go through each of the rooms one-by-one. I would just have to go as fast as possible and search inside every closet or closed space.

After looking in the living room and the kitchen, I stepped into the hallway that led down to Brooke's room and the tiny hairs on the back of my neck stood up. My heart skipped a beat and I gasped. I could feel them. The stones inside the ritual items were practically calling out to me.

Excited, I stepped forward, following some strange connection I felt deep within. I passed a closed door on the right side of the hall and my arms erupted in goose bumps. I backed up and opened the door. The room had probably belonged to one of the older Harris girls at some point, but was now set up as a basic guest room. There wasn't much here except for a queen-size bed, two bedside tables and a dresser, but it was the dresser that caught my attention.

I walked straight over to it and ran my hands down the front of each drawer, stopping as I reached the second one from the bottom. I clasped the clear glass knobs and pulled, breathing in deep to calm the flutters in my stomach.

There, nestled next to a blue velvet ritual robe was a black case and a silver cup.

THE OLD BROOKE

I REACHED INTO MY bag and pulled out two of the fakes Essex had created. I picked up the cup-shaped one, then grabbed the real silver ritual cup. I concentrated on recreating every detail of the real cup, then felt the fake transform in my hand. When the glamour was complete, I set the fake chalice in the drawer, careful to set it down in exactly the same place as the one I'd taken.

I opened the black case and removed the ritual dagger, replicating it the same way and putting the fake one in its place. Then, I put both of the real items in my bag and closed the drawer. I stepped back and studied the area to make sure nothing looked out of place.

I glanced at my watch. Only five minutes left. Crap. I still had to find the necklace.

I breathed in deep through my nose, letting a calming breath fill my lungs. If I had been able to feel a connection to the stones in the dagger and the cup, I would definitely be able to find the necklace the same way. After all, I'd worn that necklace for years. Long before I understood what it really meant.

I could tell the necklace was not here in this bedroom. I went back out into the hallway and shut the door behind me. I knew from that first night I'd stayed here that Brooke's room was at the very end of this hallway. If she sometimes wore the necklace to school, there was a good chance I would find it in her room somewhere.

As I got closer to her room, I knew I'd been right. The necklace was definitely in there.

Her door was halfway open and as soon as I walked inside, my eyes went straight to the blue stone. I nearly cried out in excitement. Even though the necklace was a symbol of the Order's control over my ancestors, it meant so much more to me than that. All my life, it had been my only connection to my mother. Every time my fingertips touched the stone, I imagined my mother's hands touching the same exact spot. It had always been such a comfort to me through the hard times.

When the necklace had been taken from me by Priestess Winter, it had felt like a part of my mom had been stolen from me. Now, taking it back was like taking a part of my life back. My confidence and power.

I crossed over to Brooke's dresser and scooped up the necklace, closing my fist around the stone and bringing it to my heart. I secured it around my neck and ran the pendant up and down the chain like I'd done a million times.

I reached into my bag and pulled out Essex's fake. It was nothing more than a thick string with a bottle cap attached. A small red stone was glued inside the bottle cap, loaded with just enough power to fuel a glamour for a week. In my hands, the fake quickly became an exact copy of the real necklace. I set it on top of the dresser and turned to leave.

That's when something under her bed caught my eye.

I leaned down and grabbed the small bronze horse. Brooke's spirit animal. It was cool against my skin, and I turned it over in my hand. From my crouched position, I could see there was more hidden there under her bed. Several horse magazines, drawings, pictures. Even a few brochures for veterinary schools. I set the small bronze horse down on the floor and picked up one of the magazines.

Brooke had earmarked several of the pages and I flipped through them, my breath catching in my throat as I came to a beautiful picture of a chestnut brown horse. Brooke had drawn a large heart around the picture. I brought my hand to my mouth, touched by that heart.

The night of her initiation, I remembered how we had sat together on the grass staring up at the fireworks. A nervous Brooke had confessed to me that she had always wanted to be a veterinarian. She'd told me about her love of horses and how all she'd ever wanted to do was work with animals.

I'd thought that side of Brooke had been lost forever, but this hidden stash showed me there was still a part of her that wanted a different life. She hadn't completely disappeared.

This was proof that somewhere deep inside, the old Brooke still existed.

I stuffed the magazine back under the bed and as I turned to leave, realized I could just make out the sound of a crow cawing on the roof.

HER SECRET DREAM

*M*Y MOUTH WENT DRY.

What had I been thinking? I should have never wasted a single second looking through Brooke's things. I should have taken the necklace and gotten the hell out of here.

Brooke's mom must have gotten home from her run.

I didn't know whether to make myself invisible or just hide out here in the bedroom until she'd gotten in the shower or something. I stood quickly and tripped over the small bronze horse just as Laura Harris poked her head through the bedroom door.

I pressed my hands tight to my jeans and tried to smile. My ears rang and my insides twisted with terror. I prayed my glamour was in place.

"Brooke? What on earth are you still doing here? I didn't even notice your car was still here." She looked down at her watch. "It's almost eight. You're going to be late for school."

Her eyes traveled up and down my body, finally resting on the horse at my feet.

She pressed her lips into a thin line and clenched her jaw. "What have I told you about those damn horses?" She leaned over and snatched it up from the floor. She gripped it so tightly, I thought she was getting ready to throw it at me. "You know you're not allowed to show any preference for your old dreams. How many times am I going to have to say it to get it through that thick skull of yours? You're never going to be a veterinarian."

I didn't dare say a word. I stared down at the floor, letting my hair fall around my face.

Mrs. Harris stepped closer to me. Her shirt was covered in sweat despite the fact that it was still relatively cool outside this time of morning. She must have been running hard.

"Do you want to mess this whole thing up for us?" she said, her voice low and tense. "I will never forgive you if Priestess Winter chooses a different family for this town, Brooke. I swear to god, I would disown you and never look back before I would give up our chance for taking control of this town."

I struggled to breathe. How could a mother say that to her own daughter? I lifted my chin and looked her straight in the eye. No wonder Brooke was so messed up.

"You know how important this is to me and your sisters," she said. "It should be important to you, too. I never want to see another horse in this room, do you understand me?"

I nodded, swallowing back my desire to give this woman a piece of my mind. Was power really more important to her than her own daughter?

"Good," she said, softening her tone and relaxing her shoulders slightly. She placed her hand on my arm, and I had to stop myself from pulling away in disgust. "I know it's been hard for you ever since Mrs. King was killed, but that was a necessary loss. She was a traitor. You understand that, don't you sweetie?"

I struggled to hide my surprise. Killed? What had they all been told?

"Priestess Winter says it's only a matter of time before we get Harper too," she said. "We just have to hang in there a little bit longer and the whole world will be at our fingertips."

I had to get out of there before I gave myself away. I couldn't sit here and listen to this woman talk about how excited she was to have me killed. "I need to get to school," I said. "I'm late."

Mrs. Harris leaned in and gave me a hug. I stiffened, unable to help myself.

She pulled away and let out a disapproving breath. "Fine," she said. "I'll see you after school."

I headed for the door.

"And when you get home, I expect you to spend some time getting rid of all this horse stuff, you hear me?"

I gave no answer as I walked down the hall, through the living room and out the front door. When I'd entered the house earlier this morning, I'd felt nothing but anger when I thought of Brooke. Now, after hearing her mother's harsh tone and seeing how she still held on to her secret dream to be something other than what the Order planned for her, I left feeling sadness and regret.

Brooke was far from innocent, but I had to remember that in many ways, she was just another victim of the Order of Shadows.

With a heavy heart, I disappeared around the corner of the house, out of the view of the cameras. I looked up to make sure Mary Anne was still on the roof waiting for me. When her blue eyes met mine, I let my image fade and flew high up into the air, following the crow back toward her village in the trees.

I expected Jackson to be waiting for me at the entrance, but as we crossed through the barrier and dropped our magic to go back to our normal selves, I noticed the rest of our group had gathered on the porch of our gray house at the end of the block.

I squinted, wondering what in the world was going on.

As I approached, I saw what had stolen everyone's attention. A girl wearing black leather from head to toe, her dark hair tied in one long braid that fell down her back. She had a blue band tied around her wrist.

"Lea," I said, setting the bag down on the steps.

She raised an eyebrow, a smirk on her face. "Princess."

I cleared my throat. I guess Jackson had already explained that whole thing to her. She seemed to have taken the news well.

"You've come to fight?"

"No," she said, her face hard and serious as she turned. "I've come to warn you."

A BEAT TOO LONG

FEAR RIPPLED THROUGH my bloodstream.

"Warn us of what?" I asked. "Does this have to do with the Resistance?"

She crossed over to the porch railing and leaned against it. "They're really going through with it," she said, her eyes focused steadily on Jackson. There was panic in her voice. "I tried to talk Andros out of it, but he's become completely obsessed. Ever since that hunter got into the Underground and almost killed his daughter he's been talking about wanting to start a real war against the Order. He wants to hurt them and he doesn't care who he has to kill to make it happen."

"Slow down," Jackson said. He pulled a chair out for her and motioned for her to sit. "Start from the beginning. I thought we'd convinced him not to go through with any attack against the gates."

Lea took a deep breath and waved away the chair. "After you left, he started bringing up his old plan more and more in our meetings," she said. "He said destroying the gates was the only answer to bringing down the Order. You've heard all his arguments a thousand times."

She was still talking to Jackson as if it were just the two of them sitting here. He may have heard Andros' arguments, but the rest of us hadn't. We only knew what little Jackson had mentioned to us earlier.

"Not all of us have heard it," I said. "Give us some idea of what we're dealing with here."

Lea looked around, really looking at me for the first time. She didn't exactly look thrilled to see me. "Andros and many of the others in the Resistance believe the best way to destroy the Order of Shadows is to close the demon gates," Lea explained. "If the gates were all closed, the Order would have no way to bring more demons across to this world. Andros thinks it's the best way to end the war."

A chill ran up my spine. I lowered myself onto the top step. "But that would also mean killing everyone connected to the gates," I said. "You're talking about thousands of lives. Maybe hundreds of thousands. Humans and demons."

"Yes, but Andros sees it as a necessary loss," she said. "A one-time sacrifice to save our world forever."

"I thought we'd convinced him to look at other ways of fighting the Order," Jackson said. "Like, only going after the High Priestesses."

"I thought so, too," she said. She pushed off of the railing and paced the length of the porch. "But after what happened with the hunter, he went right back to his old way of thinking. Seeing his daughter captured by the hunter really scared him."

"I saved her life," I said, frustration seeping into every fiber of my being. "So, his response is to kill me and everyone like me?"

"What happened with the Hunter?" Angela asked.

"When Harper was living in the Underground, a hunter tracked her and managed to get inside," Jackson said. "She held Andros' little girl captive and threatened to kill her unless they turned Harper over."

Just thinking about that day brought my anger rushing to the surface. "The hunter never would have gotten inside if one of Andros' most trusted men hadn't betrayed him," I said. "Yet, he still blamed me for her being there. And you know what? I could have run. I could have gone out the back door before anyone realized it, leaving his daughter to pay the price, but I didn't. I chose to fight, risking my life and Aerden's life to save them. Now, he's going to repay me by coming after primas like me? By murdering thousands of innocent humans and demons?"

"Regardless of how the hunter got in, it was you she was after," Lea said. "If you hadn't come there, she never would have tried to get in in the first place."

"That was a risk their council took when they decided to let me stay," I said.

"What's his plan now?" Jackson asked. "He can't seriously be planning on destroying the gates?"

"I tried to talk some sense into him," she said. "Believe me, I tried. Only, the more he talked about it, the more the rest of the council started agreeing with him. The commanders of the Resistance army were on board from the beginning. They've been looking for an opportunity to fight. It didn't take long before I was outnumbered on the vote."

"This is murder they're talking about," I said, rage burning like a fiery pit in my belly. "Don't they realize that?"

"Like I said, they see it as a necessary evil," Lea said. "To them, the demons who have already been enslaved are as good as dead, so killing them doesn't seem like murder."

"And killing the humans is what? No big deal?" I said. "Human lives aren't important at all?"

"The humans they would be killing aren't innocent," Lea said. "They're witches who chose to join the Order of Shadows."

"When a witch is brought to her initiation ceremony, she has no idea about the demons," I said, standing. I was too angry to sit down any longer. "These women are manipulated and lied to. I'm not saying they're perfect and blameless, but they don't deserve to be murdered."

Why did I feel like I'd had this same argument thirty times? Why couldn't people understand that just because a witch was a member of the Order, it didn't automatically mean she was evil?

"No one wants to go around killing witches and demons without purpose," Lea said. "Andros believes it's a smarter way to attack. A kind of sacrifice for the greater good. Destroying the gates will weaken the Order's numbers significantly, and it will also keep them from rebuilding. Eventually, once all the gates are closed, it will bring them down completely."

I narrowed my eyes at her. "You sound like you agree with him."

She groaned. "This is not easy for me," she said. "I wish there was a way to keep my people safe without killing anyone, but the Order makes that impossible. Until we close these gates permanently, they'll continue to find a way to kidnap our kind and turn them into slaves. What other options do we have?"

"We have the chance to possibly reverse the ritual that created the gates in the first place," Jackson said.

"What? How?" Lea asked.

"Didn't Andros tell you?" he asked her. "He gave us a diary before we left the Underground. In it, there are instructions on how to basically undo the connection that holds a demon gate open. We're pretty sure if we can perform this spell, we can free both the demons and the witches tied to any gate without killing any of them."

"I don't understand," Lea said, leaning back against the railing. "If Andros had access to a spell that could free the demons, why didn't he tell us? Why did he give it to you instead of testing it himself?"

"Maybe he didn't really believe it would work," Jackson said.

"Or maybe he just wants to kill everyone," I said. "Who knows?"

"Maybe he gave us the book to give us one last chance to change his mind," Jackson said. "He didn't give us much time to follow through with it, but maybe that was his reason for passing the book off to us when he did."

I closed my eyes and tried to still the pounding of my heart. As if there wasn't already enough riding on this reversal ritual. When Andros had given me the book, he'd said he felt my destiny was tied to it. What a load of crap. He hadn't even given us six months to try it out.

"How long do we have?"

Lea sighed. "Not long," she said. "Andros has already activated the first part of his plan. As we speak, teams of assassins are gathering information about primas all over the southern half of the United States. They're planning a coordinated attack that will go down in four days."

I crumpled back down onto the stairs, hanging my head in my hands. Only four days? My head pounded. "This can't be happening."

Our time-line had just been bumped up another few days, and we had already been stretched too thin.

"How long have you known about this?" Jackson asked.

"Two weeks," Lea said. "I tried to get word to you sooner, but you don't understand what it's been like for me. After Jericho's betrayal, Andros watches us all like a hawk. He's become so paranoid about every move we make. He didn't even want me talking to Mary Anne anymore because she's human and he doesn't trust her. He's completely obsessed, not wanting to let any of his top council members out of his sight, even for a minute."

"Then how did you get away long enough to come here?" I asked.

Lea swallowed, her jaw tense. She turned to meet my eyes, then paused, her silence stretching out a beat too long.

"Because I agreed to be the assassin who kills you."

THE BOMB LEA HAD JUST DROPPED

*T*HE QUIET VILLAGE erupted in shouts.

I lunged at Lea, but Jackson gripped my arms and held me back. He pressed his mouth to my ear. "She's not actually going to do it. Calm down."

"How do you know she's not planning to do it?" I asked. "She's hated me from the first time she laid eyes on me."

Angela and the others all shouted over each other, trying to make sense of the bomb Lea had just dropped on us.

"Everyone sit down," Jackson said, his voice rising above the rest. "Give her a chance to explain herself."

I yanked my arm away from Jackson's grasp and straightened my clothes, my face and neck hot with anger.

Through all the commotion, Lea said nothing. She waited for everyone to quiet down and settle back into their seats before she spoke.

"Of course I'm not planning to actually go through with it," she said. "You should know me well enough by now to know I wouldn't do that."

I stared ahead, my teeth clenched and my breath fast and uneven. How could I possibly know her well enough when she'd always kept me at arm's length?

"I knew this was the only way to get away from Andros in order to warn you about the Resistance," she said. "If I'd come to you any other way, Andros would have labeled me a traitor and thrown me in the dungeons."

"I don't understand why you couldn't convince him that Peachville needed to be left alone," I said. "He couldn't at least start on the other side of the country? There are gates in Europe. He couldn't start there? Even if the demons in the Underground don't all like me, a lot of them were friends with Aerden. Killing me and closing the gate means killing him too. How could they do that to their friend?"

"Unlike Jackson, most of them don't hold out any hope that Aerden can be saved." She fidgeted. "Besides, I didn't exactly volunteer for the job. Andros and the council offered it to me. They told me it was a way to end your life and get Jackson back for myself."

I started toward her again, but Jackson's hand gripped mine.

"So you lied and said that's what you wanted?" Jackson said, emphasizing the word lied.

"Yes," she said, her eyes focused on my face. "Even if you don't believe me, I've let go of the idea that Jackson and I can ever be together. I can't say I understand it, but I see how he feels about you. I know there's nothing I could ever do to change that. Not even if I killed you, which I won't."

I settled into a chair beside Jackson on the porch, letting her words sink in. "How exactly do you plan to get out of this?" I asked. "Don't you think they'll notice if I'm still alive in four days? They'll just send someone else after me, right? What then?"

"I hadn't gotten that far," she said. "I thought maybe you could go into hiding. How far are you from attempting this ritual you were talking about? If we could go to Andros and show him proof the shadow demon slaves can be freed, it will change everything."

"Why kill so many all at once anyway?" I asked. "You said the Resistance plans to attack the gates in the south right? That's got to be at least, what, a hundred gates?"

"One hundred sixteen," Zara said. She'd been so quiet, I'd almost forgotten she was here. "All gates under my mother's rule."

"Andros wants to hit as many as he can all at once in order to maintain the element of surprise," Lea said. "If he started with one, that would alert the Order to his plan and they would set up guards for the primas and the portals, maybe even send the primas into hiding for a while. Each gate would become a full-on battleground, which is what he's trying to avoid in the first place. If he kills them all at once, they'll all be taken by surprise and he can close over a hundred gates in a single day.'"

"That's why he's sending these assassins out early, then?" Jackson said. "To investigate the town and the primas?"

"Yes," Lea said. "Each team has a lead assassin who has already been sent out to their assigned town. Their job is to watch the prima and figure out her schedule. They need to see how often the portal is used and how difficult it will be to get to when the time is right. That sort of thing. Andros gave us two days to gather the information we need before we're supposed to go back and give him an update and assemble the rest of our team. Then we'll have one day to get in place before the actual assassination. The fourth day, we're supposed to kill the primas at eight in the morning."

"That only really gives us three days to attempt the ritual," I said. "There's too much that still has to be done."

"You'll have to find a way to move faster," Lea said. "Short of this ritual working and demons going free, there's no way Andros is backing down from his plan."

I leaned over, my head in my hands. Three days? I had no idea how, but we were going to have to find a way to pull this off.

The future of both our worlds depended on it.

SO MANY SECRETS

*J*ACKSON OFFERED TO show Lea to one of the rooms he and Essex had cleared out in the blue house where Angela was staying. Lea didn't have much with her, only a small bag and a few weapons.

She stood, but as she passed behind Zara, her eyes flickered to the family tree Zara had been working on all day.

"What's this?" Lea asked, her eyebrows cinched together in the middle.

Zara turned. "Harper asked me to write down everything I can remember about my family's history," she said. "I decided to write out a family tree going all the way back to Eloisa Winter, the first priestess of the Order of Shadows."

Lea set her bag back down and leaned over the paper, studying it with great focus.

"What is it?" Jackson asked. "Do you recognize someone?"

"Look at this." Lea ran her index finger across several lists of daughters. "Don't you find it a little bit odd that each generation has exactly three daughters?"

I walked around to see what she was talking about. I studied the tree for a moment and realized she was right about each generation except the first one. Eloisa had been one of five daughters, the original sisters who created the Order. Eloisa had three daughters of her own. Her oldest daughter also had three daughters. Every single prima since her had also had exactly three daughters.

"Hmm," Zara said, tapping the page with her sparkly green pen. "I don't know why I never noticed this before. It makes perfect sense, though, since each of the three has a very specific job to do."

"What kind of job?" Mary Anne asked.

"We all know the oldest daughter becomes the prima, or in this case, the next Priestess Winter," Lea said, pointing to the names of the oldest daughters in each generation. "But what about the two younger daughters?"

Zara sat up straight as if a teacher had asked her a question. "Thirds, like me, are guardians and trainers," she said. "My Aunt Mary and my Great Aunt Kathryn are my mother's most trusted guards. They live with us at Winterhaven and are usually watching over the portal stone and the house unless mother needs them."

"They never married?" I asked.

Zara shook her head and her voice became softer. "No, thirds are not allowed to marry or have children of their own. We are taught from a young age that our role will be to protect the priestess and the home."

"What about the seconds?" Angela asked. "What job do they have?"

Zara stared at the names she'd written on the family tree. She bit her lower lip, her expression troubled.

"What's wrong?" I asked. I'd never seen her so upset, except maybe when her mother had tried to kill me.

"It's very curious," she said. "This doesn't make any sense. I've studied my family tree for years hoping to find answers about the change in my own mother, but never once until this moment did it occur to me that I have never met any of the seconds except my sister Honora. In fact, I don't even know where they are. I don't know if they're alive or dead."

"Your mother never talks about her sister Cora?" I asked, looking at the names on the paper. "Or her Aunt Janine?"

Zara shook her head. "It's as if no one remembers they existed," she said, her normally cheerful voice cracking slightly. "Isn't that the weirdest thing?"

I shivered, thinking of Lydia Ashworth's sister. No, it was not the weirdest thing. I knew exactly what it meant when no one could remember you existed.

It meant you'd been sacrificed. Or at least that's what it had meant in Lydia's sister's case. Was the same thing happening to the seconds in the Winter family? And if so, what were they being sacrificed for?

"What is it that the seconds do?" Angela asked.

"What do you mean?" Zara asked. She seemed dazed.

"Their job. You said that each of the three daughters have their own specific purpose," Angela said. "What's the second's purpose?"

Zara stared ahead for a long moment, her lips parted slightly. "I should know the answer to this," she finally said, "but for some reason I can't tell you. I can't remember."

"Your memory's been altered," Angela said, placing her hand on Zara's. "I have a lot of experience with memory spells, and I recognize the signs in your tone and demeanor. If no one had pointed this out to you, you probably never would have realized it on your own."

"Why?" Zara asked, her face crumpling. "What do you think happened to them? Why would someone try to hide it?"

No one answered her, because no one knew the answer. Except maybe me, but I was still trying to put things together in my mind. I didn't want to upset Zara any more than she already was.

"There's something else here that's odd," Lea said.

Jackson peered over my shoulder. "What?"

"The dates each new Prima took over," she said. She pointed to the dates on the paper when the reigning Priestess Winter died and her eldest daughter took over as Prima. "2004, 1977, 1955, 1929, and so on. These dates are significant. These are all years when some of the largest and most powerful demon gates in this area of the country were massacred, the gates closed and all of their witches and demons murdered."

I gasped. "Are you sure? How do you know that?"

"I've been studying this since I first came to the human world almost fifty years ago," Lea said. "I always wondered if there wasn't some kind of pattern or significance to the dates, but I could never figure out it. Sometimes there were 25 years between the massacres, sometimes there were thirty years or more. There were some smaller gates destroyed along the way, but it was the big ones that were always spread out like this. I could never put a pattern to it."

"You're talking about the killing of an entire demon gate coven, right?" I asked. "Like what you showed me in Aldeen when Priestess Winter cut that prima's throat?"

Zara clasped a hand to her mouth and sat down. I cringed. I hadn't meant to be so heartless. Did she not know what her mother was capable of?

"That's exactly what I'm talking about," Lea said. She pointed to the dates on the tree when the oldest Priestess Winter died in each generation. "Aldeen was small, though. Every single one of these dates marks the death of the most significant demon gates on this side of the United States. Gates with powerful prima demons and more than a hundred witches in their covens."

"Wait a second," Jackson said. He pushed toward the front and ran his finger furiously along some of the dates. "Zara, you said you were five years old when your mother took over as prima right?"

Zara nodded, her light eyes wide and scared.

"That's when you said she started acting strange and different, as if she wasn't herself," Jackson said. "Look at the birthdays of all the third daughters, and then look at the dates each Priestess Winter died."

Zara's hand moved to her mouth and tears ran down the side of her face. "Each time the new prima took over, her youngest daughter was exactly five years old," she said in a whisper. She looked up at Jackson, doubt and fear in her eyes. "What does this mean?"

"I don't know," he said. "But it's got to be significant in some way."

"Each Priestess Winter has died before the age of 65," Lea said. "Doesn't that seem strange to you? Primas are supposed to be notoriously difficult to kill. That should be especially true of the priestesses. So what did each of these women die of so young?"

"Zara?" I asked, putting my hand on her shoulder. "What did your grandmother die from?"

She shook her head. "I don't know. I can't remember." A sob escaped from her mouth and she clamped her hand over the top of it.

"It's possible someone messed with that memory too," Angela said. "Most people know how their grandparents passed away, especially if it happened at such a young age, like sixty-one."

"Ever since I was a little girl, I felt something strange was going on in my house, but I didn't want to believe it," Zara said, her eyes red and full of sorrow. "I had no idea there were so many secrets being kept from me."

"We're going to figure this all out," I said, trying to keep my voice calm for her sake. "There has to be a reason why things always happen in this pattern and why someone took special care to alter your memories."

Zara turned and buried her head in my shirt. She began to cry, sobs shaking her body. I knew those sobs all too well, and it broke my heart to hear them coming from someone like Zara.

They were the sobs of a girl who'd only just realized the true pain of betrayal.

DARK MAGIC

I SAT AT THE small table in the house Jackson and I shared, staring at my notes about Zara's family. The key to understanding Priestess Winter was here somewhere, I could feel it. If we could figure out a weak spot, we would have a real chance to bring her down. But what was I still missing?

The pieces of the puzzle were scattered across the table. I'd been over them at least twenty times since dinner. Jackson had already gone to bed, but I couldn't sleep. The clock was ticking now, with the Resistance expecting Lea to murder me in just three days.

I sighed and went over the details again.

Each first or Prima Futura in the Winter family always had three daughters of her own. The first daughter would always grow up to become the next Priestess Winter. The second daughter was a mystery, possibly sacrificed for the sake of dark magic? The thirds became guardians of the priestess, trained to fight and to protect, and never allowed to have families of their own.

Each time a third turned five years old, two major events occurred within that year. Her grandmother died, making her mother the reigning Prima and Priestess Winter. Also, a major demon gate was destroyed, killing hundreds of witches and demons.

What could those two things possibly have in common?

Were those witches fuel for another sacrifice of some sort? I knew the answer to Priestess Winter's power was here in front of me. I just couldn't seem to put it together.

I fell asleep at the table hours later, dreaming of ritual daggers and dark magic.

TENNESSEE—1995

"*I* MISSED SOMETHING YESTERDAY," Lea said when she joined us at breakfast the next morning.

The whole group had gathered to discuss the day's plan and talk about what we knew so far.

"Something about my family tree?" Zara asked. Her eyes were still red this morning. Had she been crying all night?

"Yes." Lea ripped a piece of bacon in two and popped one half into her mouth. "Last night, I kept going over the dates in my head. I knew I was missing something, so I wrote down every demon gate I could remember that had been destroyed in the last fifty years."

She pulled a small piece of paper from the pocket of her black leather pants. I reached for it and she leaned over the table to pass it to me. There were eight dates listed. Five in black and three in red.

"What are the ones in red?" I asked.

"Those are the major towns. The ones I was saying had the most powerful prima demons and at least a hundred or more witches in the coven. Those dates correspond with the year Priestess Winter died and her oldest daughter became the new

Priestess Winter." Lea paused until I looked up and met her dark gaze. "All of them except one."

I looked at the dates and noticed one at the very bottom was circled. Tennessee - 1995. I suddenly felt as if I'd had the breath knocked out of me.

"That's the year I was born," I said.

"Exactly," Lea said, raising a single eyebrow. "This was a large demon gate town with an extremely powerful prima demon. Besides the original five gates like Winterhaven, this was probably one of the most powerful gates in existence. According to the pattern, Priestess Winter should have died that same year. Only she didn't. The Priestess Winter who murdered that town's prima didn't pass away until 2004. It has to mean something."

My head pounded. I'd barely gotten any sleep, trying to see the meaning in all this information. Now, she was giving me another piece that seemed to show I was stuck in the middle of all this somewhere. But how?

Angela took the small paper from me and studied it. "1995," she said. "What town did you say that was?"

Lea leaned forward, elbows against the table. "A small town just outside of Nashville, Tennessee. Clement, I think it was called."

My head snapped up. "Clement?" I asked, my heart racing. My breath stopped in my chest and the world began to spin as I remembered my conversation with my father. "Clement is the name of the town where my grandfather died."

Angela put her hand on my arm. "The year makes sense," she said. "That's the year my father left. When he went back to the demon world to take over as the King of the South. Maybe our grandfather was the prima demon there in Clement."

I put my hand on my chest. "He couldn't have been the prima demon in that town. Lea, you said it was an older gate, right? One of the earliest ones created?"

She nodded. "It was opened sometime around 1915."

"See? Our grandfather couldn't have been trapped in Clement since 1915," I said. "He was ruling the Southern Kingdom when our father first came to Peachville in 1985. None of this makes sense. Why would he have been killed along with the rest of that town? Is it possible he was pulled through for a regular initiation?"

Jackson shook his head. "No way. The hunters never would have chosen someone as powerful as your grandfather for a normal initiation ceremony."

Angela brought a hand to her temple. "Then why would he have even been there?" she asked.

I took a deep breath and looked at Lea. "There's only one way to find out."

WHAT HAPPENED
THAT DAY

*L*EA SHOOK HER HEAD. "NO."

"I want to see it for myself," I said. "This could be the key to understanding how all of this fits together. Why my grandfather died. Why Priestess Winter usually dies after she kills a large demon gate town. We need to know the answers to these questions before it's too late."

Jackson shook his head. "I don't know if that's such a great idea right now," he said. "It takes an extreme amount of power to recreate an event that took place so many years ago. Don't you remember what happened last time Lea showed you a memory? The Order found us and took you away from me. What if they tracked her magic before and that's how they found you?"

"They knew I was with Lea that time," I said. "This time they probably don't even know she's come back to the human world. Besides, it's worth the risk. Something happened that day to throw off the pattern. We need to see what it was."

"I agree with Harper," Angela said. "We need to know what happened in Clement that was so different. And what did our grandfather have to do with it? I think it's worth a look."

Jackson stood and paced behind my chair. "It's too dangerous," he said. "We can explore the truth of what happened there after we free Aerden. I don't think it will make any difference in whether our ritual works or not."

"In order to perform this ritual, we're going to have to reactivate the blue portals. Priestess Winter is going to feel it," I said, standing. "She'll come for us. If we don't figure out what her weaknesses are, it won't matter if the ritual works to free Aerden, because we'll all be dead."

"We've survived this long," Jackson said. "Freeing Aerden won't change that."

I shook my head. "Don't you see? Freeing Aerden will change everything," I said. "You think Priestess Winter has been coming after me with everything she's got? She's sent an insane tiger, a few undead hunters, and her daughter. Not once has she actually come after me herself. Not once have I had to fight her. So far, she's been going easy on me compared to what she's capable of. My father said she's abnormally powerful. More so than any regular prima or witch. We can't win against her without some help."

Jackson ran a hand through his hair. His jawline tensed. "I don't like this."

"Can you do it?" I asked, turning to Lea.

"Yes," she said. "I've recreated memories of places and events from much farther back than this. But Jackson's right. It will take way too much power. I would be drained for days. Maybe a week. We don't have that kind of time."

"Courtney," I said, turning to Mary Anne. "She's at Lark's right now, but she would be able to recharge Lea's power. Can you go get her? You should be safe once you get past the Chen's security system."

Mary Anne nodded. "Should I bring everyone? Or just Courtney?"

"Bring Lark and her mom too if they're willing to come," I said. I'd been dying to see Lark ever since we first got back to Peachville. "We could use their help too."

Mary Anne and Essex ran off to get three more wristbands from inside.

"Will we all be able to go see the vision?" I asked Lea.

She shook her head. "It's easier if it's just you and me," she said. "It would take too much energy to bring everyone."

I looked at Angela. "Are you okay with that?" I asked. "It's your family as much as it is mine."

Angela stood. "I'm not sure I want to see what happened that day," she said. "To watch my own grandfather be murdered is a memory I don't really want, to be honest with you."

Her words weighed heavy on my heart. I hadn't even considered the emotional impact of watching his death. I was too focused on getting the information to even think about how it might affect me. Would I be able to handle this?

I swallowed down any doubt and turned back to Lea. "Then it's just you and me," I said. "Please do this for me. We need to see what happened that day."

She looked to Jackson and their eyes locked. My heart beat faster as a silent conversation passed between them. Finally, Jackson slowly nodded, then lowered his head.

Lea turned to face me. "All right," she said. "You owe me one."

I CAME TO SET
HER FREE

*L*EA AND I stood together in the center of the village. My heart beat double-time in my chest. She placed her hands on my shoulders.

"Are you ready?" she asked.

I pressed my lips together firmly and nodded, trying to control the roller-coaster in my stomach.

She spoke in her demon tongue. Chills rippled down my arms.

We turned to black smoke, disappearing from the crow village and landing in a large room. Dim lights buzzed overhead.

I brought my palm to my forehead and squeezed my eyes shut. Even after all my practice shifting into demon form, I wasn't prepared for the violence of Lea's time travel. I felt as if I'd been slammed against the ground.

"The demon gate is in here?" I asked, finally able to open my eyes and look around. We were in some kind of basement from the looks of it. The floor was gray cement with dirty boot prints and water stains. A set of metal stairs led up, but Lea pointed in the opposite direction.

"Yes," she said, and motioned for me to follow. "In the bigger demon gate cities there aren't large open fields or deep woods anywhere, like in Peachville or Aldeen. The Order needs to hide their portals away from the rest of the world, so in cities like this, or D.C. or New York, the gates are deep in the basements and bottom levels of buildings. Sometimes they're in houses, like in Winterhaven, and sometimes the portal is in the basement of a normal-looking office building, like this one."

"I thought you said Clement was a small town."

"It's more like a wealthy suburb of Nashville," she said. "Lots of attorney's offices and banks and such."

"You've been here before?" I asked.

"I've been to them all," she said.

My eyes widened. "Them all? As in all of the demon gates that were closed?"

"No. Them all as in all of the demon gates in the world."

I swallowed. She'd been to every gate? But there were thousands. I guess I hadn't really given much thought to what Lea had been doing for the past fifty years. She'd originally come through to the human world to find Jackson, but when his power had been entombed in the statue in Peachville, she'd moved on to look for other ways to fight against the Order.

I knew she and the other shadow demons in her group had spent a lot of time visiting demon gate towns and trying to convince the witches of the Order that what they were doing to the demons was wrong. I hadn't realized how extensive her travels had really been.

"It's just down this hallway," she said. "Can you hear them?"

I listened, at first hearing only the sound of our footsteps. Then, in the distance, the hum of words spoken in unison. My skin began to tingle.

"I hear it."

"We're close."

Lea lengthened her stride, and I jogged to keep up. The humming grew louder.

"This is it," Lea said. She met my eyes in the semi-darkness, then opened a door labeled 'Employees Only'.

Light flickered across the walls inside.

No one looked up as we entered, and I had to remind myself that to them, we didn't exist. We were ghosts eavesdropping on the past.

The portal stone in the center of a five-pointed star glowed a deep ruby red. The witches of the Order all wore black robes similar to ones I'd seen in Peachville. The prima stood at the top of the star, hood drawn. I recognized her by the ruby necklace around her neck. It was identical to mine except for the color of the stone.

She chanted and the stone glowed brighter.

Screams echoed in the hallway and I turned, fear closing my throat and making it harder to breathe.

A girl, naked except for the red cloth draped around her middle, was carried into the room, her body trembling. Her eyes wide as saucers.

Her initiation ceremony.

It was so similar to the ceremony I'd watched in Peachville the day Brooke had been initiated. The fear in this girl's eyes was the same, too, and I knew instantly no one had prepared her for this night. I wanted to close my eyes, but I forced them open.

A figure in a blue robe stepped out of the shadows to examine the girl. She lowered her hood, and I gasped. Her white-blonde hair. Her pale blue eyes. This wasn't the Priestess Winter I knew, but then, it wouldn't be. She had only taken power eight years ago.

"Zara's grandmother?" I asked in a whisper, forgetting no one could hear or see us.

"Margaret Winter," Lea said. "A cold bitch if there ever was one."

This older Priestess Winter stepped toward the naked girl, her pale eyes gleaming. She lifted one pale, wrinkled hand to the girl's face, caressed it, and gripped her chin tight. Their eyes locked for a moment, then the young girl began to cry silent tears.

Priestess Winter released her, and waved her hand toward the red glow of the portal.

My stomach twisted. This woman took joy in the fear of others. She hadn't touched the girl to offer words of comfort or welcome. She'd merely gone over there to see her terror up close.

I shuddered and turned away.

"I have a feeling you'll want to see this," Lea said.

I took a calming breath, then returned my eyes to the ritual. "Do you know what happens?" I asked.

"No, but I have a good guess," she said with a sinister smile.

Her smile confused me. Was she enjoying this? She couldn't be.

The five witches on the pentagram knelt down at the points and began to chant. The initiate's body went rigid, hovering over the portal as the swirling mist of red over the portal stone began to glow brighter. My pulse quickened, waiting for the arrival of her demon.

The prima raised her hands high into the air, opening her mouth to speak the demon's name. But before she uttered a word, a bright light flashed like lightning across the portal. Witches all around the room gasped and backed away.

"What's happening?" I asked.

"Just watch," Lea said.

I trained my eyes on the red portal stone. Another flash of bright light, then a slow burn. White smoke rose up as if the portal itself were on fire. The prima threw her hood off and backed away from the stone, fear in her eyes.

Priestess Winter grabbed the prima's arm and shoved her back into her spot on the pentagram. "Finish the ritual," she growled.

The prima shook her head. "Something's different," she said. "Don't you feel it?"

"I said finish the ritual." Priestess Winter slapped the prima across the face. "Bind the demon, now."

"Calixto, demon of the shadow world, we bind you." Her voice trembled. "Enter into this holy vessel, we command you."

The red mist below the initiate's body seemed to bubble up. With a loud crack, a rush of white smoke poured forth. Only, instead of entering the girl's body, the demon wrapped itself around the neck of one of the witches forming the pentagram. She grabbed her neck, but her fingers went through the smoke as if it were only air. In seconds, she fell to the ground, a bloody mark around her throat.

Another strand of white flew from the portal, then another. The room erupted in screams and cries as more and more demons materialized. Witches tried to run, but a white demon blocked the doorway, slicing witches from top to bottom with a silver sword.

In the chaos, I didn't know where to turn my eyes. Blood rained down as more than fifteen demons sliced through the first row of witches.

I covered my mouth. I felt ill. I wanted it to stop.

Then, suddenly it did. Demons froze mid-motion, trapped between smoke and beast.

Priestess Winter stepped to the middle of the room, blood coating the bottom of her robe. She held up a tight fist, her face gnarled in anger.

The witches of the coven slowly backed away from the frozen demons, terror in their eyes.

"Don't fear them," Priestess Winter said. "Bind them."

A few brave witches stepped forward, binding the demons with their magic. Some of the demons became trapped in boxes of ice while others became bound with fiery rope. Each of them was brought to their knees, their demon form forced to become human and powerless.

All were bound except one. A tall powerful form hovering over the portal stone. The first to come through. A silver sword in his hand, its hilt decorated with jewels. I gasped. I'd held that sword in my own hands.

Priestess Winter walked to the front of the pentagram, her eyes trained on him. Keeping her right fist clenched tight, she reached out with her other hand, putting it straight through the heart of the smoky form.

He crumpled to the floor, forced to become human.

I instantly recognized his silver eyes. They were just like his son's.

"King Ryen," Priestess Winter said. "I should have known you would show your face here eventually. Did you think you could save her after all these years?"

The king struggled to stand, but the priestess pushed him back down with only a flick of her wrist. Iron shackles appeared out of nowhere, rising to clasp his arms and pull him farther toward the ground.

"No," he said, struggling against his chains. "I came to set her free."

The priestess cackled, throwing her head back. The sound filled my body with terror.

"Free? She will never be free," she said.

The king lifted his chin in defiance. "Death is freedom."

Priestess Winter held her hand out to the shivering prima at her side. The woman pulled a silver dagger from her robe and placed it in Priestess Winter's hand, a red stone sparkling in the light.

"You alone will find such freedom today."

"You're wrong about that," the king said. "You will join me."

He pulled his arms tight to his chest, then raised them up with a terrible force, the chains shattering like glass. He shifted into white smoke, moving so fast my eyes couldn't follow. Then, with a cry that shook the walls, he reformed behind the priestess and plunged his sword deep into her back. Its tip pushed through her gut and came out the other side.

I gripped Lea's arm. Had he killed her?

Priestess Winter dropped to her knees, her hands grasping for the sword, as if trying to pull it from her body. Her face began to change and wrinkle, aging rapidly as blood the color of burgundy poured from her wound.

The king lifted his boot to her back, using it as leverage as he pulled the sword from her body. He raised it again, this time aiming for her heart.

FEAST OF SOULS

I WRAPPED MY ARMS tight around my body, breathless.

I watched as the king's sword moved toward the witch's heart, my own cheering him on, forgetting for a moment the reason we were here.

Priestess Winter dodged his sword before my mind could comprehend what had happened. The king stumbled forward, then attempted to shift. Her spell caught him mid-way between man and demon. His body turned to stone. Only his eyes were still human. A stormy silver, darkening to a deeper gray as he watched the priestess.

Her face wrinkled and changed as she stepped toward the town's prima. The woman bowed her head, her lip trembling.

Priestess Winter put a bloodied finger under the prima's chin and lifted it up, meeting the woman's tear-filled eyes. "Your family has been loyal to the Order," she said, coughing. "This line has been filled with powerful leaders who never wavered in their faithfulness, and I hate to end your reign so abruptly."

The prima's head pulled back slightly, her eyes searching the face of the aging priestess. "I don't understand," she said, her tone uncertain.

"I need power to heal," Priestess Winter said. She placed her wrinkled hand on the prima's cheek, stroking it slowly. "Such a shame."

She began to chant in Latin, words I had heard before. In Aldeen.

How would this ritual heal her? I didn't understand.

With one quick motion, Priestess Winter raised her ritual dagger to the prima's throat. The blade sliced clean across her skin.

Priestess Winter held out one hand and a silver cup flew across the room toward her. She lifted it to the prima's neck, catching the blood inside.

I turned away, covering my eyes with my hand.

Lea gripped my shoulders and turned me back toward the scene. "I know it's difficult, but this is the part you came to see."

I stifled a cry, my fist pressed hard against my mouth.

Priestess Winter stumbled, nearly dropping the chalice as the prima fell to her knees. Blood trickled over the side. Summoning her strength, the priestess made her way to the eye of the red portal, then poured the contents of the cup across the large stone. It bubbled and hissed. All at once, the witches of the Clement coven fell to the ground, their faces locked in a death-gaze.

With a loud crack, the portal stone broke into a million pieces.

"Stop," I said, falling to my knees. "I can't take any more."

"Wait," Lea said. She crouched down beside me and placed a hand on my arm. "What's she doing?"

I expected the priestess to go straight to my grandfather, but she didn't. Instead, she fell to her knees on top of the ruined stone. Slowly, she lifted her hands upward in a V, chanting again in a foreign tongue.

I shook my head. "Did this happen in Aldeen?"

"I don't know," Lea said. "We didn't stay long enough to find out."

I waited with breathless anticipation as a mist began to form above the body of each fallen witch. "Oh my god," I said, my flesh erupting in goose bumps. "I've seen this before."

The white mists hovered over each dead body, each taking on a light of its own, just like when Coach King had passed on. The mist over the prima's fallen body was so bright, I had to shield my eyes.

"I have, too," Lea said, her voice trembling. "But never here in the human world. Usually when a witch dies, there's no sign of the demon's spirit. I don't understand it."

I waited for the mists to fill with shimmering color like Coach King's spirit had done, but it didn't happen.

"Why aren't they passing on?" I asked. Dread pooled in my stomach.

Priestess Winter stood, her face unrecognizable now. She stretched her arms out wide, and leaned forward as she released all the air from her body. With a terrible gasping sound, she let her head fall backward, sucking in a loud breath as her jaw practically came unhinged.

The white spirit of each demon lifted up, then moved through the air toward the priestess. One by one, they were sucked into her open mouth. She consumed them all, her wrinkled body becoming younger with each demon that entered her. The trickle of rust-colored blood at her side stopped as her wound healed over. Her hands lost their wrinkles and her face became smooth and young.

Finally, only the prima demon's spirit remained. A single bright mist in a room full of death.

Priestess Winter walked over toward the statue that held my grandfather captive. Tears flowed from his eyes, wetting the stone beneath. "Your Queen will never be free," she said. "Her fallen spirit will fuel my withered heart for an eternity to come."

Priestess Winter inhaled again, pulling the bright spirit into the dark cavern of her mouth.

Finished with her feast of souls, her jaw snapped shut. Then, she licked her lips and smiled.

I'VE SEEN SOMETHING LIKE IT BEFORE

*W*E RETURNED TO the crow village in an instant.

Lea fell to the ground, gasping for air. Courtney ran to her side, but I didn't even look around to see who else had arrived since we'd been gone.

"What did you do?" I shouted, my body feverish. "We have to go back. He was still alive."

"I can't," Lea said. She coughed, her shoulders shaking violently.

Angela ran inside the blue house nearby and came back with a blanket. She threw it over Lea's shoulders, then looked up at me, worry in her eyes. "What happened? Did you see our grandfather?"

I paced, my steps quick and frantic. I drew a shaky hand through my hair, images of death burned in my mind.

Jackson took my hand, but I pulled it away. I didn't want to be comforted. I wanted to make sense of what I'd seen. I wanted to go back there and see the rest of it.

"We saw him," I said. "We saw..."

My voice gave out. I struggled to breathe. What had Priestess Winter done back there? What exactly did we see?

"You're scaring me," Jackson said. "Tell me what happened."

"Harper?"

I looked up to see who had spoken. It was a voice I hadn't heard in months.

Lark stepped forward, her eyebrows drawn together in concern. Seeing her face brought down my walls, and I threw my arms around her, holding her tight. She hugged back.

"I missed you," she said. "I was so worried about you after my mother told me what the Order tried to do to you. Thank god you're okay."

"I don't feel okay, right now," I said. I pulled away and collapsed into a nearby chair. I leaned over on the large table and put my head in my hands. "I don't even know where to start."

Jackson, Lark, Angela, Zara and Mary Anne all sat down at the table with me. Courtney and Lea sat on the ground near us, meditating together to restore Lea's power. Essex stood behind Mary Anne, his hand on her shoulder. All eyes were on me, waiting.

"It was horrifying," I said, my voice catching. I cleared my throat. "The ritual started as a regular initiation. Some helpless girl. But once it started, we could tell something was wrong. Priestess Winter was there, but not the one we know now. Her mother."

I looked to Zara.

"Your grandmother," I said.

She pressed her lips together, then looked down at the table, her hands fidgeting in her lap.

"Instead of just one demon coming through the portal, there were more than a dozen," I said, reliving it in my head. "They slaughtered as many as they could before Priestess Winter stopped them. She was so strong, she made them powerless with just a flick of her wrist."

I paused to catch my breath. My heart was still beating a hundred miles an hour.

"My grandfather led the demons through. I think they planned on killing everyone," I said.

"Why?" Angela asked. "Why would he do something like that?"

I rubbed my forehead, then met my sister's gaze. "Because our grandmother was a slave there," I said. "She was the prima demon of that town. He said he'd come to set her free. To release her spirit by killing her and the woman she was trapped inside."

Angela gasped and lifted the back of her hand to her mouth. "I had no idea."

"I don't think he was expecting Priestess Winter to be there," I said. "Either that or he'd completely underestimated her power. She was too strong for the small group he'd brought with him. He tried to fight back, and for a minute, I thought he'd killed her. It was the strangest thing. He was able to surprise her. He stabbed her straight through the stomach and she was bleeding really badly. But..."

How did I explain what happened next? I replayed the scene in my memory.

"When he wounded her, something weird happened to her. She began to age really fast. Her skin shriveled up and her face changed," I said. "I thought she was going to die right there, but then she got free and before he could defend himself, she turned my grandfather into stone."

"She killed him?" Mary Anne asked.

I shook my head. "No, she just trapped him there so he could watch." Tears filled my eyes. "Priestess Winter said something about needing to heal her body, then she slit the prima's throat, performing the same ritual we saw her perform in Aldeen when she killed the whole town. Every witch in the room fell dead right there in front of us."

"Why would she do that?" Essex asked. "Why would she kill her own people?"

"She needed them," I said. "She needed what was inside of them. The demons."

Jackson's mouth opened in surprise. "What are you saying? The demons didn't die when the witches died?"

"They died," I said, searching for the words to explain what I'd seen. "But it was as if the death of the prima and the breaking of the portal stone freed their souls. It's hard to explain. Their spirits rose up from the bodies as mist. I saw it when Coach King died. It was exactly the same, as if they were preparing to pass into the Afterworld."

"Oh, my god," Jackson said. He brought a hand to his forehead. "The broken portal set their spirits free."

"I think so," I said. "But they didn't shimmer and disappear like Coach King's spirit. They just hovered there for a minute, until..."

My voice cracked, and I had to take a deep breath to compose myself.

"Until what?" Angela asked.

I glanced up at Zara. I knew this would be difficult for her to hear. She might have hated her grandmother, but this was still her family I was talking about.

She swallowed and straightened her shoulders, as if readying herself for the news.

"Until Priestess Winter inhaled them," I said finally. "She sucked them in as if she was drinking them."

"They healed her," Mary Anne said, her eyes wide and her expression blank.

I nodded. "How did you know that?"

"I've seen something like it before," she said. She glanced toward the alter at the center of the village. "I've seen the Mother Crow eat the souls of the dead, but I never understood what it was. I never realized they were demon spirits."

Everyone around the table grew silent and still.

"I only saw it once," she said. "When I was a little girl. She brought a witch up here and slit her throat like you were saying. Only, she didn't exactly inhale the spirit. She used a stone."

"What kind of stone?" Essex asked.

"A soul stone, I guess," Mary Anne said. "I can't remember exactly. It may have been red, though, instead of black. She pulled the spirit into the stone, then she ate it."

"Then what happened?" I asked, sitting on the edge of my seat.

Mary Anne stared ahead, as if seeing the ritual play itself out before her. "She became younger," she said. "Not exactly beautiful or anything, but somehow less grotesque. And stronger."

I lay my head in my hands. The similarities were obvious. Both Priestess Winter and the crow witch had somehow eaten the demon spirits to give them power and strength. "But the crow witch was how old?" I asked. "Over a hundred years old, right?"

"Yes," Mary Anne said. "About one hundred and twenty."

"And she was in rough shape," I said, remembering the old woman's leathery skin and clawed hands. "Priestess Winter was still young and beautiful. She was only, what? Fifty back in 1995? Fifty-one? She didn't even look that old at first. I don't understand why she aged so fast when she was wounded. It doesn't make any sense."

"It makes sense to me," Lea said, standing to join us. Her strength had returned completely thanks to Courtney's abilities.

"How?" I asked.

"Because she wasn't just fifty years old," she said. "She was two hundred."

THE GREATER THE COST

"*T*HAT'S NOT POSSIBLE," Zara said. "You think my grandmother lived for two hundred years?"

"I think she's still alive," Lea said. "You yourself said you didn't think your mother was the same after she took over as Priestess Winter."

"This is completely ridiculous," Lark said. "No one can live that long."

"Don't you see?" Lea slammed her hand down on the table and everyone jumped. "She's been keeping herself alive all this time by using dark magic. She's powering her own body with the souls of demons. That's why she keeps killing those demon gate towns. She needs the demons' power."

I shook my head. Was this really possible? Could Priestess Winter really have kept herself alive for that long? If the crow witch had been able to do it for over a hundred years, didn't it make sense Priestess Winter could keep it going for much longer? She was so much more powerful and had access to a lot more demon souls.

The skin on my arms erupted in goose bumps.

"Her fallen spirit will fuel my withered heart for eternity," I said.

All eyes turned to me, questioning.

"Those were the last words we heard her say before we left the vision in Tennessee," I said. My pulse raced. "Priestess Winter was telling my grandfather that his wife would never know freedom because her soul had become fuel. She plans to live forever."

"Are you telling me that my mother really isn't my mother?" Zara asked. "That I was right about her?"

"That's exactly what I'm saying." Lea rubbed the back of her neck. "I think the original Priestess Winter, the oldest sister who started the Order of Shadows, has never died. I think she's been using the spirits of the dead to keep her looking young."

"But she looks just like my mother," Zara said.

"A glamour," Lea answered. "All she would have to do is use a glamour to switch places with her oldest daughter when the time came."

"There's no way she could keep that up twenty-four hours a day," Lark said. She stood from her place at the table, a frown on her face. "I think this whole thing is a stretch. Maybe you didn't understand what you were seeing."

"I know what we saw," Lea said.

"There is a way to make a glamour permanent," I said, remembering Lydia Ashworth's story. She'd said all magic has a cost. "Almost any spell can become permanent if you sacrifice a life to create it. A memory spell, a glamour, anything. The greater the magic, the greater the cost."

"All she would have had to do was sacrifice a human life in order to make the glamour last a very long time. Years, even," Lea said. Then she gasped. "That's why there was usually twenty or thirty years between one Priestess Winter and the next. Maybe her glamour was starting to fade."

"But who would she have sacrificed?" Lark said. "Don't you think someone would have noticed if all these people kept going missing or being murdered?"

"That's the beauty of it," Lea said. "She sacrificed the oldest daughter. The one who was next in line to become priestess. No one noticed she was gone because as soon as she took her daughter's life, she switched places with her. To everyone else, it looked like the grandmother had died and her oldest daughter had taken over as the next priestess. In reality, it's been the same woman changing faces every twenty years or so."

Zara made a choking noise. "I knew it," she said, clutching at her heart. "I knew something terrible had happened to my mother."

"But how does she keep having children if she's so old?" Angela asked.

"She doesn't," Lea explained. "That's why she waits until the oldest daughter has three daughters of her own. That way there's always an heir who will grow up, have three children of her own, and then die. It's brilliant."

"So when my oldest sister Selene has three children, you're saying my mother will kill her?" Zara asked.

Lea nodded. "When Selene's youngest daughter turns five. She'll kill her. Then she'll become her," she said. "It's a never-ending cycle of sacrifice."

I shuddered at the thought.

How could someone be so cold-hearted that they would be willing to sacrifice their own daughters and granddaughters, generation after generation? I thought of my own mother and how she had done the opposite.

She had been willing to sacrifice everything to keep me safe.

Someday, if I ever had a daughter of my own, I knew I would do the same. I would never let power become so important I would sacrifice someone I loved to have more of it.

"I still can't believe this is happening," Zara said. She pulled her knees up to her chest and hugged them tight to her body.

Jackson stood and walked over to put a hand on Zara's shoulder. "It's been a long day," he said. "This is a lot to take in. I think we should take a break, rest for a little while and think this through. Some of us have been through a lot lately."

I nodded. We still had a lot to do to get ready for the battle ahead, but for Zara's sake, I knew he was right. Angela had already finished the wristbands and sent them out, so more people would be arriving throughout the evening and in the morning. Now was a good time to rest and let all this soak in.

The group dispersed, people pairing off or going to their rooms to be alone.

I stood and took Jackson's hand in mine. Together, we walked up the steps to the gray house we shared. We stepped inside and closed the door behind us. Without a word, I fell into his arms, holding tight to him, wishing I never had to let go.

PROVEN

"WE NEED A PLAN," I SAID.

Jackson sat at the table drinking a cup of coffee. I was glad we had a place we could go to be alone. I needed to talk to him without everyone else's noise in my head for a few minutes. Since we'd come through the portal back to Peachville, it had been one revelation after another.

My mind was about to explode from all the new information.

"What did Zara find out about the master stone?" Jackson asked. "None of this matters if we don't have all of the original ritual items."

"Lark actually confirmed it for us," I said. "I talked to her about it earlier and forgot to mention it to you. She asked her mother and found out that the portal stone is actually referred to as the master stone in the older ritual books."

Jackson sighed in relief. "This might actually work, Harper," he said, his eyes sparking with hope.

"As long as we can keep Priestess Winter away long enough to give it a shot."

"If Lea's right and Priestess Winter really is the original two-hundred year old Eloisa, the oldest of the five sisters who created the Order, maybe we can use that to our advantage," Jackson said.

"How?" I asked, sitting down across from him. "She might be old, but what I saw in Clement explains why she's so extraordinarily powerful. She has hundreds of demon spirits inside of her, using them like a battery to keep herself alive. According to the pattern, that power lasts at least twenty years or more. It's only been eight years since she last powered herself with a major town. And Aldeen was only what? Six months ago?"

Jackson nodded.

We both sat quietly, thinking this through.

Had my father been right all along in saying Priestess Winter was an impossible enemy? I'd watched her almost single-handedly take out fifteen demons, one of them a powerful king. I hadn't actually seen his death, but I knew she'd killed him.

How could I fight against that kind of power?

"We have to be smart," he said. "What about Zara's protection spell? Couldn't she make stones for all of us to carry that would protect us from Priestess Winter's magic?"

"She could probably do it, but that won't last forever," I said. "Honora cast maybe three or four spells at me before my stone cracked, and she isn't half as powerful as Priestess Winter."

"Maybe if we used bigger stones?" he asked.

"We'd have to ask Zara," I said. "The thing is, we're all taking a big risk inviting so many people here to the village and explaining our plan. If any of them are spies or traitors, Priestess Winter will know everything we plan to do. I wish I could say I trusted everyone with all my heart, but I don't know anymore. The whole world feels like it's upside down."

"So who can we trust?" he asked. "Without any doubts?"

"Each other," I said.

He smiled. "That's a given," he said. "Who else?"

"Angela," I said.

"Mary Anne and Essex."

"Zara."

He nodded. "They've all proven themselves in big ways."

"That's it," I said. "If we're truly talking about people we can trust without even a hint of a doubt."

"We can trust Lea," he said. "I know she isn't the easiest person to get along with, but I know her. I know she would never betray us. Especially not to the Order."

I bit my lip and stared down at my hands. "I can't believe it's come to this," I said. "That we're sitting here talking about our friends, trying to decide if any of them are possibly about to betray us to our enemy. It makes me feel sick to my stomach."

"Me too," he said. "What's worse is that the list of people we know we can trust is very short."

I nodded.

"So we talk to Zara in secret," I said. "Ask her to make larger protection stones for the seven of us and hope that in the end, it buys us enough time to fight back."

"How much time do you think we'll have before Priestess Winter shows up?" he asked.

"There's no way to know," I said. "I think we have to go in there assuming she'll be waiting for us, just in case someone does betray our plans to her. To the group, we'll say we expect her to arrive in fifteen minutes. As soon as the blue portal reactivates, she'll know."

"Every witch in Peachville will know," he said.

I put my head down on the table. This was impossible. Was I about to get everyone killed?

"We'll need someone on the other side," he said. "Someone we can trust with the blue ring."

I nodded. I'd been thinking about that too. In order to reactivate the blue portals, we'd have to put the anchor back in place. That meant sending someone to the quarry of blue stones in the Southern Kingdom. But who?

"I need Mary Anne, Angela and Zara down in the ritual room with me," I said. "Do you think Lea would go?"

He shook his head. "We need Lea on this side with us since she'll have a blue protection stone," he said. "Can you think of anyone else we could trust with the ring?"

I ran a hand through my tangled hair. Who else was there? It would have to be someone strong enough to fight against hunters, yet trustworthy enough not to hand over the ring.

I suddenly remembered my father's words. He'd said the people of the domed city were my people. That they would lay down their lives for me. That they could be trusted. I lifted my head.

"I know who we can ask."

WOULD THEY HELP US?

By MORNING, PEOPLE had started to arrive.

Lea had contacted the other demons. Cristo, Erik, Mordecai and Joost. They arrived first, blue wristbands in hand.

Lark's mom came soon after, pulling me into a tight hug. "So glad you're safe," she said. Several other Peachville witches followed her inside.

I knew more would be arriving throughout the day with their wristbands. One by one, I explained to them why they'd been asked to come. I told them I was the daughter of a demon king. I gave them information about the journal we'd found.

Jackson slipped away in the middle of the morning, careful not to be seen or followed. He needed to be sure no one saw him go back through the white roses to the domed city. When he got there, he would talk to Piotrek, Liroth and some of the other guards and ask them to join us in our fight.

I worried my father would be angry with me for asking the guards for help, but since we weren't asking them to come here to Peachville, I knew he couldn't argue too much. The guards would be doing what they always did. Fighting hunters and keeping the Southern Kingdom safe.

If they agreed, Jackson would give them the ring. It was a leap of faith, but I felt that we had come to know those guards really well during the two months we'd lived there. They would never betray their king and country. They would die before they would hand that ring over to the Order.

Jackson also took a special stone with him that Essex had made for us. When the time came, I would be able to signal Piotrek to let him know when to return the ring to the quarry.

I waited nervously for Jackson to return and let me know the plan was in place. For now, we were the only two who knew about it, but later, if the guards agreed, I would fill everyone in on the plan.

He was gone much longer than I expected, leaving me to worry whether something had gone wrong. Finally, just before dark, he slipped back through the barrier. My eyes sought him out and waited for a sign. Had they accepted? Would they help us?

His eyes locked on mine and slowly, he gave a subtle nod.

TOGETHER WE ARE STRONGER

*E*VERYONE GATHERED IN the pavilion.

They sat on rows of stone benches, anxious looks on their faces as they stared up at the altar where I stood with Jackson.

The weight of the moment pressed against my heart. I had never asked to be a leader. I had certainly never imagined myself to be the kind of person who would start a revolution or set out to change the world.

Yet here I was.

And one way or another, after tomorrow, everything would be different.

"I can't tell you how much it means to me that you're all here," I said. "I know it's a lot to ask of you. There are no guarantees the ritual will work. There's no way to know if any of us will even make it out of there alive."

I studied each face. Zara had given up everything to stand by my side and fight against her own flesh and blood. Mary Anne had risked her life several times to save mine. My sister had sacrificed her own freedom to wait for me. Lea had left behind her friends in the Resistance to warn me of their plan. Every person sitting there had given up something valuable in order to do what was right.

"But there are some things I do know." I swallowed the lump that had formed in my throat. "I know that what we're doing is noble and good. I know that together we are stronger than any one of us would be alone."

I took a deep breath, determined not to cry in front of all my friends.

"Tomorrow, we have a very specific plan in place, and each one of you has a very specific role to play," I said. "In the shadow world, some dear friends of ours are in charge of reactivating all the blue portals. When they do, every witch connected to a blue demon gate will probably feel the change, including Priestess Winter. It may take them a few minutes to put two-and-two together, but we can expect to be attacked within fifteen minutes of those gates going active."

I cleared my throat. Saying our plan out loud made it all seem so real. So final.

"The Sullivan family is in charge of creating a diversion," I said, looking to the prima family from Cypress. I was touched they had come, but wanted to keep them as far from the real action as possible. "It's supposed to be a stormy day tomorrow anyway, so you'll be in charge of amping up that storm. Especially on the roads between downtown Peachville and Shadowford."

"How bad do you want the storm to be?" Caroline asked. "Are we talking tornadoes and hail? Or just some strong winds?"

"I'll leave it up to your judgment," I said. "I would say go as strong as you can without drawing unnecessary attention to yourself. If things go terribly wrong tomorrow, I want the three of you to be able to act as shocked as everyone else that all this happened. I don't want Priestess Winter to know you had any idea what we had planned."

Eloise Sullivan sucked in a nervous breath and nodded, clutching the hands of both her daughters.

"Everyone else will be coming with us to the ritual grounds," I said. "Only six of us will go down into the ritual room to perform the actual ceremony. Zara, you'll play the part of priestess. Angela, Mary Anne, Courtney, Lark and myself will stand on the five points of the star that surrounds the portal stone."

I picked them each out of the crowd and they all nodded in understanding.

"The rest of you will be with me up top," Jackson said. "We will form three rings of defense around the area. Lea will head up the front line where all of the demons will stand. We'll set up heavy traps and protection spells here, so if any of you know a special spell that will help, this is where you will cast it before the ritual begins. If the battle is able to make it through this first line, they'll hit the second line, which will be led by Essex. That line will consist of all the witches who have joined us from nearby towns."

I looked out, amazed that so many had come. Angela had sent out wristbands to only about twenty witches, but some of them had brought friends. People who wanted a way out and resented the Order's lies.

"The inner circle of defense will answer to me," he said. "All of the witches from here in Peachville will make up this inner circle. Our primary job is to protect the entrance to the ritual room so that no one gets down there."

Lark's mother, Mayor Chen, put an arm around her daughter.

"As soon as the portal becomes active, we'll begin the reversal ritual down below," I said. "We have no idea how quickly Priestess Winter or any of her followers will get here, but we need to be ready from the minute the ritual starts."

Nervous energy buzzed through the crowd.

"The most important thing is that we are able to get through the entire ritual," I said. "If it works, we'll have set all the demons free and no matter what happens from that moment forward, the world will be a different place. Even if Priestess Winter defeats us, all it takes is one person to spread the word about what we accomplished."

I straightened, my pulse racing.

"Tomorrow will be one of the most important days in the history of both our worlds," I said. "If we're successful, it will only be the beginning. We may start a war that will take decades to fight and practically a miracle to win. But I promise you, we will never give up until every demon and every witch is free."

I lowered my head for a moment, wanting to find the perfect words.

"My whole life, I thought I had nothing to lose. I thought I was completely alone in this world, and that I always would be." I turned to Jackson and took his hand. "When I moved to Peachville, I realized for the first time just how powerful it could be to love someone. And to be loved. There isn't a human or demon here who hasn't had something or someone they love stolen from them by the Order of Shadows. It's time we started taking it back."

THIS ONE NIGHT

I COULDN'T SLEEP.

I tossed and turned for hours before finally giving up and heading down to sit on the front porch steps. I stared out across the crow village. Zara's flower lights had long been turned off and there was only the soft light of the moon streaming through the clouds.

I wondered if we would ever make it back to this place. I'd given so much thought to the ritual and the battle; I hadn't really taken time to think about what might happen after all that. Jackson's brother might be free. I might be free.

Where would we go? Would Jackson want to go back to his home in the Northern Kingdom? Or would we stay here in Peachville?

If the ritual didn't work, everything would fall apart. The Resistance would go ahead with their plan, killing hundreds of primas and their covens. So many would die in an instant. How would the Order hide that from the world? So far, they'd found clever ways to manipulate memory or provide explanations for why an entire community of women died together. How would they explain a hundred towns all losing their most powerful women in a single day of carnage?

And what would happen when Andros realized Lea hadn't killed me? Would he send someone else after me?

I pulled my knees tight to my chest.

My whole life I'd felt like the world was against me, but never before had it been so true. I was grateful for my friends and for those I loved and trusted, but would it be enough? Were we strong enough to win?

There would no doubt be losses on both sides. The thought of losing any of the people I loved brought tears to my eyes.

The wood creaked behind me. I turned to see Jackson standing in the open doorway. The sight of him took my breath away.

I will die if I lose him.

"What are you doing out here?" he asked with a yawn. "Come back to bed."

"I can't sleep," I said.

He joined me on the steps. "You need to try to get some rest," he said. "What are you down here thinking about?"

I leaned against him, his body warm and solid.

"I can't seem to turn my mind off," I said. "I keep going over all the possible outcomes in my head."

"I know what you mean," he said. "On one hand, I could see my brother again for the first time in over a hundred years. But on the other, I could watch the last real hope of freeing him slip away."

His words created an ache in my chest.

Jackson angled his body toward mine, then gently caressed my cheek with the back of his fingers. "What's really got you up this late?" he asked.

My breath caught in my throat and my eyes stung. "What if this is the last night we ever have together?" I asked in a whisper, afraid if I said it too loud, it might actually come true.

"Tomorrow has never been certain," he said, wiping away a tear that escaped down my cheek. "Not for any of us. All we can do is love each other as much as possible every single moment we do have."

I lifted my eyes to his. "I don't want to lose you."

"You won't," he said. "We're a part of each other now. Down to the core of our souls. Even death can't erase that."

His lips brushed against mine, soft and gentle. I put my hand against his chest, wanting to feel every breath as it entered his lungs. Every beat of his heart. To know that he was alive and no matter what tomorrow may bring, we had this one night, this one moment, together.

My lips parted, drawing him closer. Deeper.

I let myself live inside his kiss, all my worries and fears forgotten for the sake of loving him with my purest self.

Jackson stood, lifted me into his arms, then carried me through the doorway to the old gray house.

NOT A DAY FOR FEAR

I WOKE WITH A START.

Today's the day everything changes.

The realization hit me like a truck. Everything had been leading us to this day. This one thing. Would we be able to set Aerden free? Or would we lose him forever?

Would we survive?

Jackson put his hand on my arm. "What is it?" he asked, his voice sleepy as he sat up.

I leaned against him. "I don't suppose you have a drawing that shows us how this all turns out?" I asked.

"I wish it could be that easy," he said. "But we're going to have to find out as we go."

I closed my eyes and took in a slow breath. "I'm scared," I whispered. It wasn't the kind of thing a leader was supposed to confess, but he was the only one I could bare my soul to. He was the only one who would understand how I could be afraid and confident at the same time.

Jackson kissed my shoulder and put his arms around me, his body still warm from sleep. "Me too."

We sat there together for a long time, watching as the sun came up outside our window.

I let my fears wash over me. I faced them with honesty, raw and real, understanding that this could be the last calm moment of my life. My last chance to show any weakness.

When I'd admitted them all to myself, I set my darkest fears aside. I got out of bed and settled on the floor of the bedroom, crossing my legs, palms up. I connected with the power deep inside my soul. I drew my strength into myself and held onto it with iron fists.

Today was not a day for fear.

NO TURNING BACK

*T*HE MORNING WAS a flurry of activity. Everyone spent their time talking through their plans, sharpening their weapons, and practicing for the battle ahead.

I knew Piotrek, Liroth and the other guards would be getting ready for battle on their side of the portal. Jackson told me they had not hesitated to volunteer for the job of protecting the ring. In fact, he said they were proud to live in service to their princess.

I had no idea how I would ever repay them. I simply prayed I would someday have the chance to thank them in person.

The Sullivan women took off around noon.

"Nature seems to be working in our favor," Eloise said. "It's rainy and overcast already. All we have to do is add some heavier rain and some bad winds. It should look very natural."

She lowered her head for a moment, then reached out to take my hand.

"My mother always told me it was an honor to be named after one of the original priestesses of the Order," she said. "It doesn't feel like much of an honor now."

I squeezed her hand. I hadn't even thought of the connection and how similar their names were. "It's not our names that determine who we are," I told her. "It's the choices we make. You're nothing like Priestess Winter and you never will be."

She pulled me into an embrace and Caroline and Meredith joined in.

"Just promise me you'll get out of town as fast as you can if anything goes wrong. I don't want Priestess Winter to take her anger out on you or the witches in your town."

"We promise," Caroline said.

The three of them left together, and as I watched them go, I felt the pressure of the coming hours. Had we thrown this together too fast? I wished we'd had more time to plan, but with the demon Resistance planning to assassinate over a hundred primas tomorrow, we had no choice but to act now.

When it was time, the rest of our large group gathered near the entrance.

I stood looking over the faces of my friends. My heart beat fast, but I took a deep breath to steady my nerves. This was it. There was no turning back now.

I wiped my sweaty palms on my jeans. What did you say to a group of people who were heading into a battle they might not survive? How did I thank them for all they were about to do?

In the end, I said nothing. I knew there were no words strong enough to say what we all felt in our hearts.

I AM NOT YOUR ENEMY

*T*HE RAIN POURED down as we reached the ritual circle. I was relieved to find that there were no witches waiting for us. No sign of Priestess Winter. The woods were quiet except for the sound of the rain on the leaves.

Everyone immediately got to work on their preparations. Lea walked around the circle creating traps. I recognized her archers with their purple flames, bows drawn in anticipation. I'd faced them myself, once before, what felt like a lifetime ago.

Zara worked her way around the inside of the traps, erecting protection spells that shimmered in the light of the purple flames. I knew this would be no match for someone as powerful as Priestess Winter, but I hoped it might slow her down. Her or anyone else who came to fight against us.

Essex and Jackson stood near the demon statue, discussing their defensive plans.

With everything under control up above, I descended the stone steps leading into the ritual room. Mary Anne, Courtney and Angela sat on the floor going over the ritual chants one last time. My eyes widened.

"Where's Lark?"

Courtney shook her head. "She left the village early this morning," she said. "She told me she had to get something from home before the fight."

I wiped the rain from my face. Without Lark, we wouldn't be able to even attempt the ritual. It had to be getting close to three. We needed to start exactly on time for the spell to work. Where could she be? No one was supposed to leave the group. What could she possibly have needed to do back home?

I ran back up the steps to look for her and stopped cold at the sight that greeted me. A gust of wind whipped violently at my wet hair.

Andros stood in the center of the circle dressed in red and black, the tip of his sword pressed against Lea's throat.

I felt the color drain from my face. What the hell was he doing here?

I glanced around and saw a small army of Resistance fighters gathered in formation near the edge of the ritual circle. They stood at attention, their eyes trained on their leader.

"I knew I couldn't trust you," Andros said through clenched teeth. His eyes focused on Lea with an anger so intense it made even Lea look nervous. "She stole the man you love away from you, yet you still couldn't end her life."

"I still have a day before the assassinations," Lea said.

Andros lifted his upper lip in a snarl. "You were never going to hurt her," he said. "I should have known that. I came here to check on you. To make sure you were going to go through with it, but here you are. Working side-by-side with these witches. Did you ever really care about our cause?"

Despite the small stream of blood trickling down her neck, Lea stood her ground, not taking even a single step backward. "Of course I care, but if we murder all those witches, how does that make us any better than the Order?" she said. "Besides, Jackson deserves a chance to try to free his brother before you would have him killed. He's our friend for god's sake. Can't you just let them try?"

Andros looked around, taking his eyes off Lea for the first time. "Who do you think gave them the diary in the first place?" he said. "Is it my fault they waited so long to come back here?"

"What's happened to you?" Jackson shouted, stepping into the circle toward Andros. "You used to believe in fighting for good, not evil."

Andros swung his sword in Jackson's direction. "They tried to kill my little girl," he said, his eyes wild. He gripped his hair with his fist and pulled, his face contorting into an angry scream. "Why can't you realize my way is the only way? Freeing the ones who were taken is impossible. Everyone knows that. The only way we can truly fight against the Order is to kill everyone associated with them, including your precious prima."

He turned the sword at me now, the blade swinging dangerously close to my cheek.

"You're one of them," he said. "Maybe not by choice, but it doesn't change the fact that you're a part of the Order."

Fury surged through me. I connected to my energy and created a shield around my hand. I reached up and grasped his blade. I pulled it down, away from my face. Andros' eyes narrowed and he tried to wrench it from my hold, but I wasn't giving it back.

"How dare you come here and threaten me." I said, the sky darkening as thunder clapped in the distance. "Yes, the Order tried to kill your little girl. They tried to kill me too. We've all lost someone important to us, but that doesn't justify what you're doing. It doesn't make it right to murder innocent people."

With all my strength, I pulled the sword from his hand and flung it into the grass.

"These women aren't innocent," he said. ""They chose to be a part of the Order."

"Some, yes. But not all of them," I said. "I never chose this for myself. Most girls who join the Order have no idea what they're getting into. They have no clue about the demons or the evil their leaders are capable of. So many witches are victims too, unable to leave the Order for fear of being killed or turned into a hunter. Would you really rather kill them than find another way?"

I gathered my power in my hands, standing tall.

"There is no other way," Andros said. He turned around in a circle, his hands shaking at his side. "No matter how hard or how long we fight, their numbers only grow. Don't you see? The only way to fight them is to kill them."

"No," I said. "Not if killing them also means killing the innocent. Your plan means killing demons, too. How do you justify that?"

"You think I want to kill demons?" he shouted, pointing at himself, his expression exaggerated. "This is war, Prima, sometimes the innocent have to die for the cause."

Something about the way he called me prima, the way his voice was drenched in judgment and hatred, started to piss me off.

"I don't expect someone like you to understand," he said. "You're one of them. You're the enemy."

His words were the final straw for me. As he stepped toward me, I shifted into smoke, whipping around behind him and coiling my power around his neck. I forced him to the ground. He gasped, his eyes bulging as he stared at my empty spot on the grass.

I returned to human form, but kept my smoky chains around him. Not enough to cut off his air, but just enough to let him know I was in control. I leaned down and whispered in his ear. "I am not your enemy," I said. "I may be a human prima, but I am also a demon like you. I'm innocent in this. Caught between a history I can't control and a future I have to fight for every day. Don't tell me I don't understand."

I released him and pushed him down to the ground. He fell against his palms, his head lowered and body shivering in the cool afternoon air.

"I didn't know," he said, his voice weak and trembling. He raised his eyes as I came around in front of him. "How?"

"My father is a demon. The King of the South." I crouched low to meet him at his level. "Can't you see? We're fighting against the same enemy here. The Order of Shadows has taken so much from all of us. But the lines between good and evil aren't as cut and dry as demon versus human. And I refuse to kill anyone there might be the slightest chance we can save."

Andros' eyes filled with tears.

I offered my hand to him. "Fight with us," I said. "Help us complete this ritual and free someone we love."

He stared at my hand, his face wrinkled with doubt. "Do you really think it will work?" he asked. "The ritual from the journal?"

"Yes," I said, believing it with all of my soul. "It will work."

I waited, my heart beating fast in my chest. If he didn't want to work with us, I knew we would have to fight to stop him. And we were running out of time.

Slowly, he raised his hand to mine.

THE END OF IT

*L*ARK FINALLY ARRIVED at ten minutes to three.

"Thank god. Where have you been?" I asked, pulling her into a huge hug. "I was worried something had happened to you."

I glanced around to see if her mother had decided to join us, finally spotting Mayor Chen in the center group near Lea. I sighed with relief.

"I'm sorry. I had some last minute things I needed to take care of," she said. "My grandmother can be very demanding."

I tilted my head. "Your grandmother? Is she visiting or something?"

"You could say that," she said, her smile forced. "I'll fill you in later."

I eyed her. Something was off about Lark tonight. I couldn't really put my finger on it, but she was acting strange. Distracted. Was she just nervous?

I didn't have time to worry about it. We needed to begin the ritual exactly at three in the afternoon. We had to get down there and into place before it was too late. I looked around the ritual circle one last time before descending the stairs. Across the grass, near the demon statue, Jackson's eyes met mine.

I lifted my fingers to my lips in a kiss, then turned my palm toward him, sending my love through the space between us. His lips parted slightly, love and worry and hope mixed in his expression.

Would I ever see him again? I wanted to run to him. To tell him one last time just how much I loved him. But he already knew.

"Are you ready?" Zara asked. She took my hand, her usually cheerful attitude turned gloomy and serious.

The three of us made our way down the stairs to where Mary Anne, Courtney, and Angela already waited. The ritual room itself was dark without the magical orbs to light it. Only a single black candle shone in the darkness. Angela held it out to me as I passed her.

The other rituals items lay on the floor by the portal stone.

The chalice.

The ritual dagger.

The necklace.

The matching blue stones glittered in the dim light, all of them chipped from the much larger stone in the middle. In the quiet chamber, I felt the energy and power of these items. They belonged together.

My heart fluttered and I had to work to keep my breathing steady.

Zara nodded to me, then took her place at the head of the five-pointed star. A descendant of the one who created this portal a hundred years ago. She leaned down and placed her hand around the hilt of the ritual dagger. She looked at me, questioning.

A chill ran through my body, a mix of fear and excitement. My hand trembled as I held it out to her and nodded.

"Mary Anne, bring the chalice," Zara said.

Mary Anne wrapped her hands tight around the base of the cup. She stepped forward and held it under my outstretched hand.

Zara's shoulders tensed and her lips pressed tight together. With a nervous breath in and out, she placed the tip of the dagger on the tender skin of my palm. I braced myself for the pain as she sliced through my flesh in one swift movement.

I winced and clenched my jaw. A blue stream of blood flowed from my hand, pouring into the ritual chalice. The blue stone embedded on the side of the cup began to glow.

"Now the necklace," Zara said, nodding to Angela King. "It's important to get the scene set up exactly like it would be at the end of the binding ceremony."

I closed my palm, then cradled it to my chest. Angela stepped forward and secured the necklace around my throat. I lifted my hand to the stone and rubbed my fingertip across its smooth surface.

Zara secured the dagger in her belt, then carefully reached for the cup. "Take your places," she said. "We're ready."

The five of them stepped onto the points of the pentagram drawn on the floor of the ritual room. Everyone but Zara knelt down on the floor and placed their left hands on the small blue stone embedded in the floor.

I retrieved the communication stone from my pocket and rubbed my finger over the top of it until it began to glow. I thought of Piotrek in the shadow world. Caroline Sullivan at the edge of town. Jackson up above on the ritual grounds. They each held a similar stone which now glowed bright with my signal.

Were their hands shaking like mine?

With timid steps, I took my place in the center of the star, the light from my candle creating five flickering shadows on the walls behind us. I closed my eyes and breathed in deeply. My heart thundered in my ears. I held the air inside my lungs until it burned, my body tense. After all these months of pain and frustration. After all Jackson's years of sorrow. After so many like Brooke had been forced into a life no longer their own. This would finally be the end of it.

I released the breath from my body, surrendering myself to the power of the ritual.

Electricity surrounded us. Anticipation. Great longing.

The scene was set. It was time to begin.

A CRACK IN THE BOND

"*COGNATUS AB ADNEXUS.*"

Zara held the blood-filled cup high in the air as she recited the words of the original ritual backwards.

I held my breath, unsure what to expect. We were in unexplored territory now, at the mercy of the ritual. At the mercy of our own hope.

At first, nothing happened. My ears hummed with the silence that surrounded us. I held my body tense, waiting, terrified. What if we couldn't get the ritual to work? What if something had happened to Piotrek and he'd been unable to place the ring in the right place? What if we'd risked everything for nothing?

Then, in a rush, light erupted from the portal stone. The force of it seized my body, pulling my neck backward as my feet lifted off the ground. I hovered in the air, parallel to the stone floor. An invisible power bore down on my chest, and I gasped for air.

A breeze swirled around the room, whipping my hair like ropes across my face. My lips parted as my head stretched back. Something deep in my veins burned, and I cried out.

The ghostly body of a woman in white formed on top of mine. My ancestor, Clara. The first Peachville Prima. Mary Anne gasped as the room filled with the ghosts of an entire coven of women. The memory of the first day, the creation of the Peachville gate, became visible to us.

We watched the last moments of the binding, as if watching a movie in reverse.

I felt Clara's terror as her jaw wrenched open, the black smoke of a demon ripped from her body.

Aerden.

Our connection burned within me. The bond boiled in my blood. Then, as the last of his essence left Clara's mouth, the necklace lifted from my chest. Aerden's spirit passed through the stone, and I felt a strange distance open between us. A crack in the bond. He coiled around us, swirling wildly as he tried to break free.

"It's working," I said, having to raise my voice over the force of the wind.

Lark, Mary Anne, Angela and Courtney stood and began to chant ancient ritual words in reverse. Mary Anne stepped forward, her fingers trembling as she unclasped the necklace and pulled it from me.

She held it over the chalice of blood. *"Moderatus compingere animus."*

She opened her fist and let the pendant fall deep into the chalice. The blood bubbled up, overflowing and spilling down the side of the cup.

Zara took my wounded hand in hers. Slowly, she poured the blood onto my palm. Wide-eyed, we all watched, breathless as the blood soaked back into the cut. Lifting the dagger from her belt, Zara retraced the scar, gasping as it disappeared, erased from my skin as if it never happened.

Like a mirror image, the ghostly forms around us went through the original steps of the ritual from a hundred years ago, only this time in exact reverse. Hope filled my heart as Aerden's essence uncoiled itself from me, his bond growing more distant.

Continuing to follow the steps, Zara fell to her knees beneath the swirling black smoke. Her light blue eyes appeared white, glowing as she lifted both palms high into the air. "Animus efferri accio."

Aerden's dark essence was sucked back into the stone and the wind around us died suddenly. The portal's light extinguished and the ghostly vision dropped from sight. Whatever force held me up disappeared, and I fell.

My head slammed against the portal stone with a crack, and I cried out in pain and panic. Fear gripped my heart with its tight fist as blood trickled down my neck.

What happened? This couldn't be right. I struggled to sit up, a scream lodged in my throat.

Angela rushed to my side. "Why did it stop? Is it over?"

"I don't know," Zara said. Panic filled her voice. "Maybe I did something wrong."

A rumbling above caught my attention. "Shhh," I said, lifting my eyes to the ceiling as bits of earth and dirt fell on us.

"What was that?" Mary Anne asked.

Shouts rang out in the clearing above and adrenaline shot through me like a lightning bolt.

"They're here," I said, holding my hand out to her. "Help me up, quick."

I stood and ran toward the stairs, but an invisible power pushed past me. Before I could reach the top, an onyx barrier rose up, closing off the exit. I'd seen a barrier like this before when the tiger witch used it to lock me out of the domed city.

Dark magic.

The candle went out, plunging us into complete darkness. We'd been sealed inside, the ritual room silent and dark as a tomb.

A stream of light from below raced toward us, its beam separating into four points. With a popping sound, the points exploded as they barreled into the chest of the girls standing behind me on the stairs. Mary Anne. Zara. Courtney. Angela. All frozen in time, their mouths open in various stages of a scream. Their bodies still like statues.

Something skittered through the darkness below. I swallowed, my throat thick with fear. Someone was down here with us, but how? Where had they come from? How did we miss that? I stretched my hand out and formed a small orb of light, then sent it down into the heart of the room.

There, at the bottom of the stairs, surrounded by five scorpion monsters, stood Lark. She wore a strange smile on her face, her dark eyes watching me carefully.

My first instinct was to rush down to her. To warn her. But something in those eyes stopped me cold.

They held no fear.

"Lark?" I asked, my tone uncertain.

She sighed and shook her head. "This is the part I've been dreading," she said. She glanced at the monsters next to her. "I never wanted to hurt you, Harper. Why couldn't you have just cooperated with the Order? Things would have turned out so much better for all of us."

Her words took my breath away. The room began to spin, and my knees went weak. I couldn't seem to make sense of what was happening.

"I really didn't want to have to be the one to do this," she said. "My grandmother told me I didn't have a choice."

"I don't understand," I said, shaking my head. I took a few steps forward, holding on to the wall beside me for support.

"Maybe this will help," she said. She spun around, her body shrinking to a tiny blue butterfly.

I fell to my knees on the hard stone steps, her betrayal piercing my heart. I brought my hands up to my head, the truth coming in waves.

Anyone could be anyone.

An image of the blue butterfly tattoo on her back flashed into my mind and I opened my eyes. She fluttered around me, then reformed on the steps by my side.

"You're one of them?" I asked. "You're a Winter? But how?"

Lark giggled. "I know it's hard to believe," she said. "My mother and I don't look a thing like them, but that's because of the glamour. I would drop it, but it's permanent. The real Chen family had to be sacrificed years ago, of course, but it couldn't be helped. Grandmother needed a spy on the inside, someone about the same age as the future prima, just in case you ever came home. Someone who could gain your trust. Teach you special spells to make you think we were friends."

"The glamours," I said.

Lark stood and walked back down to where the scorpions waited. "My job was to seduce you with your own power and with the idea of acceptance and friendship."

"I can't believe I trusted you," I said, anger and sadness twisting in my stomach. "I should have seen the signs. The butterfly tattoo. The insane amount of security at your house. The fact that you knew spells none of the other girls knew."

"Don't be too hard on yourself," she said with a frown. "I can be a very good actress. I learned it from my mother. All seconds are trained in the art of deception from the day they are born."

"Seconds?" My eyes widened. "Your mother was a second?"

She nodded. "Yes," she said. "All seconds are eventually placed as spies in demon gate towns. That's why no one can remember them. Seconds become someone else. The priestess has eyes everywhere."

Everything was finally becoming clear. No wonder Zara never knew where the seconds were taken. They weren't being sacrificed. They were becoming a part of some evil network of spies, sending information to the priestess about each individual coven. That must have been how Priestess Winter knew about gates like Aldeen. Gates where the witches had begun to protest the slavery of demons.

A loud rumbling above sent more debris raining down on us.

Lark looked up. "I'm afraid I don't have any more time to talk," she said. "Grandmother is expecting me to deliver you to her soon so we can end this once and for all."

With a snap of her wrist, she sent a stream of light toward me. It was exactly like the one she'd frozen the other girls with, but I was too fast for her.

I shifted into white smoke and flew down to the back of the room, disappearing into the shadows.

Lark cursed and whipped around, her black eyes searching for me. She formed a bright orb in her palm, then commanded the scorpions to find me.

I had to think fast. It had taken everything Jackson and I had to fight just one of these things. Luckily, I already knew their greatest weakness.

I reached inside my core and dragged my power to the surface. Flames danced across my fingertips as the scorpions skittered toward me. With a fierce cry, I fueled the white-hot fire with my pain. I had trusted her. Loved her. And all along, her friendship had been a lie.

Tears streamed down my face, but rage burned in my heart. I sent the fire out in a circle around my body, burning the scorpions' shells to a crisp until their green blood boiled within. The sounds of their final screams mirrored the agony I felt inside.

When the scorpions were dead, I turned to Lark.

I would mourn our friendship later, but now, I would have my revenge.

I TRUSTED YOU

LARK'S EYES GREW wide, surprise and fear sending her stumbling backward toward the stairs. She kept shaking her head, unable to take her eyes off the sizzling corpses of the scorpions.

I raised my hand in the air and the stone beneath her feet obeyed my command, rising up in a wave to send her sprawling, head-first into my arms.

I gripped her shoulders tight. "Look at me," I said, my voice trembling with anger.

She choked out a sob and ran her hand under her dripping nose. "I can't."

I reached up and grabbed her jaw between my thumb and index finger, forcing her eyes to mine. I stared straight through them, hoping to send my message straight to her soul. If she had one.

"I loved you as a sister," I said, my heart breaking. "I would have given my life for yours."

She raised her hand to my wrist and pushed, trying to escape my grip, but I wasn't ready to let her go.

"I don't give my trust easily, but I trusted you," I said. "I should kill you for this. For putting us all in danger."

A whimper escaped from her lips as she struggled against me.

I looked toward the entrance to the ritual room where the other girls stood frozen. "Release them," I said. "Whatever spell you're holding them with, undo it."

I let go of her jaw and forced her to turn around. With shaking hands, she cast a new spell, sending a darker stream of energy toward the others. With audible gasps and chokes, they came back to life, stumbling against the stairs, horror written across their features.

The others came down to stand beside me.

"How could you do this?" Angela asked, staring at Lark. "This whole time, it was all just an act?"

"I never wanted it to be this way," she said. "This was Harper's choice."

"Now, the barrier," I said. We didn't have any time to waste. "Take it down."

Lark shook her head. "I can't," she said. "The way the magic works won't allow anyone to open that barrier except Priestess Winter herself."

I lifted my hands, flames springing to life. Lark cowered.

"Priestess Winter knew we were coming this whole time, didn't she?" I asked. "You told her about our whole plan. This was an ambush."

Lark pulled away, attempting to run. I sank my power deep into the earth, then lifted up with all my might. A cage of stone rose up from the ground, trapping her inside. She beat her hands against the barricade, but it held firm.

"Tell me why the ritual failed," I said. "It was working at the beginning. I could feel it. What happened?"

She shook her head, scratching her nails furiously against the stone until her fingers were bloody.

"You must have known we wouldn't be able to free Aerden," I said. "If it had any chance of working, Priestess Winter never would have let us get as far as we did. What did we do wrong?"

She stopped clawing at her cage and stared at me through prison bars made of earth.

"Tell me," I said. "I need to know."

She sniffed, tears running down her face. "You were missing one piece all along," she said.

I shook my head. "That's not possible," I said. "We went over it a dozen times. We had every item from the original ritual."

"Every item except one," she said. "You never had the master stone."

My breath stuck in my throat. "But the master stone is here," I said, looking back at the large blue gemstone embedded in the floor. "The portal stone."

"No," she said. "You assumed the portal stone and the master stone were the same thing. I just confirmed it for you, making you think you were right all along. The ritual was never going to work without the master stone. Priestess Winter wanted you to believe it would so that you would put the ring back where it belongs and reactivate the blue demon gates."

I brought my hand to my forehead.

"Piotrek and the others?" My head pounded.

She lifted her chin. "Probably dead by now," she said. "Once they placed the ring near the stones, more than a dozen hunters appeared to take them down. Hunters led by an old friend of ours. Lydia Ashworth. Or what's left of her."

I clenched my teeth together. This was my fault. I'd trusted the wrong person and now my friends were dead. I had to find a way to make this right.

I had to find the master stone and complete the ritual. I searched my memory for any reference to another stone during the rituals I'd witnessed, but there was nothing.

"Where is the master stone?" I asked. "Does Brooke's mom have it?"

"The stone belongs to Priestess Winter," she said. "Like the ring, there's only one for all the blue demon gates. I've never seen it, but I know she keeps it with her at all times. You'll never be able to get it from her."

Above us, a loud boom shook the earth. More of the ceiling caved in around us. I lifted my hands over my head and moved toward the stairs. We had to get out of here before this whole thing fell in on us. The others followed me.

Lark, trapped in her earthen cage, fell to her knees, her straight black hair falling down around her face.

"Please, let me go," she said, coughing as bits of dirt rained down on her. "I don't want to die down here."

I stared down at this girl who I'd thought was one of my best friends. "You should have thought of that before you betrayed us," I said.

I placed my hand against the stone, knowing that with a single push it would cave inward, crushing her beneath its weight.

"Harper, don't," Mary Anne said, coming to stand beside me.

Tears of rage welled up in my eyes. "She deserves to die," I said, but I knew Mary Anne was right. I couldn't kill Lark.

Instead, I brought my hands together, squeezing the rock tighter to create solid walls. At the very top of the stone enclosure, I left a tiny hole. Big enough to let air in so she could breathe, but just small enough that a butterfly couldn't pass through.

MY DESTINY

A BATTLE ROARED ABOVE US.

"We have to get up there," Mary Anne said, pounding against the black barrier. "Essex is up there."

"Jackson's up there too, but even if we find a way out, we're going to need a plan." I grabbed her arm and pulled her back toward me.

"There's no time for a plan," she said. I'd never heard her voice so full of panic. "Listen to it out there. They need our help."

"We won't be able to help anyone if we're all dead," I said. "We have no idea what the situation is up there or who is in control."

"What should we do?" Zara asked. She wrapped her arms tight around her body.

My mind raced ahead, searching for some solution. I looked up, remembering the battle with the crow witch. When she left this room, she hadn't bothered with the steps. She blew a hole in the roof and flew away.

"I know how we can get out of here," I said. "But then what? From the sound of it, I think the fight has already reached the inner circle."

"Please," Mary Anne said, her eyes begging.

I knew she was right. We didn't have time for some elaborate plan. "Okay, but I'm going first," I said. "As soon as I give you the signal that it's safe, you can come up."

"Where do we go?" Zara asked.

"Get into the woods, hide somewhere in the trees," I said. "Don't rush into anything. Watch the battle and see if there's a safe place to join the fight."

They stared at me with wide eyes full of fear.

"If we're losing and there's no hope, get the hell away from this town as fast as you can."

"What are you going to do?" Angela asked.

"I'm going after the master stone," I said.

Energy rushed through me. The ritual may have failed at the end, but we'd almost completed it. All that was missing was the master stone, and Lark had said Priestess Winter kept it on her at all times. If I could just find it and get it down here, maybe I could still complete the ritual. It was our only hope.

I turned and started up the steps, but Courtney reached out to grab my hand.

"Here," she said. "Give me your other hand."

I placed both hands in hers as she poured new power into my body. It filled my core, as if someone had plugged me in to some never-ending source.

"Thank you," I said, a strong current flowing beneath the surface of my skin.

I pushed everyone back against the stairs, then gathered my strength in the palm of my hands. I reached out to grab the earth above the ritual room. With a great yell, I pulled the ceiling down, rocks and grass and dirt falling to the floor.

A massive hole opened up, the dim light of the dreary day pouring in around us. I stepped forward, climbing over a mountain of earth, upward toward my destiny.

BLOODBATH

I ASCENDED INTO HELL.

Spells flew through the air. Trees blazed with orange fire. A misty haze hovered above the area, blocking out the sky. Lights flashed all around like gunshots in the darkness.

I swept my gaze across the area, quickly taking in the scene from one side to the other. I searched for Jackson, praying he was still alive. Still fighting.

Lea commanded a group of archers to my left, their purple arrows flying deep into the woods.

Andros and the Resistance held the perimeter against the advancing witches of the Order. I saw faces I recognized fighting against us. Brooke's mother. Ella Mae. The sheriff. The ground beneath them was scorched and dead, demon power sucking the land dry.

No one had gotten through to the center of the ritual circle yet. I motioned to the others below.

"There," Mary Anne shouted as she joined me. She pointed toward Aerden's statue. "I see Essex. He's alive!"

My heart skipped a beat as I followed her gaze, searching for Jackson. He was supposed to be commanding the center line of defense, but he was nowhere to be seen. "Everyone spread out, find a place to join the fight. I have to find Jackson."

I shifted into white smoke, then shot straight up through the air, getting far above the trees so I could get a better view of the battle. Nausea rolled over me in waves. Everywhere I turned, bodies littered the ground like rose-petals, their bright red blood flowing across the scorched earth. The carnage turned my stomach.

My father was right. I had underestimated the Order. Underestimated my own friends. This was a bloodbath.

What have I done?

I had led both humans and demons to their deaths, betrayed by one of my closest friends. Someone I thought I could trust. Hadn't I learned my lesson by now? I couldn't let this be the end.

I needed to find Jackson. I needed to make this right.

I searched the battlefield again as I hovered in the air. There was no sign of him. I knew I needed to calm down. To focus my energy on finding our special connection. But my being filled with panic and turmoil as the battle raged below.

If I didn't focus, I would lose him forever.

I took a deep breath in, then released it, pushing away thoughts of the battle. I let go of my worry and guilt. I let go of all my doubt and fear until I finally came to focus on the one person who was most important in my life. The one I couldn't live without.

My heart stilled. The noise of the attack fell away. I searched for him in my soul, connecting to the bond I only shared with him. It radiated through me like a warm sun, bright and strong. I let it fill me completely. I let it lead me.

Our connection rose up from the battlefield, binding us together.

Pain seared through me, but it wasn't my pain. It was his. Somewhere among the slaughter, Jackson was in agony.

My eyes flew open and my head snapped to the right. I'd been searching the ground and the woods, expecting him to be lost somewhere in the bloodshed below.

But he was up. Here above the trees.

I saw him through the haze. His arms and legs were shackled. Mayor Chen held the right side in chains while Honora held him on the left. The three of them floated on some kind of platform just above the forest. Priestess Winter hovered behind him, her hands passing in a circular pattern above his head. Her lips moved as she cast a spell that had Jackson writhing on his knees.

I didn't wait for her to see me.

I dipped into the well of strength in my core, then rocketed toward her. I slammed into her with amazing force, wrapping my arms around her waist and pulling her with me as we fell down, down toward the forest floor.

She screamed, struggling against my grip. We tumbled faster and faster. I barely shifted in time, releasing her and flying out to the side, then up again. She hit the ground, bones cracking. Hope filled my heart as she lay there, her body bent at an awkward angle. Had I killed her? Could it possibly be that easy?

I wanted to search her. To see if I could find the stone. But Jackson's pain called me to him.

I turned my attention back toward the floating platform. I flew up, circling it once before coiling ropes of demon smoke around the shackles Lark's mother held in her hand. I broke the chains in two, then grabbed one end and yanked until she stumbled and fell to her knees. I dropped the chains, ready to face Honora.

Before I could, Jackson pulled her forward with his free hand. No longer bound by whatever Priestess Winter had cast on him, he shifted to black, slipping out of his restraints.

For a brief moment, he was human, his green eyes seeking mine.

The love I saw there fueled my strength. I whipped around, my focus settling on Lark's mom. A second in the Winter family. A spy and a traitor. A murderer. But as I made my move, an invisible power wrapped around my chest, knocking the breath from my body.

I tumbled in circles, spinning out of control, unable to move my arms or control my powers. I thrashed with all my strength, struggling to breathe. To fight. The barren ground above the ritual room barreled toward me at great speeds. I skidded across the rocks, skin scraped from my cheek and arm. I winced and tried to stand, but my legs failed me.

On the ground, a blue stone glittered in the light of the fires that burned all around us.

Zara's protection stone. I scrambled forward, my palm closing around it just as the black heel of a boot ground into my forearm.

I looked up, taking in her blue skirt and white button-up shirt. So prim and proper for a battle. She must not have expected to get her hands dirty today.

I pulled my arm from under her foot and lifted my eyes to hers, hoping she could see the hatred I held inside.

"Did you really believe this was a battle you could win?" Priestess Winter asked with a sinister laugh. "Your kind has been underestimating me for centuries."

Warm blood trickled from the wound on my face and I was pretty sure my leg was broken. Still, I braced against the pain and forced my body to a standing position. "This isn't over yet," I said.

She narrowed her eyes at me, and I moved to shift, planning to come around behind her. Before I could change forms, two hands grabbed me from behind, breaking my focus. I turned to see my captors and instantly knew them by their white-blonde hair and light eyes.

Zara's aunt and great-aunt. Thirds, like her. Guardians trained to protect the priestess. They twisted my arms tight around my back while Priestess Winter approached.

"You're wrong," she said, gripping my chin in her hands. "It was over the moment you came back to Peachville."

AFTERWORLD

I CRIED OUT, PULLING and twisting to try to escape.

"Look around you," Priestess Winter said, motioning to the circle of fire and destruction that surrounded us. "Your battle is lost. Your friends are dying. Soon, your precious Jackson will be locked in a statue next to his brother and your throat will be split wide open, your essence transferred to a new family."

"No," I said, my voice a cry and a shout. A prayer. "You're wrong."

If I could only figure out where she was keeping the master stone, I might have a chance. If I could somehow find it and take it from her, she might grow weak enough for me to injure her. It was my only chance.

My eyes hungrily searched her for any sign of the stone. A ring. A bracelet. A pendant of any kind. She wasn't wearing a single stone that I could see. Nothing shimmered or glinted under her clothing. But I could feel it. Its power hummed in the air around us.

She had to be hiding it somewhere.

"There's no point in struggling," she said. "This will all be over soon."

She cupped her hands together and a bright light formed inside. The heat of her spell radiated from her, and I pulled back, desperate to get away. The thirds gripped my arms tighter and I winced.

I tried to focus. To shift. But I was too aware of my human form.

I closed my eyes, breathing in. I started to let go, but panic washed over me and my eyes snapped open again. I thrashed and kicked, screaming out in frustration.

This was the moment. Do or die.

I couldn't let this be the end. I had to be strong.

I searched my soul, dipping into a hidden well of power just as Priestess Winter sent the light flashing toward me. I shifted, slipping from the hold of my captors and reforming just beyond their reach.

They recovered faster than I expected and three spells hurled toward me at once. Energy hummed through the air and I screamed, unable to shift again in time. I stumbled backward as each spell made a direct hit.

Zara's stone burned my palm as it absorbed some of their magic. But it wasn't strong enough to take it all. I opened my fist and the stone fell onto the ground, shattering to pieces.

I stumbled again as pain ripped through my body.

I fell to my knees, reaching toward the sky as if hoping to find something I could hold on to. Something I could use to pull myself back up.

But there was nothing.

My strength faltered, and I collapsed.

The two guardians began casting spells, and I knew they were meant for me. I pushed myself back up, refusing to give up.

For the sake of everyone who had ever fought against the Order of Shadows and everyone whose lives had been destroyed by them. I would fight until I had nothing left.

A flash of light and a ball of flame rocketed toward me. I pushed my hand away from my body, palm out, forming a shield around myself. Their magic turned to black sand against my shield, and I tasted the dry blackness of the guardian's hearts. Their dark magic.

It choked me, and I doubled over, coughing uncontrollably.

Metal clanked as Priestess Winter conjured iron chains that rose up from the ground. Shackles closed around my wrists and neck. She pulled forward and the chains shortened, bringing me to my knees.

Everything moved so fast and happened all at once.

One of the Winter guardians sent a spell flying toward me, but just before it hit, a red light crashed into it, causing it to explode to early. Mary Anne appeared at my side, her hands glowing deep red. She shot her power out toward the guardian like a laser.

Essex joined the fight, coiling thick black smoke around the throat of the other guardian.

Priestess Winter conjured half a dozen small knives that hovered in the air in front of her. I'd seen her conjure the chains before, so I should have known she was talented with metals, but I hadn't been expecting blades.

I thought she would turn them on me, and I prepared to shift.

But then I followed her eyes and saw that I was not her target this time.

Her gaze was locked on Mary Anne. I shouted her name, but she couldn't hear me over the roar of the battle around us. I pulled against my chains, time seeming to move so slowly as Priestess Winter launched the daggers toward my friend, their tips ripping through the air.

I shifted, slipping from the chains and launching myself across the ritual circle. I moved faster than I ever had before, the world a blur around me.

The blades caught me mid-air. They sliced through the flesh in my side, my arm, my thigh, then disappeared into thin air. Their damage done.

I fell to the ground, the force of the fall knocking the breath from my lungs. I breathed in, but no air came. I panicked, clawing at my neck, begging for life.

Finally, my lungs opened up and I inhaled with a terrible gasp that left my throat raw and sore. I exhaled and struggled to draw another breath.

My wounds sobbed, blood gushing forth like tears.

My body grew cold, and I began to shiver. I hugged my arms tight around myself and closed my eyes. A battle drum beat inside my ears, my blood pumping fast, spilling onto the barren earth that cradled me close.

When I opened my eyes, the air in front of me shimmered and for a moment, I wondered if this is what it felt like to die. Was this my demon spirit leaving my body?

I waited for the end to come, feeling no regrets. Knowing I had given my everything. Done all that I could. I had been a true warrior. If my father had been here, he would have been proud of me.

Then, suddenly, he was.

He leaned over me, his silver eyes filled with tears.

"Dad?" I said, lifting a bloodied hand to his face. I was sure I was hallucinating.

"I'm here, Harper." He glanced down at my wounds, then ran a shaky hand over my hair. He pressed his lips tight to keep them from trembling.

He seemed so real. A welcome vision to my weary eyes.

"I'm dying," I whispered.

He shook his head. "No," he said. "You're being reborn."

He placed a hand over my heart and a great warmth radiated in my chest.

I lifted my hands to his, running my fingers across his skin to see if this was all a dream. "Are you real?"

He laughed through his tears. "Yes," he said. "I'm sorry I didn't come sooner. You were right. I was afraid. Like so many others, I lost everyone I ever loved to the Order of Shadows. My mother. My father. Claire."

He paused at her name, closing his eyes to hide his pain. I gripped his hand tighter, letting him know that I understood.

"I was so scared that if I loved anyone again, the Order would take them too," he said. "I let my fear keep me from really spending time with you and getting to know you. I let my anger and my pain close my heart off from you and your sister. I told myself that if I didn't let myself love you, it wouldn't hurt when you were taken from me."

The warm energy he poured into me reached all the way down to my toes, rolling through me like a wave, healing me from the inside. My strength began to return and I lifted my head slightly.

I drew in a startled breath and my mouth fell open. A shimmering dome of light covered us, locking the two of us inside. Spells of light and poison erupted against its surface. Priestess Winter beat her angry fists against the dome, but nothing could penetrate his shield.

"But I loved you anyway," he said. "I've always loved you. You and Angela, you're a part of me, and I had turned my back on you. When I realized it, I gathered my people together and we came here, but I was too late. I saw you fall to save your friend and my heart broke all over again."

I reached my other hand up to his shoulder and gripped it tight, wanting to tell him I loved him, too, but unable to find the words.

"You were right, Harper." He placed a second hand over my heart. "Some things are worth dying for."

Light and power and love rushed through me. The ache of the wounds and broken bones disappeared and I felt my open flesh close in and heal over.

I shook my head, finally understanding. "Wait," I said. I tried to sit up. To pull at his hands and make him stop. "Don't go."

He smiled down at me. "It's the only way," he said. "My life for yours."

My face crumpled and tears filled my eyes.

"In my culture, an elder passes from this world at a moment of his own choosing," he said. "I choose this moment with pride, knowing your life is a worthy one. Knowing you are the true leader our people have been waiting for."

His eyes began to close and his voice faded as his energy left his body.

I rose as he fell. I lowered him gently onto the ground, then buried my face inside the folds of his uniform. Tears of gratitude and sorrow soaked into the golden fabric as he hugged me close.

"I love you, Father," I said, sobs shaking my body as I felt his life slipping away.

He struggled to reach something at his side, and I sat up and wiped my eyes. He lifted a silver sword from its sheath, then lay back against the ground, his breathing labored as he passed it into my trembling hands.

The jewels embedded in the hilt shone in the light of the glimmering dome overhead.

"My father's sword," he said. His voice was barely a whisper. In the tradition of his people, he emptied the last of his power into one of the stones. A final sacrifice. "Set them free."

With one last exhale, his body went still.

Slowly, a white mist lifted up and hovered over him. It sparkled with a radiant light.

I lay the sword across my lap, and pressed my hands tight against my heart, the skin still warm from his healing power.

I watched in awe as the mist shimmered and sparkled, filling with lights of every color imaginable as his spirit passed into the Afterworld.

SHE WAS MINE

I KNELT AT MY father's side, his body now just a shell, empty of power and spirit and life.

I felt his energy pulsing in my veins. His sacrifice. His choice.

I didn't know if I deserved this, but I was determined not to let his death be for nothing. Strength and sorrow coursed through me as I lifted my chin. I would end this now.

I closed my eyes and let my breath and the beating of my heart become the only sounds I could hear. I felt my demon-self rise to the surface. The normal panic tried to take hold, but I overpowered it, refusing to be afraid.

For the first time, I rose above my fears and truly embraced the demon side of my power.

I became my father's daughter, letting go and surrendering to the truth of who I really was.

My body disappeared, shifting to white smoke, then taking form again, not as human, but demon. Mist swirled around me, a strange power lighting me up from the inside. I felt so alive, every sense heightened. Empowered.

I stood and stepped through the shimmering dome my father had created, seeing the world as if for the first time. Light surrounded every living being. I could see energy vibrating all around me. And I could pull life from anything. Anyone.

The battlefield had changed. The tide had turned as guards and citizens from the domed city joined the fight.

Angry spells zoomed toward me, but I deflected them easily, their power nothing compared to what I had become.

I inhaled, but instead of pulling in air, I pulled in life. I drew it from the roots deep inside the earth. From the trees that surrounded the battlefield.

I sucked it from the marrow of the two guardians who came rushing toward me. Their beautiful white-blonde hair grew brittle and fell from their heads. Their skin wrinkled and decayed as they both sank to the ground, clutching their throats in agony. I used their life-force to fuel my own, then turned my eyes to Priestess Winter.

Lightning cracked, striking the ground beside her. She jumped, fear flashing in her eyes as she stared at the lifeless bodies of her two most trusted guardians.

I lifted my hand and the ground beneath her feet obeyed. It rippled up, knocking her down. Her knees hit hard and her eyes widened. She tried to stand, but the ground trembled again at my command, causing her to stumble and land face-first in the dirt.

Before she could stand again, I gripped her with the force of my magic, lifting her with invisible hands. She struggled, kicking her legs in anger, but it was no use. She was mine.

I opened my palm and called the silver sword to me. It rose from the ground and I closed my fist tightly around the jeweled hilt. The stone in the center that held my father's power shone bright, illuminating the area around us.

I approached the priestess, my heart beating in time with each footstep that carried me forward.

I looked deep into her light blue eyes. "This is for every family you've destroyed," I said. "Every child whose parent you stole. Every dream you crushed beneath the boot of your greed."

I gripped the sword tighter.

"This is for my father."

I thrust upward with all my strength, burying the sword deep in her belly.

She curled inward, her hands scraping at the weapon as rust-colored blood oozed from her wound. Just as it did in Clement, her body began to age. Her hands grew old and her face grew wrinkled and dry. Her features changed as one glamour faded and the next appeared like layers being slowly peeled away.

I lowered her to the ground and pulled my sword from her, knowing next time I would pierce her heart.

You act as if Priestess Winter has a beating heart.

The tiger witch's voice echoed in my memory and suddenly, something clicked deep in my mind. I turned my gaze on the priestess and searched her with my new demon eyes. I searched for her life-force. Her power.

On the outside, she was a shell. Underneath her glamours, she was nothing more than a decaying mass of bone and dust where no life remained.

But there, inside her chest, was the source of her prolonged life.

Not a beating heart.

A stone.

She has a cold stone where her heart should be.

The master stone, pulsing with the light of a thousand demons. Their stolen spirits trapped deep within, fueling her magic. Keeping her young.

Her greatest secret.

Her only weakness.

I sank the tip of my grandfather's sword into the dirt next to me, then raised my hands up. With all that I was, I thrust a smoky coil forward, deep into her chest. Through her glamoured skin. Through the decaying bones of her ribcage.

Her eyes bulged and her body went rigid.

I closed my smoky fist around the glowing stone, gripping it tight. With all my might, I pulled it from her body, ripping it from her chest.

A scream of such terror tore from her mouth that the very ground beneath our feet shook. Everyone on the battlefield, both witch and demon, stopped to cover their ears, some falling to their knees in agony.

The fighting stopped and all turned to see.

Priestess Winter fell to the ground, scratching and clawing at the gaping hole in her chest. Without her battery of souls, she aged with horrifying speed. Her face wrinkled and changed, taking on the features of each of the futures she had sacrificed for her own evil purpose. One by one the glamours were stripped away, showing but a glimpse of each stolen life, until finally, her true face emerged. Old and withered. Paper thin.

I shifted back to my human form, the glowing blue stone gripped tight in my hand. Dark red blood, old and lifeless, covered its surface. I watched; eyes wide, as the blood turned to dust, carried away by the wind.

The armies on both sides became still, terror and awe etched on their faces as they witnessed the gruesome end of a woman who had been responsible for so much heartbreak and so much death.

Priestess Winter curled her bony hands up toward the sky as if to ask for forgiveness. But no god would forgive her now. No magic would ever answer her commands again. Her skin shriveled and dried and turned to fine dust that blew around her like a tornado. The skeletal frame that remained doubled over, desperate for the hope of one last breath, then finally collapsed into a pile of ancient bones.

FREE

HE MASTER STONE shook against my palm. The shimmering spirit of every demon she had trapped inside the stone came pouring out, flying toward the sky. A bright mist hovered in the air over the battlefield for a moment, then filled with color.

I stared up at the beautiful sight, crying tears of joy as the demon souls left this world that had held them captive for so many years, and finally passed into the Afterworld.

Those who remained on the battlefield stood in silence, open-mouthed, their war forgotten.

I felt their eyes turn to me. Their prima. Their princess.

I grasped the glowing blue stone within my hand, the day's victory not yet complete. I still had one final task.

I turned and searched for familiar green eyes among the crowd, my heart leaping as I found them. The truth of this moment intensified as he crossed the barren field to stand by my side. We didn't say a word.

There were no words strong enough to say it all.

This was everything we'd been waiting for. Everything we'd hoped for.

He offered his hand to me and together we descended into what was left of the ritual room. Rock and dirt covered the portal stone. Jackson lifted his free palm and the earth obeyed, clearing our way to the blue stone below.

I raised the master stone over the portal and a bright blue light shot upward, the force of it nearly knocking me back.

My heart beat fast as I opened my mouth to speak.

"Unum mundum fit duo."

The final words of the ritual echoed through the broken room as the master stone was pulled from my hand. It hovered in the light, glimmering with such intensity we had to shield our eyes. Jackson and I stepped backward as a rumbling sounded deep beneath our feet. My breath caught in my chest and my heart thundered against my ribcage.

Hope burst through me as a tiny crack formed at the edge of the portal stone.

Adrenaline rushed like a river in my veins as more cracks formed, separating the stone into a thousand pieces. The earth shook with a mighty force, the noise deafening. Jackson and I both lost our footing, tumbling to the ground. Holding tightly to each other.

Then, stillness.

We held our breath, our eyes locked on the shattered pieces of the stone, our hands entwined. Time stood still.

A second rumbling began deep inside the earth as one by one, demons poured forth from the stone fragments. Spirits flew free, their slavery and torment ended. They rushed up into the air, unbound. Alive.

Demons on the battlefield sank to one knee, bowing their heads in thankfulness and disbelief.

Loved ones who recognized each other were reunited after decades of sorrow.

Witches clutched their chests as their demon slaves were ripped from their bodies.

And finally, once all the spirits linked to the witches of Peachville had been released, one final spirit flowed from the ruins of the ritual stone. I felt his essence cut from me, our connection severed for all eternity.

Aerden rose up with a mighty roar, soaring high into the air. Arms stretched wide. Eyes lifted heavenward.

Free.

THE CENTER

*J*ACKSON AND AERDEN met in the center of the ritual circle. I stood back, giving them their moment together. My friends gathered around, our eyes filled with tears of joy. Mary Anne's arm circled my waist. Essex stood to her right, his hands clasped tight as if in prayer. Angela laid her head on my shoulder and looped her arm in mine. Courtney stood just behind us, pressed close.

I searched for Lea, finding her alone. She glanced my way and offered a single nod of her head, the corners of her mouth lifting in the smallest of smiles before she turned away, wiping a hand under her eyes.

In the circle, the two brothers clasped hands. Then, after a hundred years of being apart, they pulled each other close, locked in an embrace.

THE LINES BETWEEN
GOOD AND EVIL

*T*HE GROUND RAN red with the blood of witches from both sides of the fight. Many demons had also lost their lives that day, passing on to the Afterworld.

Andros and other soldiers of the Resistance had taken on the task of separating the dead from the wounded, stacking bodies on one side of the field.

The wounded from both sides had been taken to a temporary hospital in Ella Mae's old house behind Brighton Manor. Jackson and Angela healed anyone they could. Courtney helped recharge their power once it was used, so they could continue to heal long after they normally would have been spent.

The rest of us walked the battlefield, separating the dead from those who needed care. Still, there were others who deserved a different fate.

"What do we do with the witches who were fighting against us?" I asked. "Some of them no longer have the demon inside of them, but that doesn't mean they aren't still powerful. They still have their witch's powers, even if they aren't as strong as they used to be."

"I say we throw them all in the dungeons in your father's castle," Mary Anne said. She placed her small hand on my arm and gave a sad smile. "Your castle."

"I guess technically it belongs to both me and Angela," I said. It was something I hadn't really thought about. Someone would have to take over as Queen of the South. I wasn't sure I was ready for all that just yet.

"They won't be able to cast their magic down there so it will keep everyone safe until we decide what to do with them," she said.

The city guards who had been so faithful to my father and who had followed him here to this battlefield had rounded up the evil witches, binding them in a temporary cell created by walls of dirt and stone pulled from the damaged ritual room.

I looked over the faces of the women inside the structure. Sheriff Hollingsworth. Ella Mae. Several faces I recognized from Peachville and witches who must have come here with Priestess Winter. Honora and Selene were also among the crowd.

"How did you know which ones to hold captive and who to let go?" I asked, knowing the lines between good and evil weren't always obvious.

"Easy," Piotrek said, tapping a notebook he'd been keeping with all the names of his captives. He'd joined us here in the human world after he and his small group had killed all the hunters who attacked them in the shadow world. Including Lydia Ashworth. "We asked the demons who had been trapped inside them for so long. They were more than willing to tell us the true hearts of the women they lived inside."

I narrowed my eyes, searching the faces again.

"What about Laura Harris?" I asked. "And her daughter Brooke?"

Piotrek lifted the page on his clipboard, searching for their names. "Laura Harris perished during the fight," he said. "Her daughter Brooke was released to go home. Her demon told us she'd never been happy about being a part of the Order of Shadows. That her real passion had been something else entirely."

"Horses," I said with a sad smile.

He eyed me questioningly and I waved him away, not wanting to hold up his work any longer.

So in the end, Brooke hadn't been evil. I wasn't sure we'd ever really be friends or anything, but at least now we knew that deep down, she was a good person. She'd just been taken down the wrong path.

Mayor Chen sat near the very back of the enclosure, her legs pulled tight to her chest. Her face streaming with tears.

"Wait," I said.

Piotrek turned back to me.

"There was a girl," I said. "Lark Chen. Is she on the list?"

He ran his hand down the list of names until he paused. "Lark Chen was killed," he said. "We found her body in the ritual room under a large pile of debris."

My hand rose to my mouth and tears stung my eyes. I'd left her there, trapped inside a cage of stone. When the rest of the ceiling fell in during the battle, she must have been crushed underneath its weight.

Even though the pain of her betrayal still stung, I was sorry she was gone. It would be a long time before I would really be able to come to terms with the fact that nothing we shared had ever been real. She'd been a Winter spy all along, her every smile a manipulation.

"Thanks," I said to him, lifting my hand to wipe away the tears that had gathered on my cheek.

Across the field, Caroline waved as she ran to meet me. She threw her arms around me. "It looks like you guys had a really hard time here," she said. She looked toward the bodies that still littered the area. "There are so many who didn't make it."

I lowered my head. "There were great losses on both sides," I said. "But in the end it was worth it. The demons are free and Priestess Winter is gone."

Eloise, her mother, stepped forward and placed her hand on my shoulder. "What you've done here is truly a miracle," she said. "Generations of women have been forced to be prima, or to join the Order, never able to follow their own dreams or find their own way in the world. Even the men we marry and homes we live in are picked for us. There are thousands of prima families out there who are going to be anxious to find freedom of their own."

She paused, staring down at her two daughters. "Even mine."

I looked at the three women from Cypress, trying to imagine how they must be feeling after all this. The women in Peachville were free and we now had a way to free all of the blue demon gates, but what about the other colors of gates out there in the world. Gates like Cypress?

"If you're willing, we can work together to find the master stone and the ring for the Cypress gate," I said. An emerald. But which of the four remaining sisters was in charge of the green gates? And would we be able to find her once she found out what we'd done to her sister?

"We all want to help," Meredith said. I think it was the first time she'd spoken since she arrived.

"You're sure you don't want to be prima?" I asked. When I first met her, she'd seemed to enjoy the prestige and attention that went along with the role.

She shrugged. "I don't see why we can't still plan to have covens with primas and everything," she said. "We'll still all be able to cast some kinds of magic, even without the demons. We just need to start some new traditions."

I smiled. "That sounds perfect to me," I said.

I left them, walking around the battlefield one last time.

So much death, but so much new life. Everyone would now have choices they had never had before. Dreams they could follow without having to worry about being punished for them. Demons would be able to return home to the shadow world. To see their families again.

But Eloise was right. There were still so many gates to free. So many in the shadow world who would now have a new hope.

The hope of being reunited with the loved ones they thought had been lost to them forever.

THE DEMON LIBERATION MOVEMENT

*A*NGELA AND I spread our father's ashes among the white roses at the edge of Brighton Lake.

I held my sister's hand as we watched them scatter in the wind.

We knew this was nothing more than the outer shell of who he'd been and that his real spirit lived in peace in the Afterworld. Still, we felt it would be good to leave a piece of him here, split between both of the worlds he loved so much.

Afterward, when all our tears had been cried, we gathered on the porch of Brighton Manor to celebrate our first victory over the Order of Shadows. With Mrs. Shadowford gone, the house was truly mine. It still needed some fixing up and some major cleaning, but with everyone's help, it was starting to feel like home.

"We should come up with a name for ourselves," Aerden said. In his human form, he looked almost exactly like his brother. Only his deep brown eyes set him apart.

Lea raised her eyebrows. "We already have a name," she said. "The Resistance."

Jackson shook his head. "No, that's the old name," he said. He pulled me onto his lap and I giggled, throwing my arms around him. "The Resistance was an army of demons who were going to take this world by force, killing everyone if they had to. The future is different now. Our mission is to set people free. We need a new name to go along with it."

"What about the Demon Liberation Movement?" Courtney said. She so rarely talked, everyone paused to look at her, shocked to hear her sound so confident.

"I love it," I said, laughing. "It has a certain ring to it. Of course, we'll be liberating humans too."

I thought of Brooke and wondered what her life would be like now that she was no longer a slave to the Order's mission. Now that her mother was gone. Would she find the courage to stand up and follow her own dreams?

At least now she would have the choice.

It was a choice every young girl deserved to have, and I knew we wouldn't stop until everyone was free.

A FUTURE HOPE

I STARED AT THE demon statue in front of Peachville High School.

I traced my index finger along the widening crack in the stone. Hard to believe Jackson's power had once been contained inside this cold rock. I still felt the slight tingle of power inside as my skin touched it, but I knew the real essence of Jackson's power had been completely restored to him.

And we'd need it in the years to come.

The Demon Liberation Movement had only just begun its work against the Order of Shadows. There were still four of the original sisters out there enslaving demons. The closure of the blue portals would hurt them, but really, it was just a drop in the bucket compared to the number of gates still open.

There was also the issue of the mysterious High Priestess. A woman no one seemed to have any information about. Yet, deep in my gut, I knew she was more dangerous than all five of the sisters combined.

A shiver ran down my spine as I thought of the dangers that lay ahead.

"Are you just going to ogle that statue all day long? Or are you actually coming to class today?" Lea smacked my butt as she walked past.

I laughed and rubbed the stinging spot.

The rest of the group had insisted we all go to school together to keep up the illusion that we were just normal students in Peachville. Soon enough, Priestess Winter's sisters would come looking for the people who had killed her. Our hope was that it would take them a long time to figure out what had really happened and who had been responsible. The more normal our lives looked on the outside, the less suspicious they would be of us.

My sister would continue to coach the cheerleading squad, only this time they'd learn actual cheers instead of magic. Lea and Aerden enrolled as seniors so they could have classes with Jackson. Zara, as the youngest of us all, had decided to enroll as a freshman with Mary Anne and Essex, despite the fact that her home schooling would have tested her out of even the most advanced classes here at PHS.

I trailed behind Lea, clutching my books to my chest. I watched the teens of Peachville High School as they rushed past. Some laughed. Some stared ahead with a more-than-bored expression on their face. Couples walked hand-in-hand. Friends huddled together in various nooks, sharing secrets and talking about their crushes or their homework or what they planned to do this weekend.

I bit my lower lip to hide a smile as I made my way to my locker.

Most of the teens here had no idea just how much this town had changed in recent weeks. They had no clue demons had been enslaved in Peachville for over a hundred years. People like Drake still weren't aware of the impact the Order had on their lives.

If I had anything to do with it, they'd never have to know.

I twisted the dial on my locker, trying to remember a combination I hadn't used in forever. When it finally popped open, a single sheet of drawing paper fluttered to the ground.

Confused, I set my books inside the locker, then leaned over to pick up the page.

I flipped it over, gasping as I stared at the elaborate drawing. I looked from side-to-side, searching the halls for his familiar leather jacket and black boots.

There, near the end of the hallway, Jackson stood, one foot propped behind him on the cinderblock wall. Our eyes met and one side of his lips curled up in a sexy half-smile that made my heart pound in my chest.

I looked back down at his drawing, a lump forming in my throat.

He'd taken care with this one. This wasn't one of his quick sketches done with a dull pencil. No, this had taken some time. The shading and colors were just right, every detail filled with love.

And hope.

How long had he known this was our future? How long ago had he seen this picture in his mind?

Tears formed in the corners of my eyes. I memorized the scene, then pulled the paper close to my heart.

Here was proof of a future hope for us and for both our worlds. No matter what the days ahead would bring. No matter the war that faced us now. Someday, this would be our life.

Jackson and me, sitting together in the garden of my father's castle. Our hands entwined. A crown upon my head. Our eyes fixed happily on a small child playing among the roses.

A boy with silver eyes.

Our son.

ABOUT SARRA—

 Sarra Cannon writes contemporary and paranormal fiction with both teen and college aged characters. Her novels often stem from her own experiences growing up in the small town of Hawkinsville, Georgia, where she learned that being popular always comes at a price and relationships are rarely as simple as they seem.

She has sold over a quarter of a million books since she first began her career as an Indie author in 2010.

Sarra is a devoted (obsessed) fan of Hello Kitty and has an extensive collection that decorates her desk as she writes. She currently lives in South Carolina with her amazingly supportive husband and her adorable son.

Connect with Sarra online!
Website: SarraCannon.com
Facebook: Facebook.com/sarracannon
Instagram: instagram.com/sarracannon
Twitter: twitter.com/sarramaria
Goodreads: Goodreads.com/Sarra_Cannon